FINDING
CAMLANN

FINDING CAMLANN

A NOVEL

SEAN PIDGEON

HARPERCOLLINS*PUBLISHERS*LTD

Published by HarperCollins Publishers Ltd

First Canadian edition

HarperCollins Publishers Ltd
2 Bloor Street East, 20th Floor
Toronto, Ontario, Canada
M4W 1A8

www.harpercollins.ca

Library and Archives Canada Cataloguing in Publication
Pidgeon, Sean
Finding Camlann / Sean Pidgeon.

ISBN 978-1-44341-102-8

1. Title.
PS3616.I34F56 2013   813'.6   C2012-906057-7

Book design by JAM Design
Map by David Cain

Printed in the United States of America
1   2   3   4   5   6   7   8   9

For my father

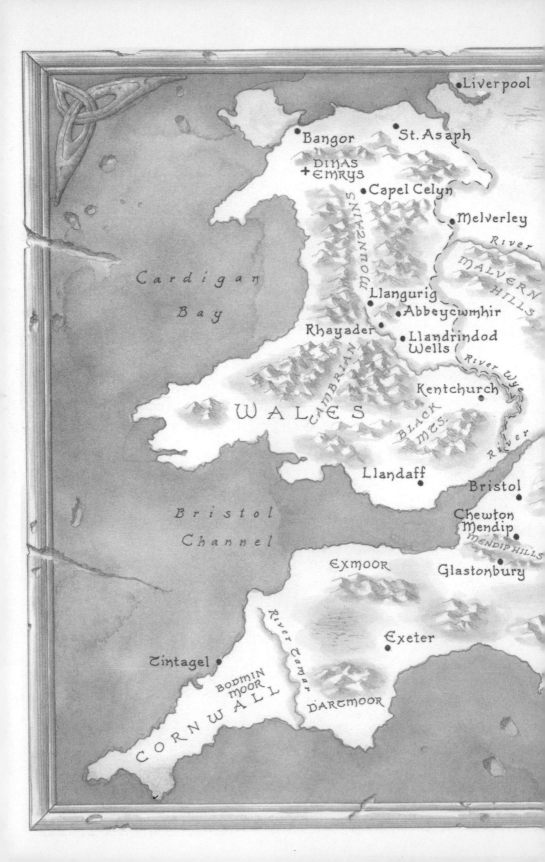

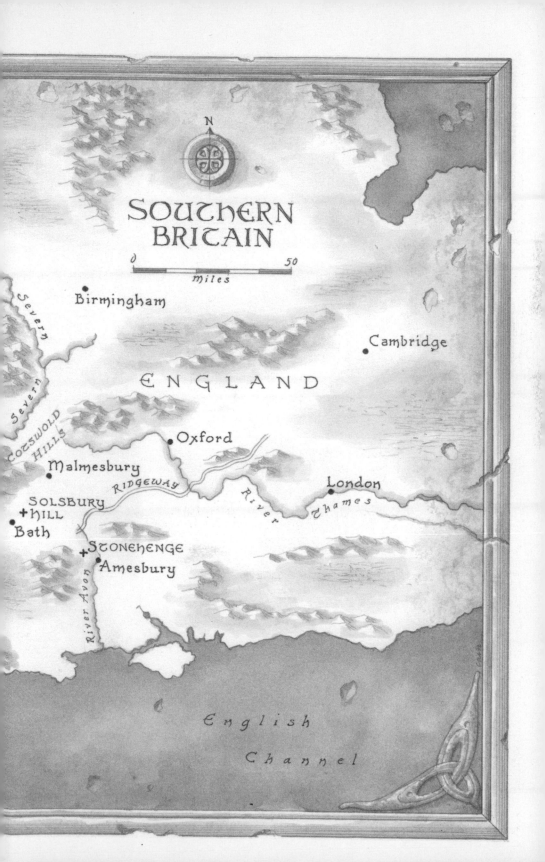

Contents

While I was dizzied thus, old thoughts would crowd,

Belonging to the time ere I was bought
By Arthur's great name and his little love;
Must I give up for ever then, I thought,

That which I deemed would ever round me move
Glorifying all things; for a little word,
Scarce ever meant at all, must I now prove

Stone-cold for ever?

WILLIAM MORRIS, *The Defence of Guenevere*

FINDING
CAMLANN

Enigmata

As HE NURSES his pint in a quiet corner of the Smoking Dog pub on Malmesbury High Street, turning distractedly through the pages of his unfinished manuscript, Donald Gladstone feels the first stirrings of a familiar dissatisfaction. By now, he should be at the comfortable stage of fine-tuning his work, correcting minor errors and infelicities of style. But he cannot help noticing a troubling patchwork quality to the text, a sense of disparate concepts stitched hurriedly together. He can hear the ancient voice of his sixth-form history teacher whispering in his ear. *Always strive for perfection, Gladstone. If in your own mind you have not achieved that exalted standard, you must start again at the beginning.* If Mr. Pankhurst were here with him now, reading over his shoulder, he would doubtless be dispensing the same impractical advice.

Donald puts down his pencil, retrieves his half-empty glass from the corner of the table and leans back in his chair. On this cool autumnal Sunday, the pub is filled with the comforting sounds of mild inebriation, a buzz and hum of mellow chatter. Fragments of

conversation drift in his direction: yesterday's second-half performance by Bristol Rovers, a new curate making enemies up at the
abbey, rumours of a black panther on the loose in Devon, the relative
merits of damson and quince. Bursts of raucous laughter accompany
the telling of a rambling story up at the bar, an account of the previous Saturday night's exploits in Shepton Mallet. At the next table,
tucked in close to a fireplace burning logs the size of elephants' feet,
two elderly men are quietly absorbed in a game of Scrabble.

The proprietor of the Smoking Dog, stoutly built and with a
fresh sweat beading on his brow, comes by on his way to stoke the
fire. In the years since Donald and his father first made this place
their habitual weekend rendezvous, he has become almost a friend
of the family. 'Ready for a refill, Mr. Gladstone?'

'No thanks, George, I'll wait for my dad.'

The publican glances down at the manuscript. 'How's the book
coming along?'

'It's not as finished as I thought it was,' Donald says. Something
in George's earnest expression prompts a different thought. 'Can I
ask you something, though?'

'Course you can. Nothing too hard, mind you.'

'If I say King Arthur, what are the first three things that come
into your head?'

'Sword in the stone . . . Merlin the magician.' George hesitates,
narrows his eyes in exaggerated contemplation. 'The quest for the
Holy Grail? Not that anyone would come here looking for it.' He
laughs good-naturedly at this, then goes on his way.

With a small, wry smile, Donald returns to the opening page of
his narrative.

Popular historians have conjured an apocalyptic vision of the centuries that followed the Roman withdrawal from Britain. This,

they inform us, was a twilit age, a period of encroaching darkness illuminated only by the candlelit scribbling of monks in exile on windswept headlands and rocky island sanctuaries. This was a fateful era, we are told, in which pagans sailing across the eastern sea threatened to bring about the ruin of Christian civilisation in the west. This was the heroic time of the Siege of Mount Badon, of the peerless Arthur as leader of battles.

Donald's intention has been to introduce a quietly provocative tone from the outset, to paint a vivid but ambiguous picture that will set the scene for his controversial retelling of Arthur's story. But now, as he glances through this well-worn text, it occurs to him that he has looked at it so many times that he has lost all sense of its likely impact on the reader. These evasive, prevaricating sentences perfectly encapsulate his challenge in writing the book. For he has set out to show, by combining the evidence of modern scientific archaeology with the long-established traditions of documentary scholarship, that almost everything that has ever been written about the historical Arthur is wrong.

There is a tense silence now at the Scrabble table. The player nearest to Donald, dressed in a fraying tweed jacket, is being let down by his technique. With his letters arranged in alphabetical order, AEGIMNT, he is staring at his tiles, chin in hand, glancing only occasionally at the board. Tweed-jacket's opponent, with a flat cap pulled down low over his forehead, is flicking through the dog-eared pages of a small dictionary. Donald checks his watch: half an hour until his father is due to arrive. He reads on through his second paragraph.

Perhaps no other period in the history of the world has attracted so much misguided scholarship. A sober assessment of the literary and archaeological evidence should cause us to question the traditional symbolism of the sun setting inexorably on the Roman world, of a dark age that was to be ended only by the wisdom and enlightenment of the later Saxon kings, of Alfred and Edward and Athelstan, four hundred years in the future. To arrive at a proper understanding of our British history, we must abandon this dramatic interpretation of what has come to be known as the Age of Arthur: even if, in so doing, we diminish what has seemed to many of us the most truly evocative period of our insular past.

Passages such as this have become a source of tension in Donald's conversations with his editor, Felicity Wickes. It's not enough to be a debunker of popular misconceptions, Felicity would say, however elegantly and convincingly you may do it. You have to tell the reader what really happened. If Arthur was not a war leader in post-Roman Britain, then who was he?

This is the very question that Donald has been striving to answer, but it is no small thing that she asks: this is a challenge that has defeated fifty generations of scholars who have come before. Of one thing, at least, he is perfectly sure. The Arthurian story as it has been interpreted by popular historians, invoking a valiant battle-leader who, for a while at least, stemmed the rising Saxon tide in fifth-century Britain, does not properly express the true nature of Arthur. He is a far deeper mystery than such stories of war and adventure would suggest.

Letters are placed ponderously on the Scrabble board. HA is attached to CAPE, making AH and PA as well. Fourteen points. With fastidious movements that do little to disguise his evident self-satisfaction, flat-cap pencils a new total on his side of the score sheet. 'A hundred and five plays seventy-two,' he says, taking a deep pull on his pint as he replenishes his tile rack.

Donald picks up the local newspaper from the basket near the fire. The headlines speak of rising damp in the local primary school, the thirty-year tenure of the town's librarian. He begins doodling in the margin, embellishing it with cross-hatched loops and burgeoning spirals, his thoughts meanwhile running on the challenge of meeting Felicity's latest deadline. His central argument is that Arthur was not so much a flesh-and-blood warrior as an archetypal hero, a god-like figure whose exploits were beyond mortal reach. Stated in these simple terms, it is not such a radical thesis; but it is not enough merely to accept this with a shrug of the shoulders and move on. What is important is to get back to the origins of this pervasive mythology of Arthur, to understand where, when, and how it arose. Such is the impractical challenge that Donald has set for himself.

'That's me finished,' says tweed-jacket. 'Can't do a thing.'

'Don't give up on me now, Jack,' says flat-cap, though this seems less than a heartfelt plea. 'I'm just getting warmed up.'

'Sorry, Harry, but I'll have to be going. I promised Beryl I'd give her a hand up at the market.'

'Chalk another one up to me, then.' Raising his voice a notch, Harry gestures in Donald's direction. 'Unless our friend here wants to step in for you?'

'Yes, why not?' Donald tucks his manuscript back into its folder, returns it to his battered leather briefcase. He has just settled himself in Jack's chair when he hears the publican's voice cutting across the room.

'Mr. Gladstone? Telephone call for you.'

With an apology to Harry, and conscious of curious eyes on him, Donald makes his way up between the tables to the bar. 'It's your father on the line,' George murmurs to him. 'He doesn't sound too special today.'

Donald picks up the receiver left dangling on its cord. 'Is every-thing all right, Dad?'

'Nothing terminal, I dare say.' James Gladstone's hoarse voice is barely audible. 'Just a touch of cold—but I shan't be joining you today, I'm afraid.'

A small wave of disappointment washes over Donald. Their plan was to have lunch together, then decide on where to go for their usual Sunday walk. 'I had a good idea for us today,' he says. 'Let's try again next weekend, if you're feeling better. I'll give you a call during the week.' He hangs up the phone, makes his way stoically back to the Scrabble table.

JULIA LLEWELLYN DRAINS the last drops from her second glass of wine. She briefly considers a refill, thinks better of it. For now, she tries to distract herself with a volume of Welsh poetry that her father has sent her. She smiles as she thinks of him, Dai Llewellyn of Dyffryn Farm. He will often send her random books and liter-ary fragments, articles and leaflets and pages torn from newspapers, usually with some dramatic arrowing or encirclement of the critical text. A thread of yellowed old string bookmarks a poem by Dylan Thomas, one that she knows well but has not read for many years.

> Now as I was young and easy under the apple boughs
> About the lilting house and happy as the grass was green . . .

As she reads, she finds herself computing the rhythms in the lines, the poet's use of stress, alliteration, and rhyme in perhaps uncon-scious imitation of the Welsh *cynghanedd* verse style. It is not purely a blessing, the way her mind works, always analysing, looking for patterns and codes and symbols. *Just read it as the writer intended*, her father would say, knowing the way she is. *Imagine he's there in the room, speaking the words out loud.* She forces herself to start again from the beginning. On this second reading, the poet's evocation of an untroubled pastoral youth, the lyrical intertwining of his verses, brings a dream-like nostalgia that merges into an inchoate sadness as the chill of mortality enters the wistful lines. In a sense, this is her own childhood, growing up at Dyffryn, though she wonders why her father should choose to remind her of it now.

Pulling her shawl more tightly around her, she closes the poetry book, uses her napkin to dab away a small drop of wine. The cover bears an unusual design, a Welsh upland landscape with green foothills rising to stark mountain peaks, dark storm-clouds roiling overhead. A narrow track leads through a gentle wooded valley before climbing into higher, more rugged terrain. There is a portentous quality in this picture that her father would find appealing, though she does not. She can hear him lecturing her about choices, taking the right path, even if it is not always the easiest. Taking the wrong path is sometimes harder, she would say in return. Taking the wrong path is sometimes right.

Julia glances at her watch: a quarter to two. Her husband is more than an hour late for their rendezvous. By now, her faint irritation has evolved into a more insistent anxiety. This was to have been a celebration of sorts, the fifteenth anniversary of their engagement, a return to one of their favourite pubs from the early days. Hugh is on his way back from the Mortimer family property at Ty Faenor, near Rhayader in central Wales, where he and his sister Ruth have been supervising recovery efforts following the heavy rains that have flooded the riverside lands. In a bulletin delivered by telephone the night before, he explained the situation to Julia in the careful, didactic manner that he reserves for such conversations. The drains around the old manor house had become badly clogged, he said, sending two feet of water into the cellars. With a couple of pumps going, everything would be under control by the morning. He would have to stay up there overnight, but an early start should see him to Malmesbury in plenty of time.

In a habitual nervous gesture, Julia begins twisting her wedding ring back and forth, prying it loose, working it over the knuckle. She swaps it to her right hand, slips it on to the third finger, begins the process in reverse. When she tries to imagine what is going through Hugh's mind, it feels like she is striking against a dark impenetrable wall. As usual, there will be a reasonable explanation for his lateness. He will have stayed at Ty Faenor to the last minute, determined to remain in charge at the moment of crisis. He will be on the road somewhere now, driving too fast, reinventing his poor awareness of time as a heroic dash to Julia's rescue.

In other circumstances, on another day, in another year, she would have found it charming. But this is not the first time in recent months that Hugh seems so casually to have lost his sense of the importance of things. She takes a piece of paper from her bag, begins mentally drafting a short, matter-of-fact note to leave for him at the bar; then folds the blank sheet and puts it in her pocket, continues playing nervously with her ring.

Her meditation is interrupted by a brash announcement from the bar. 'Mr. Gladstone? Telephone call for you.' She sees a tall man get up from a table in the opposite corner and approach the far end of the bar. He has reddish-brown hair cut short, the weathered face of an outdoorsman, strong parallel frown-lines tempered by a gentleness in his expression as he reaches for the telephone. A memory replays itself: the steps of the Ashmolean Museum in Oxford, a book falling from her bag, white with an orange spine, a heavy volume of Welsh history. It was picked up by a tall, awkward boy who happened to be following her up the steps. He made some dry comment, said he was reading it too, and he didn't know it had become such a blockbuster. On the strength of this introduction, they spent an hour together in the new Egyptian exhibit at the Ashmolean, then afterwards went for tea across the road at the Randolph Hotel.

Now she watches curiously as Donald Gladstone hangs up the phone, turns and walks back to his table with an air of quiet disappointment. She remembers liking him at the time, though her interest was purely theoretical; in those days, she was intensely preoccupied with a third-year student at Jesus College by the name of Hugh Mortimer. It is perhaps not so great a coincidence, seeing Donald here, but still she feels a faint unsettling tug of superstition.

❖ ❖ ❖

HARRY HAS GONE up to the bar to get them both a refill, leaving Donald under some pressure to deliver an impressive score. He is convinced there is a seven-letter word somewhere in Jack's hand. MINTAGE would work, but there is nowhere to put it. He reaches into his briefcase, pulls out the top sheet of his manuscript, writes the letters down, scattershot, at the foot of the page; then taps unsuccessfully through various permutations with the tip of his pencil.

'I think it's *enigmata*.' These words are spoken from behind his left shoulder, a quiet voice with an unmistakable Welsh lilt.

Donald turns to meet the gaze of a woman in her thirties, dark-brown hair cut to shoulder length, a pale complexion, striking green eyes behind narrow-framed reading glasses. A long embroidered shawl is wrapped loosely around her shoulders. She is achingly familiar to him, somebody he once knew.

'You just need to use the loose A down there,' she says, pointing to the bottom right-hand corner of the board. She picks up his discarded pencil, goes through the letters in sequence; then pauses, gives him a searching look. 'You don't recognise me at all, do you?'

Something in her expression brings the memory back, crystal clear. It must be sixteen years ago at least, perhaps seventeen, his second year at Oxford. He found himself behind her on the steps of the Ashmolean Museum just as a large book fell from her bag and tumbled down towards him. Picking it up for her—it was John Davies' *A History of Wales*—he mentioned that he had been reading the same book, which indeed was true. She laughed at some poor joke he made, and he decided straight away that he was going to fall in love with her. 'It's good to see you, Julia,' he says.

There is the flicker of a smile. 'Now that you've remembered me, are you going to ask me to join you?'

'Of course. I insist on it, in fact.' He stands up, a little too quickly, pulls a chair across from a nearby table. 'Will you have something to drink?'

'What about your game?' she says. 'Your friend's on his way back.'

Harry returns to the table, his hands shaking with the effort of carrying an overfilled pint precariously in each. He sets them down, glances from Donald to Julia, sizes up the situation with a knowing look. 'Seems to me I might be superfluous to requirements.'

'I'll be glad to finish the game—'

'I haven't the heart for it anyway, truth be told. On you go now.'

Brooking no further argument, Harry settles himself back down, pulls his cap more firmly on to his scalp and begins the cheerless process of returning the tiles to their green cloth bag.

'I'll find us somewhere else to sit,' Julia says, matter-of-fact. 'Dry white wine for me, please.'

Up at the bar, George stops just short of winking. 'Friend of yours, Mr. Gladstone?'

'I think so,' Donald says, in a low voice.

The publican assumes a more philosophical expression as he busies himself with the drinks. 'Right you are,' he says. 'She's been sitting there a long time, all on her own. Either way, these are on the house.'

Julia circles her fingers around her wine glass, pulls it towards her. Her fingernails are short and perfectly manicured, except for one or two raw patches where she has pulled at the peeling skin. 'So what have you been doing with yourself all these years?'

'Mostly scraping around in the mud and dust.'

'Archaeology? I remember, that was your thing at Oxford. You gave me quite the lecture on scarabs and cartouches.'

'I'm very sorry about that. I must have bored you to death.' At the time, she was like no one Donald had ever met. There was a forbidding sort of cleverness to her, an abruptness and a remarkable intensity in the questions she asked him as they made their tour of the Egyptian exhibit. After the Ashmolean, they went for tea across the road at the Randolph; and then, at the end of it all, there was a matter-of-fact goodbye on the corner of Broad Street. Maybe he even tried to kiss her clumsily on the cheek. He remembers seeing her a couple of weeks later, hand in hand with another man.

'Well, I'm glad you kept going with it.' Julia takes a sip of her wine, looks at him with a surprising familiarity. 'Archaeology suits you, somehow.'

'I'm not sure how to take that.'

'As a compliment, of course. Unless there's something disreputable about your profession.'

'There is a certain stereotype.'

She tilts her head to one side, dark hair falling across her face. 'You should probably grow a beard, maybe invest in some slightly shabbier clothes.'

'Don't worry, I have the complete wardrobe at home.' Donald sips at the foam spilling over the edge of his glass. 'So that's me, anyway. What about you? How did you get to be so good at anagrams?'

'It's an occupational hazard.'

'You compile crosswords for a living?'

'Not quite,' Julia says, straight-faced, 'though I wouldn't mind that. I work as a researcher on the *Oxford English Dictionary*.'

'What kind of research?'

'It's to do with words—long words, mostly.'

'Now you're just mocking me.'

'It was a funny question.' Julia seems momentarily preoccupied as the door of the pub creaks opens, admitting a breath of cool air and a group of latecomers, men in discoloured orange boiler-suits who go straight up to the bar to get their orders in. She drinks most of what is left of her wine, smiles at him in a distracted kind of way. 'So what brings you to the Smoking Dog on a Sunday lunchtime?'

'Just catching up on some work. My dad was supposed to meet me for lunch, but he didn't feel up to it. And you?'

Julia hesitates, and he senses a faint anxiety directed at him or perhaps elsewhere. 'I was supposed to meet someone here as well.' It seems at first that she might expand on this statement, but instead she empties her glass, lays a hand on the sheet of paper with the anagram: the first page of Donald's manuscript. 'Is this what you're working on?' she says. 'Do you mind if I have a look?'

He has no choice in the matter, anyway. She has already begun to read, a small frown-line creasing her brow. When she looks up at him, it smooths itself out, leaving just a faint trace behind. 'If all this scholarship is really so misguided, why don't you go ahead and correct it?'

'It's not quite that simple,' Donald says, wishing he had chosen some less pompous phrase.

'Why not?' Julia's gaze is disconcertingly direct.

It is exhilarating, in a way, to be so directly challenged. 'My point is that we won't ever know very much about that period of British history, and it's a mistake to try too hard to fill in the blanks.'

'In which case, is there really anything left to write about?'

'Yes, I think there is.' Donald picks up his glass, pretends to study its contents. 'The problem with the history we read in books is that it's too full of dramatic turning points, heroic leaders and decisive battles, as if these events alone were responsible for the sub- sequent state of the world.'

'Would the historians agree with you on that?'

'Probably not.' Donald takes another mouthful of beer, feels a sudden surge of eloquence. 'But here's an example of what I'm talk- ing about. Imagine you were trying to trace the historical origins of King Arthur, to understand how he came to be celebrated as his country's greatest hero.'

'I'm imagining,' Julia says. 'Go on.'

'Well, it's not as simple as you might think, because all we can really say about the Arthur of history is that his name appears in a battle-listing of unknown antiquity that was copied down by a medieval monk, and again in two entries in the *Annales Cambriae*, the medieval Welsh Annals. That's all there is, two possibly indepen- dent sources for the famous battles of Arthur, and no one has been able to demonstrate convincingly that those battles ever took place.'

'Which doesn't necessarily mean there were no battles.'

'That's true,' Donald says, 'and because our enduring image of Arthur is the heroic leader who turned the tide against the invading Saxons, it's natural to assume the battles did actually happen, even if we know nothing about them. The popular mythology of these events, the interpretation that is the most appealing to us, is that the battles were real.'

'So it's a circular argument, in a way,' Julia says. 'Arthur as battle-hero is something we want to be true, but there's no proper historical evidence, so we improve on the history by making up stories about it—and those stories become established as the popular perception of what really happened. Is that what you're saying?'

'Yes, absolutely yes.' Donald thumps his fist on the table, then grabs at his glass to rescue it from a dangerous wobble.

Julia laughs, a silvery, girlish sound. 'Not that you feel very strongly about it.'

'Sorry about that. But you've hit on such a crucial point. Generations of Arthurian enthusiasts have been so anxious to find a real Arthur who matches up to our expectations of him that they have felt compelled to say he really did exist, and this is who he was, and this was his heroic role in defeating the Saxons. But if you take away all the wishful thinking, the evidence just doesn't support it.'

Julia picks up the manuscript page again, reads to the end. 'Is there more?' she says. 'I want to know what the archaeologist has to say about Arthur.'

He has a momentary fantasy of reaching into his bag, taking out a handsome volume bound in dark blue leather: *The Origins of Arthur*, by D. E. Gladstone. 'Yes, there's a whole book, but I haven't quite finished it.'

'I'd like to read it, when you do.'

Donald cannot help wondering whether she means to make herself quite so intriguing, sitting there watching him with her ironical half-smile. He hesitates now, stares down into his last two inches of beer. 'There's a place not far from here,' he says. 'I was planning to go there this afternoon with my father, but he couldn't make it. Would you like to come along with me instead?'

On Badon Hill

J ULIA GLANCES AROUND the inside of the antique Morris Traveller, dark green with a rear section framed in honey-coloured wood, takes in the austere simplicity of its controls, the worn leather seats, the interior trim polished to a smooth dark patina. 'This belongs in a museum,' she says.

'My mother had it before me,' Donald says. 'I suppose it's become a kind of family heirloom.'

He turns the key in the ignition, reaches for the starter. The engine answers his muttered incantation, coughs half-heartedly into life. Shifting noisily into gear, he pulls out into the sparse Sunday afternoon traffic. Julia remains silent, picking at the ragged skin next to her thumbnail as the text of the note she left for Hugh plays itself relentlessly back to her. *I ran into an old college friend. You weren't here, so we decided to go out for a drive.* She tries to imagine how he will interpret it, hopes he will simply shrug his shoulders, turn around and drive home; but her inadequate sentences keep returning to disturb her peace of mind. If this is an act of revenge, there will be precious little vindication in it.

Her anxiety begins to ebb away as they head out of Malmesbury to the west, joining a minor road that carries them rapidly into the farther depths of the English countryside. Soon they are crossing earthy red farmland, curving fields broken by dense stands of beech and oak whose autumn colours brighten and soften the afternoon sunlight filtering deep into the gold-shadowed recesses of the wood.

'It's good that you find time to spend with your father,' Julia says. In the silence that has gathered, her words fall more abruptly than she intended.

'We're both on our own now, so it's not so hard.'

Glancing across at Donald, whose attention is focused almost too fiercely on the road ahead, she considers the complexities of his state-ment, wonders which one of them was not on his own before. His father, presumably, at some point; and Donald as well? At the very least, she would like to ask him about his mother, but something in his expression seems to forbid the question.

'What does your father do?'

'He's a geologist, retired a long time ago.'

Julia sees a diagram, complex strata with neatly lettered labels down either side. 'It's all about layers,' she says, speaking the phrase that comes fully formed into her head.

Donald's expression is amused rather than surprised. 'I think I know what you mean,' he says.

'His layers in the rock, your human layers on top. It's a connec-tion between you.'

'We meet somewhere in the middle, I suppose. Over the years, he's taught me pretty much everything I know about the British landscape.'

They have come to a small crossroads, signs to Hullavington and Norton to the left, Tetbury and Easton Grey to the right. Donald reaches down next to his seat, pulls out a well-worn Ordnance Survey map. 'We should probably make sure we know where we're going.'

'Show me,' Julia says.

He finds a stub of pencil under the dashboard, traces out the route. They are to head south-west along the line of the Fosse Way—the old Roman road from Lincoln to Exeter—then cut off just past the Somerset border and follow the back-roads from there to their destination, a small steep-sided hill on the far side of the village of Northend.

Julia takes the map out of his hand, deftly refolds it and flattens it out on her lap. 'I think there's a shorter way,' she says. 'I suggest you turn left at the next crossroads we come to.'

Soon they are making steady progress along the western fringe of Wiltshire, following the rectilinear fragments of modern road that preserve, in spirit at least, the original line of the Fosse Way. Just beyond the Three Shire Stones, where thick slabs of rock mark the meeting point of three ancient counties, they turn on to a narrow lane, almost a tunnel beneath tall hedges on either side. Walls made of local limestone are buried deep within the foliage, slowly crumbling into pale shards that have mixed with the thick mud thrown up into a ridge along the centre of the lane. As they drop down into Northend, they meet a tractor lumbering up the hill towards them, its driver eyeing them with guarded curiosity as Donald squeezes the Morris into the hedge to make enough room for him to pass.

On the far edge of the village, they pull off the road next to a church whose grey-gold stonework glows faintly in the hazy sunlight filtering through a thickening layer of cloud. Donald turns off the ignition, brings the engine stuttering to a halt. The ensuing silence seems almost absolute, broken only by the faint pattering of the raindrops that are now beginning to fall on the windscreen. The churchyard in front of them is neglected and overgrown, gravestones tilting here and there through the weeds. Beyond the church, a tall grass-covered hill rises steeply to a flat summit.

There is a tight knot of anxiety in Julia's stomach. By now, for sure, Hugh will have arrived at the Smoking Dog. She imagines him opening the door of the pub, breathless, expectant, to find only her terse note left with the barman.

'We can walk up past the churchyard,' Donald says, 'but first I need to explain why we're here.' He reaches for his pencil and a scrap of paper, begins to outline a large irregular shape. 'This is Britain, circa 500 AD.' He adds three large arrows, from the west, north, and east. 'For the past century, since the Roman withdrawal, the island has been under siege from at least three different directions. Here,' he says, stabbing at the first arrow, 'Irish pirates have been raiding the western shores. Here, Picts from Scotland are harassing the North Britons. And here, the Saxons and other Germanic tribes are landing in increasing numbers on the eastern and southern shores. According to popular tradition, this is when Arthur emerged as the hero who roused the British defence.'

The rain has progressed to a fine drizzle, making small rivulets on the glass that soon join up to form an intricate watery landscape. There are pictures in it, too, plump grey sheep on a distant hillside, the rugged contours of a steep-sided valley. Julia thinks of home, the upper slopes of Moel Hywel above Dyffryn Farm.

'When I was growing up near Rhayader,' she says, 'my father used to tell me stories about the great warriors of the past, Arthur and Llywelyn and Owain Glyn Dŵr. He said they started out as pure Welsh heroes, to be spoken of in the same breath, but Arthur's story was stolen and corrupted by the English. All the talk about round tables and magical swords was a lot of nonsense concocted as a means of legitimising the English monarchy.'

'That's not very far from the truth,' Donald says.

There is something vexing to Julia in the guarded way he says this. 'I think it's precisely the truth. The English were not content with taking our land—they had to steal our favourite stories as well.'

'I'm so sorry.' Donald puts his hands up in self-defence. 'I didn't steal them.'

She laughs at him now, at the wry expression on his face. 'You mustn't get upset at me. I'm my father's daughter, that's all. How did you get to be so interested in Arthur, anyway?'

'I suppose it started when I went up to Bangor to do my Ph.D. My thesis advisor was a terrifying Welsh bulldog by the name of John Evans. He wanted me to write about the archaeology of the famous dark-age citadels of the Cambrian mountains, but I was much more interested in the mythical traditions connected with those sites. Before I knew it, I was making a full-blown study of the legendary heroes of Wales, including Arthur and Owain Glyn Dŵr. Evans thought it was a frivolous topic for a student of archaeology, and told me to stop. He threatened to throw me out of his research group, which made me all the more determined.'

'What happened in the end?'

'We came to an agreement. I got to write what I wanted to write, but I had to put in a lot of gritty archaeology as well. I spent two years digging trenches on the top of Dinas Emrys.'

It is a place Julia knows well, from visits with her father. She smiles at this image of a youthful Donald stranded in a ditch on the fog-bound hilltop. 'Shall we go for our walk? You can tell me more on the way up.'

On the far side of the church, they find a steep muddy track that takes them on a zigzag path between thick clumps of scratching gorse. The rain has backed off, though threatening to return in full force. Ahead of them, the path opens up to a long gentle upward sweep over close-cropped turf towards the summit. In the distance, to the east and south, waves of rounded hills spread out to the horizon. To the south-west, the Georgian city of Bath makes a dramatic splash of cream-coloured stone that fills the valley and spills up the surrounding slopes.

At the brow of the hill, they find a small sign put up by the National Trust: *Little Solsbury Hill, Ancient Monument*. A modest earthwork rampart, all that remains of the iron-age fort that once occupied the hilltop, encloses a broad grassy space grazed by half a dozen lugubrious dairy cows.

'It's a lovely view,' Julia says. 'But I'm still not quite sure why we've come here.'

There is something charmingly professorial in the way Donald walks away a few paces, then turns back to face her, using his hands for emphasis as he talks. 'Do you remember the Arthurian battle-listing I told you about? It was written down in the ninth century, in a book called the *Historia Brittonum*. The manuscript includes a list of twelve battles in which Arthur supposedly took part, including one at a place called Mount Badon.'

'Is that where we are now? On Mount Badon?'

'I'd like to think it was here. This is one of several sites that have been proposed, and I think it's a plausible location.' Donald shrugs, defensive or perhaps dismissive, she cannot tell. 'The archaeologist in me wants to know for sure, but the precise geography doesn't really matter. The more interesting question is whether a warrior known as Arthur was the leader of the Britons that day.'

The afternoon has descended into a chilly gloom, the sun now

lost behind swirling cloudbanks driven from west to east by a fresh-
ening breeze. Bowing their heads into the wind, they walk on to the
farther edge of the hill and stand there for a while looking down a
long slope studded with small birch trees and dense thickets of the
dark-green gorse. It must be four o'clock at least, no more than a
couple of hours until sunset.

'Is there more to the story?' Julia says.

'Yes, there is a little more.' Donald motions for her to sit down next
to him on the grass-covered bank, and she cannot help liking the bold,
casual quality of this gesture, as if they were truly old friends rather
than people who once spent half an afternoon together. She wonders
what Hugh would think, if he could see her now. Of all the people in
the world, he is the first to leap to a jealous conclusion.

Donald takes out his hand-drawn map, flattens it across his knee
to protect it from the breeze, taps a finger on the south coast of
Wales. 'Somewhere here, in about 540 AD, a monk called Gildas the
Wise wrote a chronicle of the events of his time. According to Gildas, the Britons had some success in defending themselves against
the Saxon invaders. They probably held the line roughly here.' He
traces an arc across the south-western corner of Britain. 'Some time
near the end of the fifth century, as Gildas tells the story, a British
force defeated the Saxons at Mount Badon, and the battle led to a
peace that lasted for over fifty years. The problem is, Gildas doesn't
say who actually fought in the battle, and he doesn't mention Arthur
at all, either in his description of Badon or anywhere else in his writings. This might lead us to think that no one of that name played a
major role in the events of the time.'

'So that's your answer, I assume? Arthur wasn't there—someone
made that part up.'

Donald smiles grimly, folds the sheet of paper and puts it back in his pocket. 'That could be true. But if Arthur was not the hero of Mount Badon, I need to find out who he really was.'

For Julia, there is a certain audacity in this challenge that Donald has set for himself, but also a flaw in his logic. 'It doesn't seem surprising to me that the historical Arthur is beyond our reach,' she says. 'My father would say he is purely a hero of the imagination. He's sleeping somewhere in the otherworld, ready to awake in the Welshman's hour of need.'

Donald stands up, takes a few steps away, picks up a narrow rounded stone lying half-buried in the grass. 'Even in Gildas's time, I think it's probably true that Arthur was more an idea than a real person. He was seen as a peerless mythical hero against whom contemporary warriors might be compared.'

'But that still doesn't really answer the question?'

'No, you're quite right, it doesn't.'

By now, the rain has gathered itself into a steady, chilling drizzle. Julia stands next to Donald, shivering faintly, watching as he hefts his stone and launches it on a long, low trajectory along the flank of the hill and into the trees beyond.

She pushes the damp hair back from her forehead, takes gentle hold of his arm. 'Let's get back to the car,' she says.

※ ※ ※

DAYLIGHT IS FAILING by the time Donald pulls up in front of his rented cottage at Iffley, just above the Thames on the southern outskirts of Oxford. He can hear the telephone ringing inside. Sprinting through the soaking rain, he forces the key into the lock, shoulders open the protesting door, drops his briefcase at the foot of the stairs and grabs at the receiver as he scuffs off his muddy shoes.

'Have you heard yet?' The familiar voice sets him instantly on edge, irritated at his ex-wife's assumption that he knows precisely what is on her mind. When he first met her, Lucy Trevelyan, the brash young visiting scholar from California who had invited herself to join his summer archaeological dig in Dorset, he was intrigued by her directness, her forceful, earthy brand of intelligence; but her eccentricities have long since become purely vexing to him.

'Heard what, Lucy?' Water is still dripping from his hair as he stands there in the semi-darkness with the night-time illumination of the west front of St. Mary's Parish Church, projected through a mist-like sheen of rain, casting an unearthly glow across the grave-yard and into his front room.

'The news from Devil's Barrow. I thought you might have spoken to Paul Healey.'

'No, I haven't.'

'In which case, you had better watch me on the BBC news tomorrow.'

'What on earth—'

But Lucy has already hung up on him. She will score this conversation as a victory, understanding her ex-husband well enough to know he will now be suffering from an intense, almost painful curiosity that will remain unsatisfied until the next day.

Donald switches on the corner lamp, draws the curtains together so that they almost meet in the middle. The fabric is printed with a curious animistic design, a series of wide-eyed bird and animal totems tessellated in a clever and disorientating way so that one merges seamlessly into the next. The downturned beak of an eagle becomes the head-dress of a great owl-chieftain, whose left eye is shared with a sideways-facing crow, whose upraised wing is also the shoulder of a giant black bear. The curtains were a gift, of sorts, from Lucy. There was a memorable day back in the spring when, a couple of weeks after their divorce was finalised, she arrived at the cottage with a car-bootful of towels and linens and assorted kitchen paraphernalia, determined not so much to make him comfortable as to remind him that he would be lost without her. The curtains were brought out last of all, Lucy's *pièce de résistance*, her very own bedroom drapes from her Californian childhood. He might have said no, understanding very well that their installation in his sitting room was designed to ensure that, across his long and solitary evenings, she would be always on his mind. But he has found himself surprisingly immune to Lucy's psychological assaults. The grinning totems, far from spying on him, have become his benign and eclectic companions, helping to bring this austere space just a little bit to life.

The disappointments of marriage are, in any case, far from Donald's mind as he walks through to the spartan kitchen, finds bread and cheese and a beer in the fridge, brings them into the front room and sits down at his desk. *Julia Llewellyn*. He writes the name down on a scrap of paper, repeats the lilting syllables to himself. It seems to him that Julia is beautiful in an unobtrusive way, as if she is somehow hiding herself away from the world.

As he retraces their conversations from earlier in the day, he finds that there is something remarkable in the way she has arrived at her own quite natural answer to a difficult question that has absorbed him deeply for years of his professional life. At Solsbury Hill, she explained how her father always thought of Arthur as a pure Welsh hero, to be spoken of in the same breath as Owain Glyn Dŵr and Llywelyn the Great. This idea of Arthur as a shape-shifting hero of the imagination, an ageless warrior who will return to the aid of the Celtic peoples in their moment of crisis, is a familiar one. But something in the way Julia expresses it, as a tradition handed down to her by her father—and presumably to him by his own father—gives it a powerful new resonance, invoking an Arthur who is the inheritor of a long and varied oral tradition.

A sudden squall of wind sighs around the eaves of the cottage and down the old brick chimney. Donald gets up from the desk, switches on the television just in time to catch the weatherman expounding excitedly on the severe conditions that are to come to southern and western parts. Settling himself on the sofa, he picks up his notebook from the coffee table and turns through the pages near the front, where he has made detailed notes on the earliest written evidence for the historical Arthur.

First there is the famous sixth-century poem *Y Gododdin*, in which the bard Aneirin, speaking of the exploits of one heroic British warrior, tells us that 'He glutted black ravens on the wall of the fort, though he was not Arthur.' Then comes the battle-list from the ninth-century *Historia Brittonum*, evoking a series of conflicts set in an epic landscape of forests and rivers and mountains. This list concludes with the siege of Mount Badon where, according to the presumably unreliable chronicler, 'there fell in one day 960 men from one charge by Arthur; and no one struck them down except Arthur himself, and in all the wars he emerged as victor.' And there is a further entry in the Welsh Annals, the *Annales Cambriae*, describing Arthur's last battle:

> *Gueith Camlann, in qua Arthur et Medraut corruere.*
> The strife of Camlann, in which Arthur and Medraut fell.

These fleeting early references are crucial to understanding the historical basis of the Arthurian legend, and yet there is no way of knowing which of them, if any, might contain some distant memory of real events. It is an old debate and an important one, but for now Donald is too tired to keep the arguments straight. He puts his notebook to one side, settles himself to watch a BBC documentary on the fate of the ancient woodlands of Britain. He knows his father will be watching as well, at home in Chewton Mendip, and it is an oddly reassuring thought.

The weather continues to worsen as the evening draws on. Outside, the rain comes in sheets that slam against the glass, rattling the windows in their old wooden frames. A heavy gusting wind seeks out the nooks and crannies of the aging stonework, making small cold draughts that creep and whisper about the cottage. Later, Donald dreams of the wind rushing past the beating wings of a black raven that lifts up his lifeless body from the blood-soaked ground and carries him back towards a castle wall. High above, on the dizzying parapet, a dark-haired woman prepares to make a desperate jump. He will not get there in time to catch her. 'Not Arthur!' the raven shrieks. 'Not Arthur!'

JULIA HAS NEVER been very fond of the house she shares with Hugh, an ornately gabled Victorian red-brick construction of the kind traditionally occupied by the upper strata of the Oxford academic establishment. She feels an almost physical discomfort now as its elaborate outlines loom above her in the squally, cloud-laden dusk. *Cair Paravel* is the name on the sign next to the darkened front door, the legacy of a noted C. S. Lewis scholar who once lived here. As a child, she was never quite transported by the tales of Narnia, but there is at least a pleasing mellifluous Welsh quality in the name.

The Land Rover is not there in the drive, Hugh's absence offer-

ing relief and disquiet in equal measure as Julia works the key into
the lock. She walks through to the kitchen and switches on the light,
bringing to life a bright modern landscape of tastefully polished
surfaces, everything in its place, dun-coloured tiles merging into
off-white walls, glossy brown cabinets above a geometric green-tiled
floor. Her brain chooses to process it differently today: this feels like
a dangerous place, a harsh perpendicular terrain with sharp angles
separating smooth surfaces from long dark vertiginous drops. It
will be better not to be in the house when Hugh gets home; he will
know where to find her.

Julia opens the back door and walks out into a darkened world
filled with crashing waves of sound as the gale takes hold in the
treetops. Running down the path to her studio, she hears the sudden sharp crack of a branch stretched past its breaking point. She
does not stop to look, hurries on to the studio door and slams it
closed behind her, takes a few deep breaths before reaching for the
light switch. The old Bakelite fitting engages with a loud click, illu-
minating a long, low-ceilinged room furnished with sturdy wooden
benches, a scattering of chairs and painter's easels, trays and boxes
overflowing with paper, brushes and paint bottles crowding the
shelves, a long wooden work-table facing a window with a view back
up towards the house.

One wall of the studio is filled with pencil sketches, bold chiar-
oscuro landscapes of hills and caves and trees and old stone walls.
This is Julia's father's work, Dai Llewellyn's vision of an untamed
Wales. The drawings seem to plumb the depths of blackness while
glowing with an unearthly light: this is the only way she has found to
describe them. If you asked him to explain why he chose to draw in
this style, he would say only that he hoped to capture some essence
of the *hiraeth*, the old Welsh yearning for the homeland.

Julia's own artwork, displayed on an adjacent wall, is something else entirely, colourful, vibrant images deconstructed and reassembled in a style dominated by geometric shapes and interlocking planes. An art critic who once visited, an old school friend of Hugh's who meant to offer encouragement, commented that her paintings reminded him of Mondrian's earliest cubist work. What she has never told anyone, not even her father, is that these are pictures of people, how she sees them in her mind's eye. There is one she made of Hugh, a great dark obsidian wall with fractures high up beyond her reach and a pale orange light glinting through the cracks from a hot fire burning somewhere within.

At the far end of the room is an expanding collage made from photographs of people Julia has known, familiar and half-forgotten faces and scenes pasted together from left to right to form a giant mosaic of her life. The past year has seen only a few additions: her mother on her sixtieth birthday at the Rhayader town hall, dressed up in an elegant blue satin dress; her father with shepherd's crook in hand, leaning against a wooden fence-post on a steep hillside. At the right-hand edge are her Wadham College friends at a recent reunion, looking proportionately older and less carefree than the images of their younger selves that are to be found several feet to the left.

Except perhaps for her mother's kitchen at Dyffryn Farm, this is the room in which Julia feels most completely at home. It is a place where she can find a certain easy solitude, make her small works of art with no pressure to please anyone but herself. Above all, this has become a private space, a refuge rarely visited by Hugh, though she has never asked him to stay away. In its Victorian heyday, this was an extravagant summer-house built for the fortunate children of a wealthy Bishop of Oxford, since then used variously over the years (or so Julia likes to imagine) by pipe-smoking philosophical dons, by tragic young poets, surely by more than a few clandestine lovers. She is not a superstitious person, but it seems to her that all this imbibed experience is still somehow present in the room, memories held deep in the coats of paint on the walls, the warped wooden panelling, the windows touched by many generations of hands. There is some essence of this structure, a tangible, comforting spirit of place, that goes far beyond its mere physical history.

She has tried unsuccessfully to explain this feeling to Hugh, who pretends to understand her but, on the rare occasions when he comes down here, sees only timber and glass and the accumulated human and structural assaults of the years. She thinks of Donald's layers in the landscape, his father's layers in the rock, her own layers in the living fabric of this building. *It's all about layers.* This seems a strong, satisfying way to explain the sense of belonging that she feels in this place.

Julia sits down at the table, looks through the window at the blackness outside, the rain now whipping against the pane. A light comes on up at the house. She sees Hugh at the back door, torch in hand, sweeping the beam over to the garden fence where a heavy limb has come down from one of the old oak trees. He goes back inside, returns with a large bow saw. After that, she loses him in the darker shadows at the side of the house. He must have seen that she is down here in the studio, though he does not come to find her. This at least she can understand: it is a simple, predictable reprisal for her earlier act of abandonment.

The telephone is ringing when she walks into the kitchen. She answers it just as Hugh comes back inside, and she is relieved to hear the kindly familiarity of her mother's voice.

'How are you, love? I was wondering about you, so I thought, why not just pick up the phone?'

Hugh is still wearing his waterproof jacket. He takes it off, shakes the rain from it and hangs it carefully on the back of a chair. He throws an inquiring glance in Julia's direction, then turns and leaves the room. She can hear his heavy footfalls on the stairs.

'I've been tidying the bedroom cupboards,' Cath Llewellyn is saying. 'I found a few old things of yours—do you want me to send them?'

'If you like. How's Dai?' From an early age, she began calling her father by his Christian name, a habit her mother still only grudgingly accepts.

'Your father's not been very well, these past few days. I've got him tucked up in bed.'

'Why didn't you say so?'

'I've just told you, now.' Julia's mother, an Englishwoman born and raised in Sussex, has picked up something of the lilting intonation of central Wales in her long years at Dyffryn Farm.

'Has the doctor been out?'

'Your dad's a little over-tired, that's all. Nothing to worry yourself about.' Cath Llewellyn's small self-conscious cough signals a switch to her favourite weighty concern. 'How are things with you?'

'Everything's fine, Mam,' Julia says.

'You're not happy, though. I can hear the catch in your voice.'

'I really can't talk about it now.'

Julia fights off her mother's astute enquiries as best she can, hanging up only after promising to call back as soon as she has a chance. She is left with a vague unsettling sense of guilt: she has been neglecting her parents, too wrapped up in her own concerns. It will be good to get up and see them some time soon, make a long weekend of it, get her hands into some real work on the farm.

Hugh comes back downstairs in a clean white shirt and jeans that give a knowing emphasis to his height and his dark good looks. In his hand is a small white paper bag decorated with a looping Celtic motif. He pulls out a chair and sits opposite her at the kitchen table. 'For you,' he says, pushing the bag towards her.

'Thanks,' she says, casually enough. It does not seem the right moment to open it.

There is something in Hugh's body language, a certain way he carries himself, to which Julia has always been susceptible. He can turn it on at will, and he does so now, looking at her with a certain directness and sincerity in his dark-brown eyes. 'I'm so sorry about today,' he says, frowning slightly. 'We got the cellars pumped out all right, but the top fence up at Cwm Cyncoed came down in the wind during the night. I had to make sure everything was shipshape before I left. I dropped Ruth off at the station, then drove down to Malmesbury as fast as I could.' He stretches out his hand and lays it on top of hers, the long fingers gripping with a warm pressure.

'It doesn't matter very much,' Julia says, resisting a powerful urge to draw her hand away.

'Of course it matters,' Hugh says, and there is a faint edge now in his voice. 'I know today was important to you.'

'To us, Hugh. Important to us.' She immediately regrets this pious statement, but the damage has been done; now Hugh is the one to remove his hand.

'You're making it hard for me to apologise,' he says. 'Is there something else you're not telling me?'

'My father's not well. I'm a little worried about him, that's all.' Feeling a sudden overpowering sense of sadness, Julia gets up too quickly, catches her knee painfully on the leg of the table. 'We'll talk later, OK?'

Upstairs, she locks the door of the bathroom, sets the hot water running. Sitting on the edge of the bath, she takes out Hugh's paper bag. Inside, wrapped in many layers of tissue paper, is a finely wrought wooden figurine: a young woman reclining beneath a tree with a book in her lap, the details meticulously rendered in a vigorous realist style. The artist has etched a title along the spine of the book, *Welsh Dictionary*, and the open page bears the definition of a single word, *cariad*, love. It is a whimsical but also a beautiful gift for Julia, and it is this image of Hugh, searching the gift shops in Rhayader for just the right thing to buy, that finally brings the tears rolling down her face.

A Magical Thing

WHETHER BY DESIGN, or merely through the accretions of the years, the cramped, cluttered, earth-toned, vaguely musty offices of the Oxfordshire County Archaeology Service seem perfectly attuned to the psychic comfort of their occupants. In his corner of the second-floor labyrinth, Donald is hedged in on one side by a wall of shelves stacked with several decades' worth of surveys and site reports, all organised into their proper strata. Perpendicular to this is a row of antique wooden filing cabinets of unknown provenance. The window behind him offers a view across a diverse landscape of rooftops dating from all centuries between the sixteenth and the twentieth, and beyond to a half-built housing estate whose farther edge adjoins a series of ancient tree-lined fields ploughed dark brown for the autumn planting.

A familiar, comforting sound from the direction of the kitchen advertises the approach of Betsy, the tea-lady, pushing her trolley stacked with rattling pots and urns. 'The usual for you, my love?'

she says, in her rhetorical way, handing him his St. John's College mug already filled with tea just this side of stewed. 'There you are, my dear.' With this, she proceeds amiably to the next stop on her early-morning round.

Donald takes a sip of the bitter brew, puts the mug down and paces over to the window. The world outside seems grey and damp and beaten down, the trees disturbed by a ragged gusting wind, the last gasp of the overnight storm. He stands there for a while in a disconnected sort of way, watching the lapwings wheeling over the distant fields; then goes more resolutely back to his desk. He takes the local phone book out of a drawer, leafs rapidly through it, writes down a number on a slip of paper.

The noise level in the office begins to pick up as the latecomers straggle in. Hearing the voice of his young assistant raised in laughter, Donald walks over to find him. Tim Watson is a newly minted Ph.D. from Bristol, tow-haired and pink-faced, with a strong line in fatalistic irony that will see him go far in the archaeological profession.

'Morning, boss. What's today's adventure?'

'Listen, can you do something for me, Tim? See if you can get through to the Cambridge group, ask if there are any new developments at Devil's Barrow.'

'Right you are, Dr. Gladstone.'

Back at his desk, Donald begins doggedly working his way through a stack of neglected paperwork. Tim has done a good job with it, weeding out the rubbish, responding to the routine correspondence, leaving only the more interesting reports and conference announcements, copies of the inevitable contracts and waivers and other outputs of the county bureaucracy. Near the top of the pile is a thick envelope postmarked in Trowbridge, the engineering plans for the Amesbury bypass. Because of his expertise on the early medieval period in southern Britain, Donald has been asked to assist his Wiltshire colleagues with a preliminary assessment of a site thought likely to preserve traces of sixth-century occupation. He opens up the package, lays out the blueprints, absorbs himself for a while in the minutiae of site selection and mapping.

Tim Watson is back within fifteen minutes. 'I couldn't raise a single helpful soul at Cambridge,' he says, 'but I did find this in the morning post.' He hands over a sheet of paper filled with a small printed text circled dramatically with a thick red pen, a press release from Downing College.

A team of Cambridge archaeologists led by Professor Paul Healey has made a remarkable discovery at Devil's Barrow, one of a series of earthworks long thought to have ritualistic associations with the nearby stone circle at Stonehenge. Upon excavation of the barrow, which lies directly along the path made by the rays of the rising midwinter sun as it intersects the outer ring of sarsen stones, Healey's team uncovered a deep pit in which were found fifteen human skeletons. Although the entombed remains were devoid of clothes or weaponry, several Roman coins of the Emperor Honorius suggest a tentative date of the fifth century AD.

'It was not a happy ending for these people,' said Professor Healey. 'All but two of them were apparently subjected to a particularly gruesome kind of ritual sacrifice, in this case by crushing of the skull, impalement through the abdomen, and finally— the *coup de grâce* for any unfortunate enough still to be alive—by drowning in the pit, which we believe would have been filled with water to a considerable depth.'

The most dramatic discoveries of all were made in the upper

section of the burial mound. Interred directly above the sacrificial victims were the upper cranium and antlers of an Irish elk,
Megaloceros giganteus, a species long extinct but famous in the fossil
record for its remarkable size. Holes drilled in the skull indicate
that the antlers were intended to be worn as a headpiece, probably by the human male—a man of unusual stature and physical
strength—whose remains were found directly above it. At the
top of the funerary pile, the team uncovered the skeleton of a
solitary female. Buried with her, still clutched to her chest, was a
ceramic cup decorated around the rim with abstract or possibly
animistic images. Inside it were discovered traces of animal or
perhaps human blood, suggesting the possibility of a ceremonial
or religious significance for the object and its owner.

According to Professor Healey, the apparently high status of
this man and woman is reinforced by the fact that they alone
avoided the terrible 'threefold death' that was meted out to the
warriors interred beneath them. Instead, each seems to have been
killed by a single thrust of a sword or spear. 'This is truly a
remarkable discovery,' said Healey, 'a once-in-a-century find.'

Though hesitant to speculate on the significance of the
remains, Healey was willing to advance one tentative hypothesis.
'If the dating is correct,' he said, 'we may wonder whether this
discovery is related to the Saxon incursions that were taking place
at that time into southern Britain.' Citing the medieval historian Geoffrey of Monmouth, Healey explained that Stonehenge
has long been associated with the burial of a group of British
'leaders and princes' who had fought against the Saxons. 'This
was a period of great fear and confusion in post-Roman Britain,'
said Healey, 'and also of great heroism on the part of the British
defenders. Some have called this time the Age of Arthur.'

The Devil's Barrow finds will be the subject of a forthcoming archaeological symposium at Tintagel in Cornwall.

'What do you make of it, boss?' Tim says. 'Could be a media feeding frenzy on this one?'

'You can be sure of it,' Donald says, distractedly, as he tries to work through the implications of what he has just read. He knows Paul Healey from the days when they were both lowly hack archaeologists employed by the Historic Building and Monuments Department. Paul's big break came on a dig in Turkey, when he was lucky enough to discover a remarkable Hittite inscription on a clay tablet unearthed at the site of the ancient city of Troy. Less than a year later, greatly assisted by a previously unsuspected talent for publicity, he landed a generously funded readership at Cambridge. In Donald's opinion, Paul Healey is a crass attention-seeker and, even worse, a starry-eyed romantic who imagines there is a new Troy to be discovered in every farmer's field.

The press release is classic Healey: without explicitly over-interpreting the finds, he hints at a dramatic explanation that is surely not justified by the evidence at hand. In effect, he is challenging others to prove that he has not, after all, uncovered the tomb of fifth-century British princes and their famous king and queen. Donald has not forgotten what Julia said to him at the pub in Malmesbury. *If all this scholarship is really so misguided, why don't you go ahead and correct it?* And it is true, something needs to be done about Paul Healey.

Tim Watson is still standing there, waiting for a more definitive reaction. 'I'll leave you to think about it, shall I? Let me know if you need anything else.'

As Donald looks up at his resourceful assistant, it strikes him that Tim has a happy archaeological knack of finding interesting things quite by chance. 'Will you come to Amesbury with me on Thursday? I could use your help down in the trenches.'

'I'll try to remember my gardening gloves,' Tim says, walking away with a self-satisfied smile.

After he has gone, Donald picks up the receiver and dials the number from the scrap of paper on his desk. On the second attempt, he gets through to the main office of Oxford University Press, asks to be put through to Julia Llewellyn's extension. As her phone begins to ring, it occurs to him to wonder what precisely he is going to say to her.

※ ※ ※

HAVING SLEPT LONG past her alarm, Julia awakens to an unaccustomed stillness in the bedroom, muted birdsong from outside, weak sunlight filtering through the blinds to catch the dancing dust-motes. The other side of the bed is empty and cold. She stares blearily at the clock, finds that she is already late for work. There are heavy weights on her forehead, steel bands around her arms and legs, pinning her to the mattress. Somehow she breaks free, forces herself to get up. She slides her feet into slippers, throws on her dressing gown against the chill in the air. As she looks at herself critically in the mirror above her dressing table, the previous evening's uneasy conversation with Hugh comes back to her. She resolves to go downstairs and talk to him, tell him what is on her mind.

He is at the kitchen table, casual, with coffee and newspaper in hand. 'I didn't want to wake you,' he says.

'I could make some breakfast, if you like?'

He looks up at her, faintly quizzical. 'I had something a while ago, thanks.'

'I was wondering about taking the day off,' Julia says. 'I thought we might go into town together.'

'Good idea.' Hugh folds the paper, pushes away his coffee cup. 'Just to warn you, though, Ruth's on her way over. She promised to look over the Merton paperwork with me. We can go out afterwards, if you like.'

It was always Ruth's project, Hugh's career in the high-end property market. After his political ambitions came to nothing, she persuaded him that he was nevertheless a born salesman, just the right person to hawk a certain kind of property to a certain kind of buyer. This is perhaps his biggest transaction so far, the divestment by Merton College of its ancient landholdings in and around a small Leicestershire town.

'I wish you'd told me she was coming.'

Hugh looks at Julia now with the particular kind of earnest expression that is most likely to irritate her. 'It's Monday. Usually you go to work.' He gets up from the table. 'I'm sorry, but I need to catch up on some reading before she arrives.'

Half an hour later, Julia is showered and dressed and listening to the throbbing cadence of a diesel engine outside. She watches from the kitchen window as Hugh's older half-sister climbs out of the taxi and approaches with small and deliberate steps up the drive. When the bell rings, she counts to thirteen before walking into the hall and opening the front door.

'Hello, Ruth.' She forces herself to smile.

'Ah, Julia. I didn't expect you to be at home. I hope I haven't missed Hugh—he promised me he'd be in this morning.' Ruth Mortimer speaks hurriedly, neither looking Julia fully in the eye nor allowing the words to interrupt her momentum as she continues on into the house. She is a thin woman with a long neck and features that have become more angular with the passing years. Her improbably dark hair is drawn up on top of her head in an elaborate twirled construction, securely pinned with a large blue lapis lazuli butterfly.

'He's in the study—'

'I'll go on through, shall I?'

'Yes, do, you know the way.'

Julia long ago gave up trying to analyse her lack of mutual understanding with her sister-in-law. At one time she would have made more of an effort, invited Ruth to share something of her presumably interesting life experience as a barrister attached to Gray's Inn and Keble College, Oxford. But the years have worn away Julia's tolerance for Ruth's brittle personality; and Ruth, in any case, has always been less likely to pay real attention to her than to offer veiled reprimands for her evident inattention to Hugh's well-being.

'It feels chilly in here,' Ruth says. 'Is the heating on? I'll just turn the thermostat up a little, if you don't mind.'

Julia does not reply, resists her reflexive response. She follows her sister-in-law through to Hugh's study at the back of the house. A tall window looks out to the strip of grass that runs parallel to the garden fence, where fresh-cut sections of the fallen oak branch have been stacked in a neat geometric pile. There is a narrow mahogany desk, and behind it a bookcase whose contents are arranged carefully according to size rather than subject. The opposite wall is filled with a diverse assortment of artwork. Farthest from the door is Edward, the Black Prince, on his knees in prayer beneath a gilded archway, and next to him a poster featuring assorted British freshwater fish species gazing lugubriously into the room. Salvador Dalí's *The Broken Bridge and the Dream*, with its skeletal, wraithlike figures melting into a gold and indigo sky, is mounted directly above Edward Burne-Jones' *The Beguiling of Merlin*, the magician lying

trapped in infatuated subservience at the feet of the lithe enchantress. Finally, closest to Julia, is a large and elaborate family tree
mounted in a heavy wooden frame.

Hugh is stretched out in a leather armchair in the corner, reading from a battered history journal. He looks up, smiles at his sister
with what seems a sincere enthusiasm. 'I've been reading about one
of our Mortimer ancestors,' he says.

'Some rapacious Norman knight, I expect,' Ruth says. There
is something caustic in her voice. 'Don't forget, I'm not especially
proud of our illustrious family history.'

Hugh lifts his hand in a gesture of frustration, then drops it with
a barely audible sigh, offers a small conciliatory smile. 'Don't get
worked up, Ruth. It's not worth it.'

Julia is irritated to see that he is still a little frightened of his sister. As their desultory exchange continues, she finds herself studying
the family tree on the wall beside her. It is a minor work of art, a
vanity piece commissioned by Hugh's father when he began what was
to have been his grand retirement project, a genealogical treatise on
the ancient Mortimer family. Robert Mortimer, who ended his military career as a lieutenant colonel in the Shropshire Light Infantry,
was an avid horseman and a heavy drinker of vintage port. He was
killed along with Hugh's mother, Sarah Mortimer, when the car he
was driving soon after finishing half a bottle of a 1963 Colheita went
through a guard-rail in the Malvern hills. At twenty years old, Hugh
inherited the family estates and also the task of bringing to a conclusion the voluminous *History of the Mortimer Family of the Welsh March*.

At the left-hand edge of the frame, in an ornate typeface, are the
words 'Wales' and 'England', from which two genealogical branches
advance to meet somewhere in the middle, then split again into two
new branches that continue to the right-hand edge. The first name

listed on the Welsh branch is Coel Hen, Old King Cole of the nursery rhyme, who died c. 800 AD. The English line, meanwhile, begins
with the Saxon Ecgbert, King of Wessex (died 839 AD). The two
lines meet in the year 1402, with the marriage of Sir Edmund Mortimer, a great-grandson of Edward III, to Catrin, daughter of Owain
Glyn Dŵr, Prince of Wales. Seeing Glyn Dŵr's name there reminds
Julia of her conversation with Donald, her small ill-tempered tirade
against the English theft of the Welsh heroic tradition. She regrets it
now, wonders just how strange and intense he must think her.

The upper right-hand branch of the family tree meanwhile
continues through the dynasty of John of Gaunt, then the Tudors,
the Stuarts, the House of Orange, the House of Hanover, and the
Saxe Coburgs, with the modern Windsors at the farthest edge. The
lower right-hand branch consists of a single unbroken line of Mortimers, father to son, from 1402 to the present day. It ends with Hugh
Edmund, the only son of the late Robert and Sarah Mortimer, with
Ruth Alice Mortimer, the product of Robert's first, short-lived marriage to a distant cousin, awkwardly attached by a faint dotted line.

'How many years has it been?' Ruth is saying, referring to Hugh's
work on the family history. 'Seventeen? Eighteen?' She speaks in an
ambiguous tone, almost light-hearted, though there is a trace of
venom in it. 'I think it's time to move on—don't you agree, Julia?'

This is a common and insidious device of Ruth's, to turn her
frustration with Hugh back on to Julia, whom she has always con-
sidered an unwelcome addition to the family. As Julia stands there
under her sister-in-law's condescending gaze, the idea of spending
any more time in her presence seems out of the question.

'I think I'd better leave you to it,' she says. 'I've remembered
something I need to finish off at work.'

She is on her way to the back door before they have a chance to react. She takes her bicycle out of the shed, wheels it down the path and out through the back gate behind her studio. Pedalling hard, she tries to blank out all conscious thought, lets the cool air wash over her as she makes her way along the familiar leafy avenues to the more crowded, urban streets of Jericho, then Great Clarendon Street and the home of the Oxford English Dictionary. She locks up her bicycle in its allotted space just inside the gate, blowing on her hands to take away the chill of the handlebars as she climbs the steps to the door.

'Morning, Miss Llewellyn.' Colin, the security guard, whose reddened drinker's face is in perfect counterpoint to his turbulent crop of white hair, gives every appearance of having only recently returned from the pub. 'Running a bit late today, are we?'

'Mondays,' Julia says, with a smile. 'I really hate them.'

'I'm right with you there, miss. There's always Tuesday, of course.' Colin chuckles quietly at this, waves her through the inner door. 'On you go, now.'

The dictionary's offices are tucked away in the corner of a modern addition to the mostly Georgian edifice that houses the larger Oxford University Press. Julia walks through to an open-plan space whose near-silence is disturbed only by the faintest of murmured conversations, the aggregated whisperings of pages turning, papers shuffling, pencils annotating in margins. As she heads for her desk, she glances across the room at her friend Otto Zeiss. Otto is a rounded, jovial man of about sixty, a specialist on Indo-European languages who moonlights at the OED three days per week. For now, she is glad to see from the glazed expression on his face that he is off on some far-away train of eastern thought, travelling through an exotic world of Sanskrit and Tocharian B.

Stacked neatly on Julia's chair is a new batch of word-slips sent in by the dictionary's network of readers around the globe. These tiny bibliographic infusions are its lifeblood, its arterial connection to fourteen centuries of English literature. It is easy and calming work to go through them, and Julia is glad of it this morning. First she organises the slips alphabetically, then scans them for obvious ambiguities that will need to be resolved later, and finally begins the much slower and more painstaking process of cross-referencing to the dictionary itself. From time to time she sets aside a usage that particularly catches her attention, to be shared later with colleagues.

Belomancy. 1646 SIR T. BROWNE Pseud. Ep. 272 A like way of Belomancy or Divination by Arrowes hath beene in request.

Snippets. 1664 BUTLER Hud. II. iii. 824 Witches Simpling, and on Gibbets Cutting from Malefactors snippets.

Sorryish. 1793 A. SEWARD Lett. (1811) III. 330 You would be sorry-ish to hear, that poor Moll Cobb is gone to her long home.

In this way, word by word, the morning hours tick comfortably by. Just before noon, her telephone rings, a familiar voice on the line. 'Julia? This is Donald Gladstone. I hope you don't mind—'

'Of course I don't mind.' Her reply is more terse than she intended, though this has the useful effect of disguising just how glad she is that he has called. 'What's new in the world of archaeology?'

'The usual stuff, I suppose—holes being dug, reports being written and filed away.'

Julia has a vision of Donald buried somewhere deep in an underground maze, surrounded by great towers of worthy paperwork ready to collapse on top of him. 'How romantic you make it sound.'

'I don't mind it at all, really. But listen,' Donald says, more animated now, 'I was just reading something that made me think of you, and how you challenged all my narrow-minded English assumptions on our walk up Solsbury Hill. I was wondering if we might meet up somewhere to continue that conversation.'

'I'd like that,' Julia says, the words coming too easily. She forces herself to stop and think. If it is the wrong thing to do, it should be harder to say yes. 'Do you mind if I ring you back tomorrow? We can make a proper plan then.'

At lunchtime, she declines Otto's offer of a sandwich in the canteen, keeps on working for an hour or more. By mid-afternoon, there is a dull throbbing pain in her right temple. Thinking to clear her head, she steps outside into fitful autumn sunshine with gusts of winds swirling up the yellowed leaves from the sycamore trees in the park across the road. She turns to the right on Walton Street, cuts through to St. Giles, then makes her way down into the medieval heart of Oxford. The streets are filled with a busy traffic of dour-faced pedestrians, students on rattling bicycles, a legion of raucous buses. High above, the declining autumn sun catching the uppermost ramparts of the old college buildings bathes them in a soft, rose-coloured light.

Julia crosses Broad Street to the music shop on the corner, wonders about going inside, instead continues along Turl Street to the neo-gothic archway and heavy wooden gates that mark the entrance to Jesus College. It is years since she has been here, but the porter seems to recognise her, waves her cheerfully through as if she last came this way the day before yesterday.

It was here in the springtime of her first year at Oxford that she sat down next to Hugh Mortimer at a seminar on medieval Welsh poetry given by Hugh's academic mentor, Caradoc Bowen, the long-time Professor of Celtic Studies at Jesus. She had first met Hugh back home in Wales, a few months before her sixteenth birthday. He was staying with his grandfather, Sir Charles Mortimer, who lived at Ty Faenor just a few miles along the valley from Dyffryn Farm, and he seemed the most mysterious and intriguing person she had ever come across. At the time she could do no more than worship him from afar, weaving her own secret stories of how they would fall in love, run away together into the mountains and never come back. Now, at eighteen, ambitious, poised, confident in her half-formed opinions, she was determined to make him her own.

During their first evenings together in Oxford, Hugh explained to her about his branch of the Mortimer family, a deep-rooted aristocratic dynasty with a long history in the border country between England and Wales. She remembers one night with a special clarity, sitting outside shivering faintly on a cool May evening at the Turf Tavern as Hugh described the happy Welsh summers of his childhood. He would be packed off every August to stay with Sir Charles, an intensely serious but kindly man who in his later years had come to value the Mortimer family manor of Ty Faenor above all else. His death when Hugh was seventeen precipitated a bitter conflict with Hugh's father, Robert, who had always favoured the expansive family estate at Melverley in Shropshire over the wilder and less productive Welsh lands. From that time, Hugh rejected the prospect of the patrician life his parents intended for him, instead devoting himself to political causes that were opposed to everything they stood for. He came to consider himself a true Welsh nationalist, having learned from his grandfather that he was descended not only from the Anglo-Norman Mortimers, but also from the royal Welsh dynasty of Owain Glyn Dŵr.

Hugh spoke to her with a surprising intensity in those days, but had a way afterwards of laughing at himself, of shrugging off all such pretension. Beneath his confidence and easy charm, he seemed burdened by a certain world-weary nobility and sadness. For Julia, this was a heady concoction that left her in no doubt as to what she wanted.

She walks on past the dining hall, through the connecting passage to the Second Quad. The entrance to Hugh's rooms was here, through the last door on the left and up the stone staircase to the top floor. It was all once as familiar to her as her own space at Wadham. She remembers Hugh running down these steps on the day he left Jesus College for the last time, vowing never to speak to Caradoc Bowen again.

As she walks around the perimeter of the quad, she sees eyes in the darkened windows, dozens of them all looking at her at once, the tall Dutch gables with their semi-circular pediments making haughty eyebrows that arch a little higher at every move she makes. It occurs to her that Bowen, though surely by now in his eighties, is still here somewhere: perhaps even now watching her, stern-faced, remembering how she took Hugh Mortimer away from him. She hurries on, glad to complete her circuit and escape through the gate to the anonymous, bustling safety of the Oxford streets.

The afternoon brings a merciful break from routine, an annual meeting of editorial staff from across the press. The first presenter is the OED's Chief Editor, Peter Harington, who is to give a progress update on the new edition of the dictionary. Julia arrives early, sits in an empty row near the back of the room. In due course she is joined there by Otto Zeiss, who proceeds to entertain her with his usual trenchant asides.

Before long, Harington is standing up at the front of the room in characteristically fulsome flow. 'For those of us who are lucky enough to have a close acquaintance with the OED,' he says, 'it seems a very contradictory sort of beast. Its ongoing care requires a labour simultaneously of the highest forms of human expression and of that harmless drudgery of which Samuel Johnson was the first and most distinguished exponent. Its content, meanwhile, is of serious interest to rather few, yet remains of inestimable importance to world scholarship.'

'*Und so weiter,*' Otto murmurs, his face set in a mask of solemnity. 'He gave the same talk five years ago. And ten and fifteen years ago also. The world will come to an end, and still he is giving this talk.'

'We are the taxonomists of a vast evolutionary structure,' Peter Harington is saying, 'a genetic encoding of the English language that captures with equal precision the most high-flown and the most mundane of human utterances. The work we do now will surely persist, in one form or another, for countless generations to come. It is proper that we remember this as we bend our arm to the daily lexical toil.'

There is a good deal more in this vein, followed by upbeat presentations from other divisions of the press, those concerned with the publication of scientific journals and medical textbooks and the classics of world literature. After the meeting has finished, there is an early move for the OED staff to the Old Bookbinders Arms, a Monday afternoon ritual of long standing. Today's expedition is invested with a special significance as a celebration of the completion of the letter *C*.

Julia is content to sit in a cosy nook at the Bookbinders, drinking the glasses of wine that others put in front of her. She does her best to fend off the Chief Editor's enthusiastic questions about her Welsh childhood, then listens patiently to Otto as he proceeds to expound at length, in his grave Viennese way, on the possibility that the Phoenicians influenced the vocabulary and syntax of Old High German, prompting the suggestion that this great seafaring people may have established settlements as far north as the Baltic Sea.

She stays an hour longer than she meant to, rides her bicycle reluctantly home through the darkened streets. The house feels empty at first, and she is glad of it, but her sense of reprieve is short-lived. Hugh has settled himself quietly in the living room with a stack of paperwork and two fingers of whisky in a heavy crystal glass. The television is on for the evening news, with the volume turned almost all the way down.

'Good time?' he says, not looking up. He is wearing his reading glasses, which give him less the look of a scholar than of a politician striving for empathy.

'Just the usual Monday crowd.' She sits down in the opposite corner of the room, close to the television. The mellowness from the wine is fading into a commonplace exhaustion.

'I have a question for you.'

Something in his voice puts Julia on her guard. 'What is it, Hugh?'

'If I needed to find out more about the history of the Merton College landholdings, where would you suggest I look?' His tone is matter-of-fact, as if it were not almost unheard-of for him to ask for her help on a work-related question. It crosses her mind that he is making an effort to connect with her, that he is perhaps trying very hard. She wonders whether he will want to make love to her tonight; whether she should be the one to make the first move.

'Best to go to the Merton library,' she says. 'I know someone over there—I could set it up, if you like.'

'If it's not too much trouble.'

Julia looks at him sharply, wondering if she has misinterpreted him. But he has returned to his paperwork, making a show of turning pages, underlining passages of text. Now her attention is caught by something on the news; she reaches to turn up the volume.

'Some are calling it the archaeological discovery of the century. To help us put it into context, we are joined by the leader of the excavation, Professor Paul Healey of Cambridge University, and by Dr. Lucinda Trevelyan of St. Anne's College, Oxford, who has also had an opportunity to examine the finds.' The seasoned interviewer, Miles Johnson, gravely furrowing his brow, speaks with an authoritative staccato delivery honed by several decades at the BBC. 'Paul Healey, you have not gone quite so far as to say that you have discovered the bones of King Arthur and Queen Guinevere, but neither have you denied it.'

Healey is a small, weatherbeaten man in his fifties, quick to smile in a twinkling, insubstantial way. He now adopts for the camera what seems to Julia a carefully calibrated expression of wry incredulity, a projected irony that is reinforced by a hint of a Merseyside accent. 'I have of course said nothing of the sort. What we have discovered is a quantity of ancient human skeletons—in my experience, they don't come with name tags attached.'

'That's not really an answer, though, Professor Healey?'

'It's an archaeologist's answer, Mr. Johnson. I can only interpret the evidence that I see in front of me.' Again, the ready smile. 'Anything beyond that is pure speculation.'

Johnson turns his attention to the other studio guest. 'Some enthusiasts are saying, Lucy Trevelyan, that the ceramic cup found at Devil's Barrow might be the Holy Grail itself. What do you make of that?'

Lucinda Trevelyan, who has remained tight-lipped during the initial exchange, is a tall woman in her late thirties, oddly but not inelegantly dressed in a long flowing dress decorated in a dramatic abstract motif. Her face has a narrow, hawkish kind of beauty to it, though firmly set in deep lines of disapproval.

'That's nonsense, of course,' she says, 'insofar as you are speaking of the Grail as a Christian symbol derived from medieval French romance.' She speaks with a restrained fervor in an American voice that is low-pitched and soft but devoid of all self-consciousness, her arguments brooking no opposition. 'And this is, in any case, entirely the wrong question to ask.'

'Which would be the right question, in your opinion?'

Lucy Trevelyan is careful to avoid eye contact with her fellow studio guest. 'I should like to ask Professor Healey how he was able to conclude that the burials date from the fifth century AD.'

Paul Healey, now wearing a look of faint amusement, has evidently been expecting this question. 'As I have made very clear, that was a preliminary conclusion only, based on the evidence of Roman coins discovered in the pit—'

'People drop coins by mistake, or deliberately throw them into holes in the ground for good luck. This is quite an ancient practice, I think you will find.'

'—and as my distinguished colleague is well aware, a formal carbon dating of the organic remains is now under way.'

Johnson steps in adroitly to bolster Healey's flagging argument. 'That's right, is it not, Dr. Trevelyan? We'll have a definitive answer soon enough.'

'Well, yes, I imagine a proper dating of the bones will settle the question. In the meantime, there are other kinds of evidence that are generally reliable. For example, the ritual cup discovered in the burial pit was still enclosed in the embrace of its protector, suggesting to me that it is unlikely to have been a random accretion, something that just happened to be thrown in there. In my opinion, the style and decoration of this artefact point to a far earlier date, possibly fifteen hundred years earlier than has been suggested.'

Paul Healey's laugh is perhaps intended to be scornful, though he puts a little too much good nature into it. 'That's pure speculation, of course—'

'Speculation that is informed by many years of careful study.' Lucy Trevelyan now turns to face her adversary with an expression of pure insouciance. 'I believe you have entirely misinterpreted the archaeological evidence, Professor Healey. As your own team has noted, the woman whose remains were discovered at the top of the funerary pile was a person of high status. She is, in my opinion, most readily identified as a priestess of the matriarchal culture that was widespread across Old Europe prior to the Indo-European incursions that finally reached Britain in the latter part of the second millennium BC.'

By now, Julia is completely caught up in this oddly compelling exchange. Despite Lucy Trevelyan's obvious eccentricity, there is an appealing passion in her, a kind of intense, charismatic self-belief that cares nothing for correctness or convention.

Lucy, who is entirely in command of the camera, pauses significantly, and Miles Johnson cannot help but take the bait. 'That seems a rather dramatic claim. Does the evidence in fact support it?'

'The evidence must of course be allowed to speak for itself, but I believe it is plausible, indeed likely, that the female remains from Devil's Barrow are those of one of the last keepers of an ancient matrilineal civilisation that once held sway across the European continent. This was a culture that persisted for many centuries in Britain before it was utterly destroyed by the Celtic warrior elites who swept across the island from the south and east.'

'Are you suggesting,' Johnson says, 'that this woman was killed in some kind of last-ditch defence of her people?'

'I would not make such an extravagant statement as that. I merely observe that her lifeless body was thrown on top of a heap made from the corpses of the warriors who died with her, and that they in turn seem to have been killed in some perverse act of ritual sacrifice. They were made to suffer the threefold death, a gruesome practice known to have been a hallmark of the incoming Celts. This was their own dreadful, contemptuous corruption of the ancient British reverence for the triune gods of earth, sun, and moon, and of the places made sacred by the power of three.'

Paul Healey, who has been listening in bemused silence, now takes his chance. 'If I may say, this is a quite remarkable and impressive leap of the imagination. Of course there's nothing in the archaeology that would directly support such an interpretation.'

Lucy turns her calm gaze on him. 'As you know, Professor Healey, I am not a strong believer in the received wisdom of the archaeological establishment.'

'That's all very well, Dr. Trevelyan,' Miles Johnson says, 'but you have not really answered the charge that is laid against you. Our viewers might like to know where your ideas have come from.'

'From a careful evaluation and interpretation of the evidence,' Lucy says, speaking now with a steely self-assurance, 'combined with numerous personal observations of similar sites throughout central and eastern Europe. The woman buried at Devil's Barrow bears the hallmarks of one who wielded a great spiritual power as representative on earth of the mother goddess whom her people revered above all others. She was a weaver of spells, a powerful spiritual leader presiding over a ritual of renewal and rebirth at the great stone circle. We may see in her an embodiment of one the Greeks called Artemis, the divine huntress and protector of womanhood. At the centre of her power and her art was the beautiful ritual chalice that she carried with her to her death.'

As Johnson reaches for a response to Lucy's astonishing discourse, it is Hugh who speaks into the brief, awkward silence. *'Belakneskato she was named, the death-wielder.'*

Julia notices that his glass is empty, wonders how much he has drunk. 'What was that, Hugh?'

'It's a line from one of the poems Bowen used to recite to us. Something she said made me think of it.' There is a fleeting intensity in his expression, broken straight away by a dismissive wave of the hand. 'It's not important.'

It is almost shocking to hear him refer to Caradoc Bowen, whose name he would never ordinarily mention. This is a part of his life that has been closed to Julia for fourteen years at least, since the events that led to Hugh's bitter falling-out with his former mentor. Sensing an opportunity for some kind of liberating conversation, she tries to press her advantage. 'I'd like to hear about it,' she says.

'It hardly matters, Julia.' Now she hears the familiar tone of mild irritation, shutting off the possibility of further discussion. 'I'm a little tired. I think I'll head upstairs, if you don't mind.'

The BBC man is meanwhile bringing things to a close. 'I would like to ask you both one last question. What, in your opinion, was the purpose of the ceramic cup? Paul Healey?'

Healey seems back in his element. 'I'll admit it's a beautiful object, fit for a British queen,' he says, the twinkle in his eye fully restored. 'The presence of traces of blood might suggest some sort of ritual significance, but in my view there's no need to look for complicated explanations. In the end I suspect it was nothing more than a superior kind of drinking vessel.'

'And Lucy Trevelyan? Do you agree with your colleague's rather prosaic analysis?'

For the first time, Lucy smiles austerely for the camera. 'The chalice was, and is, a magical thing, that much is clear to me. Perhaps we should not attempt to interpret it beyond that?'

Lucy has the last word, and the interview is wrapped up. Hugh is now standing in the doorway that leads to the stairs. 'Will you come up soon?' he says.

It is a clear enough invitation, and Julia finds herself wishing he would simply take her by the hand and lead her to bed, as he would in the old days. 'I won't be long,' she says.

In the end she stays up for another hour or more, finding unopened post to go through, counter-tops to wipe, things to tidy up, her mind racing all the while on Hugh's startling reference to Caradoc Bowen and his poem, on Lucy Trevelyan's vivid description of the woman of Devil's Barrow and her magical chalice.

The Song of Lailoken

CUTTING ACROSS LONELY chalk downlands, the train skirts the northern border of Cerdic's ancient kingdom of Wessex, crossing the line of the old soldiers' road from Corinium to Calleva, then following the Vale of the White Horse as it runs through the lands of the Brigovantes to the east. To the right, the long escarpment of the Berkshire Downs marks the line of the Ridgeway path, for over four thousand years the most important road of southern Britain. Here on the grassy uplands, in earthy mounds and cold stone barrows, lie buried the greatest leaders of bronze-age Britain.

As Donald gazes out through the half-fogged glass at this landscape of rolling fields and curved green horizons, the soporific cadence of the wheels on the track carries him along the pleasant dreamy verge of sleep. He awakens some time later with a start, reaches into his pocket for his handkerchief to wipe a small dribble of saliva from his chin. Crossing the Thames at Goring, the train coasts on through Pangbourne with its vistas of neat suburban houses dispelling all sense of history.

At Reading, the carriage fills up with London commuters. It seems to Donald, as he watches them unfurl their salmon-pink newspapers, that these people are uncommonly calm, focused, in control of their professional lives. He tries to gather his thoughts for the upcoming meeting with his editor. Felicity will gently try to steer him, as she always does; they will have the kind of conversation they always have. He takes out his manuscript, turns through the pages one more time, still hoping to find the essential, decisive insight that will make sense of it all.

Meanwhile, he cannot stop thinking about Lucy and her excruciating television interview. Paul Healey, having failed to recognise the strength and agility of his opponent, came off far worse in the exchange, but at least he did not abandon all his scholarly principles. As to how Lucy was able to get sight of the Devil's Barrow finds and then insinuate herself into the BBC newsroom with Healey, perhaps it is better not to ask. In some ways, Paul and Lucy make a likely pair; they are, after all, two of the most successful self-promoters in British archaeology. It occurs to Donald, with a surprising twinge of jealousy, that Lucy may have slept with Healey in return for sundry academic favours, then taken her chance to stab him in the back on national television.

Outside the window, Windsor Castle makes a dramatic silhouette of towers and battlements on the southern horizon. The train rattles on past deciduous suburbs, along brick-lined Victorian canyons carved through Northolt, Greenford, and Ealing, and finally through a railwayman's maze of rusting steel into the cavernous dimness of Paddington Station. Stepping out on to the platform, Donald is immediately caught up in the crowd pressing forward in the direction of the main concourse, the *Financial Times* readers rushing to save precious seconds in their twelve-hour days. Despite the chaos of humanity, this is a familiar and comforting space, with its high curving roof, timetables clicking overhead, the announcer's voice rising resonant and lifeless above the throng. He heads straight for the taxi rank, climbs into a waiting cab, and is soon being driven through watery London sunlight towards Belgravia.

The offices of Crandall & Boyd, Publishers, are situated in an imposing 1830s town-house with a polished brass nameplate at the door. The receptionist, tweedy and efficient, looks up at Donald with an overly practised smile. 'If you'd like to take a seat, Mr. Gladstone, Miss Wickes will be with you shortly.' She directs him to a cluster of straight-backed chairs arranged in front of a tall bookcase displaying a selection of titles from the publisher's two and a half centuries of history. On the top shelf is an impressive array of leather-bound volumes, amongst them the arrestingly titled *Zoonomia, or the Laws of Organic Life*, published in 1796 by Erasmus Darwin, who did not live long enough to see his work eclipsed by that of his more famous grandson. Placed unfortunately, or whimsically, next to the elder Darwin is a Victorian edition of the biblical chronology of James Ussher, seventeenth-century Archbishop of Armagh, according to whom the world began on the morning of 1 January, 4004 BC.

Donald searches in vain on the lower shelves for his own book, published two years earlier by Crandall & Boyd. It was a surprising success at the time, *A Dark Age Landscape: The Archaeology of Sub-Roman Britain*. Intended as a serious academic study, it gained some traction in the bookshops largely (Donald has always assumed) because of the publisher's insistence on a highly marketable title. On the strength of this achievement, he was able to negotiate a second contract for a book aimed more squarely at the popular market.

'Donald, how are you?' A plump young woman in a shiny black skirt and purple blouse comes striding across the room towards him. 'Good to see you again,' she says, grasping his hand. 'How was the journey? Packed in like sardines?'

'No, it was fine,' Donald says. 'I like the train. It's a good place to think.'

'Good. Excellent. Let's go upstairs, and we can have a proper talk.'

Felicity's office is a jumbled papery landscape. 'Sorry about the mess,' she says. 'People will insist on sending me their life's work.' She taps her hand against a large green bin at the office door, brimming with countless hours of profitless literary effort. 'At least I can offload the slush pile to Emily—she's been a great help.' Emily, who is rapidly turning pages in a small office across the corridor, looks very clever, though much too young to be behind a desk.

Donald sits in a leather armchair next to the tall sash window with its striking view across the road to the tightly wooded edge of Belgrave Square Gardens. He digs into his briefcase, pulls out the cardboard folder. 'I've made a few changes to the version I sent you,' he says. 'I took out some of the denser background material on Geoffrey of Monmouth.'

'Well, I'm glad to hear it, Donald. When I was reading the previous draft, I couldn't help wondering why there was quite so much of Geoffrey. He seems mostly incidental to the story, don't you think?'

The charming look of uncertainty and contrition on Felicity's face persuades him she is not joking. Geoffrey's fanciful history of the British monarchy, the *Historia Regum Britanniae*, with its heroic narrative of Arthur and its famous prophecies spoken by the young Merlin, was responsible for the transformation of these characters from largely unfamiliar names in the old Welsh tales, little known beyond the Celtic lands, into the most celebrated figures of medieval romance. The implausible historical writings of this twelfth-century scholar have been a central theme of Donald's research from the outset. 'Don't forget, he's the reason we have all heard of King Arthur.'

'I'm sorry to be such a poor student,' Felicity says, grimacing faintly. 'I do very much admire what you've done.'

Donald finds himself smiling in sympathy with his editor as she stretches her diplomatic skills to the limit. 'Why don't you tell me what you really think?'

She hesitates now, choosing her words cautiously. 'Your writing seems so full of caveats and qualifications. I'm hearing about who Arthur was not, rather than who he really was.'

'That's exactly the point,' Donald says. 'If there ever was an Arthur of history, he is lost to us. All we can do is try to understand the origins of the story, and why it became so pervasive in European mythology.'

Felicity, despite her ignorance of the twelfth century, is a dependable literary pragmatist. 'I think your readers are going to want something a little more positive than that. If Arthur is so tenuous, historically speaking, could you perhaps get a little more creative, try to reconstruct him as he might have been?'

Donald is rescued from answering this question by a loud knock at the door. 'But now here's Madeleine,' Felicity says. 'We can ask her what she thinks. You remember Madeleine, of course?'

Madeleine d'Alembert, director of sales and marketing at Crandall & Boyd, would be a difficult person to forget. She is slim, elegant, dressed in black with lipstick and nail varnish in a coordinated dark crimson. Her face is frozen in an arctic demeanour that perceptibly chills the air as she walks into the room. She smiles, and the ice cracks momentarily.

'Hello, Donald,' she says. There is the faintest hint of a French accent. Her nails dig in a little as she shakes his hand. 'I hope you haven't quite finished your book yet, because I have something for you—but I expect you have seen this already?' She hands him a cutting from the *Guardian* newspaper, a short, whimsical article from the bottom of the front page.

(Un)Holy Grail Discovered in Wiltshire Field

Despite the lofty ambitions of her mythical quest, Dr. Lucinda Trevelyan of St. Anne's College, Oxford would be the first to admit that she is far from being the perfect Grail knight. She is female, of course, and half-American on her mother's side, neither of which were attributes of Sir Perceval; though it is true that she, like Sir P., was removed at an early age from the corrupted world of chivalry (England), to be brought up by her mother in rural obscurity (California); and that she, being precocious in the acquisition of knightly skills, was determined to return to the royal court at the earliest opportunity. This she did in fine style some ten years ago, having first obtained her doctorate from Berkeley, and has since made her reputation at Oxford as an outspoken nonconformist scholar working at the thinly populated intersection of women's studies and archaeology.

Dr. Trevelyan's unusual characterisation of the ritual cup discovered in an excavated pit near Stonehenge as a 'magical' object has led to some speculation that the Holy Grail has at last come to light. While scholars may choose to enter into prolonged and elaborate arguments about provenances and dates, and amateur enthusiasts may wonder quite how Joseph of Arimathea came to lose his prize possession in a Wiltshire field, Dr. Trevelyan consciously distances herself from such debates. 'In ancient times,' she avows, 'the Grail was revered as a pure symbol of the feminine divine. Medieval France is solely to blame for its brash appropriation by the Christian faith as the holy vessel of the Last Supper.'

With such trenchant opinions as these combined with her dramatic presence and fearsome erudition, Lucinda Trevelyan seems likely to become something of an icon herself. When this newspaper tried to reach her by telephone at St. Anne's, we were told that she was engaged in an interview for the *Daily Mail*, and would call us back later.

Donald exhales deeply and slowly, unsure whether to laugh or to cry. 'From this morning's paper?' he says.

'Yes, this morning,' Madeleine says, 'but of course you know about this already? This is your wife we are speaking of, this lady who so disdains my noble country?'

'My ex-wife. We were divorced a few months ago.'

'I am so sorry, Donald.' Madeleine's regret seems entirely sincere. 'She is such a remarkable woman.'

Felicity has a familiar discerning expression on her face. 'Should we be sorry?'

'Not in the least. You should be happy for me.'

'But of course this is perfect,' Madeleine says, the French coming back more strongly into her voice. 'We can put our clever English scholar up against the crazy woman from America.'

Donald cannot help smiling. 'I'm not quite sure what you have in mind.'

Madeleine picks up the cutting, flaps it melodramatically in front of his face. 'You can use this in your book somehow, surely? The discovery of the Holy Grail?'

'I've decided I'm not going to take that suggestion seriously.'

'Archaeologists can be so dull.' Madeleine's smile is a flash of crimson on white. 'If we're quick, we can be first out on the street with our version of the story. You could do a documentary, Donald, become the new face of TV archaeology. What do you think, Felicity?'

'I'm not sure our author is quite convinced,' Felicity says.

Half an hour later, nursing a second pint of Fuller's ESB at the Prince of Wales pub, Donald is feeling quite sure of his opinions. 'You seem to have mistaken me for the kind of person you assume Lucy would be married to,' he says. 'She was once my wife, but not any more. And even if we were still married, you would never persuade me to write that sort of book. It's almost the opposite of what I set out to do.'

Madeleine casually swirls the umbrella stick in her vodka martini. 'So your book will become the opposite of a bestseller, is this the idea?'

'Leave him alone,' Felicity says. 'He can't help having principles.'

'I was never troubled by them, darling.' Madeleine empties her glass in one go, winking at Donald. 'Sorry, but I must be getting back—I've got some sales figures to muster up for the boss this afternoon.'

'Please don't pay any attention to her,' Felicity says, in the calm that follows Madeleine's departure. 'She likes to pretend she works for a more glamorous company. I'm with you on this, Donald. I'm not at all interested in publishing something that's a fake.'

※ ※ ※

JULIA IS DUE to spend the day in the section of the Bodleian known as Duke Humfrey's Library, where she has privileged access to materials from one of the most extensive medieval collections in the world. She heads in early, cycling down the Woodstock Road to St. Giles, then cutting along the path that skirts the leafy parkland behind St. John's College. At the main entrance to the library on Catte Street, she finds a small knot of people gathered in wholesome silence in the courtyard, familiar zealous faces waiting patiently to go in. She smiles at some of them, acquaintances of a sort though they rarely exchange more than a few words during this long-standing morning ritual.

When the doors are opened, she is the first to walk up the stairs and into the cool, dark, silent gallery of Duke Humfrey's, with its extraordinary painted ceiling and ranks of heavy book stacks on either side. She makes her way through the older part of the library to her favourite reading desk, tucked in at the far end with an unobstructed view through the westerly window to the grounds of Exeter College. Once she is seated there, she feels the first infusions of a familiar tranquillity, a renewed sense of the order and importance of intangible things. It is a feeling that often overtakes her in a great calming wave as she adjusts to the mood of this hallowed literary space. Here, through a mixture of educated guesswork and pure serendipity, she hopes to find some of the earliest recorded uses of words in the English language. When things are going well, this is the part of her job that she likes most of all, the thrill of lexical discovery, the small rush of elation that accompanies the unsuspected literary find. She rarely tires of it, finds that her hours spent at the Bodleian resist all notions of the routine.

Taking out her thick marbled notebook, Julia finds her bearings by flicking through the pages from the beginning. This particular book, the latest in a long series, runs from the middle of the letter *C* to the start of *D*. Each page is devoted to a single word written boldly at the top: *coolly, coolness, coolrife, coolth*. Some of the entries are crowded with her small neat script, excerpts from sundry texts prefaced with essential bibliographic data, the word of the moment underlined in their midst, while others are almost entirely blank, signifying hours or sometimes days of fruitless searching. She keeps on turning the pages, *coolung, coolweed, coolwort, cooly*. Then comes a word that gave her some trouble a year or so before: *coom* or *combe*, deep hollow or valley, one of rather few loan-words that made the jump from early Welsh into Old English. In her quest to find an earlier usage of this word than any previously discovered, *combe* presented her with a particular challenge because (as she noted near the top of the page) a very early quotation had already been found in an Anglo-Saxon charter of the eighth century AD:

> 770 in Birch *Cartul. Sax.* I. 290 (No. 204) Of þære brigge in cumb; of þam cumbe in ale beardes ac.

To go back further, she decided to begin her search with the medieval Anglo-Welsh ecclesiastical materials, on the provisional hypothesis that the earliest extant uses of *combe* might be found in English translations of documents relating to the Welsh monasteries (which were often situated in remote valleys). Beneath the citation she wrote:

> Welsh monastic establishments, fifth to seventh century. Try Bowen's poetry book from TF?

Reading this last sentence, Julia's fragile serenity is disturbed by a powerful sense of *déjà vu*. At the time, she did not pursue this particular lead for *combe*. It was in any case highly speculative, and it prompted unwelcome memories of Caradoc Bowen, Hugh's mentor

at Jesus College. She rests her head in her hands, casts her mind back
to a talk of Bowen's she once attended with Hugh. The topic of his
presentation that day was a book of poetry he had discovered many
years before in a manuscript collection that was then still held at the
manor house of Ty Faenor. Professor Bowen described to them a
particular poem he had found in this book, an extraordinary narrative depicting a series of heroic battles from the distant past. She can
see him standing there at the podium, focusing all the energy of the
room into his voice as he recited glowing fragments of ancient verse.

This is the text that Hugh was quoting from the night before,
Julia is quite sure of it. Something Lucy Trevelyan said about the
Devil's Barrow finds made him think of it. Caradoc Bowen's poetry
book suddenly seems of far more than academic interest. It might
have something to tell her about Hugh's intense relationship with
Bowen, a part of his life she has never quite been able to come to
terms with. Perhaps there is a clue to be found in this poem that so
inspired Bowen and lodged so indelibly in Hugh's memory of that
time, something that might help her to understand. For now, all
thoughts of lexicography are forgotten.

The librarian on duty at the main reference desk is one of the old
hands, long accustomed to such unusual enquiries. 'That's a tricky
one,' he says, running an earnest hand across his balding scalp. 'We
could give you special access to the entire collection, if you think
that might help. But if I were you, I'd try to speak to the boss—this
sounds like Dr. Rackham's sort of thing.'

Julia walks along the corridor to a heavy panelled door bearing
the words *Bodley's Librarian* embossed in gold. She knocks firmly, is
invited to come in by an authoritative female voice. The door opens
to a spacious interior flooded with light from a pair of tall windows
that look out on a startlingly green vista of the Fellows' Garden of

Exeter College. The walls are lined with fine antiquarian maps and prints. In the centre of the room, seated at a massive desk of apparently medieval construction, is the venerable Dr. Margaret Rackham. She has thick grey hair and piercing blue eyes that make her seem, at first glance, to be somewhere in her sixties; but this initial impression is belied by an extraordinary network of deep wrinkles around the eyes and across the cheeks, evidence of a long life spent in contemplation of the written word.

'It's Julia, isn't it, from the OED?' she says. Despite her decidedly aristocratic accent, any lingering sense of imperiousness vanishes instantly. 'You came to me once before, to ask if you could have a look at Junius II, the Cædmon manuscript.'

'Yes, that's right. I'm surprised you remembered.'

'Such is the librarian's curse. I remember a great many things, sometimes rather more than I would like. What may I do for you, my dear?'

As Julia relates her story of Bowen's poetry book, she judges from the growing expression of curiosity on the librarian's face that she has come to the right place. 'There was a time when I saw a good deal of Caradoc Bowen,' Margaret Rackham says. 'I was a junior postgraduate when he first became a Fellow of Jesus College, and it must be said that there was something both attractive and mysterious about him in those days. He was by far the cleverest person I had ever met, and a naturally gifted poet, too, being closely related on his mother's side to the Powys family of literary fame. But he was also in some ways a strange and difficult man. I'm afraid I have rarely spoken to him in recent years.'

To Julia, Margaret Rackham's words seem imbued with a faint wistful sense of lost opportunity. She finds herself transported to another era, imagining a striking young Caradoc Bowen, the brilliant new Oxford don, and the youthful Margaret, sharp as a knife and beautiful too, admiring him from afar. 'Did you know him very well?' she says, then regrets her careless question.

The librarian fixes her with a cool gaze. 'Before I answer that, I should like to know why you are so interested in this book of his.'

Julia feels entirely unready to confess her vague presentiments and intuitions to such an august authority. 'My main interest is in Welsh loan-words that found their way into Old English,' she says. 'I'm looking for new materials that might help me with my research.'

'Which makes it seem rather a large effort to hunt down such an obscure manuscript, unless you already have an idea of what you hope to find?'

Something in Margaret Rackham's candid expression seems to invite the sharing of confidences, but Julia is careful not to say too much. 'There was an old battle-poem—Professor Bowen gave a talk on it once, a long time ago. I was hoping to track down the original.'

Julia is made to feel the full weight of disbelief in the long, contemplative look the librarian gives her. 'I do wonder if there's something you're not telling me, my dear. Be that as it may, I believe I know precisely what you are looking for. Give me just a moment, would you?'

The Bodley's Librarian turns to her card catalogue, throwing up faint clouds of old library dust as she opens and closes the small wooden drawers. Some minutes pass as she follows an apparently complex bibliographic trail. Eventually, a faded manila file emerges from a massive filing cabinet. 'Why don't you start with this?' she says. 'Meanwhile, I'll see about having the original brought up for you to look at. Won't be a tick.' To Julia's surprise, rather than pick up the telephone, she gets up from her desk and walks briskly out of her office, closing the door firmly behind her.

The room falls into a near-silence filled with the resonant ticking of a carriage clock, previously unnoticed on a corner shelf. Julia opens the file, takes out a hand-written letter and its original envelope bearing a postmark from nearly fifty years in the past.

My dear Margaret,

I write to you today from Ty Faenor House, where I find that my amiable host, Sir Charles Mortimer, has inherited his due share of the antiquarian sensibility that has run so strongly in his family for the past three hundred years. Sir Charles has allowed me to remain as his guest for a week longer than I had planned, with the happy result that my research in the medieval manuscript collection held in the library here has at last borne sudden and unexpected fruit in the shape of a previously unknown manuscript dating from the fifteenth century.

I do not propose to dwell here on the manner of its discovery, save to say that it was experienced as something closer to fate than to happenstance. I had been searching for early sources relating to my main subject of study, the poet Siôn Cent, when my eye was drawn inexorably, as it seemed, to an outwardly unremarkable volume in a plain monastic binding of the kind often produced in the Welsh scriptoria. Upon taking this volume down from the shelf, I was disappointed to find the earliest parchment folios, twelve quires of eight leaves each, destroyed beyond repair or restoration by a penicillium mould whose inexorable progression had erased all immediate evidence of the title, authorship, and provenance of the manuscript. The later pages had fortunately for the most part been spared, and there I was able to read a series of previously unknown poems written unmistakably in his customary meter of *cywydd deuair hirion* by the bard whom I have come to know almost as a companion and friend, Master Siôn Cent. This was precisely what I had been seeking, the earliest poems of Siôn Cent whose work had previously been known only from the austere religious pieces composed in his later years at Kentchurch Court.

Though this was perhaps a sufficient revelation in itself, there was more to follow. It was almost that I heard a siren voice in my head, urging me to *turn the leaf, turn the leaf*, until I came upon a remarkable text presented under a title, the Song of Lailoken, that will not be entirely unfamiliar to you from your knowledge of the Welsh mythical canon (Lailoken, as you may recall, was the original Welsh model for the prophet Merlin), though the lines written beneath it most assuredly will.

One other observation may be of interest. At the head of the first folio of this poem, our bard adds a short and stirring preamble, informing us as follows: 'I relate here the true story of Arthur's return, that all Welshmen may know of him, and his rise to glory, and his fall to earth, and that hidden place where he entered the gates of the otherworld. Let none doubt the veracity of this tale, for I have taken it from the words of Merlin found in Cyndeyrn's book which fate has brought to my hand.'

It is better, in any case, that the poet be allowed to speak for himself. I therefore enclose herewith my free translation from the curiously archaic Welsh of the original text. I ask merely that you study it very carefully, and in due course do me the kindness of sharing with me your observations upon this most unusual text.

Yours sincerely,

C. H. R. BOWEN

Attached to Bowen's letter with a rusty paperclip are two further hand-written sheets on which he has presented his English translation of Siôn Cent's original Welsh text.

THE SONG OF LAILOKEN

The crab I am called, safe-keeper of wisdom
Guardian of ancient songs, voice of the red dragon
Whose beating wings are heard in mortal hearts
Soaring far above the three-tongued serpent
Gorged on its own children's flesh.

Fiercely we battled them in those days, red against white
Fire scorched the mountainsides
Rivers turned black with blood
Winds alone scattered the pleading death-moans
Of their pale-winged god.

First at the sky-temple, giant-wrought circle
Our foe standing proud upon her charnel-stone
Belak-neskato she was named, the death-wielder
Draining blood of men three-times slain
To slake the white serpent, three-times thirsting
Sky-devil who bore the giants' ring from farthest west
To make this hallowed killing-place.

It was Arthur gave life to our courage
Strove with her twin protectors, Araket and Madarakt
Painted petty-gods on earth, their strength availed them nothing
The first meeting Arthur's blade, the second flew the field

Then our champion leaping high struck down the black enchantress
Tore her from her gruesome perch.
I did not heed her last-breath's screeching
Threefold life she promised me, and threefold death
My doom the venom on her tongue.

Thence to the black water we came softly at dawn
Strong in battle, we slew eagerly with silent blade
Swift was the fate that felled our enemy that day
Awoken from sleep, their morning feast was bitter
Sent by bright sword's edge to the dark river water.

On a green hilltop we made our stand, spear-tips trapping gold of
    sunset
Bold herald of darkness and the dread that ensnared us
Arthur alone bore our courage on his shield
His ardour undiminished, our grim-blooded scourge
Nine times our number cut down in that terrible charge
At nightfall we fell like thunder down the slope.

Then at the last, to the crooked vale where the three rivers fall
We strove for the heights but they held us there
Caught us at sun's falling, trapped at axe's edge
Grimly we gathered, in close rank, certain of death
Crags raised red like bloodied fists above us
The distant water rushing, whispering, sighing
The river, a wolf's-head smile carved far below.

In purest air we heard it in the thudding of our hearts
Great wingbeats in the eastern sky, our foe was upon us

White serpent circling, thirsting for the certain feast
Our champion Arthur stepping forward
The giant Madarakt beckoned him to his doom.

To the crooked vale we came, in fleeting joy beheld
The beast cast down by Arthur's sword
All saw him do it, heard the sighing of the wind
Watched the dying of the evening light
As he too was felled by this creature's mortal strike.

We bore him up to the highest cliff-top, gate of the otherworld
Laid him beneath a linden tree, the shield-wood powerless now
The words unspoken on his lips, the life we saw still behind his eyes
No more than the trick of light and shadow on the rock.

Thus our champion fell to earth, not dead but deeply sleeping
Listening for red dragon's song, faint echoes from the valley
Breaking earthly chains, three times we rise to dragon's cry
Twice more to greatness, twice more cut down
Fire glows dim in dragon's failing gasp.

Have we the strength, we carry the last flame
Our blaze burns bright in mountain fastness
Rage moves winds to howl and seas to rise
Hope brings warriors to the call
We strike the loathsome white beast coiling
Rend its scaly claws from our sacred soil.

As Julia reads these remarkable verses, she has the uncanny
impression that someone is speaking the lines out loud to her. She

imagines it is Caradoc Bowen whose voice she hears, his refined Welsh tones roughened with age or emotion as he recites the poem with an almost disturbing dramatic intensity. She has another reaction, too, as she reads about the warrior Arthur and his battles across this landscape of rivers and mountains. These lines make her think of Donald and his lost battle-sites. It is all no more than a coincidence, perhaps, but she feels a frisson of real excitement; above all else, she must share this discovery with him.

She walks over to the window and looks out across the garden towards the familiar, enduring stonework of Exeter College. At the centre of the scene is the ancient mulberry tree that reputedly once inspired Tolkien to create a race of timeless creatures to inhabit the great forests of Middle Earth. Two groundsmen are at work on it, gently cutting away the dead wood with a long-handled pruning saw. As the words of the Song of Lailoken continue to play in her head, Julia watches them load the last of the cut branches into a hand-cart. In her mind's eye, she sees flames dancing around the edges, lapping up the sides of the funeral pyre.

The spell is broken soon enough by the return of Margaret Rackham, who comes back into the room wheeling a scarred old leather-bound volume on a wooden cart. 'To answer your earlier question,' she says, abruptly, 'I am not at all sure whether Cranc Bowen— I always called him by his childhood nickname—whether Cranc would ever have allowed me into a close friendship with him. What I can say for certain is that his discovery of this manuscript, and the effect it had on him, made such a relationship entirely impossible.' She lifts the book reverentially to a velvet pad on her desk, then hands a pair of white cotton gloves to Julia. 'The official designation of this manuscript is TF 97B. Its original title, if ever there was one, has been lost, and in lieu of this it has informally been referred to as the poetry book of Siôn Cent. You may have a look for yourself. Please take the utmost care, especially with the early folios where the damage is the worst.'

Julia slides a gloved finger under the fractured front cover and lifts it gently. The opening page is a map of a post-apocalyptic world: a dwindling archipelago of faded brown parchment surrounded by spreading oceans of greenish blue. As she cautiously turns the pages, she finds that many of the leaves are so firmly stuck together that they cannot be opened without risk of damaging them further; and those that can have not escaped the insidious mould.

'I'm afraid we are rather too late.' The librarian speaks with a kind of grim professional resignation, as if she were a physician commenting on the status of a terminal patient. 'This manuscript has never been touched by the conservators, you see, nor has there been a formal dating.'

'Surely Professor Bowen would have asked for those things?'

'You might have thought so, but Cranc was insistent that the manuscript not be touched, for fear of further damage. In reality, I think, he wanted to keep it to himself, though no one challenged him on it. Those were very different times.'

'Could it not be remedied now?'

'Perhaps, at least to some extent. The first thing we need is for someone to show some interest, to tell us what we might be looking for. Cranc brought this book here from Ty Faenor not long after he wrote the letter I showed you, and it has remained in the Bodleian ever since. I have double-checked the records, and it seems that only two people have asked to see this manuscript since then. Cranc Bowen is one of them, and you are the other.'

'I'm not quite sure I understand.'

Margaret Rackham sighs deeply. 'In the beginning, there was

some interest in Cranc's discovery. He wrote up a detailed study for a medieval studies journal—you should look it up, I'm sure they'll have it across the road—and that paper, controversial though it may have been, was given a polite enough reception. But later on he seems to have become obsessed with the Song of Lailoken. He made some very far-fetched statements about it, which lost him a good deal of credibility with his peers. As far as I know, he never published on the topic again, and certainly his standing in the field never quite recovered.'

'So the entire manuscript was simply ignored after that?'

'I'm afraid that is what has happened, yes. It is rather a question of being tarred with the same brush.'

Julia has meanwhile continued to turn through the obliterated pages. About half-way through, there is a change from the fragile parchment to a heavier vellum, which has remained largely untouched by the mould. Areas of well-formed script can now clearly be seen, a patchwork text written in medieval Welsh: this is a version of the language she knows well enough from her years at the OED. Here she finds the early bardic poems of Siôn Cent, sombre, finely crafted verses in the *cwydd* meter, seven-syllable lines in rhyming couplets. At the end of the manuscript, written in the same strong scribal hand, there is one poem composed in a different style. The title can easily be made out, *Cân Lailoken*, the Song of Lailoken.

Margaret Rackham has been watching Julia closely. 'There is one thing you may not have noticed,' she says, her voice shifting subtly to a higher, more didactic pitch. 'It is not obvious to the untrained eye, but this manuscript was rebound when the new folios were added. The first section consists of a low-grade parchment, and the inferior quality of the materials probably accounts for the catastrophic effects of the mould damage. The later section, a further nine quires made of a more durable vellum, seems to have been added much later. This is where Siôn Cent's writing is found.'

'Do we know where the manuscript came from originally?' Julia says.

'Not definitively,' the librarian says, 'though there is strong evidence connecting the entire collection to the scriptorium at Cwmhir Abbey. We believe the manuscripts were removed from the abbey for safe-keeping in the early years of the Reformation, probably in the 1530s, and later found their way to Ty Faenor when the manor house was built in the mid-seventeenth century. We assume, but cannot say for sure, that this manuscript originated at the abbey and remained with the collection throughout this period.'

Julia turns back to one of the opening pages, looks more closely at the ruined surface of the parchment. She imagines some priceless story waiting there to be discovered, a lost epic by Homer or Virgil, a forgotten work of Dante Alighieri. 'Is there no chance of restoring it?'

'I rather think those pages are beyond redemption,' Margaret Rackham says. 'But only a proper analysis will tell.'

'Can we do that?' Julia says.

The librarian meets her in the eye. 'I dare say I could call in a favour or two,' she says. 'But do be careful.'

Her tone is surprisingly sharp, and Julia, thinking that she is being scolded for carelessness, pulls her hand away from the book. But the expression on the librarian's face makes it clear that she means something else altogether.

'This is an odd thing to say, I know, but I want you to be aware that this manuscript has brought nothing but misfortune to Caradoc Bowen. I have watched it all with a great sadness. My advice to you is to keep your distance, don't get too involved with it.'

If she had intended to encourage the precise opposite of this, Margaret Rackham could not have phrased her warning any more effectively. As Julia leaves the office of the Bodley's Librarian, she is filled with a kind of cautious exhilaration. Her most pressing thought is to call Donald and tell him what she has found.

From Farthest West

HE LOBBY OF the Randolph Hotel makes a dignified but curiously lifeless setting, heavy with wood panelling and richly upholstered furniture of the kind that absorbs all ambient sound. As Donald sits there waiting interminably, it seems, fending off the advances of the elderly, hush-voiced waiter, he finds himself beginning to regret his choice of venue. This strikes him now as a superficial world of polish and veneer, a space too self-consciously designed to invite the decorous sharing of confidences.

At last he sees Julia coming through the door, gets up from his chair, his pulse quickening. She seems happy, radiant with a concealed excitement. 'Over here,' he says, and she walks over to join him.

'Am I late?'

'No, I was early. It's a bad habit of mine.'

Julia takes off her coat, sits down on the plush red sofa. Without her glasses, she has a charming, faintly myopic look. Donald has the strange impression that he is seeing her properly for the first time.

'I hope you don't mind meeting here?'

'Where else?' she says, in her half-satirical way.

The hovering waiter offers them tea or coffee, a slice of a rather fine fruit cake if they would like something to go with it. They opt for the tea on its own, causing the waiter to acquiesce with a reverent but faintly disappointed nod. He makes a small annotation on his pad, paces solemnly away along his well-worn path.

Julia reaches for her bag, then seems to change her mind, leaves it where it is. 'Have you ever come across the work of Caradoc Bowen?' she says.

Donald smiles at the lack of preamble; still, the question stirs a flicker of interest. 'I have a book of his at home. It's the best thing I've read on Glyn Dŵr, though it's quite old now. His later work has been mostly dismissed or ignored, as far as I know.'

'Do you have any idea why that might be?'

'I couldn't say for sure. My thesis advisor at Bangor used to say that Bowen's poetry went to his head, and the historians stopped taking him seriously after that. Why do you ask?'

Julia takes two copies of a thin stapled document out of her bag, hands one of them to Donald. 'I'd like to know what you make of this,' she says.

It is an article from a back issue of a medieval studies journal, nearly fifty years old; its author is listed as C. H. R. Bowen of Jesus College, Oxford. The title immediately compels Donald's attention: *Arthurian resonances in the mythology of Owain Glyn Dŵr and the Welsh rebellion, 1401–15.* He skims the first page, then reads it again, more slowly, soon finds himself deeply absorbed in Bowen's description of his discovery, quite by chance, of a previously unstudied book of poetry in a manuscript collection held at the manor house of Ty Faenor in Radnorshire, the Welsh seat of the Mortimer family. The collection was originally assembled there in the seventeenth century by Sir

John Mortimer, a well-known antiquarian and a leading member of the border aristocracy.

When Donald reaches the end of Bowen's translation of the Song of Lailoken, he looks up to find that Julia is watching him closely. 'This is extraordinary,' he says. 'How did you find it?'

The waiter chooses his moment to return with the tray, settling it wordlessly on the table between them. Julia lifts up the pot, deftly pours tea into bone china cups. 'A friend of mine at the Bodleian told me where to look,' she says. 'Keep reading to the end, then I'll explain.'

Bowen goes on to give a brief account of Owain Glyn Dŵr and his Welsh rising. In 1401, this shrewd politician and tenacious fighter seized power in Wales from the English under Henry IV, proclaiming himself *Owynus dei gratia princeps Wallie*—Owain, by the grace of God, Prince of Wales—in the presence of emissaries from Scotland, France, and Castile. For a while it seemed that Glyn Dŵr might succeed in securing the borders of an independent principality, but his vision was destroyed by the faithlessness of his French allies and by the overwhelming strength of his adversaries. Following a bitter defeat at Harlech castle, he spent his last desperate years in hiding in the remote high country of Wales. It is not known when or where he died, nor has his burial place ever been found. He became a legendary figure even in his own lifetime, one of the greatest heroes of the Welsh imagination.

Caradoc Bowen then makes the critical assertion that the poet Siôn Cent in his earlier years held a singular position in the Welsh bardic order as prophet and seer of Owain Glyn Dŵr's rebellion. The Song of Lailoken was composed while Siôn was in hiding at the Cistercian Abbey of Cwmhir (the remains of which are to be found not more than a mile away from Ty Faenor house) as a cel-

ebration of Glyn Dŵr's famous battles against the English crown.
Claiming inspiration for his verses from Lailoken, a Welsh bard of
the sixth century who was the historical archetype of the prophet
Merlin, Siôn wrote in a highly archaic style, drawing deeply on the
imagery of Arthurian battle-verse and Merlinic prophecy to pro-
mote the idea that Glyn Dŵr was 'Arthur' returned to the aid of his
people. He intended to bequeath to his former master a cult-like
status as one who, like Arthur, would never truly die. In so doing,
he would give solace and encouragement to future generations of
Welshmen in their ongoing struggle against the white serpent of
English hegemony.

At length, Donald lays the article back down on the table. 'That's
quite a story,' he says.

Julia calmly hands him a full teacup. 'When I was a student at
Wadham, Caradoc Bowen gave a talk on the Song of Lailoken. It
was the news about Devil's Barrow that made me think of it again.
There was an archaeologist from St. Anne's talking about it on the
BBC.'

There is no avoiding the confession. 'That would be Lucy Trevelyan,' Donald says. 'I used to be married to her.'

Julia's scrutiny is not entirely comfortable. 'How long were you
together?'

'Six years. No, five.' It has become an unfamiliar arithmetic. 'We
were divorced a few months ago.'

'I'm sorry about that.' There is something ambiguous in the way
Julia says this, as if she might want to take Lucy's side. 'I thought she
had some interesting ideas.'

Reflexively, Donald finds himself on the defensive. 'Interesting
in what way?'

'As I was listening to her, it crossed my mind that the description of the first battle in the Song of Lailoken seems to match the discoveries at Devil's Barrow—the terrifying woman perched on her sacrificial stone, the remains of the British warriors subjected to a gruesome death.'

Donald looks sceptically at the opening lines of the poem. This is exactly the sort of dubious leap of faith that he most dislikes. 'Are you suggesting that the poem might be an account of what happened at Devil's Barrow?' He picks up his cup and saucer, takes a slow sip.

'I'm not suggesting anything that might make you choke on your tea.' Julia smiles at him now, entirely disarming. 'But I did want to see how you would react. It's at least an interesting coincidence, don't you think?'

He forces a smile in return, cursing himself for his petulant reaction. 'Not really, to be honest with you. Siôn Cent was writing in the early fifteenth century, so the poem can't have been composed until at least nine hundred years after the events at Devil's Barrow. I would say that the two are entirely unconnected. Siôn took the motif of the threefold death straight from the old Welsh story of Lailoken, then dramatised it a little, gave it a Merlinic aura to make it more inspiring to his listeners.'

Julia takes this in her stride. 'That's what I thought you would say. But the giants' ring? Is that a coincidence too?'

'It could mean almost anything,' Donald says. 'If Siôn wanted to add a convincing reference to a stone circle, there were plenty in Wales for him to choose from.' This is really not an argument he wants to engage in; he tries to steer the conversation in a different direction. 'The last I heard, Bowen was still going strong at Jesus College. We could try asking him what he thinks about Devil's Barrow?'

There is a small silence now, Julia tugging at a fingernail. 'I would rather not have to speak to Caradoc Bowen.'

'Why is that?'

She looks up, meets him in the eye. 'Did you ever happen to know someone at Oxford called Hugh Mortimer? He was a student of Bowen's at Jesus, studying for a doctorate in politics.'

'I don't think so. Is he related to the Mortimers of Ty Faenor?'

'Yes, the Ty Faenor estate has always belonged to his family. Hugh spent his childhood summers there with his grandfather— that's where he first met Caradoc Bowen, who later helped to secure a place for him at Jesus. As soon as Hugh got to Oxford, Bowen invited him to join a Welsh political group he had founded. They called themselves Tân y Ddraig, the Dragon's Fire.'

'I used to see them sometimes,' Donald says. 'At the Eagle and Child on a Thursday night.' At the time he thought them merely foolish, these self-important young Welshmen sitting in a circle next to the fire, debating their weighty topics with a kind of fake messianic intensity. 'They were militant Welsh nationalists. I'm not sure I would have described it as politics.'

'I know that now,' Julia says. She picks up her empty teacup, stares down into it as if to divine some essential truth in the tea-leaves. 'But I didn't really understand it at the time. Certainly I was worried about Hugh when I realised how deeply he had become committed to the group, even though he had promised me they had no interest in any kind of violent action.' She sets her cup down on its saucer, rotates it to some precisely defined angle. 'Hugh and I have been married for fourteen years,' she says. 'I'm sorry, I should have told you earlier.'

'That's all right, I never asked.' A memory comes back to Donald now, Julia on the arm of a tall, dark-haired man, walking along

Brasenose Lane only a couple of weeks after their visit to the Ashmolean. Silently, he forces his way past a sharp spike of jealousy. 'Is there more to the Bowen story?'

'Yes, there's more. The year we were married, the government announced a plan to dam up the Cwmhir valley in central Wales to supply drinking water to the English midlands. The farmhouse where I grew up, where my parents still live, is at one end of that valley. The Ty Faenor estate, which belongs to Hugh's family, is at the other. Later the same year, one person was killed and another was badly injured in an explosion at an office in Rhayader where some of the engineering work for the dam was being done.'

'I remember hearing about it when I was up at Bangor,' Donald says. 'I thought it was ruled an accident, though.'

'That was the verdict of the official inquiry,' Julia says, 'but most of the local people thought it was just a government whitewash. There was a lot of speculation that the more militant members of Tân y Ddraig were involved. Hugh certainly thought the rumour was true. He had a bitter falling-out with Caradoc Bowen, and they haven't spoken since. I am quite sure Bowen blames me for it.'

'It was a long time ago. Why should he still care?'

'Because I think he was a little bit in love with Hugh, and I was the one who took him away.'

'Let me speak to Bowen,' Donald finds himself saying, though it seems almost an irrelevance now. 'I can ask him what he thinks about the Devil's Barrow finds.'

They say goodbye at the corner of Broad Street, the same place where they parted nearly seventeen years before. Donald's easy wave of the hand as he walks away from Julia is meant to disguise the surprising, bitter disappointment that he feels. There is no logic to it, but Hugh Mortimer, a complete stranger, now feels like his enemy.

IT IS A cheap red wine, bitter on Julia's tongue. She refills her glass nevertheless, takes another sip, balances the cork on the rim of the bottle where it sits silently reproaching her. She makes herself focus again on the final page of Caradoc Bowen's journal article. As she rereads the closing paragraphs, she thinks back to the early days with Hugh, when he would tell her about Bowen's strange poems and prophecies, the stirring lines he would recite to fire up the nationalist spirit in his protégés during the weekly meetings of Tân y Ddraig. There is one passage in particular that catches her eye.

That the Song of Lailoken draws abundantly on Merlinic themes is evident even to the casual observer. Geoffrey of Monmouth, through his prophecies spoken in the voice of the famous sorcerer, was primarily responsible for the medieval cult of Welsh deliverance from the Saxon impostor. It was quite natural for Siôn Cent, writing his poem some three hundred years after Geoffrey's time, to tap into this well-matured nationalistic spirit by claiming the 'words of Merlin' as the basis for his own mythological concoction. Owain Glyn Dŵr was an ardent disciple of the Merlinic cult, a man who believed himself—or, at least, wished others to believe him—chosen for a singular role in shaping the destiny of his country. In the inspiring imagery of the Song of Lailoken, we may read for ourselves Siôn's bold intention to fortify this image of Glyn Dŵr as a predestined Celtic hero, to make of him a new Arthur.

To make of him a new Arthur. It strikes Julia now with great force, as she thinks back to the Oxford days when Caradoc Bowen had his eye so much on Hugh, that these words took on a very personal meaning for Bowen. It was Hugh who bore the mark of greatness, who was to carry the flame of Welsh nationalism in modern times, to act the part of Glyn Dŵr to Bowen's Siôn Cent, prophet of a great new rebellion. For the first time, she begins to comprehend the powerful forces that were at play during her early relationship with Hugh.

As the evening wears on, she sits alone in the silent house, sketching an elaborate abstract design on the back of Bowen's article, a chaotic vision of overlapping circles. By now, her head is throbbing, her eyes smarting with fatigue. She wants nothing more than to curl up in bed and sleep, but she decides instead that she will wait for Hugh to return, try to talk to him about his past with Caradoc Bowen.

It is after ten o'clock by the time he walks in. He seems tired and a little drawn, though surprisingly mellow. 'Thanks for waiting up,' he says, taking her by the hand, and for a moment she imagines he is going to kiss her. Instead he releases his grip, takes a whisky bottle from the cabinet and pours himself a generous measure. It has become a familiar evening ritual.

'How did it go today?' Julia says. At her suggestion, he has been over to the Merton College library to look up the original estate records relating to the Leicestershire landholdings. She wants to ask why he is back so late, but does not.

Hugh sits down at the table, takes the cork off the rim of the half-empty wine bottle. 'I found what I needed,' he says. 'Do you want some more of this?'

'Yes, why not?' Looking at her husband now, as he refills her glass almost to the brim, Julia finds herself removing the years from his face, searching for the old Hugh beneath the lean, careworn features, looking for the irresistible young firebrand she knew in her youth. His glance in return is quizzical, amused.

'Can we talk?' she says.

'Of course, what's on your mind?' Hugh is placid still, though there is a hint of wariness now in his voice.

'I found this at the Bodleian the other day.' She turns over the journal article, pushes it towards him.

Now there is a small, tense silence as Hugh flips the pages. 'You just happened to come across it?' he says.

'When you mentioned Bowen's battle-poem the other night, I remembered it from a lecture of his we once went to, a long time ago. I was curious, that's all.'

Hugh frowns slightly, sits back in his chair. 'Do you remember what he was like, Julia, the extraordinary grandiosity of the man? He imagined himself as some kind of prophet, a Merlin for our modern times. That's why he was so obsessed with Siôn Cent and the Song of Lailoken.'

Julia has been reflexively twisting the stem of her wine glass; now she stops herself, pushes the glass to one side. There are questions she desperately wants to ask, but she lets him keep talking.

'Caradoc Bowen thought the poem would show us the way, that we could go striding out into the Welsh wilderness and discover the valley where Owain Glyn Dŵr went into hiding at the end of his life, the place where he was last seen on earth. Bowen was convinced he would find some essential spirit of Glyn Dŵr still lingering there. We spent long days tramping through the mountains, looking for the crooked vale where the three rivers fall, but we never did find it.'

Hugh reaches for the whisky bottle, refills his glass to the same level, drinks some of it down. 'Then one day he asked me to come and see him at the college. I remember he looked terrible, as if he had not slept at all. He said he had dreamed of drowning in a torrent of water, and then in the morning there was a phone call from someone he knew in Whitehall, telling him about the plans for the Cwmhir dam. It hit him hard, because he had always felt a special kinship with that valley, almost as if he had lived there in some former life. He said we must abandon the idea of looking for missing fragments of the old Wales. We should devote our energies to what could still be saved. As far as he was concerned, the greatest possible English crime was the drowning of the valleys.'

Julia speaks gently to him now. 'I suppose he wanted you to see it the same way.'

'He knew I was angry enough about it.' Hugh focuses on the last of his whisky, avoids Julia's gaze. 'I didn't need much persuasion.'

It is crystal-clear in her memory, a warm afternoon in late June, not long after they were married and still in the idealistic days when they imagined they might take up farming for a living, make a go of things together at Ty Faenor. She is up on the hillside above Dyffryn sketching with Dai when Hugh arrives at the farmhouse. He talks first to her father down at the gate, then walks up through the fields to meet her. From the look on his face, the first thought she has is that somebody has died. What he tells her instead is the news he has just heard from Caradoc Bowen, that the British government is planning to dam the valley of Cwmhir and turn it into a reservoir to supply the city of Birmingham. The rising waters will drown not only a sacred piece of Wales, including the remains of Cwmhir Abbey and the grave of Llywelyn the Great, but also a large part of the Mortimer family estate and the manor house at Ty Faenor. He is more emotional than she has ever seen him. He owes it to his grandfather's memory, he says, to make sure the dam does not get built.

'My father had cut a deal with the government years before, when the idea was first proposed by his Tory friends in the inner circles.'

Hugh's tone is bitter, though the fire has gone from his voice. 'As far as he was concerned, Ty Faenor was more trouble than it was worth. After my grandfather died, he was free to do as he pleased.'

The contours of this story are familiar enough to Julia, though she has never heard him speak so openly about it before. She is acutely aware of moving into dangerous territory, but there is one question she needs to ask. 'So what really happened that autumn, Hugh? Was Caradoc Bowen somehow involved in the explosion at the engineering office?'

He rubs his eyes, runs a hand across his forehead and through his hair. She notices that it has grown longer, almost down to his shoulders. 'To be honest,' he says, 'I'd rather not talk about it any more.'

It is there again, the dark impenetrable wall. She wants to hammer her fists against it. Instead she tries to probe a little, find a place to get her fingernails inside. 'It must have been hard for you, not wanting to disappoint him.'

'What makes you say that?' The change in Hugh's voice is slight, but devastating. 'What makes you think I would care if he was disappointed in me?'

Now Julia cannot stop herself; she can feel a small crack opening up beneath her grip. 'You must have known he was a little bit infatuated with you.'

Hugh laughs, a harsh, contemptuous sound. 'He found me useful, that's all. I don't think you ever really understood that.'

Julia stands up, disorientated. 'Do you know how patronising that sounds?' She walks away a few paces, turns to face him with her back to the refrigerator door. 'I think you were completely in Caradoc Bowen's shadow in those days. He had ambitions for you that you couldn't possibly fulfil.'

Hugh reaches for his glass. Finding that it is empty, he sets it back down too hard, cracking the rim. 'You're quite right, Julia. It's not so easy to meet other people's expectations.'

He has a tight grip on himself, but Julia can hear the anger in his voice, and a kind of contempt, too. 'I'm just trying to talk to you,' she says, quietly.

'Don't worry, there's nothing left to talk about.' As Hugh strides out of the room, blood is running down his hand from where the glass has cut him.

⊞ ⊞ ⊞

DONALD SILENTLY REPEATS a familiar phrase to himself, the advice once offered to him by the gruff, Viking-bearded York-shireman who was in charge of the first archaeological dig he ever attended. *Imagine you're Leonardo, painting the Mona Lisa . . . your first duty is not to ruin that perfect smile.* This is a lesson that has been well learned; and so it is with the lightest and most patient of brushstrokes that he resumes his dusting of the dried, encrusted mud from the surface of the small rounded object that is emerging from the floor of the trench.

'Buried treasure?' Donald's assistant, Tim Watson, is crouched down next to him.

'I shouldn't think so.' But it is with a growing sense of excitement that Donald frees up a small patch of heavily tarnished metal, begins to detect the smooth curves that indicate a high degree of craftsmanship: the trademark, perhaps, of a skilled worker in iron or bronze.

'Steady now,' Tim says, in his irreverent way. 'There's no hurry. We've a long empty morning ahead of us.'

The days since Donald's meeting with Julia at the Randolph

Hotel have passed in a foggy state of disappointment and frustration. He is glad to be outside again, to get his hands back in the
mud, to rediscover his old satisfaction in the practical details of
his trade. The two of them are in a small field on the outskirts of
Amesbury in Wiltshire, close to the River Avon, part of a team that
is working a small exploratory cut along the path of a proposed
road-building scheme. Despite the apparently unpromising setting,
this excavation is far from routine. They are digging in one of the
richest archaeological landscapes in Britain, close to the site of a late
Roman settlement that remained in continuous occupation through
the fifth century and beyond. Just a short distance to the west lies
the neolithic circle of Stonehenge.

Tim is watching closely now as the object begins to take its
proper shape. 'I hate to steal your thunder, boss, but I think I know
what it is.'

Donald has reached the same quotidian conclusion. 'It's a brass
doorknob,' he says. 'Circa 1850, if I had to guess.'

'Could be a bit before that,' Tim says. 'Maybe late Georgian. You
can see the concentric pattern with interstitial etching.'

Donald looks at him sceptically. 'I had no idea you were such an
expert.'

'I'm really not, truth be told, but it looks an awful lot like the
doorknobs in my grandma's house in Bath.'

At lunchtime, declining Tim's offer of the Bull and Butcher pub,
Donald gets into his car for the short drive to Stonehenge. It is, as
always, an equivocal experience for him to visit this most venerated
of monuments, the highest temple of British archaeology. When seen
from a distance across the fields, the great standing stones silhouetted against the long horizon of Salisbury Plain are a breathtaking
sight, the work not of humans but of the giants who carved the

primordial landscape. And yet, upon a closer approach, the modern world seems to crowd in: there are roads and car parks, foreign tourists milling from their coaches, fences to constrain them sheep-like to their proper paths across the windswept turf.

As Donald makes his way towards the stone circle, the arrival of a powerful squally shower causes the crowds to disperse, leaving him alone with just a few of the hardier enthusiasts. He surveys the inscrutable sandstone trilithons through a swirling mist of rain, tries to erase modern Britain from the scene, to imagine this great structure as it would have been when it was completed in the third millennium BC. Written history has left only the faintest of clues as to the original purpose of Stonehenge. According to the ancient Greek historian Hecataeus, a far northern people known as the Hyperboreans occupied a large island in the ocean facing the country of the Celts. There, in a magnificent circular temple, they worshipped the sun god.

'You look like a fellow who knows a thing or two.' He turns to see an older American couple standing together beneath a capacious golfing umbrella. 'My wife and I were hoping you might be able to help us understand something.'

Texas is Donald's best guess, from the intonation. 'I'll be glad to, if I can.'

'We were just wondering, how in the name of sweet Jesus did they get these stones here?'

'That's an excellent question,' Donald says, 'and it hasn't been well answered. We do know that the larger stones were dragged in from about twenty miles away.'

'Twenty miles?'

'And the smaller bluish stones you can see inside the main ring came from the far west of Wales, more than one hundred miles away.'

'One hundred——?'

'We don't really know how they got them here.'

'Divine intervention, that's what I'd call it. Well, be sure and let us know when y'all have it figured out.' The Texan man bids him farewell with a crisp military salute.

As he completes his circuit of the standing stones, trudging along with his head down into the wind, boots placed methodically one in front of the other in the mud, Donald calls to mind the line from the Song of Lailoken that describes how the white serpent 'bore the giants' ring from farthest west'. He remembers very clearly where he has seen such a reference before. In his *Historia Regum Britanniae*, Geoffrey of Monmouth stated that a British leader named Ambrosius Aurelianus called upon the magician Merlin to bring great standing stones from the far west and set them down on Salisbury Plain. His purpose in placing such a monument there was to commemorate the burial place of the British 'leaders and princes whom the infamous [Saxon leader] Hengist had betrayed'. Modern archaeology has proven Geoffrey's claim to be at least partially grounded in truth, the older Stonehenge bluestones having almost certainly been quarried in the Preseli Hills of Pembrokeshire in south-west Wales. It may never be known whether this is merely a chance convergence with Geoffrey's fanciful outpouring, whether he might equally have said north rather than west; but it is tempting to think that his story preserves a distant folk-memory of the time when the stones were first brought in, as if by some supernatural power, from a land beyond the setting sun.

Another thought occurs to Donald as he makes his way along the now-deserted path that leads beyond the car park and out across the fields. In his press release, Paul Healey made a point of citing Geoffrey's reference to the fifth-century burial of 'leaders and princes' at Stonehenge. His intended subtext, though he did not state it explicitly, was that Devil's Barrow might be the very tomb alluded to by Geoffrey. It is not impossible, after all, that Geoffrey's tale of mass interment is also, like the Merlin story, a throwback to some far-distant historical event. But to pluck a name at random from popular mythology, to suggest that Arthur was one of those buried war-leaders, as Healey appears to have done, this is a purely self-indulgent flight of fancy.

No more than a hundred yards ahead, close to the path of the great ritual avenue that once led all the way from the River Avon to the massive heel-stone of Stonehenge, is a group of battered caravans that together serve as the headquarters for the Devil's Barrow archaeological project. A large square patch of ground now covered by tarpaulins indicates the extent of the excavation.

Paul Healey is waiting at the door of the first caravan. Donald's immediate and surprising reaction is to feel a surge of affection for his fellow archaeologist as Healey greets him with his open, easy smile. The genial, salesman-like air is enhanced by an expensive suit with a cufflinked shirt and blue silk tie at half-mast, an incongruous wardrobe for a working dig.

'Sorry about the posh togs,' Healey says, catching Donald's dubious glance. The Merseyside in his voice is stronger than it was on television. 'I had the ITV crowd here this morning.'

'I'm sorry about Lucy,' Donald says, reminded of the painful BBC interview.

'Not your problem any more, son. And to be honest, it was that stuck-up git Miles Johnson who bothered me more. He was captivated by your Lucy—she had him eating out of the palm of her hand.'

The squally rain returns in force, obliging Healey to catch at the door before it slams shut. 'Come on in out of this,' he says. 'There's something I want to show you.'

The interior of the caravan, though predictably cramped and cluttered, seems mysteriously larger than its external dimensions would allow. There is a stale smell of coffee and sweat and fried eggs. Donald stoops to avoid the low ceiling, follows Paul Healey to the tartan-covered bench seat at the far end. Something about the configuration of the seats and the table, combined with the gusts of wind rocking the entire structure on its moorings, reminds him poignantly of a childhood holiday on a hillside in Scotland.

'Don't mind the mess,' Healey says, alluding to the profusion of paperwork and beer cans and crisp bags strewn along the seat. 'Just push all that stuff along to the end, there's a good lad.'

Despite feeling entirely at home in such surroundings, and thoroughly disarmed by the familiarity of his host, Donald is anxious not to lose the initiative in this conversation. 'I wanted to ask you something, Paul.'

Healey's smile is a little more guarded. 'Go on, then.'

'I was wondering why you let that press release go out. You must have known how much trouble it would cause.'

'How so?'

'Because you can't uncover a burial that dates from the fifth century AD, or so you say, with the remains of a great warrior and his queen as the main attraction, and then just happen to throw in a reference to the Age of Arthur. It was bound to create a media circus.'

Paul Healey regards him curiously for a moment. 'I've not said anything definitive at all, not yet, anyway. We've not even had the dating analysis back from King's.'

For the first time, Donald begins to understand what is really going on. Paul Healey is enjoying his moment of fame; he is in no hurry to see the scientific evidence, in case it brings the whole edifice crashing down. 'Just as long as you don't start believing your own propaganda. King Arthur and his queen dug up in a Wiltshire field?'

Healey's gaze is steady. 'I've not said that now, have I? And anyway, why should you care so much?'

Donald smiles now, remembering that Paul Healey has always kept a perceptive eye on the competition. 'Thanks to you and Lucy, my publishers want me to write about the discovery of the Holy Grail. But never mind that. You said you had something to show me?'

Healey pushes a battered file across the tabletop. 'Take a look,' he says. 'These came in this morning.'

Inside is a series of exquisite black-and-white drawings of a tall cup with gently curving sides. 'The magical chalice?' Donald says.

'The very same. Do you remember, there were some images engraved around the top, but we couldn't really tell what they were? We did some cleaning up and a proper microscopic analysis, and this is the reconstruction we came up with.'

The artist's rendering shows the chalice from four different directions. Each picture shows a striking iconic representation of an animal just below the rim of the cup. 'These are incredible images,' Donald says. 'Serpent, stag, boar, and crow?'

'Raven, I'd say.'

Looking more closely, Donald notices a curious detail, that the creature in the first drawing has not one fearsome set of jaws, but three. 'And is it a white serpent, or a red one?'

'We were hoping for a nice Celtic red for the dragon.' Healey grins at him, conspiratorial now. 'But the ochre pigments don't hold up as well as some of the others—the colour must have washed away a long time ago.'

Back at the Amesbury dig, the afternoon brings no revelations beyond the occasional pottery sherd and a substantial haul of Georgian red clay bricks. Driving home a few hours later, Donald turns over and over in his mind the exquisite images that Paul Healey showed him, the beautiful symbolic depictions of creatures from some other time and place. He has every expectation that Healey will use this new discovery to support his own analysis of the Devil's Barrow archaeology. Perhaps he will try to claim that this is the classic art of the Celtic world, one of the finest examples we have yet seen. The stag is the ancient symbol of male strength and fertility, as represented by the pagan god Cernunnos. The raven is the common representation of the goddess of war and death; she is the harbinger of doom and destruction who hovers over the fray, foretelling the outcome of the battle. As for the dragon, this is the enduring symbol of the Celtic peoples, known at least since the time of the Roman occupation of Britain. At Devil's Barrow, Healey will say, we have found the remains of a warrior elite, of men who fell defending their king and queen in the time of the great British struggle to resist the Saxon incursions: in the time of the great war leader known as Arthur.

And yet it is all hopelessly wrong. Every hypothesis advanced by Paul Healey must now be viewed as tendentious at best. So far, he has no convincing verification of his dates, only the evidence of coins tossed into a pit. It is possible, as Lucy will certainly claim, that the animistic motifs preserved on the rim of the chalice have their origins in a far more ancient world than that of dark-age Britain. The totemic imagery undoubtedly lends weight to her idea that the chalice had a greater ritual significance, that it was something much more than a simple drinking vessel. The artistry of the chalice could even support her theory of a pre-Celtic date for the remains found buried at Devil's Barrow, giving life to her vision of a glorious, peaceful, matriarchal Old Europe in which war had not yet been invented. As to which of their two interpretations is the more improbable, Donald cannot quite decide.

Outside the car, the shadowed farmland of north Wiltshire slips by, tail-lights winking on and off ahead as the road curves and dips through the rolling countryside. Donald switches on the portable radio on the passenger seat, tunes in to an oboe concerto by Albinoni that seems to lend a melancholy, dream-like flow to his thoughts. Though he has no way to describe the sensation in scientific terms, he cannot escape a perception of larger forces at play, of vast expanses of human time, of his own insignificance to the story. It is not altogether a comfortable feeling.

A road sign for Malmesbury makes him think of Julia. In her own way, she is as beautiful and unorthodox and certainly as clever as Lucy. Not that it matters, anyway. She is happily married, unapproachable, unattainable; someone he might have hoped to have known at a better time, in a better place, in another life. This is what he tells himself as he drives on through the twilight into a darker rural hinterland.

Whispers

ONALD FINDS HIMSELF quarantined by Mrs. Violet Frayne, Caradoc Bowen's long-serving and augustly indifferent secretary, in the chilly, narrow space that acts as an ante-chamber to the professor's rooms at Jesus College. While he waits, he occupies himself with a thin blue monograph he has brought with him from home, Bowen's *Notes on the Welsh Rising*, given to him in his postgraduate days by John Evans at Bangor. More than forty years old, it is still the most compelling description of Owain Glyn Dŵr's rebellion he has read. The author is perhaps a little too poetical, a little free and easy with his historical detail, but he captures the tragic intensity of those years in a way that other, more fastidious writers have failed to do. His Glyn Dŵr is a brilliant, intense creation, a worthy inheritor of his people's hopes and dreams of Arthur's return.

Donald skims through the pages, reminding himself of the outlines of this Shakespearean tale of hubris and tragedy. He reads more closely as Bowen arrives at his final scene, in which he offers his own interpretation of the laying to rest of Owain Glyn Dŵr.

It is a bleak enough place, and a bleak enough day now descending into twilight, the slate-coloured sky emptied even of the soaring carrion-birds as the wind swirls up from the valley and cuts across the high plateau. In the shelter of a long grassy mound near the edge of the cliff, a dozen men marked fresh with the scars of battle stand shoulder to shoulder around their leader's mortal remains laid out on the ground beneath an ancient twisted lime tree. These mourners are chanting not a Latin mass, but a song in the Welsh language, a fitting requiem for the passing of Owain Glyn Dŵr. None standing there would say that their leader had truly departed: for it was told by the *brudwr*, the prophetic poets of that time, that Owain, like Arthur, did not die, but went to sleep in the otherworld, that he might return in his people's hour of need.

Donald's contemplation of this passage is interrupted by Mrs. Frayne's brisk instruction to enter the professor's study. He opens the door with a creaking of hinges, walks through into a substantial and imposing space imbued with a faded, damp austerity that stands in striking contrast to the bright autumn day outside. The sixteenth-century stonework, the plain wooden furniture and sparsely adorned walls, all lend a vaguely ecclesiastical air to the room. This ascetic quality is barely alleviated by the modest trappings of academic life: ranks of leather-bound volumes on the shelves, a large old-fashioned blackboard presently occupied by an indecipherable text, an ancient electric kettle and a grimy cluster of cups and saucers beside a small sink in the corner.

The elderly man behind the desk does not look up at first, continues scribbling on a thick sheet of writing paper that keeps curling up from the bottom. He smooths it out again and again, each time with a small muted exhalation of breath, though he does not allow this inconvenience to interrupt the uncompromising flow of his tiny, ornate script across the page. He is hunched down low to his work, presenting to the world a pale, bony forehead incised with deep lines, most of them parallel to the brows, some cutting across at a steep angle with rows of oblique little crossroads at the joins. The mane of white hair tumbling from his scalp seems to catch the tempo of his work, oscillating gently as he writes.

Finding himself ignored, and the only other chair occupied by a tall stack of encyclopedia volumes, Donald walks over to the window, looks out across the quad towards the gothic façade of Jesus College Chapel. The old glass in the panes is thick and uneven, distorting the bright rectangular view, detaching it slightly from reality. Down below, undergraduates in groups of two and three make their way untidily around the edge of the grass and on towards the main gate. Donald tries to discern some spark of above-average ability in these future Nobel prize-winners, poets laureate, pillars of British government; then remembers himself at a similar age, lanky and a little foolish, bursting with knowledge but with no sense of how the world was supposed to work.

The minutes begin to stretch uncomfortably. Donald turns away from the window, begins an unobtrusive examination of the nearest bookshelf. There in the top row he finds the Welsh poets of the past six hundred years, from Iolo Goch to R. S. Thomas and Albert Evans-Jones. It is tempting to take down a book and look inside, but this seems too great a presumption. His eye is drawn instead to a large map of central Wales that occupies the wall next to the dormant fireplace. It is one of the early Ordnance Survey sheets, issued in the first two decades of the nineteenth century. The heavy, portentous shading of the more extreme relief depicts a mountainous country almost uninhabited save for the small towns and villages clustered sparsely in the valleys.

'Perhaps you are familiar with that part of Wales?' Donald turns to find that Caradoc Bowen has set down his pen at last and is looking up at him. The professor's expression is difficult to read through his old-fashioned spectacles, thick round lenses whose disturbing effect is to emphasise the intensity of his bird-like stare; though the imagined fierceness is perhaps, after all, nothing more than a distant amiability, his eyes not so much penetrating in their gaze as merely old and tired. 'Those particular lands, which once formed the *cantref* of Maelienydd, have been held in hegemony by the Anglo-Norman aristocracy since the eleventh century.' Bowen's voice, which is surprisingly strong for so slight a frame, carries a trace of Gwynedd or Ceredigion worn smooth by his many decades at Oxford.

'It's a fine old map,' Donald says, wishing straight away that he might have found some less facile comment.

'It is indeed a fine map of a once-glorious country that has seen only ruin and destruction at the hands of the noble Englishman. Do you not agree?'

This time, Donald pauses before answering, gives a more careful consideration to his response. 'Wales is a glorious country still, in my opinion, if not what it once was.'

Bowen seems to look at him more closely now, as if noticing him properly for the first time. 'But now I am afraid you have distracted me, and I have entirely forgotten my manners. Caradoc Bowen, at your service.' The professor speaks these words with a genuine feeling, but stiffly, as if they have not been much used in recent years. Rising with a surprising vigour from his chair, he offers a firm handshake, dry as dust. 'I trust that I have not made you feel unwelcome. Do by all means sit down, if you prefer. You need only eject the *Britannica* from his perch. Just move him up here to the corner of the desk, if you would be so kind.'

'Yes, of course.' As Donald begins self-consciously lifting the volumes off the chair in twos and threes, Bowen offers an unexpected running commentary.

'This, as you may have noticed, is the ninth edition, published from 1875 to 1889 under the editorship of T. S. Baynes and William Robertson Smith. I must say it's no longer so useful as it once was, though it does contain some of the finest scholarship to be found anywhere in the world.' Bowen takes one of the volumes in hand, turns almost deferentially through the pages. 'Swinburne wrote in here of Keats that "the rawest and the rankest rubbish of his fitful spring is bound up in one sheaf with the ripest ears, flung into one basket with the richest fruits of his sudden and splendid summer." That is to say, even the most talented person makes mistakes in his youth, and, I might add, they invariably contaminate everything he does thereafter.'

Donald removes the last of the volumes, sits down amidst a creaking of old tenon joints and a cloud of fine dust that settles gently on to his trouser-legs.

'There, that's a little more civilised,' Bowen says. 'Now, may I offer you some tea?'

'I don't want to take up too much of your time. We spoke on the phone yesterday—'

'Quite so, you're the archaeologist. Are you by chance an Oxford man?'

'Yes, I was an undergraduate at St. John's.'

The professor makes a small disparaging gesture with his hand. 'And you have some education beyond those narrow confines, I trust?'

'I studied for my doctorate at Bangor, under John Evans.'

'I am glad to hear it. Evans is no fool, and neither does he suffer them.' Bowen is on his feet again, busying himself with the tea things. 'Will Darjeeling suit? Or do you prefer Earl Grey in the afternoon?'

'Darjeeling would be perfect.'

In due course, the professor hands Donald a chipped, heavily stained mug decorated with a painting of St. David's Cathedral. 'What is your particular archaeological speciality, may I ask?'

Something in Bowen's demeanour makes this feel like an invitation to confess to a crime. 'My main area of professional interest is the archaeology of sub-Roman Britain,' Donald says, formulating his answer with special care. 'I have worked most recently on the correspondences between the archaeology of that period and the mythological traditions that have arisen from it.'

The professor gives a short, sharp laugh. 'Well, that is a refreshingly ambitious topic to choose. Good luck to you, young man. *Audaces fortuna iuvat.*'

Donald decides to risk a further qualification. 'More specifically, I'm writing a book on the origins of the concept of the warrior Arthur in the Celtic tradition.'

Bowen takes off his glasses, lays them down significantly on the desk. 'As to the origins of Arthur,' he says, leaning back in his chair with his hands clasped behind his head, bony elbows drawn forward next to his ears, 'I am not at all sure I can help you. Whether he is real or imaginary, he is an irreducible mystery, and surely intends to remain so. Perhaps that is what you had better write in this book of yours.'

The thought occurs to Donald, as he absorbs this presumably dismissive response, that Caradoc Bowen is very much unaccustomed to having his opinions directly challenged. 'I agree with you to some extent,' he says. 'But surely there are some things that are known, or might possibly be known, about Arthur? For example, there is a chain of tradition and transmission that led to the recording of the twelve Arthurian battles in the *Historia Brittonum*, even if we choose not to interpret that text in a literal way.'

'In point of fact,' Bowen says, as if responding to some quite different question, 'I don't much believe in searching for indelible truths about people or things, in history or anywhere else.' He has a curious habit when he speaks, seeming to look away into some intermediate distance. 'Though I admit that there is a paradox in the case of written texts. In one sense they are the most fragile of creations, they may burn or crumble to dust, while in their essence, as arrangements of words and ideas, they are utterly imperishable.'

'And so there is an indelible part, after all,' Donald says, determined to hold his own against the professor's circuitous, idiosyncratic logic. 'If I look at a copy of some original text, I can at least be sure that the ideas the author meant to capture have been preserved, even if the original has been lost or destroyed.'

Bowen puts his glasses back on, refocuses his piercing gaze. 'No, I'm afraid that won't do at all. One cannot simply look at words that were written centuries ago and expect to find some Cartesian essence, some core of truth untainted by the author's world-view, his milieu, the literary, religious, social, and moral culture of the age in which he lived. I want to get past what is in the historian's head. His brain is like a distorting lens, and I want to see the object, not the image. No, that's not quite the right metaphor. Let me see.'

The professor gets up from his desk and walks over to the window, stands there for a while in silence, then begins pacing to and fro. 'Yes, that's better. Imagine a game of Chinese Whispers played across the centuries. Our distinguished authors sit in a circle, each separated by, say, three hundred years. Gildas starts things off by leaning over to whisper in Bede's ear. Bede, in turn, cups his hand and stretches over to William of Malmesbury, who is squeezed in uncomfortably close to his rivals, Geoffrey of Monmouth and Henry of Huntingdon. William listens carefully to Bede, but Geoffrey and Henry hear only parts of the message, and must fill the rest in for themselves. Walter of Oxford, who is sitting outside the circle, taps Geoffrey on the shoulder and whispers something in his other ear. But Geoffrey fails to pass on this new information to his close colleagues, instead hurrying around to deliver a murmured soliloquy to his French pen-friend, Chrétien de Troyes, who is meanwhile struggling to comprehend the mutterings of an elusive Welshman named Bleheris. The resulting information traverses Robert de Boron, Layamon, Thomas Malory. By the time Arthur's story reaches our modern ears, it is garbled beyond recognition.'

'And where do you see yourself in this great circle of historians?' Donald says, risking a faint irony.

'Me? I am sorry to say that I find no place at all for myself. I am condemned to the far periphery, to a distant orbit reserved for poets and magicians.' For the first time, Caradoc Bowen smiles. 'But you must forgive me. I have become carried away with my clever metaphor. My point is simply this. When we are speaking of the writing of history, the laws of human nature must apply. As soon as pen hits paper, quill hits vellum, distortion begins to pour undiluted on to the page.'

This is too good an opening for Donald to miss. 'Talking of which, I was wondering, Professor, whether you happened to read the press release from Downing College concerning the discoveries at Devil's Barrow?'

'Yes, and is it not an excellent case in point?' Bowen looks at Donald with what seems a genuine approval. 'Do I take it that you have as little patience as I for the absurd posturing we have seen from the Cambridge team? To say nothing of our American colleague, Dr. Lucinda Trevelyan of St. Anne's College. It is a fine Cornish name to be despoiled by such nonsense as we hear from her lips.'

Donald tries hard not to smile. If he is to keep his promise to Julia, this is the moment when he must press the case. 'Do you think it's possible, though, that there is a connection between the archaeology of Devil's Barrow and the description of the first battle in the Song of Lailoken?'

Caradoc Bowen bows his head, makes a show of polishing his lenses on the frayed lining of his tweed jacket. 'I was not aware that anyone was still reading that poem,' he says. 'I have not looked at it myself for a very long time.'

'I came across it by accident,' Donald says, scarcely bending the truth. 'I think it is quite remarkable.'

'And on what possible basis,' Bowen says, his voice suddenly rising, cracking with indignation, 'do you imagine that such a poem might be connected to the discoveries at Stonehenge? Are you forgetting that the Welsh battles it describes are removed from the events at Devil's Barrow by several hundred years at least, to say nothing of the geographical challenges?'

Donald begins to deploy his carefully rehearsed argument, trying hard to ignore the evidence of Bowen's rapidly mounting impatience. 'But would you not at least agree,' he says, 'that Siôn Cent intended those lines in his poem to be read as an allusion to Stonehenge? He speaks of a giant-wrought circle, a temple brought from farthest west by a god-like power. Does that not seem a close parallel to Geoffrey of Monmouth's description of Stonehenge in the *Historia Regum Britanniae*?'

Now the professor offers the thinnest of smiles. 'You are very astute, Dr. Gladstone,' he says. 'In this case, however, I believe you are entirely on the wrong track. Of course, I noticed the connection with Geoffrey's remark when I first came upon the poem. But over the years I have come to understand the mind of Siôn Cent. He had a jackdaw eye, picking up twinkling little images here and there across his reading. He will have known the *Historia* intimately, of course, steeped as he was in the Merlinic tradition of which Geoffrey was largely the progenitor. He merely borrowed the Stonehenge reference and adapted it to his own ends.' Bowen looks critically at Donald, one eyebrow raised almost imperceptibly. 'You may wish to invoke some other explanation, but Occam's Razor tells us we should doubt the more complicated interpretation.'

'And the theme of the threefold death?' Donald says. 'There is evidence of this practice in the archaeology from Devil's Barrow, and a corresponding reference in the Song of Lailoken. Surely, at the least, that's an interesting coincidence.' As he speaks these words, he can feel himself falling into the professor's well-laid trap.

'My dear fellow,' Bowen says, 'you seem to be losing touch with the essence of Siôn Cent. His clear intention was to embed a sense of authenticity in his poem. It is no accident that he named it the Song of Lailoken. Perhaps you will recall, from your study of Celtic mythology, the story of St. Cyndeyrn's encounter in the forest with the bard Lailoken, who had been driven to the brink of madness by visions of death and gruesome battle. He told Cyndeyrn that he knew the manner of his own death, that he would be killed three times, by stone, stake, and water. This episode is related in a twelfth-century manuscript now preserved in the British Library, which suggests that the story was widely known by that time, and would certainly have been familiar to Siôn Cent writing three hundred years later.'

This analysis does not quite seem to answer the question, but Donald has no chance to respond. Caradoc Bowen rises abruptly from his chair and steps to the blackboard behind his desk. He uses an old yellow cloth to erase the cryptic text that is written there, snatches up a piece of chalk and begins fiercely scribing circles and lines.

'It is clear,' Bowen says, 'that Siôn Cent was greatly concerned with verisimilitude, and that he deliberately populated his verses with totemic figures who seemed to speak of a distant mythical past. On the side of the white serpent, we have the one called Belak-neskato with her twin protectors, Araket and Madarakt.' Bowen writes these names in the three circles on the left. 'Speaking for the red dragon, we have the one called the crab, together with his warrior-champion whom Siôn has named Arthur.' Bowen fills in the circles on the right. 'Why, you might ask, should he write of Arthur when he might have spoken of Glyn Dŵr? The answer is clear. It is because he wanted to leave no doubt in his listeners' minds that Owain Glyn Dŵr was a true Celtic hero, that he was Arthur returned to them in their time of trouble. He wanted his audience to believe they were listening to authentic Merlinic prophecy, symbolic words that came straight from some ancient mythological substrate.' The professor underscores this last point by shading a vigorous layer of white at the foot of the blackboard, joining it with dotted lines to the encircled names. 'Our poet went so far as to claim that the Song of Lailoken represented the very words of Merlin taken from an old book that happened to fall into his hand, though we may of course dismiss his book of Cyndeyrn as a convenient fiction, a clever ruse borrowed from Geoffrey of Monmouth. Perhaps by now you begin to understand the sophistication of Siôn Cent's method?'

'I see what you mean,' Donald says, feeling the full weight of Caradoc Bowen's scrutiny. 'But do you think this is the only possible interpretation of the poem?'

Bowen does not seem to hear him, barely pauses for breath. 'All of this, of course, was preparatory to our poet's rousing coda, in which he turns from past victories to future glories, making a prophecy to stir the heart of any true patriot. These closing lines were intended as a clarion call to the men of the red dragon, Welsh peasantry and nobility alike, to rise against the English impostor. The words have the greater power in the archaic Welsh of the original, though few can now follow that language. If I may make so bold?'

'By all means,' Donald says. He slides his chair a little way back from the desk, then watches in fascination as Bowen stands with his hands behind his back and delivers a dramatic Welsh rendition of the final two verses of the Song of Lailoken.

Fel hyn y syrthiodd ein harwr i'r ddaear, nid marw ond mewn
    trymgwsg
Yn clustfeinio am gân y ddraig goch, atseiniau gwan o'r dyffryn
Yn torri cadwyni daearol, deirgwaith y codwn i gri'r ddraig
Ddwywaith eto i fawredd, ddwywaith eto fe'n torrwyd i lawr
Pyla'r tân yn chwythiad edwinol y ddraig

A yw'r nerth gennym? Cludwn y fflam olaf
Llachar y llosga ein tân yng nghadarnle'r mynyddoedd
Dicter a bair i wyntoedd udo ac i foroedd chwyddo
Dena gobaith filwyr i'r alwad
Bwriwn y bwystfil gwyn ffiaidd sy'n ymdorchi
Rhwygwn ei grafangau cennog o'n pridd cysegredig.

The professor pauses for breath, and then, with an almost equal intensity, delivers the same lines in English, his accent coming through more strongly than before.

Thus our champion fell to earth, not dead but deeply sleeping

Listening for red dragon's song, faint echoes from the valley

Breaking earthly chains, three times we rise to dragon's cry

Twice more to greatness, twice more cut down

Fire glows dim in dragon's failing gasp.

Have we the strength, we carry the last flame

Our blaze burns bright in mountain fastness

Rage moves winds to howl and seas to rise

Hope brings warriors to the call

We strike the loathsome white beast coiling

Rend its scaly claws from our sacred soil.

'Do you not hear the dragon's song?' Bowen says, his eyes bright with some inner fire. His voice is hoarse, and there is a faint sheen of sweat on his brow. 'Can you not feel the power of the poet's call? Glyn Dŵr, he tells us, is neither alive nor dead, but granted safe passage to the otherworld. We must not forget him, nor become heedless to the perils that face our homeland, for he will assuredly return to help his people in their hour of greatest need.'

Donald decides to say nothing, allows Bowen to sit himself down, wipe his forehead with a large white handkerchief taken from his jacket pocket. He seems more frail, drained of some vital energy. 'You must forgive my sudden access of enthusiasm,' the professor says. 'It is many years since I last allowed myself to speak those lines. I trust, however, that I have helped you to apprehend with a little more subtlety the remarkable mind of Siôn Cent.'

'I am indebted to you, Professor Bowen.' Donald decides to risk one further question. 'I was wondering, though, why you have not written on this subject in recent years?'

'Because, quite simply, I have nothing more to say.' Bowen's tone is peremptory, but then softens. 'I approve of your persistence, Dr. Gladstone, in challenging what others may take for granted. I encourage you to persevere in this approach to your work. Now, if you will kindly excuse me, I am feeling a little tired.'

As Donald makes his way back down the stairs to the quad, he decides that he likes Caradoc Bowen rather more than he expected to. He walks out of the Jesus College gate on to Turl Street just as the sun breaks free of cloud, lighting the old college stonework in glorious tones of amber and gold.

IN THE WAY of those dreams that remain etched in the mind for days and weeks to come, he finds that he can see everything in exquisite detail, the weft and the warp of the threadbare blanket that covers him, the burgeoning pattern of green and yellow lichens on the walls, the last light of sunset glancing through the window to touch the letters carved into the heavy stone lintel. Lailoken: this is the name that is spelled there. It comes to our dreamer with a distant familiarity, as if it were a garment he once wore himself. It is a comfort to see it written in stone; a sense of permanence and sanctity seems to flow from this extemporaneous alliance with the solid rock. Now he feels himself falling more deeply asleep, going to some more distant place, a dream within a dream, as he murmurs the closing lines of an old familiar poem.

When he opens his eyes again, the world has darkened. There is a cool wind blowing in the trees. He is alert and fearful, his limbs frozen in place, his hearing attuned to a distant, insinuating voice that seems drawn from deep within the rock itself.

> *Do you not see me, crab blinded by shame?*
> *Black raven I am called, the dream-maker*

Sending you my last-breath's curse
To blight your darkest sleeping

Three times reborn, three times you will die
By stone, by stake, by water I send you
To sate the white serpent, three-times hungering
Wind-lord whose breath awakes the raging storm
Whose wrath tears thunder from the sky
Whose magic woven through my voice
Will still your mortal sighing.

The breeze turns bitter cold, rises swiftly to a howling storm such that this rough shelter will not long withstand. As our dreamer awakes into his present world, the great lintel-stone is tumbling down upon him.

▨ ▨ ▨

JULIA HAS SPOKEN no more than a few unavoidable sentences to Hugh in the few days that have passed since their disastrous conversation. Somehow they are still sleeping in the same bed, finding reasons to go up at different times, and she is shocked at the ease with which they have been able to avoid one another. The routines of life continue, but the silence between them has grown until it fills the house like a toxic gas.

She is in her studio on a bright Saturday morning with the shouting of children in the next-door garden drifting through the open window. They are playing hide-and-seek, three of them in turn portentously chanting from one to twenty, followed by the happy sounds of discovery in dense rhododendron thickets, behind trees and potting sheds. Julia finds herself tuning in to their game, smiling at the intensity that they bring to the task at hand; envious that they can be so much in the moment, not looking beyond the next half-minute of their lives. These are good kids, Will and Richard and Anna Speedwell, clever and polite, products of what has always seemed the unlikely pairing of Emma, a diminutive and voluble ward-sister at the Radcliffe Infirmary, and her lanky and diffident classicist husband Tom, Fellow of Christ Church. Emma has been a good friend to Julia, as has Tom, in his way, to Hugh, the two men from time to time staying up to the small hours over a bottle of single malt.

The children's game continues for some time in this mode of happy repetition, until a distant shout of lunchtime from the matron brings the proceedings to an end. Hugh would like to have children, Julia knows this, but motherhood has remained a frightening and inaccessible place for her. When she tries to think of it, she sees a remote plateau surrounded by unscalable cliffs. Dismissing the confusing, wistful thoughts that try to enter in, she returns her attention to the parcel on the table in front of her. The address has been written in her mother's usual elegant, precise style, with the name of the house, Cair Paravel, segregated inside perfectly crafted quotation marks as if to emphasise Cath Llewellyn's disapproval of such pretension.

Julia unwraps the fraying string, strips away the brown paper wrapping to reveal a cardboard box sealed so comprehensively with sellotape that it takes a long battle with scissors to break through to the seams. Inside, she finds some of her old things: a collection of diaries bound with a pink ribbon, some strange amorphous figures that she once carved out of a wooden block, one of her father's sketch pads, yellowed with age. A page has come loose, a pencil drawing of a dramatic tilted rock-face set in a landscape of rugged tree-clad hills beneath a gleaming cloud-filled sky. The patterns of light and shadow in the rock, the luminous quality of the cloudscape, have been picked out with exquisite care. There is a short caption beneath, *Craig-y-Ddinas*, and the tiny initials in the corner, DRL.

At the bottom of the box is a scrap-book with a dark green cover and a stout ring binding. There is a note stuck inside it, in her mother's writing. *I want you to have this, no arguments now.* A name is boldly written in rounded girlish handwriting on the inside front cover, Catherine Maud Pursey. The pages are filled with the tokens of her mother's young and happy life in Sussex, invitations to birthday parties, tickets to the Brighton pantomime, blurred family photographs taken at the seaside. Later on, there are cartoonish drawings of schoolteachers, notes scribbled by friends, various boys' names written in the margins. One name appears more often than the others, Peter K., the blameless Englishman whom Julia's mother would have married were it not for a holiday in Aberdovey and Dai Llewellyn standing there at the dock when she stepped off the ferry-boat.

Julia turns to a page at the back of the book. It is another of her father's sketches, a young woman at a window, seagulls in the sky, small fishing-boats on the water beyond. Her hair is tied back in a scarf decorated with tiny loops and spirals. The beautiful Catherine Pursey, aged twenty-one, looks out across the Dyfi estuary with a gently mocking half-smile on her face.

Setting the scrap-book to one side, Julia unties the pink ribbon and lays the diaries out on the tabletop, four of them bound in the same bright red leather. She opens the first one and begins to turn through the January pages. The daily spaces are filled with a bold writing in pencil, a painful coming-of-age documented with all the ordinary entangled emotion of her lonely fifteen-year-old self writing these words in her room at Dyffryn Farm. There is a tug of memory now as she comes upon the entry for Valentine's Day.

14 FEBRUARY

I had a card today from Ralph Barnabas. I think he really has a thing for me, but he's very quiet about it, I suppose he's a bit strange really. Maybe we have that in common. None of the other boys at school seem to like me very much, not that it matters anyway because Dai has a shotgun out in his workshop and I really think he'd use it if any one of them tried to come near me. Aunt Nia is coming over later to take me out. Not sure why she chose today but Thank God she's coming.

There are more pages written in similar vein as the winter drags on; but with springtime comes a change, even the handwriting is neater as she composes her entries with a new style and purpose.

12 APRIL

I met someone at the Black Lion last night. It was Gareth Williams who introduced us, he said here's a man I want you to meet. His name is Hugh Mortimer and he's staying with his grandfather over at Ty Faenor, one of *the* Mortimers no less. He says he's going off to Oxford University in the autumn to study history and politics. I like the way he knows what he wants from life, and the way he looks at me, too, a little bit mysterious as if he knows all about me.

Julia flips through pages filled with a surprising intense narrative, glimpses of Hugh in town on a Saturday morning, occasional awkward conversations on street corners, the time she ran into him when she was out walking with Dai, who didn't much approve of Hugh's father, and she had to pretend not to know him.

31 AUGUST

Sixteen today. Ralph was there waiting for me after school. He asked if he could walk with me for a while, and I couldn't really say no. We'd gone as far as the Rhayader bridge when we saw Hugh standing there at the other end. When I told him it was my birthday, he ran and picked a rose from Mrs. Edwards' front garden and gave it to me with a funny sort of smile. Ralph just walked away without saying a word. After that, Hugh stayed there with me and I was sure he was going to kiss me, but then he smiled in a sad sort of way and told me his grandfather had just died and he would be going away to Oxford soon. We stood there for a long time, watching the river going over the old waterfall.

There is some elusive significance in this final word, *waterfall*. It is only much later on, as Julia is preparing to go back up to the house and her eye falls on Caradoc Bowen's journal article lying there on the table, that she realises what it is. When she first read the Song of Lailoken in the original Welsh, musing over its highly archaic constructions, she concluded that this was a true anachronistic masterpiece on the part of Siôn Cent. He wrote the poem in the vernacular of the fifteenth century but with something of the character of Old Welsh, a version of the language spoken hundreds of years earlier. It is as if Geoffrey Chaucer had chosen to compose a work in the style of the author of *Beowulf*, but in such a way that it would be comprehensible to the common people of his own time.

She turns the pages rapidly now until she finds Bowen's English translation of the poem. In the description of the final battle, where Siôn's 'Arthur' fell to the creature Madarakt, Bowen renders the location of the battle-site as 'the crooked vale where the three rivers fall'. This is the line that prompted his fruitless searching for just such a mountain valley in Wales. Julia makes a small annotation in pencil, substituting a more archaic and poetic usage of the Middle Welsh *llifeiriant*, interpreting it as 'waterfalls' rather than Bowen's 'mountain rivers or streams'. The line becomes 'the crooked vale with three waterfalls'. It might be true, she thinks. It must be true. Without a moment's hesitation, she picks up the telephone.

The Importance of
Aerodynamics

I FFLEY'S LONG-SERVING VILLAGE postman seems
unaccountably cheerful as he leans his bicycle against
the garden wall and makes his way to the front door
of the cottage. Catching his eye through the front-room window,
Donald walks across to open the door.

'Popular today, sir. Is it your birthday?'

'I don't think so,' Donald says with a smile, as he takes in hand a
respectable haul. 'Thanks all the same.'

The postman climbs back on his bike, looking askance at the
heavy shower clouds now racing across the sky. 'Clearing up by
lunchtime, so they say. Pigs might fly.' With this he is off down the
lane, whistling tunelessly through his teeth.

Dropping the stack of post on the desk, Donald picks up his
pencil and the notebook in which he has been writing furiously
for the past three hours. A new idea has taken a fierce hold on him
since he arose almost sleepless before dawn. It was Caradoc Bowen's
comment about Siôn Cent and the Song of Lailoken that set him

off. Siôn claimed that his poem was taken 'from the words of Merlin found in Cyndeyrn's book which fate has brought to my hand',
and this book, Bowen said, should be dismissed as a pure invention,
a clever ruse borrowed from Geoffrey of Monmouth.

In the preface to his *Historia Regum Britanniae*, Geoffrey claims
that it is a direct translation into Latin of 'a certain very ancient
book written in the British language', *quendam Britannici sermonis librum
uetustissimum*, brought to him from Wales by Walter, Archdeacon
of Oxford. Geoffrey's mysterious source has never been found, and
most historians, along with Bowen, have found it sufficient to say
that the 'ancient book' was entirely a product of his fertile imagination, a publicity stunt designed to discredit his scholarly rivals. But
Donald has always found it an appealing idea that such a book once
existed, and that Geoffrey drew upon it in some way when he came
to create his famous history of the British kings.

So far, this is no more than wishful thinking; but now there
are other pieces of the puzzle that seem to fall irresistibly into
place. First there is the identity of the 'Cyndeyrn' whose book was
claimed by Siôn Cent as his inspiration for the Song of Lailoken. A
quick check in Butler's *Lives of the Saints* confirms that St. Cyndeyrn,
also called St. Kentigern or St. Mungo, was a celebrated northern
churchman of the sixth century AD who is known to have established a monastery at a place called Llanelwy (on English maps, St.
Asaph) in the north-eastern corner of Wales. It is St. Cyndeyrn who,
according to the old Welsh story mentioned by Caradoc Bowen,
encountered the poet Lailoken in the forest and wrote down his
prophecy concerning the threefold death.

Then there is the well-documented fact that Geoffrey, late in
his life, was elevated to become Bishop of St. Asaph, a position he
had long coveted. It is, at the very least, interesting that there is a
geographical connection between Geoffrey of Monmouth and St.

Cyndeyrn, via the Welsh diocese of St. Asaph. More intriguing still is the fact that Geoffrey's *Historia*, with its famous Merlinic prophecies, and (if Siôn Cent is to be believed) the book of Cyndeyrn each contained elements of prophecy or poetry that were claimed to have been spoken by Merlin himself.

It would be easy enough to accept Caradoc Bowen's line of reasoning, to say that Geoffrey's 'certain very ancient book' and Cyndeyrn's book were entirely fictitious. But what if the evidence, thin though it may be, is taken at face value? Could it possibly be true that both books once existed, and indeed drew on the same prophetic tradition, or even some common written source? This is the thought that struck Donald like a thunderbolt as he lay in bed in the small hours, sent him running electrified down the stairs.

It is a tantalising idea, but his excitement is tempered by the recognition that this is just the kind of loose, hopeful reasoning that he has so often criticised in the more enthusiastic popularisers of Arthuriana. For now, he is too tired to develop his ideas any further. His eyes are dry and gritty, his head pounding from the intensity of his concentration. He puts down his pencil, stretches his arms high over his head, then begins to sort distractedly through the pile of post on the desk. There is the latest volume in the *Archaeologia* series from the Society of Antiquaries, some apparently misdirected marketing pieces (Johnson's Fine Shrubs and Perennials, Ma Baker's Texas Fruit Cakes), a newsletter from the local ramblers' club, bills for electricity and water rates. He sets to one side a leaflet for the Tintagel symposium on the archaeology of Devil's Barrow, which is due to start at the weekend. Two envelopes at the bottom of the pile immediately catch his interest.

The first, postmarked in Oxford, is addressed to him by hand in a tiny flowing script. Inside is a letter written on faded paper headed with the Jesus College crest, three silver stags on a bright green field.

It is a short and surprising note from Caradoc Bowen, thanking him for his visit and expressing the wish that he should come again whenever he likes. It occurs to Donald that Bowen must have looked him up in the phone book to find his address. He feels a small surge of gratitude, almost of affection, for this curious old man. With a renewed sense of optimism, he picks up the second letter. It is from London sw1, a long white envelope bearing the sinuous blue logo of Crandall & Boyd.

Dear Donald

I'm afraid I have some bad news. You may have heard that C&B have been in some financial difficulty recently. We've been hit by rising paper prices, high bookshop returns and, frankly, some disastrous publishing decisions. Things came to a head last week, and we were asked to review all existing book contracts, particularly those that are very overdue. Yours came up for consideration, and I'm afraid I couldn't save it, in spite of what you gave me when you came up to London. It's really not finished yet, is it? I am so very sorry.

Here's my advice. Keep working on your book, and send it to me when you are truly satisfied with it. I'll either resubmit it here, or try to place it somewhere else. It's important work, and it deserves to be published.

We'll be sending you a formal contractual release in due course.

Very best wishes, and good luck.

FELICITY WICKES
Executive Editor

Donald holds Felicity's letter by one corner for a few seconds, then lets it fall to the floor. This is a not entirely unforeseen disaster, and he finds that the news brings no immediate feeling of shock or outrage. A fantasy darts into his mind, of burning his manuscript in public, page by page, perhaps on the Iffley village green, explaining to the bewildered onlookers that it was all wrong anyway. In a sense, it no longer seems to matter. If he is right about Geoffrey and the ancient book, he will have something truly important to say to the world.

He is outside at the bottom of the garden, pruning back a tough old rosebush that has survived despite a summer's worth of benign neglect, when he hears the telephone ring. At first he thinks to ignore it; then changes his mind, remembering that he is expecting a call from his father. As he sprints back through the kitchen, he notices with a twinge of guilt that an archaeological report he promised to send along, a study of Roman lead mining in the Mendip hills, is still there on the table. On top of it is a first edition of W. G. Hoskins' *The Making of the English Landscape*, which he found in a second-hand bookshop and intends to give to his father as a gift. He gets to the phone on the eighth ring, lifts the receiver and pauses for half a second to catch his breath.

'Hello, Donald. Are you there?'

It is disorientating to hear the warm, familiar voice. 'Julia—'

'Could we meet somewhere? I have an idea I want to discuss with you, about the poem. It's too complicated to explain over the phone.'

Donald's eye falls on the leaflet for the Tintagel symposium, there in front of him on the desk. 'I'm heading down to Cornwall tomorrow for a conference on the Devil's Barrow finds. If you'd like to sign up, it's not too late. I'm sure we could find some time to talk.'

'Yes, I'd like to come,' Julia says, with only the barest hesitation. 'Just tell me what I need to do.'

After he hangs up the phone, Donald picks up Felicity's cancellation letter and lays it out flat on the table. He folds it in half lengthways, opens it up again, then folds the corners down in two symmetrical triangles, joining in the middle. He makes two more symmetrical folds into the middle, folds the whole in two, then creases each side back down at an angle, half an inch below the apex, to make two swept-back wings. Finally, by making small tears in the trailing edge, he adds two narrow rectangular flaps, one at the back of each wing.

He goes upstairs to his bedroom, uses both hands to force open the narrow sash window. A breath of chilly air steals into the room. He lifts his creation from underneath, adjusts the flaps, then launches it gently through the opening. Its nose lifts at first in the breeze, then dips suddenly, forcing the plane into a steep descent that ends in a crash-landing against the churchyard wall. Two small boys on their way back from choir practice clap ironically. One of them picks up the aircraft, makes a small modification at the tail, then relaunches it. The second flight is beautiful: looping and diving, swept up by the wind, the plane performs stately aerobatics above the middle of the road before gliding to a perfect landing on top of a mildewed old tombstone. This time, all three of them give it a round of applause.

▒ ▒ ▒

HUGH IS WAITING there in the twilight as Julia wheels her bicycle in at the back gate. It will later occur to her that he meant this as a gesture of reconciliation, a throwback to a simpler time when he might genuinely have done such a thing, but now it feels more like an ambush as he steps out from around the corner of the garden shed.

'I told Ruth I would walk down and meet her in town for dinner,' he says.

Julia pushes her bike into the shed, shuts and padlocks the door. 'Please say hello from me.'

Hugh lingers by the gate, makes a show of lifting the latch and opening it. 'I was hoping we could talk,' he says. 'I'm sorry about the way I spoke to you. I'd like to try to make things right again, if I can.'

Caught off guard, Julia finds herself speaking words that she hardly meant to say. 'By having dinner with Ruth?'

'I'll cancel it.'

'It's fine, Hugh, there's no need. I wanted to ask you something, though. Do you mind if I go away for a couple of days? There's an archaeological symposium in Tintagel.'

'That's a bit of a stretch for you, isn't it?' He says this almost carelessly, though she can read the uneasiness in his face.

'It's related to the discoveries at Devil's Barrow, the thing we saw on the news.' Julia is torn by a sudden feeling of guilt and regret that is out of all proportion to what she has said to him, or not said. 'Would you like to come with me?'

Hugh looks at her for a long moment, his expression difficult to read. 'Yes, I would, but the timing's really bad for me. We're about to close on the Merton thing.'

'So we'll talk after I get back?' she says.

'Yes, we'll talk. I hope you have a good trip.' With this, he is through the gate and on his way with a backward glance and a hand raised in what seems a deliberately casual farewell.

Up at the house, Julia packs a small suitcase, working quickly and decisively; then sets it down by the front door, ready to go. Later in the evening, when the place begins to feel too dark and empty, she phones her mother at Dyffryn Farm.

'Your father's been much better,' Cath Llewellyn says. The relief is palpable in her voice. 'Just a twinge of angina, the doctor says. He's been ordered to stop smoking and leave off the heavy work. I even got him out for a walk today, just the two of us, strolling hand in hand along Cyncoed Lane. Can you imagine?'

Julia smiles at her mother's girlish enthusiasm. Her parents have been lucky in their love for one another. 'Can he come to the phone?'

'He's sleeping like a baby. I'd best leave him to it, love. Will you speak to him tomorrow?'

* * *

IT IS A brisk November morning, the air clear and sharp with an edge of early frost, the lushness now fading from the landscape as the hills and pastures take on the muted shades of approaching winter. Coaxing the Morris up the steep and twisting lanes, Donald drives carelessly on, his thoughts drifting back to his new theory about Geoffrey of Monmouth and Siôn Cent. Two days have passed since he awoke in the small hours at home in Iffley, convinced that he had found a way to solve one of the greatest riddles of Arthurian scholarship. Since then, he has hardly dared think about it, fearing that it will not seem quite such a good idea as it did in the first flush of discovery.

His proposition is that the 'ancient book written in the British language', which Geoffrey claimed was brought to him from Wales by his friend Walter, Archdeacon of Oxford, was not merely the product of a lively imagination. It was a real thing, and it drew on the same tradition, perhaps even the same original source, as the book of Cyndeyrn cited by Siôn Cent as his inspiration for the Song of Lailoken.

Caradoc Bowen would tell it differently. He would say that neither of these books ever had a tangible existence. His masterly analysis of the Song of Lailoken leaves little room for doubt that Siôn
Cent was the original author of the poem, that he constructed it
with exquisite care to meet his own purpose of exalting the memory
of Glyn Dŵr. The book of Cyndeyrn was nothing more than a
clever fiction, a ploy to legitimise his master's claim to a predestined
kind of greatness, to guarantee his seat in the Welsh heroic pan-
theon. To claim that these books were connected in some way is to
suggest only that Siôn's invented source was inspired by Geoffrey's
earlier fabrication.

In any case, Donald resolves to keep his ideas to himself until he
has found some more convincing evidence. Meanwhile, he tries to
concentrate on not getting lost in the Somerset hills. A road closure
has diverted him to an unfamiliar route, requiring him to navigate
by a sort of dead reckoning based on half-recognised landmarks and
the position of the sun. By now he has reached the meeting point
of the three minor roads that climb up from the valley of the River
Yeo to the top of the northern Mendip escarpment. To his right is
the Castle of Comfort Inn, a haven since the seventeenth century
for travellers crossing the hills to the cathedral city of Wells. A left
turn at the next junction will put him on the track of the Roman
road connecting the old lead mines with Sorviodunum and Venta,
Old Sarum and modern Winchester, to the east. He makes the turn,
skirting the northern edge of the Stockhill forest, an artificial plan-
tation whose evergreen ranks stand in stark contrast to the sparse
Mendip landscape. The road takes a kink to the right at Red Quarr
Farm, then runs in a perfectly straight line for several miles across
the high rugged farmland.

With the open road empty ahead of him, Donald crashes

through the gears, accelerating the Morris to sixty across this solitary plateau. He brings the car shuddering to a halt in Green Ore, a blank and austere village whose name recalls a lost way of life now preserved only in the warren of lead miners' tunnels reputed to lie undisturbed beneath the fields. A left turn brings him on to the main road from Wells to Midsomer Norton, dipping to the northeast over Nedge Hill and down into the Chew Valley.

Just beyond Chewton Mendip, he follows a narrow lane for half a mile, then turns on to a gravel drive that leads to a grey stone house. It is an angular Victorian building with tall symmetrical windows in need of paint, a slate roof with several broken tiles, a front wall riotously overgrown with ivy. *Grendel's Lair* carved into a wooden nameplate above the door announces the name that Donald's father gave to the house, in a rare attack of whimsy, when he first moved here from the outer London suburbs.

Donald hears the door opening as he gets out of the car. 'Hello, Dad. Sorry I'm late.'

'I was beginning to wonder what had happened to you. Traffic not so good today?' James Gladstone is tall and slightly stooped, with a long, pale face and thinning grey hair combed neatly to one side. His voice has something of wartime Britain in it, John Mills in *We Dive at Dawn*. 'Well, get yourself in out of the cold. I'll put the kettle on.'

A distillation of bittersweet memories runs through Donald's head as he kicks the gravel off his shoes and steps into the chilly front hall. It was only after a long and difficult campaign with his older brother Alec that their father was persuaded to accept an offer of early retirement from the civil service and move back to his native Somerset from the family home in Surrey, where he had lived on carelessly for several years after their mother's untimely death. For

James Gladstone, the loss of his wife was a shattering blow that entirely destroyed his enthusiasm for his career with the Geological Survey, where the two of them had met and worked together for twenty-five years. Donald was only thirteen when it happened, and still from time to time he is haunted by a vision from his youth, of his mother lying there in silence, the fire burning low in the grate, the heavy blue wallpaper with its exotic Japanese flora and fauna, the old carriage clock on the mantelpiece. He will never forget the expression on her face, no longer of fear but of sad acceptance, her faint smile meant for his encouragement but in fact only drawing his attention to the dreadful, slowing tick-tick-tick of the clock.

Alec was travelling abroad at the time, away on his summer break from university, leaving Donald to hold everything together as best he could. It was in those difficult weeks that he began to forge a new and unexpected bond of affection and common interest with his aloof and distant father. It was at that time, too, that he first became the beneficiary of James Gladstone's boundless knowledge of the British landscape. Beginning a tradition that has continued on and off over the years, they would head out together on a Saturday or Sunday, tramping across the fields and through the deciduous woodlands of the Surrey hills. It was on those walks that he learned the meaning of hedges and banks and barrows and ditches, the many-layered tracings of humans on the primal environment.

'Shall I go on through to the study?' Donald says.

'Yes, why don't you? I'll join you in a moment. If it's cold in there, you might like to get the fire going.'

James Gladstone's study is a long bright room at the back of the house, a comfortable, disorderly space strewn with half-read newspapers and library books. To the left, two formal armchairs and a settee upholstered in pale green face an ornate Victorian fireplace. A vintage typewriter stands on a burnished old walnut desk in the corner. At the rear, tall windows look out on a rambling garden planted with rosebushes and apple trees, leaf-strewn grass running down and merging into the farmers' fields that rise gently at first and then more steeply towards the Mendip escarpment. A bird table near the front of the lawn is visited sporadically by chaffinches, robins, and sparrows, the occasional dunnock and greenfinch.

Donald crumples up several sheets from yesterday's *Times* and sets them in the empty grate. Taking rough kindling from a brass container next to the hearth, he builds up from twigs to sticks to thicker cut branches, finally to the quarter-split oak logs from the cast-iron rack in the corner, then touches a lighted match to the newspaper. With the fire well set, he sits down in the nearest armchair, takes up a geological magazine and flicks idly through it, soon finds himself wrapped up in a familiar sensation of comfort and peace.

His father returns with the loaded tea tray. 'Have a ginger biscuit, won't you?' he says. 'They're rather good. Audrey Jenkins brought them over, though of course your mother wouldn't have approved.'

Donald wonders for a moment whether he is referring to the ginger biscuits—a famous dislike of Elizabeth Gladstone's—or to the role of Mrs. Jenkins of Priory Farm. He has an unexpected and faintly unsettling vision of an austere affair being conducted in secret, wonders what his mother would have thought of that. 'Not for me, thanks,' he says.

With the faintest of sighs, James Gladstone picks up the blue and white floral teapot with both hands, frowning with concentration as he pours. The sound is strangely pleasing, a thin mezzo-soprano tinkling that deepens, as the cup begins to fill, into a more substantial tenor gurgle.

'Sugar?'

'No thanks. You ought to know by now.' Donald reaches into his briefcase, takes out a small green booklet. 'I've brought you a copy of the archaeological survey you asked for. It's quite detailed on the surface markers of the Roman mine workings.'

While his father skims through the report, making occasional vague noises of assent and disapproval, Donald leans back in his chair and gazes into the mesmerising world of crackling orange and yellow, willing the flames to greater heights. At length his father closes the booklet, puts it down next to the tea tray. 'There are some useful observations,' he says, 'but still I don't feel that we're getting to the heart of the matter. We won't really know what's down there until we dig for it.'

'We've had that conversation before, Dad—'

'I know, I know, there's no need to say it. One can't dig up the whole country merely to please an amateur enthusiast like me.'

Donald reaches into his briefcase again. 'There's this, too. I found it in a second-hand bookshop.'

A smile of genuine pleasure comes to James Gladstone's face as he takes up the first edition of Hoskins' *The Making of the English Landscape*, turns reverently through the pages. 'This is marvellous, Donald. If there were one book I should have liked to have written, this would have been it.'

'It's not too late.'

'Yes, of course it is, don't be so silly. Now tell me, what have you been up to? Gadding about the country looking for the elusive Arthur? I've been reading the draft you sent me.'

'And?' Donald's forced smile is a poor camouflage for his genuine feeling of nervousness. His father's approval is more important to him than he would care to admit.

'It's very nicely done, I should say, though there was one thought

that occurred to me repeatedly as I was reading through the manuscript. Thoroughness and objectivity are doubtless of great importance in your profession, but you mustn't allow yourself to become
entirely hidebound by what history and archaeology can definitively
tell you. As generations of scholars have proven beyond a doubt,
that approach won't get you any closer to the true origins of Arthur.'
James Gladstone looks meaningfully at Donald now, eyebrows
raised, gently challenging him to refute this argument. 'A thousand
years from now, your clever Oxford people will still be debating the
reliability of the battle-listings in the *Historia Brittonum*, still searching for the location of Mount Badon.'

'I don't disagree, but I think I've said all those things in the
book.'

'Well, almost, but not quite. We all know Arthur is a slippery
sort of fellow, and you've tried to grab at him from almost every
conceivable direction. But there's one approach I think you haven't
quite done justice to.'

Donald is transported back a quarter of a century, to his father
poring over a schoolboy essay on ancient Greece or the Roman
empire, pointing out some unconscionable error of classical history
or political geography. 'What did I get wrong, Dad?'

'Just humour me in a little thought-experiment, if you would.
Let's imagine you were the first modern human to explore the British landscape, and let's say you happened to set eyes on a curiously
shaped hilltop, one that could be seen from many miles in all directions. Think of Glastonbury Tor, if you want a real example. What
would you have done?'

It is a very strange question, even by James Gladstone's unorthodox standards. Donald sits there quietly for a while until the answer
comes to him in a flash of insight. 'I would have named it,' he says.

'That's exactly right.' Donald's father looks approvingly at him. 'An unusual place like that would demand a good story to explain it—a creation myth, you might say. So you would have named it, probably by invoking some great character or story drawn from the mythology of your people. You would have called it Lud's Hill or Mabon's Throne or something like that.'

Donald is long accustomed to his father's oblique approach to such conversations; he will never tackle a subject head-on if an indirect line of attack can be found. 'Where are you going with this, Dad?'

'Well, there's an obvious inference to be drawn. If only we could get back to the original names of things, names that are settled deep into the bones of the landscape, we would learn a great deal about our distant ancestors. I suggest you think carefully about that when you come to reconsider all the rocks and caves and mountain-tops that are named for the mythical Arthur.'

'I've already discussed the toponymic evidence at some length in the book, Dad. It would be easy to over-interpret it.'

'I am merely suggesting that you should supplement the evidence, such as it is, by using your own intellect and imagination. Now then, perhaps you'll drink your tea before it gets cold, and tell me what else you've been up to. Or is it all about the book at the moment?'

Straight away, Donald's thoughts turn back to Julia Llewellyn, and what the next twenty-four hours may bring. 'I did meet someone interesting the other day.' For a moment, he imagines he sees a new candour in his father's gaze; but they have never discussed the women in their lives, and it seems too late for the breaking of ancient taboos. Instead he describes his meeting with Caradoc Bowen, tells his father about the Song of Lailoken and Bowen's interpretation of the text.

James Gladstone calmly takes all of this in, cradling his cup and saucer and smiling faintly in his usual unfathomable way. 'You may be interested to hear that I once had dealings with Professor Bowen. He wrote to us at the Survey, a long time ago now, to enquire about the prevalence of lower Devonian sandstone formations in the mountainous regions of Wales.'

'Is there something special about Devonian sandstone?'

'Well, I suppose its most notable feature is that the high iron oxide content typically gives it a rather striking dark red colour. As I recall, Bowen was especially interested in this, and also in the steepness of the terrain. For some reason, he was looking for places in Wales where he might find tall cliffs made of reddish-coloured rock. We had no idea why, but still we obliged him by sending him several large geological maps marked up with the most likely locations.'

It all seems to fall perfectly into place. In his analysis of the Song of Lailoken, Bowen made a forceful argument that the battle descriptions in the poem referred to real events, that these were the battles of Owain Glyn Dŵr as captured in verse by the bard Siôn Cent. There is one particularly vivid depiction of Glyn Dŵr and his companions trapped in the crooked valley, grimly awaiting the final English attack.

> We strove for the heights but they held us there
> Caught us at sun's falling, trapped at axe's edge
> Grimly we gathered, in close rank, certain of death
> Crags raised red like bloodied fists above us
> The distant water rushing, whispering, sighing
> The river, a wolf's-head smile carved far below.

Caradoc Bowen thought he could find this place, the valley where Glyn Dŵr made his final stand, by interpreting the clues in Siôn

Cent's poem. This was the obsession that drove him, that caused him to lose the confidence of his peers and tarnished his reputation as one of the foremost scholars of the Celtic world.

'I can tell you've an interesting idea lurking in there somewhere,' James Gladstone says, looking at his son with kindly scepticism. 'Do let me know when it has found its way out.'

'Did Bowen ever contact you again?'

'Not as I recall. It would have taken him months, even years, to visit all the places we marked on the map. If he ever found what he was looking for, we certainly never heard about it.'

'I don't imagine he ever did find it.' Donald feels a faint stirring of unease as he reflects on his meeting with Caradoc Bowen and the unexpected letter that followed. Anxious now to be on his way, he glances at his watch.

The gesture does not escape his father's notice. 'Will you stay for lunch, at least?'

'I'm really sorry, Dad, but I have a long drive ahead of me.'

Backing out of his father's drive a few minutes later, Donald is oppressed by a vague sense of melancholy and guilt. The lanky, stooping figure in the doorway recalls random scenes from half a lifetime of partings at this green door with its perennially flaking paint, memories of driving back to university after the Christmas break, of setting off on a trip to Scotland with Sally-Ann Bright, the red-haired girl from the second-hand bookshop on St. Aldates, around the time he almost asked her to marry him. It crosses his mind that it might be the most natural thing in the world for Audrey Jenkins to be standing there on the doorstep with his father; his mother, after all, never lived in this house. It has always been an austere and solitary place, with James Gladstone's slowly fading grief lying over it like a dusty shroud. Perhaps Audrey would let in some much-needed daylight.

Donald forces the Morris into first gear, gives one last wave, senses rather than sees his father turn back wearily into the empty house. He rejoins the main road in Chewton, follows it up the gentle rise of Nedge Hill to the top of the plateau. As the dim green expanse of the Somerset levels begins to open up ahead of him, forming a broad new horizon above the southern Mendip edge, his spirits begin to lift. The city of Wells comes gradually into view, the buildings of the old market town clustered tightly about their majestic cathedral. In the hazy distance beyond, Glastonbury Tor, an improbably steep-sided island, seems to float somewhere above the plain. Driving on through the narrow, busy streets of Wells, then on out to the south-west across wide-open countryside towards the distant county of Cornwall, Donald is gripped by a new sense of excitement at the possibilities of the world.

A Castle Built High
Above the Sea

ITHIN HALF AN hour of leaving his father's house, Donald is driving through a marshy landscape haunted since the seventeenth century by ghostly cries said to belong to the soldiers of the Duke of Monmouth, who was taken prisoner by the royalist forces of his Roman Catholic uncle, James II, after the Battle of Sedgemoor in 1685. Monmouth was executed for treason at the Tower of London in July of that year. He calmly paid the axe man, Jack Ketch, to do a clean and merciful job, but Ketch lost his nerve, taking five bloody strikes to relieve the duke of his head.

Then comes the cider country between lines of rugged hills to the west and south, the Quantocks and the looming Blackdown range marking the border between Somerset and Devon. The weather seems well adjusted to Donald's state of mind, showers arriving overhead at regular intervals between short intermissions of bright sunshine and crystal blue sky. On the far side of Honiton, a grim resolve asserts itself as he finds himself trapped by a series of heavy downpours in the middle of a convoy of high-sided lorries. These unstable vehicles veer from side to side as they catch the wind, their wheels kicking up huge drowning sheets of spray. He is forced to work his way through the pack, pulling out to overtake each in turn, putting his foot to the floor and hanging on determinedly as the Morris inches its way past, then finally back to the safety of the inside lane.

Thus he makes a halting south-westerly progress towards Exeter, the Roman city of Isca Dumnoniorum established in 79 AD at the south-western limit of imperial administration in Britain. In the sparsely populated peninsular lands to the west, the Roman presence was restricted to a handful of lonely military outposts and trading stations along the edges of the moors. This was otherwise deemed a rugged and inhospitable land best left to its Celtic peoples, the Dumnonii, who maintained a form of independence through four hundred years of imperial rule.

The rolling green hill-country of Devon carries Donald to the edge of Dartmoor, where he skirts to the north of the bleak rocky uplands on which Holmes and Watson heard the baleful cry of the hound. Dropping down into the valley of the Tamar, he crosses the river at Launceston, ancient capital and gateway to Cornwall. Soon he begins passing signs to numerous small villages, Tregadillett, Tregeare, Tresmeer, Treneglos, Tremail, and Trelash, evidence enough for a Cornishman that England has truly been left behind.

This is the land of Lucy Trevelyan's paternal forebears, who once held sway in the parish of St. Veep near Lostwithiel on the south Cornish coast, where they were noted for their fertile production of Tory politicians and historians in Victorian times. As far as Donald can remember, Lucy never showed any interest in renewing her ancestral ties to the famous Trevelyan clan. It occurs to him in a theoretical way, as he urges the Morris on up to the higher ground, that Lucy's disparagement of her provincial forebears is as much an expression of her need to be at the cultural centre of things as it is a rejection of the conservative values that were so firmly embedded in her Cornish lineage.

There is a more straightforward explanation, too, that Lucy's posture towards her Trevelyan kin is a simple denial of any shred of allegiance to her own father. When she was in her early teens, Philip Trevelyan, himself a scholar of some repute, was discovered *in flagrante* with a postgraduate student half his age, whereupon Lucy's embittered American mother, never at home in England, seized the moment to take her daughter and two young sons back to California. These experiences helped Lucy to grow into adulthood with a strongly developed sense of self-determination. When, in her late twenties, she arrived to take up a readership at St. Anne's College, Oxford (having already made her mark in the women's studies department at Berkeley), she was fully prepared to deploy her illustrious surname as a battle-sword of her personal academic freedom.

To the right, the land is now dropping gently away to the valley of the River Ottery. To the left rises the barren edge of Bodmin Moor, a vast and desolate tract of rocky outcrops and treeless hills where, long before the Roman occupation, tunnels were dug by bronze-age man to find the precious tin ore. The sun is low in the south-west, making sharp, craggy silhouettes of the angular granite tors that rise like puzzling sculptures on the hilltops. Somewhere high up there on the moor is Dozmary Pool, where it is said that Sir Bedivere, commanded repeatedly by the dying King Arthur, threw Excalibur into the deep dark water, there to be received by the Lady of the Lake.

Donald leaves the main road at Trewassa, heads down a narrow back road towards the coast. As the lane twists and turns interminably across the heathland, it seems to him that he has taken a wrong turning into some ancient, inescapable maze. At last he drops down a long hill into the village of Tintagel, where he finds a cluster of brick and stone buildings, old and new, assembled in homage to the Arthurian tourist trade. It is not yet two o'clock; he is more than an hour early for his rendezvous.

The Cornish tourist season is long past, leaving windblown, half-deserted streets with the atmosphere of Blackpool or Skegness after the summer crowds have left. Donald parks the car on Fore Street, walks on past the King Arthur's Arms and the Excalibur Tea Room, with its brightly painted sign depicting an imposing Arthur in full armour, visor up, sipping tea from a delicate floral cup. At the Uther Pendragon Bookshop, he stops to look in at the window display, smiles with a grim irony as he sees the predictable collection of real-Arthur potboilers set alongside various new-age enchantments that might cause even his ex-wife to blush. A serious-looking couple hovers nearby, debating quietly over the purchase of a yellow plastic sword that their young son has discovered in a large bin outside the door of the shop. Grinning broadly, the boy unsheaths this weapon from its scabbard and flourishes it in front of them.

'Look, Dad!' he says. 'Guess what sword this is?'

His father speaks to him carefully, as if confirming a difficult point of history. 'Yes, Charlie, that's Excalibur, that is.'

The lane next to the bookshop runs steeply down beneath high stone walls overgrown with ivy. At the bottom of the hill, Donald crosses a bridge over a small stream and joins an old medieval track that climbs up to a low summit where a tall, tapered stone stands half-buried in the hedge. Ahead of him, Tintagel Island rises steeply from the slate-grey Atlantic breaking white at the base of the cliffs.

A rocky isthmus joins the island to the mainland, the sea surging and foaming into narrow inlets on either side. High above, white dots of gulls and fulmars hover and swoop across the crumbling ramparts of a medieval castle, sending their mournful, avaricious cries along the westerly sea-breeze.

Earl Richard's famous castle at Tintagel is now forever entwined with the popular mythology of Arthur. Richard, the younger brother of Henry III, acquired the manor of Bossiney, including Tintagel Island, in 1233, and there established his stronghold. He was certainly familiar with Geoffrey of Monmouth's history of the British kings, which was by then well known throughout Europe. According to Geoffrey, it was in an ancient fortress on the island that the future King Arthur was conceived. This was the fanciful story that inspired Richard to build his own Arthurian citadel.

In Geoffrey's tale, Uther Pendragon sought the love of the fair Ygerna, wife of Duke Gorlois of Cornwall. The duke, who was then at war with Uther, hid his bride at Tintagel, thinking her perfectly protected from the Pendragon's assault by the great ramparts of the keep and by the steep and narrow approach to the castle gate. But Uther's love was not to be thwarted by mere walls of stone.

He called to him Ulfin of Ridcaradoch, one of his soldiers and a familiar friend, and told him what was on his mind. 'You must tell me how I can satisfy my desire for her, for otherwise I shall die of the passion which is consuming me.' 'Who can possibly give you useful advice,' answered Ulfin, 'when no power on earth can enable us to come to her where she is inside the fortress of Tintagel? The castle is built high above the sea, which surrounds it on all sides, and there is no other way in except that offered by a narrow isthmus of rock. Three armed soldiers could hold it against you, even if you stood there with the whole kingdom of Britain at your side. If only the prophet Merlin would give his mind to the problem, then with his help I think you might be able to obtain what you want.' Merlin was summoned, and he used his black arts to transform Uther into the image of Gorlois. Queen Ygerna, thinking this was her duke returned unexpectedly from the war, spent that night with Uther in the castle, and there conceived Arthur, the most famous of men.

In the 1930s, Professor C. A. Ralegh Radford excavated extensively on the island, unearthing many artefacts from the post-Roman period. Most impressive of all were the fragments of giant amphorae, jars for wine and olive oil imported from the Mediterranean. All of this, Ralegh Radford said, was evidence of an early Celtic monastery dating from the fifth or sixth century AD, the time of Arthur. Later generations of archaeologists would modify their distinguished predecessor's version of events: this was not, they said, the retreat of ascetic monks, but the stronghold of Celtic chieftains, a line of British warriors whose exploits, captured in local folklore and heroic verse, were picked up by Geoffrey of Monmouth and transformed by his prodigious imagination into a legend of Arthur's birthplace.

Something soft is nudging at Donald's calf. He looks down to find a large tabby cat staring back at him, bright green eyes wide with curiosity. It has a collar around its neck with a name-tag attached: *Galahad*, Glebe Hill Farm, Tintagel. He strokes it under the chin, and with this encouragement the cat begins purring loudly, meanwhile performing a complicated figure-of-eight loop through his legs. When Donald continues on his way, Galahad trots ahead of him.

There is a fork in the path ahead, the right-hand branch leading down towards the narrow approach to Tintagel Island. Donald's first thought is to cross over for a closer look at the ruins; but now he sees something that stops him in his tracks. At the nearer end of the isthmus, perhaps a hundred yards below him, a dozen or more people are gazing up at the castle walls. They are archaeologists, fellow attendees at the symposium, many of them people he knows. There amongst them is the tall, graceful, unmistakable figure of Lucy Trevelyan.

The cat has meanwhile continued to the left, in the direction of Glebe Cliff. Donald follows in its footsteps, picking his way up the steep track to the clifftop, sure that Lucy will have seen him by now; he can only hope that she will not try to come after him. When the path divides again, he takes the southerly branch towards the church standing alone in the fields to the left. Galahad, meanwhile, continues on his own secret quest, stepping purposefully through the rough grass without so much as a backward glance.

The Parish Church of St. Materiana, in its solitary location on an exposed promontory scourged by Atlantic storms, seems remote from modern Tintagel, a throwback to some former pattern of village life. Numerous low grassy mounds close to the church, identified as early Christian burials, confirm that the site has been sacred ground for at least fourteen hundred years. Donald enters through the lych-gate and makes his way across the churchyard, conscious of stepping on centuries of anonymous Cornish people, hundreds, perhaps thousands of them laid out beneath him, head to the west, feet to the east. Someone has laid fresh flowers, white and yellow and red, on one of the newer graves.

Turning the latch on the heavy oak door of the church, Donald steps into the dimly lit interior and drops a few coins into the collection box before continuing along the nave, footsteps echoing on the flagstones. He stops for a while in front of one of the more striking memorials, a tall brass plaque set into the floor near the entrance to the chapel.

HERE LIES JOHN ANSELL, BELOVED SCHOOLMASTER IN THIS PARISH, AND WORTHY POET, WHO DIED THE 20TH DAY OF DECEMBER, 1842. ALSO HIS WIFE MERRYN, WHO DIED THE 19TH DAY OF JUNE, 1843, FROM THE WEIGHT OF SADNESS THAT WAS IN HER HEART. MAY THEY BE REUNITED AT LAST IN PEACE.

The words of a poem are inscribed beneath, an oblique ode to Thomas Gray's *Elegy Written in a Country Churchyard*; perhaps the work of Ansell himself, penned in anticipation of his own demise.

A sleeping churchyard finds the muse
Of England's poet, framed by death
He rhymes unknown an epitaph
Of silent dust and fleeting breath.

Along this path in dreaming-space
Treads phrase world-weary, hopeful, wise
A life, unmourned, has dimly passed—
Grey stone recalls where cold bone lies.

His mind's eye in the future spies
Fair wand'rer chanced upon his tomb
She stops to read, then shake away
Chill-fingered pledge of coming doom.

What if one day such lyric gaze
Should glance across his perished lines?
How would she speak, what history tell
Fond thought regale, or truth divine?

What says the wind in yew tree's bough
Or raindrops darkening the pane?
How sings the grass grown high above
The thick black earth that bears his name?

The tale's forgot, the time long spent
The clock heard striking on the tower
All traded now for passing grace
In transient year, by vanished hour.

Let grandchild's child forget those days:
A summer's eve, a hand held fast
The skylark's song above the field
Must wane, and fade, 'tis gone at last.

Something of John Ansell's mournful valediction stays with Donald as he heads back through the lych-gate and on down a long grassy slope towards the top of Glebe Cliff. There he sits for a while on a rock near the cliff's edge, close-cropped turf beneath his feet, wind and sea enclosing him in walls of rushing sound. The sky has cleared from the west, bringing to the foam-flecked sea a dark steely hue that calls to mind the grim depths of the cold ocean. Feeling suddenly nervous, he looks at his watch. It is much later than he thought. He gets to his feet, makes his way back along the clifftop into the teeth of the rising gale.

It is only a short drive from Tintagel village to a place called Rocky Valley where a rough driveway descends steeply from the road towards a narrow, heavily wooded ravine still showing a long sweep of autumn leaves in shades of red and yellow and russet-brown. At the end of the track is a solid grey stone building next to a stream running vigorously down through the trees. Once a functioning water-mill, the building has long since been converted into a substantial guest-house. Mrs. Ennor Carwyn, the owner of this establishment, comes to meet him at the door. She is an unsmiling woman with dark watchful eyes, grey hair drawn back from her face and tied in a narrow braid at the back.

'We're glad to have you back, Dr. Gladstone.' She speaks guardedly, as if he should be careful not to make too much of her familiarity.

Having stayed at Trevethey Mill on two previous visits to Cornwall, Donald knows a little of its history. The oldest parts of the building date back to 1472, and the mill has been in the Carwyn family for at least four hundred years. There is something here of Cold Comfort Farm, an eccentric edge to the place that he finds obscurely pleasing, never a trace of sycophancy or misplaced courtesy. He also has hopes of avoiding the symposium attendees, who are more likely to put up at the conference hotel down in Tintagel village.

'Dinner is at seven,' Mrs. Carwyn says. 'Will it be just yourself?'

'I'm expecting a colleague, Julia Llewellyn. Has she checked in yet, by any chance?'

Now there is a fleeting curious look in the landlady's eye. 'No, she has not. I'll be glad to let you know when she does.'

Donald writes Julia a note, proposing a short walk along the Rocky Valley to the sea, then goes to his room and lies down for just a moment on the bed. He closes his eyes, falls into a fitful sleep in which he is tumbling in slow motion from a precipice, watching curiously as the tumultuous, wave-torn seashore rises to meet him.

When the knock comes at the door, he is saved from a certain death on the sharp-edged rocks. 'Dr. Gladstone? Your colleague is downstairs.' It is Mrs. Carwyn's voice. 'She said you had suggested going for a walk. Shall I ask her to wait for you?'

He looks at his watch, forces his brain to comprehend the orientation of the hands. Quarter-past six. Half-past three. Half an hour late. He jumps to his feet, calls back through the door. 'Yes, please ask her to wait. I'll need just a couple of minutes.'

There is a wash-basin in the corner with two thin towels and a small mirror hanging on the wall above. Donald splashes water on his face, hurriedly brushes his teeth, throws more water on to his bed-spiked hair. He digs clean clothes out of his bag, tossing aside books, a crumpled newspaper, assorted Ordnance Survey maps. When he looks in the mirror, he sees dark rings beneath his eyes, the beginnings of a reddish stubble on his chin. The frown-lines between his eyebrows seem more than usually pronounced. He takes a deep breath, lets it out again, more slowly; then picks up his jacket from the bed and makes his way downstairs.

Julia is sitting next to the reception desk in an upright wooden chair, radiant and smiling, as if some secret is about to be shared. 'I almost went without you,' she says.

'Sorry about that. I was dreaming of falling off a cliff.'

They head out of the back door of the mill to a bridge across the stream that hurries noisily down the narrow wooded valley towards the sea. Once they are in the trees, the sound of the wind in the branches seems to merge with the rushing of the water, the late-afternoon sunlight dappling the woodland floor in a bright shifting pattern of light and shade. Donald has an almost surreal sense of having stepped outside the ordinary world, of sharing this space with Julia alone. As he leads the way down the narrow winding path, he feels a strong urge to reach out and take her by the hand.

Soon enough, they are out of the trees again and climbing on to a craggy outcrop that offers a view down the valley to the place where the stream battles out to meet the ocean. They stand there for a while looking out at the Atlantic now in the full flood of high tide with the breakers crashing against the seaward rocks.

'How's the book coming along?' Julia says, raising her voice above the booming of the surf.

'Slowly, as usual.' Donald smiles in an offhanded way. Significant phrases from Felicity's letter are etched into his memory. 'I went to see Caradoc Bowen, by the way.'

Something in Julia's expression makes him regret having raised this subject. 'I didn't think you would go,' she says. 'What did you make of him?'

'He's quite a character, very clever and a little eccentric. More or less as I expected, really.'

'It sounds as if you took a liking to him.'

'Yes, in a way I suppose I did.'

Julia turns away, scuffs at the loose rock with the toe of her boot. She bends down to pick up a tiny white cockle shell, turns it over in the palm of her hand. 'What did he have to say about Devil's Barrow?'

'I'm afraid he didn't think much of the idea that there might be a connection to the Song of Lailoken. He thought the parallels were no more than coincidental. But you said you had a new idea about the poem?'

'I'll tell you about it later, OK?'

They walk back mostly in silence to Trevethey Mill, Julia apparently lost deep in thought, Donald meanwhile trying to decipher the conversation they have just had. She stops at the bridge over the stream, within sight of the mill, turns to him with not a hint that anything is amiss.

'What will you do tonight?' she says.

'There's a group reception down at the conference hotel in Tintagel, but I wasn't planning to go to it.' Donald would rather be struck dead by a thunderbolt than be forced to endure Lucy this evening, least of all in Julia's company. He recites a silent prayer. 'I was thinking we could have dinner here instead?'

⊠ ⊠ ⊠

THE OLD WOODEN stairs creak unpredictably beneath Julia's heels as she makes her way down from the top floor. She has dressed with particular care, well enough to feel good about herself but without going too far. Persistent, awkward questions keep whispering themselves to her, but she leaves them unanswered as she comes expectantly down the last flight to the reception. Donald is waiting for her there, freshly scrubbed and very good-looking, it seems to her, in a shirt with a fraying collar and a well-worn pair of jeans.

'I have something for you,' she says, handing him a faded old foolscap envelope she has brought down with her. 'I found it in a box of old things my mother sent, and it made me think of you.'

Donald opens the envelope, takes out a finely rendered pencil sketch of a dramatic tilted cliff-face set in a rugged Welsh landscape. *Craig-y-Ddinas*, the caption reads. 'For me to keep?'

'Yes, I'd like you to have it,' Julia says. 'Arthur and his knights are sleeping in a cave underneath that cliff. That's what my father told me, anyway.'

He seems surprised, but genuinely pleased. 'I'll hang it above my desk, for inspiration.'

Mrs. Carwyn has meanwhile reappeared at the reception desk. 'It's French beef casserole, if that will suit?' She ushers them into a broad open space with chipped old flagstones underfoot, the original working heart of the mill. Except for a young couple in the far corner speaking together in hushed, self-absorbed tones, they have the place to themselves. They sit down at a wooden trestle table next to a row of old millstones standing propped up against the wall.

'The main course will be fifteen minutes,' the landlady says. 'I'll bring you some wine to start with.' She soon returns with a modest bottle of Côtes du Rhône, pours about half of it into two large glasses. 'There's bread here too, if you like,' she says, leaving them with an entire loaf on a board at the end of the table.

'Well, cheers,' Donald says, lifting his glass.

'Here's to Cornish hospitality.' Julia takes a long sip of wine. 'I'm sorry about this afternoon, by the way. I was a little grumpy with you.'

'I didn't notice,' Donald says, and she finds herself liking the look on his face, the irony perfectly outbalancing the earnestness. 'Did I say something wrong, though?'

'No, it wasn't your fault. When you mentioned your meeting with Bowen, it brought back some bad memories, that's all.' Julia has an urge to tell Donald everything, to explain to him the corrosive effect that Caradoc Bowen is still having on her marriage, fourteen years after she last set eyes on him. But this is not a conversation she is ready to have with him. 'Why don't you tell me what to expect at the symposium tomorrow?'

Donald leans back in his chair, wine glass in hand. 'Honestly,' he says, 'I'm worried you might find it very boring. You'll witness a roomful of scruffy archaeologists debating over dislocated skeletons. Maybe a few arguments about the colour and consistency of certain kinds of mud.'

'It sounds perfect,' she says. Listening to Donald talk in his wry, self-deprecating way, Julia feels a surge of affection for him. She tries to imagine how she would paint his picture, something solid and strong but full of a subtle kind of light, deeply rooted to the earth, like a spreading oak tree in a forest clearing.

'By the way, I've been meaning to ask you, how does someone get to work for the OED?'

'By answering an advertisement in the *Oxford Mail*.'

'Lexicographers wanted?'

'Something like that. They happened to be looking for someone who could speak Welsh, and I was the only applicant with a master's degree in the Brythonic languages.'

'How did your father feel about your new job?'

It is a curious thing for him to say, but it seems to Julia that this is just the right question to ask. 'The true Welsh patriot whose daughter runs off to the heart of the Saxon kingdom to make a perfect record of the English language? He didn't much like the idea at first, in fact he didn't like me going away at all. But he's come around since then, I think.'

She remembers well the day she announced boldly to her father that she had turned down good offers from the Welsh university colleges, that she planned to go to Oxford instead. He explained to her in his ironic, lilting way that the inflated, bombastic old boys' club of Oxford and Cambridge was nothing more than a kindergarten for the inflated, bombastic, rapacious British government. The

English government, he would have called it, nothing British about it at all. She smiles at the memory of his smoke-hoarsened tones attacking the Anglo-Saxon establishment, extolling the virtues of Welsh independence and fresh mountain air.

'Do you get back there much, to visit your parents?' Donald says.

'Yes, as often as I can.' Julia drinks more of her wine, feels the mellowness flowing through her. 'There's not much there except for hills and grass and old stone walls, but it's still home for me. I love waking up on a spring morning and hearing nothing but the bleating of lambs and the breeze along the valley. I need to get back up there soon.'

'You seem a little bit sad about it.'

'Yes, I suppose that's true.' This simple statement disguises the complexity of what she feels, her guilt at not having spoken to her father, her resentment at Hugh for all the time he spends at Ty Faenor, just along the valley from Dyffryn Farm. With the flexibility of his property work in Oxford, he has made a habit of taking himself off to his Welsh refuge as often as he likes, usually at some erratic time during the week rather than waiting for a weekend when they might go together. There is always a vague but reasonable explanation, a new farm-hand to interview, an important project to manage on the estate.

'Do you want to tell me your idea?' Donald says. 'About the poem?'

'Yes, if you like.' Julia breaks off a small piece of bread but does not eat it, leaves it on the edge of her plate. She is nervous now, the words coming out in an anxious rush. 'I think Caradoc Bowen made a mistake when he translated the Song of Lailoken. Where he has *the crooked vale where the three rivers fall*, I think it should read *the crooked vale with three waterfalls*. It's a more lyrical and archaic translation of the Middle Welsh *llifeiriant*, which would be appropriate to the overall construction of the poem. He was looking for rivers, when he should have been looking for waterfalls.'

Donald adds half an inch of wine to both their glasses. 'I hate to mention this, but do you think it's likely Bowen would have made a mistake like that?'

'I think you're putting a little too much faith in the wisdom of Caradoc Bowen,' she says, fighting down a small surge of irritation. 'He's a poet and a historian, not a linguist. He doesn't know everything there is to know about the evolution of the Welsh language. And once he has an idea in his head, he finds it impossible to let it go. I know this to be true.'

There are loud noises from the kitchen, a crashing of pans, heavy footsteps on the floorboards presaging Mrs. Carwyn's reappearance with their main course. They watch in silence as she serves up giant portions of a thick meaty stew from a heavy stoneware pot. After she has left, neither of them moves to eat.

Donald smiles at Julia now, showing the laugh lines etched around his eyes and mouth. 'Well, I think you've made a remarkable deduction. So it's not the crooked vale where the three rivers fall, but the crooked vale with three waterfalls. What are we going to do about it?'

'I've been thinking about that.' Julia reaches for a napkin, takes a pen out of her bag, sketches an outline of Wales. She adds in the mountains: Snowdonia in the north-west, the great upland tract known as the Elenydd across the middle of the country, the Black Mountains and the Brecon Beacons to the south. 'If I were looking, I would start here,' she says, drawing a circle around the southerly ranges. 'I've heard there are many beautiful waterfalls in those hills, though I have never been there.'

And so they talk on into the evening, planning their hypothetical expedition to scour the Welsh mountains for the lost valley where, according to the Song of Lailoken, Owain Glyn Dŵr made his last stand. Donald tells Julia his father's story of Caradoc Bowen and the geological maps, Bowen's conviction that Siôn Cent's verses could be read literally in this way. Together they work through the lines of the poem, try to fix in their minds the picture of this imaginary place. Mrs. Carwyn returns at some point, emanating a faint disapproval as she circles the table, clearing away their barely touched dinner plates.

Later, they walk outside into the night air deepened by thickening cumulus clouds, a breeze through the treetops carrying the fragrance of falling leaves and the distant sound of the sea. They stop at the footbridge across the stream, stand there in the middle of the span looking down at the water tumbling through the arch, ghostly white in the darkness. Donald picks up two small sticks from the path, throws them far out into the stream, tries to follow them as they are carried back under the bridge.

Julia feels him move closer to her now, reaching out for her in the darkness. She cannot properly see the expression on his face, but there is no doubting the touch of his fingers as he brushes the hair away from her cheek, the firm grip of his hands as he pulls her towards him. She does not resist, holds on to him tightly as he bends to kiss her.

But the moment is too brief, shattered by the sound of voices, a small band of archaeologists, torches in hand, heading out on some night-time expedition. 'A pleasant evening,' says the leader of this group, an overweight, heavily bearded man who cannot take his eyes off Julia as he steps around them and across the bridge. His companions follow him in single file, some of them nodding awkwardly to Donald as they pass by.

In their wake comes a great drowning wave of guilt and humili-
ation and sadness. 'I have to go,' Julia whispers, as the last of them
disappears into the darkness of the trees. 'I'll see you tomorrow,
OK?' She is on her way back up the path to the mill before Donald
has a chance to react.

THE SYMPOSIUM IS to be held in the grand ballroom of the King
Arthur's Castle Hotel in Tintagel, a massive Victorian crenellated
construction squarely built from blocks of local granite to resemble
a medieval keep. Completed in 1899 to a design by Silvanus Trevail,
the famously depressive Cornish architect, the hotel is situated alone
on an exposed hilltop facing Tintagel Island. It seems to Donald, as
he walks towards this oddly misconceived building, that the crumbling remnants of Earl Richard's much earlier effort remain by far
the more evocative of an imagined Arthurian past.

But he is more immediately occupied with other concerns. He
has not seen Julia since she left him on the bridge, though he waited
for her at breakfast in a state of hopeful confusion. It was Mrs. Carwyn who rescued him with an emphatic serving of bacon and eggs
and the crucial information that she had seen the young lady leaving the mill shortly after dawn. She was going out for a walk, she
said, to get some fresh air. Thinking about the night before, Donald
sees one moment with perfect clarity, causing almost a physical pain
in his chest as he relives the fatal interruption at the hands of the
boorish Raymond Grint (known to him by reputation only as an
outspoken iron-age man from the University of Bristol) and his
party of blundering acolytes.

By now he is late for the start of the morning's plenary session.
He heads through the hotel lobby and along the corridor to the

ballroom entrance, slips in through the double doors, finds a seat at the end of the back row. From there, he takes his measure of a large space lushly appointed with heroic tapestries on the walls, a thick embroidered carpet underfoot, tall, heavily swagged and curtained windows at the eastern end. The whole has been thrown into twilight by the dimming of the giant chandeliers overhead. There is an impressive attendance of perhaps two hundred people in closely spaced wooden chairs.

In ordinary circumstances, Donald would be in his element amongst this worthy gathering of cautious professionals, but for now there is no question of settling his thoughts to archaeology. He scans the room, finds that Julia is nowhere to be seen. Lucy, meanwhile, is there in the front row, looking disdainfully up at the smiling, suntanned man standing at the lectern.

'It is with genuine pleasure,' Paul Healey is saying, 'that I welcome you here to the King Arthur's Castle Hotel for what promises to be one of the highlights of our archaeological year.' He continues for several minutes in similar vein, dispensing gratitude and appreciation to right and left as if he were accepting some exalted award: for best actor, this is the thought that comes to Donald as he listens with a growing sense of dismay. Healey is in his element, in full manipulative flow as he hastens to bolster his credibility in front of an apparently receptive crowd.

During the small ovation that follows this speech, Donald feels a touch on his shoulder, turns to find Julia sitting down next to him. She whispers a single word, *sorry*, but there is no chance for them to talk. The applause for Paul Healey dies away to an expectant near-silence broken by sporadic outbreaks of coughing, a restrained turning of pages, the shifting of weight in creaky wooden seats.

The opening presenter is duly introduced as Dr. Roderic Wilson, a thin, mousy forensic anthropologist from King's College, London. He takes a sip of water, steps up to the microphone to deliver his sententious opening lines. 'I surely do not need to remind this audience,' he says, 'that a careful posthumous examination of the human skeleton can tell us a great many things about the cause of death, especially if the individual's demise happens to have been brought about by a pathological condition, or by some form of excessive violence.'

Wilson continues for some considerable time in this mannered style, describing in meticulous detail the results of his examination of the skeletons discovered at Devil's Barrow. His findings, as it turns out, are remarkably consistent. Thirteen of the fifteen victims, identified as males in their twenties and thirties, appear to have died by the same combination of a sharp blow to the skull (delivered by some kind of blunt instrument, perhaps a stone axe, not large but wielded with force) followed by impalement through the abdomen and up into the ribs by a long sharp weapon, probably a spear. Whether or not they were all dead by the time they were thrown into the water-filled pit, he cannot say for sure, though he rather hopes that they were.

Donald is sitting close enough to Julia that he can detect the faint scent of lavender, the fragrance returning him with a painful immediacy to the Trevethey bridge. He has no choice but to keep his attention firmly fixed on Roderic Wilson, to try to follow the details of the talk.

'The last two sets of remains,' Wilson is saying, 'those of the apparently high-status individuals found at the very top of the pile and in close proximity, respectively, to a decorative ceramic chalice and an antler headpiece, present a rather different case. I can confirm Professor Healey's preliminary finding that they were each

killed by a single thrust from a sharp weapon. Though not the same
weapon,' Wilson adds, looking up at his audience to emphasise the
importance of this point, 'not the same weapon that was used on the
thirteen males who were buried beneath them.'

Now there is a stir at the front of the room as someone stands
up to ask a question. Recognising Lucy's unmistakable profile,
Donald feels a tight knot forming in the pit of his stomach. She
turns in such a way that she is addressing not just the speaker, but
the entire group.

'It seems to me, Dr. Wilson, that you have failed entirely to
recognise the significance of these finds. Is this not precisely the
method of threefold sacrificial killing that has been noted elsewhere
in the Celtic world at sites dating from the first millennium BC?'

The unfortunate Roderic Wilson, finding his most telling rhetorical moment fatally compromised by Lucy's interruption, makes
an unconvincing open-handed gesture to the closest members of the
audience. 'Well, I should say that was a question for my archaeological colleagues—'

'Is this not,' Lucy continues, raising her voice above the murmuring that has begun in the room, 'is this not the clearest evidence
yet of the practice of ritual slaughter perpetrated by the incoming patriarchal Celts? Can we not see, in the well-documented pattern of these cruel woundings, a deliberate, calculated profaning of
the triune mother goddess of Old Europe?' She leaves this question
hanging in the air, scans the rows of watchful, apprehensive faces,
daring someone to respond.

It is Donald, propelled by an unstoppable rush of irritation, who
gets to his feet to answer her. 'I would like to take issue with Dr.
Trevelyan's remarks,' he says, speaking loudly enough to cut across
the renewed whisperings of the audience. He is intensely aware of

Julia's curious eyes on him as he begins to formulate his argument. 'It is important for us to remember that Devil's Barrow has so far provided no firm evidence at all to suggest a specific aggressor. Indeed, the site is lacking artefacts of any kind that might suggest a Celtic presence. To suggest otherwise is nothing more than unfounded speculation.'

Lucy, still standing up at the front of the room, is for once left momentarily at a loss for words, while Donald's interjection is greeted by noises of assent and approval from all sides.

'If we take the evidence at face value,' he continues, 'it appears just as likely that the solitary female was not so much a victim of this sacrificial rite as its chief arbiter. The traces of blood found in her chalice would seem to suggest as much—and, as we have seen, she was one of only two individuals who escaped the full savagery of the threefold death. Perhaps Dr. Trevelyan would like to comment on this possibility?'

The ingratiating Paul Healey chooses this moment to step back up to the microphone. 'If I may,' he says, 'I would like to propose that our distinguished colleagues continue their discussion during the coffee break. I'm quite sure it's a valuable debate, but meanwhile we must allow our presenter to finish his talk.'

Donald sits back down in his chair, does his best to avoid Julia's gaze, though now he feels the warm pressure of her hand resting on his. 'Well done,' she whispers, leaning in close.

Roderic Wilson has meanwhile taken Healey's cue. 'In closing,' he says, 'I would like to share with you our preliminary results from the dating of the organic materials found at the site. Our goal has been to validate, or otherwise, Professor Healey's proposed assignment of the skeletal remains to the fifth century AD.' Wilson pauses, takes a sip of water, determined perhaps to deliver a final flourish.

'Unfortunately, no such verification is possible at this stage. Carbon dating of several bone samples has provided wildly varying date estimates, with discrepancies of up to two thousand years for the outliers. This suggests that there has been some degree of sample contamination, a not uncommon problem at inhumation sites such as this, where intrusions by plants or animals or later humans very often cause difficulties of this kind. A new analysis with a larger and more diverse sample set is now under way, and will hopefully lay these ambiguities to rest.'

As he steps down from the podium, Roderic Wilson acknowledges his polite applause, his face expressing a mixture of relief and frustration. Lucy has meanwhile walked over to the right-hand edge of the room, where she is standing in the semi-darkness beneath a tapestry depicting Uther Pendragon's magical infiltration of Tintagel Castle. Donald is acutely aware of her glances in his direction, and of Julia's very physical presence immediately to his left. It is an intolerable situation. He resorts to a fiercely concentrated study of the conference programme. There are two more presentations before the morning coffee break.

The next speaker is a nervous young postgraduate from Healey's group at Cambridge. Her physical analysis of the Devil's Barrow site is dry but worthy stuff, a careful exposition of the painstaking scientific practice of field archaeology. She accompanies her presentation with numerous line drawings and site maps, the occasional photograph of muddied, besweatered archaeologists and lank-haired students unearthing mud-encrusted skulls and femurs. There is a sense in the room of moving past the earlier theatrics, of buckling down to the important work.

But now there is a second interruption, enough to stop Healey's student in her tracks. The double doors at the back of the ballroom are thrown loudly open, and there is a general turning of heads to watch the measured, almost regal entrance of a tall, striking man with greying hair to his shoulders. He stands there for a moment, scanning the rows of seats, apparently oblivious to the many eyes that are on him. To Donald he seems vaguely familiar, though he cannot quite place him. Certainly he does not have the look of an archaeologist.

Julia's intake of breath is unmistakable. 'It's my husband,' she says, quietly, as the newcomer's plaintive gaze falls on her. 'I'm so sorry, but I'll have to go.' With this, she gets up and hurries along the aisle. She goes outside with Hugh Mortimer, the doors slamming shut behind them.

※ ※ ※

OUTSIDE IN THE bright Tintagel sunlight, Julia sees that Hugh's eyes are bloodshot, the grey coming through strongly in the stubble on his chin.

'Something's happened,' he says. 'I had to come and tell you.' He puts a gentle hand on each shoulder, looks her in the eye. A cold empty space opens up inside her. 'Your father passed away in his sleep last night. There was a call early this morning, from Dyffryn. I promised your mother I would try to catch up with you.'

For a small, strange moment, Julia's thoughts go back to Donald, left alone in the symposium and oblivious to this new calamity. She wants to go back in and say something to him, but it seems impossible. Their wonderful, romantic, bookish conversations belong to a separate, more carefree world, a place that only ever had a real existence in her imagination. Here in front of her now is her husband bringing back the authentic reality of life, and of death, the full crushing weight of it. 'Can we go there straight away, please?' she says. 'I need to be with my mother.'

※ ※ ※

FINALLY THE BREAK arrives, tea and coffee and digestive biscuits served out in the hotel lobby. Julia has not returned, but Lucy is there at the coffee urn, holding forth to a group of three bemused but politely attentive archaeologists from Durham University. Donald walks straight past her, heads for the front door of the hotel.

'Not so fast, Dr. Gladstone.'

'Lucy, not now, please.'

Her gleaming leaf-patterned dress hugs the long, slim contours of her body. She has carried a handful of biscuits away with her from the table, and now offers one to Donald. 'Here, take it. I think your blood sugar needs a boost.'

'Really, I don't want it. And by the way, I don't feel like having an argument with you today.'

'Why should we argue, sweetness? I was just a little curious about the dramatic exit this morning. Who was she, anyway? She seemed quite fond of you.'

This conversation is anathema to Donald, but to avoid the question will only make matters worse. 'Her name is Julia Llewellyn. She works at the OED.'

'I wasn't aware they were hiring archaeologists there. Or has she discovered a new interest in the subject? How very interdisciplinary of her.' Lucy smiles at him in her demure, infuriating way. 'Was that Julia's husband who came crashing in? I thought he was rather good-looking.'

'Leave it alone, would you, please?'

'OK, I'll make a bargain with you,' Lucy says. The smile has gone, and there is a hint of ice in her voice. 'I'll refrain from commenting on your sordid little affair, but only if you promise not to stand up in public and attack my credibility.'

In her usual unerring way, she has succeeded in finding the right buttons to push. Donald speaks to her now in a low, fierce voice. 'Just because you assert something over and over again, Lucy, it doesn't become any more true. Is it too much to hope that you will ever understand the difference between real, scientific archaeology and the telling of stories?'

'Like your tales of King Arthur, for example?'

Donald does not respond to this, merely walks away from her, the anger coiled tightly inside him as he heads out of the hotel and on along the path that leads back to Tintagel village.

Dyffryn Farm

ND SO THEY leave Tintagel in a convoy of two, driving on and on through the late morning and the afternoon to the early autumn sunset. They stop only once, at a roadside transport cafe near Monmouth where Hugh buys sandwiches and coffee for them both, does his best to make some kind of considerate conversation. Julia wraps both hands around her coffee mug, smiles weakly at him, says little in return. She finds herself counting the days since she last spoke to her father: twenty-five, almost a month since she heard his voice, and she will never hear it again. This is the thought that rises to the raw surface of her mind.

From Hereford, they head west and north in the gathering darkness to the border of Radnorshire and on across the endless Welsh hinterland. Staring blankly through the windscreen at the big square rear lights of the Land Rover, Julia occupies herself entirely with the mechanics of driving, tries to hold all else at bay. It is close to six o'clock by the time they reach the edge of Rhayader. They leave the main road and wind their way up into rain-bound hills making arcs of deeper blackness in the encircling sky. As they turn on to Cyn-coed Lane and climb the lower slopes of Moel Hywel, Julia looks up instinctively to see the lights of Dyffryn Farm glowing faintly on the hillside above.

Cath Llewellyn is waiting for them at the front door, a lonely sil-houette against the brightness that falls from the storm-lamp fixed high on the wall above. 'In you come, now, out of the rain,' she says, ushering them firmly inside with a show of normality, her courage showing through her red-rimmed eyes and the deeply drawn lines of her face. 'Will you have something to eat? There's hot soup on the stove.' For a strange, disturbing moment, Julia sees Dai standing there behind her mother in the shadows.

Hugh lays a gentle hand on her shoulder. 'Is there something I can do? Or shall I go on to Ty Faenor for now?'

'Yes, please do that.' She feels a small surge of relief and grati-tude. 'You'll come back tomorrow morning?'

After he has driven away, she follows her mother mutely into the kitchen. Since she was a small child, this is where they have always held their important conversations. It is a long, low room dominated by a table and chairs of darkened oak along the centre. At the far end, the family china is arrayed in a tall Welsh dresser, a wedding gift to Julia's great-grandmother. There is a collection of old-fash-ioned kitchen implements, heavy pots and pans, long-handled ladles and spoons, all hanging on tarnished brass hooks from the walls. A cast-iron stove set into the old original fireplace makes a great radius of warmth stretching to all but the farthest corners, doing battle with the relentless cool draughts that come creeping in past the curtains and around the edges of the door.

Julia takes all this in at a glance, all the aching familiarity of it. There is something new here as well, an unaccustomed sense of emptiness. Usually when she steps into this room she feels a reassuring essence of her forebears, the vital spirit of the Llewellyn family matriarchs who have ruled over it since Georgian times, but they are absent today. The house itself seems lost in mourning.

'Well now,' Cath Llewellyn says, taking Julia's hands in her own. 'Let me have a look at you, love.'

Julia's resolve is undone not so much by the sound of her mother's voice as by something that happens to catch her eye, her father's latest pencil sketch half-finished on his favourite chair in the corner, his tattered old fleece-lined slippers laid out ready on the floor beneath. The despair wells up in her chest, tears coming now in great shuddering waves as she gives herself up to her mother's embrace.

In time, the intensity of it subsides. Cath Llewellyn guides Julia firmly to a chair, reaches up to a high shelf for the Bristol sherry. 'Your father won't have wanted to see us moping about,' she says. 'This was supposed to be for Christmas, but there's no sense saving it now.'

And so they sit together at the kitchen table, drinking sweet amontillado from chipped enamel mugs, crying and laughing in equal measure as they share their best memories of Dai. They talk on far into the night, firing up the stove with the seasoned ash-wood logs to keep it blazing brightly against the wind and rain lashing the window-panes. There is a wrenching sadness and also a kind of fierce exhilaration in the things they have to say to each other, a mother and daughter now alone in the world, meditating as they never have before on their years spent with a man who was difficult and proud but never bitter, who was as quick to anger as he was to a smile, who was unwavering in his devotion to his wife and only child.

Some time in the small hours, Julia swathes herself in blankets on the settee in the front room, falls straight away into the deepest sleep. In her dreams she is visited by scenes from her youth, of her father admonishing her gently in Welsh, telling her she must be having a nightmare, of course he is not dead. Hugh is there too, in the background, familiar but oddly distorted as if, like Dorian Gray's picture, his features have become subtly altered since she last set eyes on him.

❖ ❖ ❖

DONALD SPENDS THE greater part of the long drive from Cornwall to Somerset reliving the events at Tintagel, breaking them down frame by frame, rewriting the script for himself. In his imagined world, every word, every gesture finds its perfect timing. By the time they walk out across the Trevethey bridge, Raymond Grint and his people have long since departed on their strange nocturnal expedition. Standing there above the rushing stream, Julia whispers to Donald that she has broken forever with Hugh Mortimer, that she never wants to see him again. She takes him back to her room, allows him to undress her in the dim half-light, to make love to her in a beautiful, natural consummation.

Scene two, the following morning at the symposium. As Mortimer enters the ballroom, Donald lays a restraining hand on Julia's arm: stay where you are, I'll go out and speak to him. There is a physical fight, perhaps, a duel of sorts (this part still needs some work); or, he defeats his opponent by weight of argument alone. In either case, Hugh Mortimer is left to limp away defeated, knowing himself to be the lesser man.

And so the miles slip by. Three hours after leaving Tintagel, Donald parks the Morris alongside a bright yellow camper van with long streaks of rust around the wheel-arches and a heavily dented roof. He climbs out of the car, stretches out his cramped limbs, stands there for a while looking up the steep grassy slope of Glastonbury Tor. Although he would find it hard to admit it to his rational self, he can feel the familiar magnetism that has drawn him back to this place again and again over the years. This surprising, dramatic outcrop rising from the Somerset plain, with its prehistoric maze of tracks and terraces and its long dark ecclesiastical history, is perhaps no more than a curious quirk of geological fate. But to many it has become a place of pilgrimage, a focus of the sacred power of Celtic Britain, the secret entrance to the otherworld: home of Gwyn ap Nydd, Lord of Annwn. Since the twelfth century at least, the Tor has been identified with Avalon, the isle of apples, *Insula Avallonis*. There, in Geoffrey of Monmouth's version of events, Arthur was taken after he fell mortally wounded on the battlefield of Camlann.

Donald begins the long ascent, settling into a satisfying cadence of evenly spaced footsteps set one above the other on the well-worn track. The day is not cold, but blustery, forcing him to lean forward into the hill against the wind that gusts across the exposed face. As he climbs higher and higher with the bright green grass all around, a feeling of calm enters in, a sense of distance from the turbulent world below. Within fifteen minutes, he has reached St. Michael's tower, the curious, desolate, hollow structure that is the only surviving remnant of a larger chapel built at the summit of the Tor in the fourteenth century. The masons would have been in no doubt that they were doing God's work up here, heaving up their stones with block and tackle, the foggy green world all laid out below. But the tower is a monument less to the glory of God than to that of a shrewd and ostentatious Abbot of Glastonbury, Walter Monington, who had every intention that the lonely church on the hill should become an iconic symbol of the town. Two hundred years later, Abbot Whiting atoned for all such vanities when he was put to death on this very spot by the troops of the Protestant Reformation, the same soldiers who were to lay waste to the abbey below.

Save for a few blank-faced sheep browsing on the upper slopes, the summit of the Tor is deserted. To the south-west, a finger of development stretches out along Wearyall Hill towards the town of Street, which itself can clearly be seen across the green water-meadows beside the River Brue. To the north-west, above the ruins of Glastonbury Abbey, the old town spreads out in an abundance of Victorian red brick that merges gradually into the newer northern suburbs. In the far distance, a bright glint of water and an uneven grey line on the horizon hint at the Bristol Channel and, beyond, the green foothills of South Wales, former stronghold of the kings of Glamorgan.

Sitting with his back to the western wall of the tower, Donald tears up fistfuls of grass and throws them high into the air, watches the wispy fragments as they are picked up by the wind and swirled away towards Chalice Hill. During the long climb, he has reached a simple enough conclusion. As much as he might wish for a future with Julia Llewellyn, she is a married woman, and she has slipped beyond his reach. For now, the part of his life that holds the greater share of his hopes and dreams is his search for the origins of Arthur. Though it is perhaps no more than a timeless calming quality in the sighing of the breeze through the ruined tower and along the secret contours of the hill, an imaginary energy flowing through him from the hallowed rocks beneath, he feels the stirring of a new sense of purpose, a quiet determination to succeed.

It is getting late, and he has a small pilgrimage to complete. He makes his way back down from St. Michael's tower and over to the northern side where he first came up, descending into deep twilight as the sun is eclipsed behind the long shoulder of the Tor. Back at the car park, a youth with a pierced eyebrow and a ragged beard is standing at the open tailgate of the yellow van, cooking up something pungent in a saucepan set on top of a small camping stove. He has an impressive tattoo on one forearm, ROBBIE + JANE entangled in an intricately wrought python, the names decorated with red roses and a grinning death's-head skull.

'I like the wheels, mate,' Robbie says, nodding appreciatively at the Morris. His accent is from East Ham or the Whitechapel Road. 'I always wanted one of them Travellers, seemed to be the right car to have, know what I mean? But Jane wanted the extra space, din't she?' He nods towards his female companion, who can indistinctly be seen pulling on a cigarette in the murky interior of the van.

Donald reaches for the right thing to say. 'More room to stretch out in there, I suppose?'

Robbie laughs, a surprising high-pitched giggle. 'Yeah, right.' He eyes Donald contemplatively, gives the contents of the pan another stir. 'You hungry? We made extra, in case there was a rush.'

'No thanks. Smells good, though.'

'Don't know what you're missing, mate.'

Donald climbs into the Morris, starts it on the third attempt, waves goodbye to his new-found friend as he sets off on the short drive into town. Robbie and Jane are latecomers, apparently, to the Glastonbury party. The summer season of bikers and mystics and mild-mannered devil-worshippers is long past, leaving quiet streets and a modest local population that seems almost as ordinary as any other in England. He parks in front of a small row of shops on Magdalene Street: a hairdresser, a florist, an aromatic pagan boutique. At the entrance to the abbey, he pays his fee to a distracted attendant who looks up from her Agatha Christie for as long as it takes to hand him his ticket and wave him on through the gate.

'Half an hour till closing, sir,' she says, her nose already back in her book.

Donald's oldest memories of Glastonbury Abbey, a series of blurred images from his childhood, are closely tied to his mother. He can remember standing here with her at the age of four or five, pretending to pay attention as she explained to him that an old ruin is a very special thing, forever caught in its own time and place. Those words come back to him now as he strikes off across the well-kept grass of the close towards the abbey. The great angular remnants of medieval stonework seem to have grown out of the earth itself, pushed up by the same subterranean forces that raised the Tor above the plain.

The historian William of Malmesbury perhaps felt some similar sense of permanence when, as a guest here some time after 1129, he began his treatise on the history of Glastonbury. In the surviving version of William's *De Antiquitate Glastoniensis Ecclesiae*, he states that the Benedictine Abbey of St. Mary at Glastonbury is the oldest church in England. There was a monastery on this site as early as the sixth century—Gildas may have spent some time there—and this in turn was established on the site of an earlier Romano-British church. The buildings as William knew them burned at the end of the twelfth century, were rebuilt, and fell rapidly into ruin after the dissolution of the monasteries in the 1530s, dismantled by the local townspeople for their finest building stone.

By now, the abbey grounds are almost deserted. The only other person in sight, an elderly gardener in a heavily patched tweed jacket, is wielding a set of rusty clippers on the branches of a large and ancient thorn tree. 'Afternoon to you, sir,' he calls out in a voice roughened with age. He goes on with his pruning, and Donald is on the point of walking past when he speaks up again. 'There's a tale that's sometimes told about the Christmas Thorn of Glastonbury, if you'd like to hear it.'

'Yes, I would, very much,' Donald says, though he knows the story well enough.

The old man nods approvingly at him, sets aside his clippers and begins what must be a well-practised discourse. 'They say Joseph of Arimathea came to the Isle of Avalon bringing the Holy Grail with him, whereupon he climbed up Wearyall Hill, over that way.' The gardener points vaguely to the south and west of the abbey grounds. 'When he got to the top, he thrust his thorn staff into the ground. He was amazed when it put forth roots, sprouted and budded, then burst into a mass of white flowers.'

'And that's the site he chose for the first Christian church in Britain,' said Donald.

'Yes indeed, and I'm pleased to see you're an educated gentle-man.' The gardener flashes a gap-toothed conspiratorial smile. 'At that same moment, up at Chalice Well, a spring began flowing and it hasn't ever stopped. That's where Joseph buried the Grail, right there at the gates to the otherworld, and nobody has been able to find it since.'

'I'm not sure it was ever worth searching for, to be honest.' Don-ald says this casually enough, then regrets his ill-judged comment as the old man turns to face him, white brows beetling.

'Some things, young man, are best left unspoken.' The gardener stares hard at him for a moment, then his expression softens. 'I don't suppose you'll set much store by the other part of this story, either.' He takes hold of a small branch and points to the tips of the new twigs, where small buds are just beginning to show. 'This fellow

now, he still blossoms with white flowers every year on Christmas
Eve. But only if you treat him right. This one and his brother in
St. John's churchyard, they're from cuttings of the old original tree
which was cut down by Cromwell's men in the Civil War.'

'Oliver Cromwell has a lot to answer for,' Donald says, striving
to redeem himself. 'He tried to drive out every last vestige of the old
English folklore.'

'That's as may be,' the gardener says. 'Now, you'd best be along,
or they'll close the gates on you. This is no place to be shut in after
dark, as I should know.' With this the old man turns away with a
low chuckle, picks up his clippers and goes back to work.

Feeling vaguely ill at ease, Donald walks on towards the main
abbey buildings, the ruins dominated by two tall, finger-like fragments that give a certain desolate symmetry to this once-majestic
structure. Inside, where the nave would have been, he finds a small
metal plaque, white lettering on brown.

SITE OF KING ARTHUR'S TOMB

IN THE YEAR 1191 THE BODIES OF KING ARTHUR AND HIS
QUEEN WERE SAID TO HAVE BEEN FOUND ON THE SOUTH
SIDE OF THE LADY CHAPEL. ON 19TH APRIL 1278 THEIR
REMAINS WERE REMOVED IN THE PRESENCE OF KING
EDWARD I AND QUEEN ELEANOR TO A BLACK MARBLE TOMB
ON THIS SITE. THIS TOMB SURVIVED UNTIL THE DISSOLU-
TION OF THE ABBEY IN 1539.

Archaeologists have found convincing evidence that an excavation of this sort did indeed take place at the end of the twelfth century. But the exhumation was shown to be a fraud, one of the more

infamous monkish hoaxes in English history. A dramatic discovery
such as this was well suited to the purposes of the presiding Abbot
of Glastonbury, Henry of Sully, who was determined to revive the
fortunes of the abbey after it burned down in 1184. It was therefore
decided that his resourceful monks should by chance unearth a hollow log containing the bones of a woman and a very tall man. To
provide a further layer of false authenticity, Henry also arranged for
the discovery in the grave of a lead cross with an intriguing inscription. It said, *Hic iacet sepultus inclitus rex Arturius in insula Avalonia*: Here
lies buried the famous King Arthur in the isle of Avalon. The cross
itself was lost long ago, though it was seen and described as late as
the sixteenth century by John Leland, the celebrated antiquarian to
Henry VIII.

Donald cannot help thinking of Paul Healey with his bones
unearthed from the Wiltshire soil, his long-limbed king and his
queen found clutching her mysterious blood-filled chalice. It is not
precisely the same thing, perhaps. Healey did not go quite so far as
to bury his skeletons first before digging them up again, though his
instinct for publicity is at least as well tuned as was Abbot Henry's
in his day. A line comes back to him, something he wrote in the
preface to his book. *Every age has its plausible charlatans; and every age has its
susceptible pilgrims and romantics, its seekers of the Holy Grail.*

As he walks back towards the gate, Donald pulls his jacket more
closely around him against the autumnal chill that has crept into
the air. The gardener has quietly disappeared into the dusk. He is
anxious now to be away from this place, with its long falling shadows and the jagged remnants of the abbey like giant gravestones
silhouetted against the sky.

AT DYFFRYN FARM, time passes for Julia in a blur of soft-voiced and kind-hearted visitors, relatives and old family friends who soon absorb her into their circle. She takes it all in, keeping her composure, not letting them get too close. Far from obscuring her other, more ordinary troubles, her father's death seems to have brought them out into the harsh daylight. Dai was always a good friend and mentor to Hugh, especially in the early days when he would often say to Julia that he saw something of his own younger self in her ardent, self-assured new boyfriend. It makes her desperately sad to think how disappointed he would be if he could see them now. She finds herself thinking often of Donald and the kiss at the Trevethey bridge, and how she abandoned him without the merest word of explanation. A few seconds longer, another sip of wine, and she might have become his lover. She would like to speak to him, to explain what has happened, but there has been no chance of making a private telephone call in the crowded farmhouse.

The funeral arrangements provide some sort of a distraction. Julia takes control, glad to be busy, to do something to help her mother just as the reality of their tragedy begins to break down Cath Llewellyn's stubborn defences. Then there is the service at St. Clement's in Rhayader, where they must look at one another, by turns resigned and desperate, as they sit huddled together with the flower-strewn coffin right there in front of them. It is Aunt Nia, her father's younger sister, who gives the eulogy, somehow steadying her voice as she stands up in front of the congregation. She speaks not of Dai the settled farmer of later years, but of the Dai she knew as a child in Llangurig, the gifted boy with a flair for landscape sketching and wood-carving in a time and a place where such pursuits were for the amusement of idle, soft-handed men who had no lambs to slaughter nor stone walls to mend. By the age of sixteen, the frustrations of youth and the mockery of his peers had subverted his talent. He fell in with a circle of fiery young compatriots, shepherds and mechanics and quarrymen who met in back rooms full of wild-eyed talk, angry reports of new English incursions on the native soil of Wales. Then, on a cold spring day at Aberdovey, he gave his hand to young Catherine Pursey of Sussex as she stepped off the ferry-boat. Cath is what he insisted on calling her (pronouncing it in the Welsh way, 'cat'), and soon enough his love for this graceful Englishwoman began to draw the bitterness out of him. In time, he was able to return to the first calling of his childhood, drawing and carving and sculpting in his old familiar style. In later years, settled and happy in the hills above Rhayader with Cath and their daughter Julia his pride and joy, he was at last content with the idea that the transcendent vision of Wales he strove to capture in his art was no more than a nostalgic landscape of the imagination.

Afterwards, the coffin is borne outside by eight men of Dai's generation, local farmers who held him in the highest esteem as a friend and fellow Welshman. They return in the vanguard to Dyffryn and lead the party through the afternoon and evening with a boxful of cheap blended whisky driven up from town by Gareth Williams, the proprietor of the Black Lion pub. These are true-blooded patriots, though their talk is more of the recent heavy rains, the state of their winter flocks and the grievances of their long-suffering wives. Hugh is there complicit amongst them as if he were a Radnorshire man himself, down from the hills. To Julia it seems a forced camaraderie on his part, an elaborate act for which she is the intended audience.

There is one of the local men who holds himself apart from this narrow fraternity, keeping his distance, brooding in the quiet corners. He has the wiry frame of an outdoorsman, dark hair cropped short, a lean, pockmarked face creased up into a habitual expression of aloofness or perplexity. It is not until late in the evening, after what is left of the party has moved to the front room and Julia is sitting exhausted at the foot of the narrow stairs, that he finally catches her eye. She watches him as he pulls deeply on his cigarette, eyes narrowing through the smoke, then taps off the ash and walks over to her, whisky glass in his other hand. She can tell he has drunk more than his share of it.

'Thank you for coming, Ralph. How have you been?'

'Well enough, considering. I'm sorry about Dai, though. He was always a good friend to me.' His meaning comes through sharply enough. Dai was a good friend, whereas Julia treated him as if he were nothing.

'I was hoping to see your father today?' The Reverend Stephen Barnabas, Anglican vicar of the parish of Rhayader, was once close to Dai. They fell out long ago, but still he might have been expected at the funeral.

Ralph takes another long pull on his cigarette. 'My dad's not been feeling well, these past weeks. I'm afraid he's on his way out.' He says this almost casually, as if discussing the price of last season's lambs.

By now, Hugh has seen the two of them talking. He breaks from his circle in the front room and comes over to join them. 'Ralph,' he says, with what seems a friendly enough nod, though there is a constraint in his expression, something held back. Ralph Barnabas has worked at Ty Faenor for more than ten years, ever since Dai persuaded Hugh to take him on, but the old grudges have never quite worn smooth.

'I'll be leaving you to it, anyway,' Ralph says, taking his jacket down from the coat-rack and heading for the front door. 'You'll not want me hanging around here, getting in the way.'

'He still has a thing for you,' Hugh says, after he has gone.

'I'm not sure why that should be. I hardly ever see him these days.'

'As if that makes a difference.' On some other occasion, Hugh's rueful smile might seem charming, but now it strikes a false, jealous note. 'I assume you'll stay here tonight?' he says. 'I'll see you tomorrow, OK?' Before she can respond to this, he has pulled on his coat and stepped out into the night.

※　※　※

A PHONE CALL at the office from Donald's father is a rare event, and his first reaction is to suspect that some calamity has occurred. Tim Watson, with whom he has been comparing notes on the Amesbury dig, catches the look in his eye and makes a diplomatic exit.

'I found something interesting in the attic this morning,' James Gladstone says, with a hint of self-satisfaction in his voice. 'I think you might want to have a look.'

'Are you going to tell me what it is?'

'It's a little tricky to explain over the phone. You'll have to see for yourself. Come over this evening, if you like.'

Donald drives straight to Chewton Mendip after he has finished work for the day. The front door of Grendel's Lair is opened by a woman in later middle age with a plump, red-cheeked face, grey-brown hair pulled back into a bun. She takes him warmly by the hand. 'Well, if it isn't young Donald Gladstone,' she says. 'Your father said he had asked you to come, though you're a little earlier than we expected.'

'Audrey, I'm very glad to see you.' Donald smiles quietly to himself, remembering the home-made ginger biscuits. Audrey Jenkins is a kind, sensible woman, a widow herself, and it is right that they should have a chance to make one another happy.

'Do come on through,' Audrey says. She ushers him into the kitchen, then heads discreetly in the opposite direction.

Donald's father is at the sink with a tea-towel and the last of the drying-up, looking intently into the darkness outside the window as if some momentous event is unfolding out there. He turns as his son enters the room, wipes his hands on the towel. 'I'm glad you could come over, Donald. Did I mention that Audrey has been keeping house for me?'

'Keeping house?' Donald smiles broadly. 'I'm happy to hear it, Dad. You'll be great company for each other.'

'I must say the place is rather more cheerful than it used to be.' James Gladstone runs a nervous hand through his thinning grey hair. 'And she has been keeping me on my toes. Did you know she has a doctorate in theology from the University of Kent?'

'Yes, you've mentioned it a few times.' Donald tries to imagine them engaging in deep philosophical debate over their toast and marmalade. 'I'm sure you'll be no match for her, intellectually speaking.'

'Quite so.' His father smiles, turns to the stack of dry crockery and starts putting it away in the cupboard. 'How was your Cornish symposium?'

'Not quite as useful as I expected.'

James Gladstone hangs the damp tea-towel on the back of a chair, looking inexplicably pleased with himself. 'Well, come along and see what I've found.'

Donald follows him through to the dining room, rarely used in the ordinary run of things except as a place to store the best cutlery. The table has been extended to its maximum length, and is now covered from end to end with large-scale geological maps of Wales. Numerous markings in coloured pencil can faintly be seen.

'What on earth have you been up to, Dad?'

'I must let you into a little secret. After we spoke about Caradoc Bowen and his maps, I went up into the attic to have a look through my old paperwork from the Geological Survey, and I found this.' He picks up a long cardboard tube from underneath the table. 'The maps were returned to me at the Survey. I had completely forgotten about it.'

'Bowen sent them back to you?'

'Well, yes—I had asked for them to be returned when he was finished with them. I have the covering note here, though it doesn't say anything very useful.'

The letter is no more than a brief, courteous expression of thanks, neatly typed up on Jesus College letterhead. It is the signature that is of most interest to Donald. The correspondent identifies himself as H. E. Mortimer, Research Assistant to Professor C. H. R. Bowen. He remembers what Julia told him at the Randolph, that her husband was once a favourite of Bowen's, a member of his radical political group, Tân y Ddraig.

'The maps have evidently been well used,' his father is saying. 'I would hazard a guess that they have been taken out in the field.'

Donald looks more closely at the nearest sheet, which shows the Black Mountains from Crickhowell to Hay-on-Wye. Several areas of upland terrain have been carefully outlined in red and blue and green pencil, all explained by a hand-written key at the edge of the map. 'You did all this yourselves?'

'Yes, of course. You have to remember that those were the good old days when a formal request to the Survey from Oxford University would be attended to without question. We put in the red highlighting to indicate the most conspicuous outcroppings of the Devonian rocks. For the most part, what you are seeing here is the

St. Maughans formation of the Lower Devonian period, known col-
loquially as the Old Red Sandstone. It is prevalent in south-eastern
and central southern Wales, as well as some parts of the border
country farther north.'

Next to each of the highlighted areas is a small cross made in
faded blue ink. 'Did you put in these markings as well?' Donald says.

'No, and I'm not sure what the annotations mean. I was hoping
you might have an idea about that?'

Donald traces a finger across the map, his father looking at him
expectantly. 'I think I could make an educated guess. Bowen wanted
to find one of the battle-sites that was described in the poem I told
you about. But I don't think he was looking for the right thing.'

'And do you know what the right thing is?'

'I have an idea about it, but we won't know until we have a proper
look.' Donald glances across the tabletop at a dozen or more maps
that together represent thousands of square miles of rugged Welsh
landscape. 'I'm going to need your help, Dad.'

'Yes, of course. I dare say I know the terrain as well as anybody,
geologically speaking. But you'll have to tell me what we're looking for.'

'We're still interested in the sandstone cliffs, but only if they are
rising above a river valley, and only if the valley also contains three
waterfalls.'

'Precisely three?'

'Yes, precisely three.'

James Gladstone raises an eyebrow. 'Well, we must do our best.'

They set to work in a state of suppressed excitement. The geology
and topography of Wales is such that many locations seem at first
glance to be strong candidates, but none of them quite meets all the
requirements. The task is made more difficult by the fact that very

few waterfalls are marked explicitly on the map; their existence must instead be inferred by studying the contour lines. A sense of futility begins to set in. An hour passes, and then another, before Donald gives a small, triumphant shout. At the edge of one of the more southerly maps, he traces his finger along a thin jagged line denoting a stream dropping down a steep valley from a mountainous terrain. There are tall rock formations higher up, outcrops of the Devonian sandstone. Lower down, a placename in Welsh catches his eye, *Rhëydr y Tair Melltith*. He will later learn that the correct translation from the Welsh is closer to 'Falls of the Three Curses' or 'Thrice-Accursed Falls', though the English placename inserted by the cartographer is an interesting variation on this, Three Devil Falls.

Borderlands

OT LONG AFTER dawn, with the cold soaking rain coming down from clouds that might be no more than a hundred feet above her head, Julia gently closes the front door of Dyffryn Farm. Behind her, the house is full of sleeping people, family and friends who failed to make it home in the groggy aftermath of her father's wake. She has in mind to escape for a while, find some space to breathe. At the back of her mind, too, is the thought that she must try to call Donald and explain everything to him. She treads cautiously around the edges of the farmyard puddles to the gate, unlatches it and swings it open. Some old nervous reflex makes her glance back at the cottage to make sure Dai is not there watching her at the upstairs window; but it is her mother who catches her eye instead, raises her hands in a questioning gesture that says, I'm coming with you whether you like it or not. Soon they are side by side in the car, driving half-blind through the rain, Julia pouring out her story as they climb up into the high country above the Clywedog valley.

'So you have two men to worry about now,' Cath Llewellyn says. There is a glimmer of mischief in her pale blue eyes. 'Three, if you include poor old Ralph Barnabas.'

'You make it sound as if I should be happy about it,' Julia says, though it is true that her spirits are lifting as they follow the narrow twisting lane up to the higher pastures that skirt the slopes of the mountains beyond. There is no traffic at all, only birds in the sodden hedgerows flying up on either side as they pass, stray sheep escaped from the fields, a large hawk glimpsed once or twice, soaring in and out of the lower reaches of the cloud.

'I remember a time when your father would have chased all three of them off with his shotgun. It's still up there on the wall of the barn, though he hardly touches it these days.'

They both notice the mistake, but say nothing of it. 'I'm thinking I'll head back to Oxford early next week,' Julia says.

'Will Hugh go with you?'

'I haven't asked him.' Julia peers out through the rain, concentrates on keeping the car out of the ruts at the edge of the lane as they climb in a series of steep curves up the flank of the hill known as Lan Goch. A question comes to her, something she has never thought to ask. 'What did you and Dad really think of Hugh when I first brought him to Dyffryn?'

'It's a bit late to be worrying about that, wouldn't you say?' Julia's mother smiles bleakly. 'In any case, I'm sure there's not much you don't already know, one way or another.'

'I'd like to hear it from you. We've never talked about it properly before.'

'Well, I'm not quite sure where to start. We had known Hugh from a distance, of course, ever since the days when he used to go to St. Clement's church with his grandpa in the summertime. And of course your father knew of the family long before Hugh came on the scene. When Dai first arrived here from Llangurig forty years ago, Sir Charles Mortimer had recently passed on the management of the family lands to his son Robert, Hugh's father. Sir Charles lived out his last years at Ty Faenor, and he was always popular in the valley, but Robert was a different story. He was the English aristocrat through and through, with his beloved Melverley estate and his horses and his cellar full of vintage port. He was obsessed with the Mortimer pedigree, even though his father's baronetcy went to an older brother who ran away to Australia and never came back. On the rare occasions when Robert did visit Ty Faenor, there was always bad blood with the hill-farmers. They used to call him Sir Robert to his face just to rub salt in the wound. So, with all that family history, we were curious to know which sort of Mortimer your Hugh might turn out to be.'

'And?' Julia says.

'It was neither one nor the other, of course, but certainly Hugh was a surprise to us. Don't forget, your father was a hot-headed nationalist in his youth, and now here comes this impressive boyfriend of yours, scion of the ancient Mortimers and obviously a blue-blooded Englishman, whatever else you might have told us about him. But then the first thing Hugh says to us is that he prefers to be thought of as a Radnorshire man. He starts talking to your father about Glyn Dŵr and the nationalist cause, even tries a little Welsh on him. Dai brushed it aside at first, thinking Hugh was just trying to charm him. It was only later that Hugh asked him about making contact with Plaid Cymru.'

Julia has a disorientating sense of old truths shifting under her feet. 'I thought Dai had broken off with them years before that?'

'Yes, but the nationalists still had a lot of respect for him. This was just after the plans for the dam were made public, and your father was in Rhayader trying to calm things down. There were a few who wanted to paint it differently, saying he was down there making trouble, but that was all just malicious gossip. It's what destroyed his friendship with Stephen Barnabas.'

Reaching back for her own memories of that time, Julia recalls only a vague sense of discord in the town, of plans being made behind closed doors, her father doing his best to keep the peace. Hugh was there too, somehow on the fringes of things. 'Dai went to a meeting at the Black Lion,' she says. 'I was away that day in Hereford with Aunt Nia, shopping for the wedding. Do you remember if Hugh went with him?'

'Yes, they went down there together. I remember Hugh saying there were some Oxford people he wanted to see.'

Julia feels it again, the old familiar landscape swaying beneath her. 'I don't think I knew that.'

'You mustn't read too much into it.' Her mother touches a gentle hand on her arm. 'Hugh was unhappy because of Ty Faenor, which would have gone under the flood, so he went to the meeting to hear what was being said. That's all there was to it. If you want my advice, love, I would leave it there in the past. It'll do no good to rake it all up.'

At last the road drops down a long hill towards the hamlet of Abbeycwmhir. They pass a small cluster of houses, a farm, a pub called the Happy Union where Julia has often been with Hugh, though she has never before been struck by the irony of it. A hundred yards farther on, she parks in front of a small stone church.

'I'd like to walk down to the river,' Julia says. 'Will you come with me?'

'No, I'll stay here, love.' Cath Llewellyn turns her knowing gaze on her daughter. 'You don't need me getting in your way.'

Julia gets out of the car and heads off along the road to a place where a path leads across a muddy field towards the Clywedog River. A plaque tells the story of the ruined stone walls and pillars that lie scattered across the valley floor, the remains of the medieval Cwmhir Abbey. The simple tranquillity of this place, the magnificence of its isolation, commended it to the wandering Cistercian monks who first came here in the twelfth century. For Julia, it has been a favourite destination since childhood, a safe and peaceful refuge, though it seems a lonely enough place on this cool autumn day. The clouds have begun to break up, showing small shifting scraps of pallid blue sky. On either side, the bare flanks of the hills are patched here and there with rough stands of evergreen trees, like threadbare clothing on an ailing child.

There was one day, early on, when they all came walking out here together. Hugh and Dai had not seen one another for a long time, not since the old days at St. Clement's, and she remembers how anxious Hugh was to make a good impression, to find common cause with his future father-in-law. Soon enough they were trading stories of Hugh's famous English and Welsh ancestors who had owned and destroyed this place, stirring tales of Glyn Dŵr and the failure of his rebellion, his fugitive existence and final disappearance somewhere high up in the surrounding hills. There was a dour intensity in that conversation, but it was also a happy moment for Julia, to see the men in her life so comfortable in one another's company, so full of mutual respect. Now her world has slipped out of balance, her poor father cold in the ground, Hugh on his own at Ty Faenor, Donald Gladstone cast aside as if he means nothing to her at all.

From where she is standing, a surviving column of the old ruined abbey frames one edge of the modern farmhouse that lies directly behind it. In the back garden, damp washing is flapping and rippling in the breeze, rows of legs and arms making ghostly disembodied children reaching for the ground. Their alter egos can be heard shouting excitedly inside the house. A thin trail of dark-grey smoke from the chimney thickens a little as somebody stokes the fire within, settling the new day into its familiar comfortable course.

If things had gone to plan, the engineers would have drowned this valley and everything in it. This was to become another of those places that have been erased from the map of Wales, turned into reservoirs for pure English drinking water. Julia can hear her father's voice, hoarse with emotion as he described to her the bitter story of Capel Celyn in the Tryweryn valley, where the villagers had to dig up their own dead before abandoning their homes to the incoming flood.

She turns away and heads back towards the road. Her mother is asleep in the passenger seat of the car. Julia leaves her in peace, continues on to the small stone church. Finding the door open and the interior deserted, she walks into the cool, resonant space, sits on a pew in the back row. She stays there for a while shivering faintly, looking up at the stained glass panels in the chancel windows. Their subjects are familiar to her from childhood: The Good Shepherd, The Crucifixion and Resurrection, I am the Light of the World, The Baptism and Agony in the Garden. But she finds no useful advice written for her there.

⬛ ⬛ ⬛

IT IS CARADOC Bowen's formidable secretary, Mrs. Frayne, who answers Donald's call to Jesus College. 'Yes, Dr. Gladstone. I believe the professor is busy, but I will check for you.'

A minute passes before he is put through. 'Three waterfalls?' Bowen says, when Donald has finished his story. His voice on the line is thin and querulous. 'You are an archaeologist, as I recall. Do you have some proper authority for this conjecture?'

'The suggestion came from a colleague of mine. She's a Welsh language expert at the OED, Julia Llewellyn.' Donald feels a small twist of guilt at the thought of her. He was able to reach a colleague of Julia's at the OED, from whom he learned only that she would be away from the office for a few days. It cannot be helped; he would have spoken to her if he could. 'I believe you know her husband, Hugh Mortimer.'

'Yes, I know the name.' There is a pause now, a hiss and crackle of static. 'We must go and have a look at this place you have described, as soon as can be arranged.'

'I suggest we meet first in Rhayader, and go on from there.' It is perhaps a reckless idea, to go to Julia's home town. Donald remembers too late the story she told him about the violence that happened there, the possible involvement of Bowen's militant nationalist group, Tân y Ddraig.

'Yes, it is as good a starting point as any,' Bowen says. 'There is a respectable inn at Rhayader, the Black Lion. Gareth Williams was the proprietor when I last visited the town, many years ago now. I suggest we meet there—shall we say, next Saturday evening? We can stay overnight at the inn, then drive together into the mountains the following morning.'

After he hangs up, Donald distracts himself with his preliminary report on the excavations at Amesbury. He asks the switchboard to forward his calls to Tim Watson's desk, tells Tim to make sure he is not disturbed. The opening sections come easily enough, a summary of the known history and archaeology of the town and its environs, followed by a standard description of the topography and geology of the excavation site. Then comes the crucial process of inventory, every last tarnished scrap of metal to be documented, every sherd of pottery, every sliver of bone. Soon he is working his way laboriously through his detailed field notes, expanding the terse annotations he made on site. *Pottery finewares are restricted to three late Romano-British sherds originating in the New Forest (context 103) . . . A fragmentary human skull was recovered from context 104 . . . A brass doorknob c. 1825 was found together with fifteen damaged red clay bricks at the far end of trench 2 (context 205), evidence of late Georgian construction-related infill.* It is dull but oddly satisfying work, the minutes ticking comfortably by as he captures for posterity the structure and contents of a muddy Wiltshire field.

THERE IS A particular quality of Welshness in a Radnorshire house, an unmistakable character that merges architecture and setting in such a way that no one would mistake it for an English dwelling. Ty Faenor, a small seventeenth-century manor house located at the eastern end of the Cwmhir valley, draws so strongly on these qualities that a casual passer-by might scarcely remark on this strongly made, compact stone building, so well does it harmonise with its surroundings. This impression of belonging is heightened by a certain fickleness in the colour of its building stone, which was brought in from the quarries at Llanddulas when it could not be pillaged from the ruins of Cwmhir Abbey. Ty Faenor chooses its moods according to the weather, glowing a rich golden-brown in the sunshine, shading dark and sombre when the clouds move in. The old wood-framed windows have lost any sense of symmetry they may once have had, giving the house a lopsided, watchful expression as it looks out across the fields to the gently rising, tree-clad hills rising on either side of Cwm Cyncoed.

Julia has the disturbing impression that this curious inanimate scrutiny is focused entirely on her as she walks up to the main entrance of the house. She has always felt a stranger in this place where the weight of Mortimer history lies a little too heavily on the land. It was here in the twelfth century (as Hugh, speaking in a half-apologetic sort of way, is fond of reminding his visitors) that an earlier Hugh Mortimer, Earl of Hereford, drove out the Cistercian monks from their first monastic establishment in the Cwmhir valley. Ty Faenor is Hugh's perfect retreat, a place he made entirely his own in the years after his father's death, returning to it some of the dignity it had lost since his grandfather's day.

Ordinarily this is a working, bustling farm, though all is strangely quiet now. Julia cannot help noticing something she has not seen before, a creeping dilapidation, repairs not attended to, gates sagging on their hinges, fences in need of a new coat of paint. These small signs of neglect seem to her the symptoms of a gradually spreading sickness, a malaise that is working its way into every human structure on the estate.

Hugh is there now at the front door, dressed in whatever clothes were to hand, scruffy blue jeans and an old cotton shirt, brown leather boots on his feet with the laces untied. Two day of stubble are showing again on his face. He carries it off with his usual air of untidy elegance; the right kind of smile, Julia thinks, the right turn of phrase, and he might become again the charismatic man she once knew, the man she fell hopelessly in love with in the distant Oxford past.

'I wasn't expecting you,' Hugh says. His tone is not unfriendly, but ambiguous; it sets her teeth on edge. 'I was going to drive over to Dyffryn later on.'

'Can I come in?' These four simple words are in themselves a confession that any sense of ownership Julia might once have felt here has fallen entirely away.

Hugh kisses her on the cheek, lays a hand on her shoulder as he guides her gently inside. It seems a finely calibrated gesture, as if rehearsed thoroughly on some imaginary wife, one who is newly bereaved and on the verge of estrangement. He leads her through a narrow entrance hall whose dark beams are gently sagging away from the perpendicular, reinforcing the impression that the house is flowing away downhill.

'Do you mind sitting in here?' Hugh says, ushering her into the panelled library where an electric heater has been switched on to take the chill out of the air.

'Of course, this is fine. Where is everyone today?'

'Ralph took them up to work on the top fields this morning.' He makes to follow her into the room, then changes his mind. 'Give me a few minutes, would you?'

Julia casts her eye about the library, the tall, mostly empty shelves where the Ty Faenor collection was housed for several hundred years before Hugh donated the manuscripts to the Bodleian. It was Caradoc Bowen who made the arrangements for the removal of the books after the plans for the Cwmhir dam were announced.

There are several heavy box files marked 'Mortimer' lying out on a table, sequentially numbered, full of materials for Hugh's family history. They are covered with a film of greyish dust. Walking over to a shelf that has been repopulated with books, Julia takes down a volume at random, a collection of early farming photographs published by the Royal Welsh Agricultural Society. The inscription on the flyleaf is written in a graceful old-fashioned script: *To Hugh, on his tenth birthday. From his affectionate grandfather, C.J.M.* Although she never met Sir Charles Mortimer, her strong impression of him from Hugh's stories is of a kindly but reclusive man who felt a strong and abiding kinship with this house. It was here that Hugh would visit his grandfather in his last years; and it was here that Sir Charles first explained to Hugh, at the impressionable age of fourteen, that his red-blooded Welsh ancestry drawn from the line of Glyn Dŵr was at least as powerful as his Anglo-Norman Mortimer descent.

The creaking of the door alerts Julia to Hugh's return. He has showered and shaved, nicking himself twice on the chin. 'I've just put those books back on the shelf,' he says. 'I had them all boxed up and taken off to storage years ago, the ones that didn't go to the Bodleian.'

It is a tenuous enough opening, but Julia seizes on it. 'Because of the dam, do you mean? Could they really have made you abandon the house?'

'Bowen was quite sure of it.' Hugh looks at her in his steady, unreadable way. 'When I first met him, he was standing just where you are now. I came into the room to find him scouring the shelves for some book or other. He had discovered the Siôn Cent manuscript here many years before, and he would come back every so often, at my grandfather's invitation, to see what else he could find. I was only a small boy, and it was terrifying to run into him unexpectedly like that, the way he turned and stared at me.'

Julia has a feeling that she is being manipulated, set up for some confession or revelation to follow. 'What made you think of that?'

'I had a telephone call from Caradoc Bowen this morning, out of the blue. Have you spoken to him recently, by any chance?'

In the long, quiet moment that follows, Julia runs helplessly through the possibilities. It is not hard to see what must have happened. Donald's conversation with Bowen has somehow raised the ghost of the professor's long-dead relationship with Hugh. A faint, creeping nausea begins to take hold. 'Why would I do that?'

'I'm not quite sure, Julia.' His voice is calm, measured, as if he is making some commonplace observation. 'Maybe it's because you can't leave the past alone, because you want to strip away the disappointing, middle-aged Hugh Mortimer, the one you don't like so much, to see if you can get back to the much better Hugh from the old days when everything was so much simpler. Am I close to the mark?'

Julia walks away to the other side of the room. She feels surprisingly self-assured, confident in what she is about say. 'I haven't spoken to Bowen since before we were married,' she says. 'But since you brought it up, here's what I think, Hugh. I think you lied to me about what happened in Rhayader that autumn. I think you got yourself caught up in it somehow, despite all your promises to me. On your own, you might have stayed away, but Caradoc Bowen forced you into it. Now I want to know what really happened.'

Hugh takes half a step towards her. Seeing the competing emotions in his face, she wonders whether he means to reach out for her hand, draw her into some desperate embrace. But he stops himself short, steadies himself, as if correcting a momentary loss of balance. 'There are some things you just can't ask me, Julia. Can you please try to understand?' He lingers there, waiting for her answer, but she has nothing more to say to him.

⬚ ⬚ ⬚

DONALD'S WORK ON the Amesbury report is interrupted by the arrival of Tim Watson, hands thrust awkwardly in his pockets. 'Sorry, boss, I know you didn't want to be disturbed, but there's a rather persistent female visitor waiting for you downstairs. Unwelcome, if I had to guess.'

Tim's encryption is easy enough to read. 'Tell her I'll be down in a few minutes.'

'Will do. There's something else, though.' He hands Donald a yellow slip of paper. 'Phone message for you. She sounded disappointed you weren't available. Julia—something Welsh?'

'Llewellyn.'

'That's the one.' Seeing the expression on Donald's face, Tim softens his ebullient tone. 'I hope I did the right thing, taking a message? She left a number, but said it would be better if you didn't call her, she'll try you again later.'

Down in the lobby, Lucy Trevelyan is in the process of unwrapping the richly embroidered, cloak-like garment that she has folded around her against the cold. She sweeps up to him and gives him a peck on the cheek. 'Don't worry, I'm not staying. But I do have some news for you, my love.'

He can tell she has been drinking: it is well disguised, but he is perfectly attuned. 'Did you drive here?'

'Don't be silly. I walked along the river.' Lucy sits down on one of the chairs next to the deserted reception desk, stretches out her long booted legs. 'Aren't you even a little bit curious?'

'I assume it's good news, if you've already been celebrating.'

'Champagne. I should have saved you some.' Lucy smiles, pauses for effect. 'I've just come from a meeting with my agent. She told me I've got myself a book contract. Aren't you proud of me? I've been asked to write about Devil's Barrow.'

Donald feels a small wave of dismay rolling over him. 'To write what, exactly?'

'I'm going to tell the story of the priestess. *The Priestess and the Chalice*, that's what I'm going to call it. Or maybe *The Last Prophetess*. Yes, I think that's better.'

It takes a herculean effort not to let his reaction show in his face. 'Do you want to tell me about it?'

'Now you're just trying to be nice,' she says, smiling. 'We'll talk another day, OK? I'm just on my way back to St. Anne's.'

'I can give you a lift, if you like.'

'Don't trouble yourself, dearest, I'd rather walk. I'll see myself out.'

Donald looks on with a tormented sort of fascination as Lucy strides out of the building and off towards the centre of town, cutting a swathe through the busy pedestrian traffic. He watches her until she is out of sight, then turns away, pushes the button for the lift.

He has been back at his desk for only a few moments when the telephone rings, a deafening blast. 'Can we talk?' The voice is very faint, as if from the other side of the world.

'Julia?'

'I need to explain what happened.'

Donald has his pencil in his hand, making cross-hatched geometric shapes on Tim Watson's yellow message slip. 'I'm listening.' He waits for her to say the expected things, that their kiss on the Trevethey bridge was a mistake, that she had drunk too much wine, that they should forget it ever happened.

'I didn't mean to run away from you. My father died suddenly, and I had to leave. I'm very sorry.'

Whatever he says now will seem hollow and inadequate. 'Please let me know what I can do to help.'

'I'll be back in Oxford next week. Can I call you?'

'Yes, of course.' These are precisely the words he has been hoping to hear; but there is a hint of nervousness, too, as he remembers what he has not yet told her. 'There's something else you should know, Julia. I spoke to Caradoc Bowen about the three waterfalls.'

'And how did he react?' Her tone seems neutral; or cold, perhaps, it is hard to tell.

'I found a place on the map that seems to fit the description in the poem. We're planning to meet in Rhayader on Saturday evening and drive out there together the following morning.'

'Where will you stay?'

'At the Black Lion.'

There is a small silence now on the line. 'Please call me when you get to Rhayader,' Julia says. 'I'd like to come with you.'

▨ ▨ ▨

HE DREAMS OF a brilliant sunlit sky, of woods and fields rising up to meet the gentle lines of the hills that frame the broad valley floor. The air seems unnaturally quiet, as if the curfew-bell has rung half a day too soon. There is a rutted cart track underfoot, an arched stone bridge across the river. As he sets foot on it, there is a familiar tug of melancholy at the thought of leaving his Welsh homeland behind, of once more assuming the disguise that has kept him safe through all the years of his exile. To his surprise, the bridge is empty, though this is a crossing much used by the local people when they travel to the English side.

But it seems he is mistaken: where there was no one before, a cloaked figure is approaching him from the far end of the span. He cannot yet see the face, though there is a distant familiarity in the tight upright bearing, the long deliberate stride, tall leather boots striking on the stones. There is something else, too, a sound like the breeze in the treetops. It grows louder as the figure draws near, a whispering, insinuating voice that surrounds him as if distilled from the limpid noontime sky.

Do you not fear me, crab scuttling sideways to your lair?
Black raven I am called, the death-wielder
Finding you in darkest dreaming.

Too late he recognises the hooded face, grasps the meaning of her words. He will use all his arts to defend himself, but already her weapons are drawn upon him, long sharpened stakes wielded with such ferocity that he has no time even to draw breath to scream.

▨ ▨ ▨

IN SOUTH-WEST HEREFORDSHIRE, the border between England and Wales follows the course of the River Monnow as it skirts the edge of the Black Mountains, turns to the east around the peak called Mynydd Myrddin, then curves again to the south before running down through low green hills to join the Wye at Monmouth. Here, from the twelfth century to the sixteenth, the Lords of the Marches— the Nevilles, the Mortimers, and the Scudamores—defended their feudal territories in the no-man's land between the western edge of the old Saxon kingdom of Mercia and the mountain strongholds of the Welsh kings. To the east, the chief threat was the capriciousness of the English king, better countered by subtle diplomacy and well-timed treachery than by force of arms. To the west, the Marcher Lords protected their vulnerable flank by building strong border castles on the river, garrisoned permanently from the thirteenth century against the incursions of Llywelyn the Great and his separatist successors.

Hunched over the kitchen table first thing on a chilly Saturday morning with the Ordnance Survey map open in front of him, Donald traces the border with his index finger, from north to south and back again. Soon he finds what he is looking for, Kentchurch Court, ancestral home of the Scudamore family. It is a large country house on the English side of the river, looking out across the valley towards the ruin of Grosmont Castle on the very edge of Wales. He turns back to the book he was reading as he fell asleep the night before, Caradoc Bowen's *Notes on the Welsh Rising*. In the final chapter, Bowen describes a portrait that now hangs at Kentchurch, said to be the work of the Flemish master Jan van Eyck. The painting depicts a priest by the name of John of Kentchurch who lived at the house in the first half of the fifteenth century, and whose reputation for the occult eclipsed his more modest declared vocation as private chaplain to Sir John Scudamore and his wife Alys, daughter of Owain Glyn Dŵr.

Deep in the Welsh Marches there arose an alchemist, magician, poet, and clergyman called John of Kentchurch, who was famous for making clever bargains with the Devil. Wonderful folktales of his exploits abound in the Marches, where he is sometimes known as Jack O'Kent (in the Welsh tongue, Siôn Cent). Some thought of him as a latter-day Merlin, one to keep alive the Welshman's hope of Arthur's return.

On his death-bed, Siôn wrote a poem, tormented lines that spoke of a great spiritual and perhaps physical pain.

> Woe to the one, woe to the many
> Who shall endure a portion of my torture
> Hear my groaning and sorely complaining
> Like a wolf on a chain.
> Do not heavenly Lord I beseech thee
> Take me from the world in a state of burning.

Donald stares out of the kitchen window at the cool grey November sky as he ponders the last words ever written by the poet Siôn Cent. At length he closes the book, stows it in the small travelling bag that is waiting by the door. It is time he was on his way.

Soon he is in the car and heading out across the Oxfordshire downland north of the River Thames, full of restless excitement and a certain liberating feeling that he is leaving some part of his former life behind. Beyond Gloucester, he turns away from civilisation into a patchwork countryside of farmers' fields set into a gently rolling, rising terrain that hints at tall mountains farther to the west. The passage to the Welsh borders, once loud with the cries of cattlemen heading for home along the old drovers' tracks, seems almost forgotten now, the road twisting its way through a tranquil landscape that lies outside the common orbit of modern Britain. Here, in the farthest reaches of the Saxon kingdoms, the west Mercian dialect of Old English was spoken for centuries after the Norman conquest. The whitewashed farmhouses with their sagging, blackened timbers seem less like human structures than modest outgrowths of the Herefordshire soil.

At Skenfrith on the River Monnow, gaunt castle walls with holes like black accusing eyes stare out at him as he passes by. The land is rising, domed hills merging gradually into the western wall of the Monnow valley and the harsher terrain of the Black Mountains beyond. The road climbs on up to Grosmont with its own dark castle, cousin to Skenfrith, perched high above. Here, in the summer of 1404, an army loyal to Owain Glyn Dŵr met a force led by the young Prince Henry. The Welshmen doggedly pursued the enemy to the gates of Monmouth, but Henry and his troops found sanctuary inside the walls of the town. That night, the arrogant young prince, grimed in the mud and blood of gruesome battle, conjured up the necessary phrases to appease his father the king, claiming his lucky escape in the name of God as a victory for the English crown.

Dropping down into the valley, Donald crosses the Monnow once more and soon becomes lost in a bewildering tangle of sunken lanes cut deep beneath heavy overhanging limbs of beech and oak. He doubles back to the river and stops to ask for directions at the Devil's Bridge Inn. It has a memorable pub-sign, a winged demon armed with flaming spears facing a sturdy priest across the span of the bridge. The bar is empty, staffed only by a small black-and-white dog who welcomes him like a long-lost friend. In the back, the proprietor can be heard muttering to himself as he clicks through the channels on his new television set.

'Sorry about that,' the landlord says, hurrying out at the sound of Donald's speculative greeting. He is large and round, his pink face crinkled up in a habitual smile. 'I don't usually expect anyone, this time of day.'

'I'm looking for Kentchurch Court,' Donald says, stroking the besotted dog behind the ears. 'It doesn't seem to be where the map says it is.'

'May I ask if you're expected there, sir?' The publican seems to appraise him anew, as if he might have mistaken him for someone of a different class. 'They usually require an appointment, you see.'

'Yes, they know I'm coming, thanks.' It was at first an awkward telephone conversation with the people at Kentchurch. Donald was interrogated as to the nature of his interest in the house, asked to give assurances that he did not work for the press. In the end, a casually delivered mention of Caradoc Bowen and Jesus College succeeded in sweeping all difficulties aside. 'By the way,' he says, 'I was wondering if there's a story behind your pub sign?'

'Not that I've heard, though they say there's always been magicians and devil-worshippers in these parts.' The landlord smiles crookedly. 'Still are to this day, judging by some of the people who come in here on a Saturday lunchtime.'

Soon afterwards, armed with a detailed sketch-map, Donald heads back out into the Herefordshire countryside. Kentchurch Court proves to be very well hidden indeed, tucked away in a fold of the hills and shielded by deep tracts of woodland. The narrow driveway seems as if it might come to a dead end, but at last the building hoves into view, layers of amber masonry and red brick forming a large and imposing edifice. Donald drives through a gate into a stable yard, parks next to a delivery van in the far corner. As he walks towards the front of the house, the heavy oak door is unlatched and pulled open by a small man with thick-rimmed glasses and a fringe of grey hair. He is carefully dressed in a patched woollen cardigan over a check shirt and plain green tie, giving him the air of a butler on his day off.

'Yes, good morning. You must be our visitor from Jesus College—Dr. Gladwell, is it?'

Donald hesitates for the barest instant, holds out his hand. 'Gladstone. Donald Gladstone.'

'My name is Gerald Rhys. My wife and I look after the house during the winter months. Please, do come in. How is Professor Bowen? He visited us several times in the old days, but we haven't heard from him in many years.'

'He's still going strong,' Donald says, pretending a greater familiarity than he truly feels. 'I saw him a couple of weeks ago.'

Rhys ushers him into a high wood-panelled hallway hung with faded portraits of cold-eyed noblemen from centuries past.

'The Scudamores?' Donald says.

'Yes, that's right. Starting with the first Sir John, at the end there.'

The painting of Sir John Scudamore, captured in confident pose circa 1430, shortly before he was dismissed by the crown from the office of deputy justice of South Wales, shows narrow features and long, flowing hair tucked into an embroidered cap.

'He reminds me a little of Richard the Third,' Donald says.

Gerald Rhys looks at him sharply, as if accusing him of some mild treachery. 'No relation. None at all, I can assure you. Sir John was persecuted by the English monarchy because he had the temerity to marry the daughter of Henry's great Welsh nemesis, Owain Glyn Dŵr. They kept the marriage secret for sixteen years. Now then, I believe it's Jack O'Kent you've come to see. Follow me, please.'

He leads Donald through a series of sumptuous Georgian rooms appointed with fine porcelain and elaborate furniture bearing the scrolled foliage and floral motifs of the Louis XV style. On the walls and ceilings, ornate plasterwork disguises the simpler lines of the building's original structure. They make their way towards a distant corner of the house, where Rhys opens a door leading into a smaller room with plain dark wood on the walls and worm-eaten beams not far above their heads. It seems a deliberately sombre refuge, a sanctuary from eighteenth-century frippery and ostentation.

'Here he is,' Rhys says, pulling back the curtain from the room's only window. At first, the dusty sunbeams fail to illuminate the painted triptych hanging on the wall, instead throwing it into a deeper shadow. As Donald's eyes adjust to the gloom, the outlines of the portrait on the central panel begin to emerge: an old man in a white robe, his cheeks sunken from hunger or illness, gazing meditatively through a window as he pauses in turning the pages of a book. There is something almost familiar in the pinched, aquiline features, the firm line of the mouth, the distant, dark eyes hinting perhaps of suffering, perhaps of long-suppressed anger or bitter regret for times long past.

Donald peers more closely at the artist's rendition of the book that rests in Siôn Cent's hands, hoping in vain that some useful detail has been preserved. 'Do you know how much of his later poetry has survived?'

'Some of his religious verses were composed while he was living in this house, and those poems have been preserved in various contemporary copies. His early work of course was captured in the book discovered by Professor Bowen at Ty Faenor. It seems he left it behind when he fled here from Cwmhir Abbey.'

Rhys has Donald's attention now. Bowen's paper on the poetry book of Siôn Cent suggested that the Song of Lailoken was written while Siôn was in hiding at the abbey. This is a small but perhaps crucial point. If the text Siôn claimed as his source, the book of Cyndeyrn, was in his possession at Cwmhir Abbey, it too might have been left there when he escaped to Kentchurch Court. 'How do we know for sure that's where he came from?'

Something in Gerald Rhys's expression suggests a schoolteacher disappointed in a promising pupil. 'As is well known,' he says, 'the secret marriage of Alys, daughter of Owain Glyn Dŵr, to Sir John Scudamore was consecrated at Cwmhir Abbey in 1414, and the witness to the marriage signed himself as *Brawd Siôn o Cwmhir*, Brother Siôn of Cwmhir. You can see the document for yourself in the National Library of Wales. The signature matches the known hand of Siôn Cent. He was wanted by the English crown because of his role in Glyn Dŵr's rebellion, doubtless to be made an example of, and so we can guess that he went into hiding as a monk at the abbey. Soon after that, presumably under pressure of English discovery, he fled to Kentchurch and remained here to the end of his life under Sir John's protection.' Rhys pauses, as if to make sure his explanation has been appropriately absorbed. 'Now, if you don't mind, I have a rather busy day ahead of me. Were there any other questions, before we leave our friend in peace?'

'Just one more thing,' Donald says. 'Can you tell me anything about how he died? I've heard he met an unpleasant end.'

'Yes indeed, that is true. The story goes that he was crossing the River Monnow when he was set upon by the Devil himself wielding sharpened stakes made to gore out the hearts of those who opposed him. Siôn was left for dead at the river's edge, his skin all scored and blistered where the weapons of the enemy had touched him. He had used all his strength to save himself, but his injuries were too great to be sustained. He took on a mortal fever, and died some days later here at Kentchurch Court.'

'Do not Heavenly Lord I beseech thee, take me from the world in a state of burning.'

'Yes, that's it,' Rhys says, looking at Donald with what seems a renewed respect. 'I can see that you have studied the matter, Dr. Gladstone.'

'I've been wondering, though, do you think people really write poetry on their death-beds?'

'Ordinary people do not, I am sure. As Professor Bowen has shown us, however, Siôn Cent was a much deeper mystery than has generally been understood.'

Abruptly, Gerald Rhys draws the curtain back across the window. Donald takes a last look at the portrait, tries to fix it in his mind, but by now the image of the elusive bard has been lost in the cracks and flakes of the brittle old paint.

Of Old Welsh Secrets

HE SIGN ABOVE the window of the ironmongers in Rhayader, Jack Edwards & Son, makes a poignant reminder of the younger Edwards, Gwyn, who would perhaps by now have inherited this business from his father had he not been killed in the explosion at the Ellis engineering works at the age of twenty-two. For Julia, walking past just after opening time on a Saturday morning, it is less a sign over a shop window than the engraved headstone of a tomb.

She is not surprised to see Ralph Barnabas standing there unkempt in his farmer's overalls and mud-encrusted boots at the open door of the shop. Gwyn was Ralph's best friend when they were growing up, and Ralph is often to be found here at the Edwards family shop. He has a dangerous-looking pickaxe in his right hand, holding it as someone else might carry a briefcase or a grocery bag.

'Are you looking to do some damage with that?' Julia says.

'Maybe, if the right person happens by.' Ralph's smile has not much humour in it, the daylight showing up new lines in the reddened, weatherbeaten skin of his face. 'Short of that, there's plenty of good Welsh rock needs breaking.'

Julia reaches for something else to say. 'How are things at Ty Faenor?'

'You'd have to ask your husband about that.' Ralph's shrug is casual, dismissive. 'He's sent me away, says he doesn't need me any more.'

This is a disturbing thing for Julia to hear, though in a way it is not very surprising. 'I'm sorry about it, Ralph. I didn't know.'

'You wouldn't have, given how it's only happened yesterday afternoon. We got into an argument, you see, shared a few home truths. It's been a long time coming.'

It is more sad than insulting to her, to hear so much bitterness layered into his voice. 'I wish I could have done something to help.'

'You're the one who married the man, as I recall.' Ralph hefts his axe, lifts it over his shoulder. 'Would you walk with me down to the river? We've a few minutes before the rain comes back.'

The overcast has broken up to form dark shower clouds chased by a brisk north-westerly breeze, mottling the streets in a restless pattern of brightness and shadow. There is a new clarity in the air, buildings and trees glowing faintly as the sun glances across them, thrown back into twilight as the racing clouds cast their dark outlines across the town. They walk to the end of West Street and then to the Rhayader bridge, stop there to watch the rain-swollen river surging over the remains of the once-famous cascade that gave the town its name: *Rhaeadr Gwy*, falls of the River Wye. The last time she was here with Ralph was on her sixteenth birthday.

'It's as high as I've seen it,' he says. 'There'll be banks overtopped by tomorrow night, with the next storm coming in.'

Julia finds it almost hypnotic to look down into the dark river water rushing through the arch of the bridge. She searches for the right words to describe the mysterious sound that it makes, the sibilance of a mistuned radio, the hissing of her grandfather's old gramophone records, the gathered whisperings of a great throng of people: the river telling its old Welsh secrets in a voice that merges almost imperceptibly with the rustling of the wind in the trees. A dead branch is carried through on the flood, making her think of Donald and his sticks thrown into the Trevethey stream. He will be on his way from Oxford by now; she imagines him persuading the Morris along some steep and lonely mountain road.

'It's beautiful to watch,' she says.

'Not if it's your best pasture gone under the flood.' Julia catches the look on Ralph's face, just as he casts his eyes to the ground. It is all written there, the feelings he once had for her, the years they have known each other, his disconnectedness from the world she now lives in. At St. Padarn's primary school in Rhayader, their different-ness threw them together early on. They were the two strange kids, always out of the mainstream, Julia with her awkward quirks and precocious insights, Ralph the eternal misfit, rebelling against his father's impossible standards of virtue and scholarship, the vicar's wayward son. In time, Julia's childhood foibles became her great-est gifts, while Ralph could never quite find the right path. What was once a real friendship became a one-sided infatuation, another reason for him to look out with a certain bitterness on a future life whose physical boundaries would be no wider than the Cambrian mountains and the valleys between.

Ralph shrugs, takes a deliberate step away from the parapet. 'Would you ask your mother if there's something I can do for her, up at the farm?'

'Yes, of course I will.' Ralph has always made an effort to stay in touch with her parents, even after his father fell out with Dai, and she has never thanked him properly for it. 'I'm sure she'll be glad of the help.'

They walk back in a heavy silence to the corner of Bridge Street. Ralph stops there and sets down his pickaxe, makes a play of rubbing his shoulder where the wooden handle has chafed. 'I'm told there's Oxford people coming up tonight,' he says.

Julia hesitates a moment too long. 'Where did you hear that?'

'From Jack Edwards. He told me Gareth Williams was bragging about it in the pub. I'm wondering if it's someone you know.'

She smiles at him, though the worry is twisting inside her. 'There are a lot of people in Oxford, Ralph.'

'Bowen's the name that was given,' he says, equably enough. 'Professor Caradoc Bowen. He's been up this way before, though not many people know it. It was just after you were married, around the time we had that trouble up at Ellis the engineers.'

The uneasy feeling comes back in full force, solid ground shifting beneath Julia's feet. She sits down on a small wooden bench at the street corner, bows her head, pulling at a ragged fingernail. Her last conversation with Hugh is still fresh in her mind. 'How do you think it really happened, Ralph?'

'The explosion, you mean? It was an accident, that's what my dad will tell you.' There is something uncomfortable now in the directness of his gaze. 'I don't think Dai was behind it, if that's what you're asking me, though I can see why some might have believed it.'

Julia's world tilts a little further off its axis. 'Why would you even suggest a thing like that, when you know it's not true?'

Ralph picks up his axe, begins to work the pointed end of it into a crack in the paving stones. 'You should speak to my father. He's the one who knows the whole story, though I'm not sure he'll tell it to you.'

◈ ◈ ◈

FROM KENTCHURCH, DONALD drives north along the Golden Valley of the River Dore through pleasant, faintly ecclesiastical villages set between undulating lines of pale-green hills. From Abbey Dore to Vowchurch and Peterchurch, the road sweeps him westward to less hallowed ground at Hardwicke, then finally back down to the Welsh border at Hay-on-Wye.

With time still in hand, he parks close to the site of the old Hay castle and walks into one of the second-hand bookshops for which this Welsh border town has latterly become famous. The shop is comfortably haphazard in its arrangement, its closely spaced shelves making numerous small passageways and cosy reader's dens, chairs and sofas placed strategically to trap the idle browser. The deep, almost oppressive silence is broken by a persistent mournful whistling that floats out from some hidden recess, *It's a long, long way to Tipperary*.

On the way to the history and archaeology section, Donald finds himself forced to squeeze past an overstuffed armchair in which a rosy-cheeked woman with round tortoiseshell glasses and a knitted Fair Isle cap is turning the pages of an early edition of Mrs. Beeton, murmuring to herself as she makes various annotations in a small notebook. Just across from her, a youth with scruffy blond hair and sideburns is sipping at something in a thermos flask as he turns casually through the pages of Aesop's Fables: The Frog and the Ox ('Self-Conceit May Lead to Self-Destruction'), The Wolf and the Lamb ('The Unjust Will Not Listen to the Reasoning of the Innocent'). From the untroubled look on his face, it seems that these lessons are not necessarily being taken to heart.

In his own quiet corner, Donald runs his eye along a shelf of local history books. Near the end of the row, a title catches his eye: *Journey Through Wales*, by Giraldus Cambrensis. This zealous Welsh churchman and scholar, who lived a generation after Geoffrey of Monmouth, is familiar to Donald as a rare critic of the fanciful histories of his time, especially those encouraged by Geoffrey's heroic tales of Arthur and Merlin. Giraldus's famous travelogue is an account of his expedition through the remoter reaches of Wales in the year 1188 with his distinguished travelling companion, Archbishop Baldwin of Canterbury. The translation is an old one that Donald has not seen before, made in the 1840s by the Reverend J. A. Giles of Corpus Christi College, Cambridge.

He takes it down from the shelf and turns to the preface, in which the essential details of Giraldus's life and work are described. As he reads, he experiences the familiar pleasing sensation of connectedness that comes from absorbing these words written long ago by one of the foremost Victorian scholars of medieval history. Giles alludes several times to his subject's preoccupation with Geoffrey, including a quotation from a long commentary by Giraldus that offers some extraordinary new insights.

I cannot neglect to tell a story I have heard of one Walter Calenius, Archdeacon of Oxford in the time of King Stephen. This Walter, however commendable in some particulars, was remarkable for his insufferable pride and ambition. Finding his archdeaconry at Oxford wanting in respect of worldly riches, he became a fawning creature of the Archbishop of Canterbury, Theobald of Bec, ready to do the archbishop's bidding in all matters however large or small, in hope of a swift preferment in the English church. Thus it was that he came to make a journey to north Wales at Theobald's behest, wherein his charge was to travel to the tiny church of Llan-Elwy, itself built on the site of the monastery established by St. Cyndeyrn some six hundred years before our present time, and there to make an inventory of certain saintly relics held at the church since Cyndeyrn's day. Walter's audit was required in preparation for the new Cathedral of St. Asaph, to which the relics were eventually to be transferred.

It is well known that another grasping man of the church, one Geoffrey who was sometime canon of St. George's in Oxford and archdeacon of St. Teilo's church at Llandaff, claimed Walter Calenius as his friend and indeed named Walter as the very instrument of the fame and fortune that attended him upon publication of the fabulous history of British kings for which his name is unjustly on the lips of every scholar in Christendom. For it was Walter who brought him a certain ancient book which he had found in the reliquary at Llan-Elwy church, and which Geoffrey duly translated, as he would have us believe, to make his own stirring tale fit for the entertainment of children, claiming for himself the corrupted histories of the bards and dressing them up as the learning of greater men.

So far was Geoffrey consumed by the cleverness of his own historical inventions that he began in his later years to believe in their authenticity, revering Walter's book to such a degree that he found himself drawn to the place of its origin. Thus we have seen that Geoffrey aspired to, and was in due course granted by Archbishop Theobald, the bishopric of St. Asaph. Against the common wisdom I have heard, that Geoffrey failed to visit his new see, dissuaded by the wars of Owain Gywnedd and the consequent dangers of travel through the border country, I must now tell the story that was given to me by an aged deacon at Llandaff who was a subordinate of Geoffrey's in his time at St.

Teilo's. This man's tale has it that Geoffrey, in a state of vexation knowing himself to be in failing health, set out from Llandaff disguised in the robes of a Cistercian monk and bearing with him his precious book. By travelling between the religious houses under cover of darkness, he hoped in time to make his way safely to his bishopric, which is to be found in the far north of the country. After many hardships, Geoffrey arrived at a small monastery then recently established at a place called in Welsh 'Cumhyr' which means 'long valley', in the lordship of Maelienydd and yet no more than half-way to his destination. There he was taken to his bed with a paralytic attack from which he sadly did not awake, and the monks not knowing what else to do buried him in their own crypt.

As Donald reads and rereads Giraldus's sly and worldly account of the final days of Geoffrey's life, he finds himself at first struggling to grasp its full significance. This commentary unearthed by the Reverend Giles has since been lost to, or ignored by, the world of Arthurian scholarship. Certainly he has not come across it in his years of studying the works of Geoffrey of Monmouth.

It is clear enough that *Cumhyr* is an earlier form of the placename *Cwmhir*: given the stated location in Maelienydd, part of modern Radnorshire, there seems little doubt of this. According to Caradoc Bowen, Siôn Cent composed the Song of Lailoken in the same valley, while in hiding at Cwmhir Abbey some two and a half centuries after Geoffrey's time. If Giraldus's story is to be believed, it would seem to place Geoffrey and his ancient book in closer geographical proximity to Siôn Cent and the book of Cyndeyrn than could otherwise have been imagined.

Donald sets the book to one side, digs in his bag for his road atlas. Rather than follow Giraldus's long coastal perambulation of 1188, via St. David's and Cardigan Bay, he traces a simpler journey up the valley of the River Wye, through the heart of Wales to Builth Wells and then Rhayader. Anxious now to be on the road, he makes his way back out of the labyrinth and rings the bell at the desk.

The source of the persistent doleful whistling becomes apparent as a large man with his head shaved to camouflage his baldness emerges loudly from a back room. 'Can I help you, sir?' he says, wiping his hands on a green towel emblazoned with the red dragon of Wales. A strong strain of north London in his voice belies any close allegiance to this flag.

Donald hands him Giraldus's *Journey through Wales.* 'Just this, thanks.'

'Not sure I'd recommend it, myself,' the proprietor says, nevertheless carefully checking the price in the front of the book before taking Donald's five-pound note and making change from a small wooden drawer. 'Wales, that is.' He underlines this emphatic statement with a westerly jerk of his thumb, alluding to the Celtic wilderness on whose very edge his cosy establishment is perched: a latter-day Barliman Butterbur at the *Prancing Pony.* 'Between you and me, mate,' he says, lowering his voice conspiratorially, 'I'd always think twice before trusting a Welshman.'

'I'll try to remember.' Donald smiles agreeably, takes his book in its brown-paper bag and raises his hand in farewell as he heads for the door.

▣   ▣   ▣

THE INTERTWINED HISTORIES of the Barnabas and Llewellyn families are very much in Julia's mind as she forces open the front

gate of the vicarage past the mass of ivy that threatens to overwhelm
it. From the time she first set eyes on this house as a seven-year-old
girl at St. Padarn's junior school across the road, she has thought
of it as a remote, even a frightening place. Some of its mystique in
those days no doubt derived from the exalted status of the Reverend Dr. Stephen Barnabas, vicar of Rhayader parish, who was as
unapproachable to a child as should be expected in a distinguished
member of the Welsh clergy. The intimidating aura of the house
was compounded by the common knowledge amongst the school-
children that the vicar's wife, who was never seen in public, suffered
from a debilitating illness that confined her to a room upstairs in
the east wing. It was generally supposed that she shared her solitude
with the aged and equally elusive Uncle Hywel Barnabas, a highly
accomplished church organist who was said to have been driven
to the edge of madness by his wartime experiences in the Welsh
Guards. Certainly the young Ralph Barnabas was never known to
speak of what it was like to live at the vicarage in those days.

An overgrown front path leads alongside a neglected shrub-
bery to a gap in a screen of tall conifers, beyond which the house
comes fully into view. It is a large Victorian structure built of red
brick with a white stucco facing, tall and elegant windows on the
lower floors and a row of small dormers on the top floor suggesting cramped, poorly lit bedrooms once intended for a household
staff. Julia reads a sadness in its expression, the loneliness of a once-
bustling residence now fallen on solitary times. She grips the lion's-
head knocker, raps on the front door, counts twenty heartbeats
as she waits. She knocks again, listens for any sign of life, reaches
twenty again before turning away.

Her disappointment is tempered by her sense of relief at avoiding
what would have been a difficult conversation. At one time, Stephen

Barnabas was a close friend of her father's, though their relationship was later damaged beyond repair. As Dai told the story, the vicar was the first man to notice him when he came to Rhayader from Llangurig, a lost sheep in search of a new fold. A quarter of a century later, it was the Reverend Barnabas who presided over Julia and Hugh's wedding ceremony at St. Clement's church. That was also the year in which the Barnabas family was visited twice by tragedy.

'The door is open, please let yourself in.' This hoarsely delivered command comes faintly through an open window, just as Julia is walking away. She does as she is told, turns the door handle and walks uneasily through to a dim, draughty hallway. There is an impression of faded yellow and brown, the sweet and musty smell of apples and old newspapers. The Persian rugs on the floor are tired and worn, the peeling wallpaper now only faintly advertising its once-charming floral design. A thin grey cat emerges from some nook or cranny, yawns and stretches itself, jumps lightly up to a sun-drenched window-sill.

'I am in the drawing room, if you would be so kind as to join me here.'

Julia follows the sound of the voice into a long bright room at the front of the house, where she finds a tall man hunched over in a wheelchair next to an unsatisfying fire of glowing coals gathered parsimoniously in the middle of the grate. She steps cautiously through the doorway.

'Do please come in. Despite what the good people of Rhayader may tell you, I do not bite.'

Julia has not seen the Reverend Barnabas for some years, and to her he seems almost shockingly aged. Though he can be no older than his mid-sixties, his deeply lined face has an almost deathly pallor to it, and his hair, which she remembers as black shot through with grey, has turned to pure white. The upper half of his body is enveloped in a thick blue woollen cardigan, the lower half in a tartan blanket that reaches to the floor.

The events that ruined Stephen Barnabas's life happened within six months of each other. First came the death of his beloved wife, just a few weeks after Julia's springtime wedding. Then, in the autumn of the same year, he suffered the terrible accident that maimed him physically and also, according to local opinion, destroyed much of what was left of his belief in God and human-kind. Though he returned in due course to his ministry, made some practical working accommodation with his damaged faith, he was afterwards known as an embittered and disappointed man. In Rhayader, on days other than a Sunday, his parishioners would give him a wide berth, for fear of becoming targets of his capricious ire. The word in the pubs and sitting rooms was that he would be best changing sides to the Methodist church, where a righteous anger such as his was in high demand.

The vicar looks up at Julia through bloodshot grey eyes, his gaze meeting hers only briefly before settling on a point somewhere closer to the floor. There is a faint tremor in his hands as they grip the armrests of his wheelchair. 'It's Julia Mortimer, isn't it? I was very sorry to hear about your father. We had many good conversations in our time, Dai Llewellyn and I.' His voice is closer to what she remembers, with its familiar tone of Welsh clerical condescen-sion, mellifluous and ponderous, perfected by a lifetime of Sunday-morning oratory. But there is also a fractured quality to it, a sense of something once broken and not fully repaired.

'Yes, he told me about that.' Julia speaks cautiously, unsure of her ground. 'He said you were very helpful to him when he first came to Rhayader.'

'As was he to me. I greatly regret that I was not able to officiate at his funeral. I have not been in the best of health, as you may see for yourself.' A smile flickers across the vicar's face. 'But you have not come here to listen to my dreary complaints. What may I do for you? If you're looking for Ralph, I'm afraid he is not here very often these days.'

'I saw him in town this morning. Actually it was you I wanted to speak to.'

'In which case, kindly do me the favour of sitting down, so that we may at least talk face to face.' Barnabas waves a hand in the direction of an armchair upholstered with fading red and pink roses. 'How is Hugh, may I ask? I have not seen him in a very long time.'

Julia has almost forgotten: the vicar has known Hugh from childhood, since the days when Sir Charles Mortimer still lived at Ty Faenor and brought his grandson to Sunday services at St. Clement's. It is strangely disorientating now to think of the young Hugh sitting there dutifully in the pews, still so tightly bound up in aristocratic convention and obligation.

'Yes, he's fine, thank you.'

'I am glad to hear it. Now, will you have some tea? There is a housekeeper somewhere, though I suspect she is upstairs with her nose in a romantic novel. That is her usual occupation when she thinks I'm asleep.'

'Please don't go to any trouble.' By now, Julia feels deeply ill at ease. Finding herself at a loss, she glances around the room, takes in the formal, upright furniture, Constable's *Dedham Vale* on one wall, Richard Wilson's *Lake Avernus* on another, dust-motes spiralling in the sunlight through the tall front windows. She feels trapped in some distant moment in time, a perception reinforced by a polished brass carriage clock sitting unwound on the mantelpiece, stopped at ten to three. Beside it is an intricately carved wooden sculpture; something about it strikes her as deeply familiar.

'Do you recognise the style?' Barnabas says. 'Your father made that piece for me many years ago. It depicts the Celtic deities Teutates, Esus, and Taranis. We were arguing about religion—he was not an overly pious man, as you will know—and I think he was trying to make a point about spiritual pluralism. As I recall, his assertion was that the old pagan religions had as much validity in their way as all the accumulated dogma of the Christian church. I suspect, after all, he was right about that, and I wish I might have had an opportunity to tell him so.'

Julia senses a premeditated quality in the vicar's telling of this anecdote, as if he is measuring her in some way against her father's beliefs. 'How did you first meet him?' she says, curious now to hear his side of the story.

The vicar smiles faintly. 'I remember it very well indeed. Dai turned up one rainy Sunday in my church, not long after he first came to Rhayader. He asked to speak to me afterwards, meaning to contradict what I had said in my sermon about the need to abandon our old enmities with our English neighbours. To me he seemed quite the most interesting man I had met in Rhayader, with a strong intelligence and a head full of wild ideas about Welsh nationhood. I think I saw in him a special challenge to my immature pastoral skills.'

There is a history here that is half-familiar to Julia, stories she has heard in passing, though she paid little attention to them at the time. 'My father said you used to stay up talking together late at night.'

'Yes, that's true. In the years before your mother came on the scene, we would often sit up into the small hours in this very room, deep into a bottle of port and some grand argument over the meaning of the world.'

A wistful thought comes to Julia now, that she is probably sitting in the same chair her father would have occupied during these long nocturnal debates. 'I'd like to understand why you fell out with him in the end, when you were once such good friends.'

Stephen Barnabas gives the faintest of shrugs, as if she is referring to some trifling thing, a regrettable but inevitable circumstance. 'I suppose there was a natural distance that grew between us over the years. For me, the demands of the church were becoming ever greater, while your father was trying to make a proper go of things out at Dyffryn Farm. And we had our differences from time to time.'

'About the nationalist cause?'

The vicar's shifting gaze comes to rest on his hands clasped together in his lap. 'That was certainly one of our areas of disagreement,' he says. 'I had seen what happened in other parts of Wales when the violence came, the terrible divisive bitterness of it, and I did not want the same affliction to visit us here.'

'My father would have agreed with you about that.' Julia's statement is blunt, combative. 'He was passionate about Welsh independence, but he was never a violent man.'

Barnabas wheels himself a half-step closer to the fire, reaches awkwardly for the poker and uses it to agitate the reluctant fire back into life. 'Yes, I came to realise much later just how true that was. At first, he was my only real connection to the more militant members of Plaid Cymru, the younger men who would sit there in a corner at the Black Lion on a Friday night, working themselves up into a fervour over the latest English insult. Dai was a calming influence on them—he knew where they had come from, you see, having made the same journey himself. Between us I thought we had the situation well under control, until everything went so very wrong in the autumn after you were married.'

'Because of the Cwmhir dam?'

'Yes, because of the dam, and God knows I was not immune to

the feelings that it provoked.' The grey cat, choosing its moment to enter the room, approaches the wheelchair with the clear intention of jumping up into the vicar's lap. He swipes at it with the poker, startling the poor creature into a hasty retreat. 'But that was not the worst of it. We might have managed things in our own way, were it not for the rabble-rousers and agitators who descended on Rhayader like carrion-birds after the news about Cwmhir got out.'

Julia feels calmer now, more in control of the conversation. 'I heard it was people from Oxford who were behind all the trouble.'

'It was always the academic types who were the worst, forever summoning up the spirit of Owain Glyn Dŵr, as if he could be of any help to us now.'

An image comes to Julia, Caradoc Bowen holding court in a shadowy corner of the Black Lion pub, his young disciples seated around him: and Hugh there too, hanging on Bowen's every word. But if Stephen Barnabas is aware of any personal significance for her in his story, his expression does not betray it. 'You must forgive my melancholic ramblings,' he says. 'I am sure this is all much more than you care to hear about.'

'It's the reason I came here today to speak to you,' Julia says. 'I've been trying to find out what happened that autumn, but nobody will talk to me about it.'

'That does not surprise me. It may not be an easy story for you to hear.'

'It's important to me.'

'In that case, I shall do my best.' A small grimace crosses the vicar's face as he reaches to set the poker back in its rack, then straightens himself as far as he can in his wheelchair. 'It was a difficult year for me, in many ways. The first blow came when my wife passed away in the middle of June. That was not so much of a surprise, after all, but still in my grief I became angry and bitter at the unfairness of the world. I hope it does not shock you to hear me say that?'

'I understand you very well, Reverend Barnabas.'

'Yes of course, I am sure that you do. Well, if you can imagine my state of mind at that time, you may also comprehend how I came to misinterpret your father's good intentions. The town was in a great ferment over the plans for the dam, and something I overheard convinced me that Dai had got himself involved, that the news of this latest English outrage had tipped him back into his old radical way of thinking. So I stood up at St. Clement's one Sunday morning and spoke out against those who might think a true Welshman should distinguish himself by fighting wanton destruction with random violence. I was looking at your father as I spoke those words, and the entire congregation was watching me. He never forgave me for it.'

Julia was not in church that day, but she can imagine it well enough for herself, the cool, austere Victorian space, the sidelong glances in the pews, the murmuring and shuffling of feet as the fiery vicar sends down his denunciation upon Dai Llewellyn standing there with an upright but wounded dignity in the front row. 'What could possibly make you think he would do such a thing?'

Stephen Barnabas bows his head, clasps his hands together more tightly in his lap; it is an almost theatrical, prayer-like gesture. 'I blame my own foolishness, nothing more. The rumour was that the militants were very well organised, that there was a secret ringleader. I had seen your father in animated conversation with some of the younger men, and I drew entirely the wrong conclusion.'

'Caradoc Bowen was the one who was behind it,' Julia says, quietly. 'Not my father.'

'Well, it is true that Wales has produced its share of zealous prophets,' the vicar says, apparently now lost in his own memories.

'As I look back on those days, I see my actions as a kind of treachery. I suppose you might say the events of the following autumn were a just retribution.'

'That's what I wanted to ask you about,' Julia says, emboldened by her indignation on her father's behalf. 'I'd like you to tell me what really happened at the engineering works.'

Barnabas moves a trembling hand to stroke the cat, which through an exercise of extreme stealth has appeared in his lap and curled itself tightly into a ball. 'It was a brave thing for you to do, to come here and ask me that question, and so I will do you the courtesy of describing the events as I saw them.'

'Thank you,' Julia says, the anxiety pressing harder on her now, a heavy weight against her chest. 'I'm sure it can't be easy for you.'

A gust of wind sighs in the chimney, briefly raising the fire to a bright orange glow. The cat uncurls just enough to stretch a paw in the direction of this new radiant warmth. 'It was a cold autumn day,' the vicar says, 'very much like today, I suppose. Since losing Angharad back in June, I had fallen into the habit of taking a walk up in the hills in the late afternoon. On this occasion my departure was delayed by some parish business, and so it was almost dark by the time I set out from the house. I decided to make a shorter circuit than usual, out to the north past St. Clement's, then just a little way up the valley and back again. My route took me past several small engineering firms whose offices were down by the old railway tracks. One of them, Ellis Engineering, had been awarded a contract by the British government to assist in the work on the Cwmhir dam.'

By now, Stephen Barnabas has settled his attention on a point in the deep distance, out of the window and beyond the garden wall. 'I remember it quite well, feeling a certain distaste as I came upon the sign on the gate. Despite all my sermonising, I could scarcely be

happy about the involvement of our most prominent local business-
man in this unfortunate project, not least because Dafydd Ellis was
a grasping sort of man without an ethical bone in his body. He's
long gone now, dead of a heart attack, may he rest in peace.'

'What happened after that?' Julia says, gently.

'Perhaps you already know the rest of the story. It was common
knowledge in the town that there were explosives stored in Ellis's
yard, ready for the blasting work at Cwmhir. As you may read for
yourself in the report of the official inquiry, it was faulty wiring that
caused the accident. All it took was a small electrical spark. I lost my
legs in the explosion, traded them in for a piece of metal the size of
a penny lodged close to my lower spine. This is why I am as you see
me now. But it was better for me than it was for Gwyn Edwards the
ironmonger's boy, who had recently signed on with Ellis as a junior
engineer. He had stayed late that day, you see, to catch up on his
work. He never stood a chance.'

'Gwyn had a lot of friends in town,' Julia says, struggling to
steady her voice as the memory of it comes back to her. 'It was hard
to believe what happened to him.'

'Yes indeed, and as to why he of all people should have deserved
it, all I can suggest to you is that—as William Cowper tells us—
God moves in a mysterious way, his wonders to perform.'

Julia once again has a troubling sense that the truth is slipping
from her grasp. 'There's one other thing I need to ask you,' she says.
'You've been honest with me about what happened back then, but
I'm wondering why everyone else is still avoiding the subject. My
husband—Hugh refuses to talk to me about it. Do you know why
that might be?'

Another grimace crosses Stephen Barnabas's face, and he reaches
a hand to rub at the lower part of his back. 'I am sorry. It is not

your question that causes me pain, though it is a difficult one. If you asked me to guess at the answer, I should say that it is out of loyalty to your family that Hugh prefers not to speak of these events. As you may recall, he came to church a few times in the weeks leading up to your wedding, and he was in the congregation when I foolishly accused your father of stirring up the mood of violence that had fallen on the town. I remember thinking afterwards that I must find a way to speak to Hugh, but I never did so. Perhaps he went away believing that what I said was true.'

A sound like distant thunder from the upper part of the house resolves itself gradually into heavy footfalls on the stairs. 'That will be Megan,' Barnabas says, sucking in his breath through a further spasm of pain. 'Having finished her novel, no doubt, she has remembered that I still exist. I'm afraid I have been sitting for far too long in this chair. If you don't mind, perhaps we might continue our conversation another day?'

As Julia makes her hurried farewell, fragments of failed conversations with Hugh come crowding in in her. *I'd rather not talk about it any more. There are some things you just can't ask me, can you please try to understand?* By the time she reaches the front gate of the vicarage, securing it behind her and glancing uneasily back through the trees at the house now restored to its habitual blankness, she has convinced herself that she has recklessly misinterpreted Hugh's intentions. His silence on the Rhayader bombing has been meant only to protect her, to avoid a discussion that might implicate her father in the attack that maimed the Reverend Stephen Barnabas and took the life of Gwyn Edwards, the ironmonger's son.

The Sign of the Black Lion

 ONALD TAKES THE back route out of Hay, urging the Morris through narrow lanes boxed in by hedges as high as London buses. Beyond Llanbedr, the road becomes easier as it drops back down towards the River Wye and the main northerly route to Builth Wells. Taller hills are rising now, pale green with patches of faded bracken turned to purplish brown in the sunshine on the highest slopes. The river is a steady companion on his right-hand side, the dark waters descended from the wilderness of Plynlimon now touched by a gleaming silvery light. Donald drives on with the windows wound down and a half-remembered mythology ringing like a dissonant poetry in his ears. *I flew north to Plynlimon Hill, where Cai and Bedwyr sat on a cairn in the strongest wind the world had ever seen.* The cool mountain air carries with it the rarefied crying of far-off sheep, countless white dots studded across the improbably steep hillsides.

Dusk is falling on the banks of the Wye by the time he reaches the long easterly loop of the river that runs beneath the wooded slopes of Gwastedyn Hill on the approach to Rhayader. It is a majestic setting, the small grey market town encircled by sweeping escarpments whose lower slopes shelter dense stands of oak and beech. It was into this high country that Owain Glyn Dŵr fled with his son Maredudd and his closest companions after the fall of Harlech Castle. As Donald looks up towards the higher ground now hidden by a descending layer of cloud, he pictures Glyn Dŵr and his followers climbing up above the trees, higher and higher, until they vanish into the mist.

He parks in the centre of town, walks along East Street to a battered red telephone box near the market cross. The cool, dank interior is profusely decorated with graffiti, the slogans of Welsh nationalism, *y ddraig goch ddyry gychwyn*, the red dragon will show the way, stirring phrases and profanities scrawled on the walls and scratched into the glass. Some of the panes in the door have been smashed, spreading small bright shards across the concrete floor. When he picks up the receiver, expecting to hear only silence, there is a clear tone on the line. He takes out a crushed yellow message slip from his pocket, dials the number that is written there.

It is an older woman who answers, a southern English accent faintly tinged with Welsh. She seems warm in a habitual way, cautious and protective. 'I'm afraid Julia isn't here, but she was expecting you to call. She asked me to tell you she'll meet you at the Black Lion later on this evening. And not to worry about Caradoc Bowen, because she will already have spoken to him by then.'

❖ ❖ ❖

IN DECADES PAST, Julia and her mother would commandeer one of the hard wooden benches on the platform at Llandrindod sta-

tion and sit with mugs of sweet milky tea in excited anticipation
of some English relative: usually an uncle or aunt from London or,
more rarely, her maternal grandparents from Sussex. It was thought
to be a great adventure in those days for the *saeson* (as Dai would
disparagingly refer to his distant, foreign in-laws) to take the train
to Swansea, then up the Tywi valley to Llandovery and finally to
Llandrindod Wells, the nearest stop to home since the old Rhayader
station was closed down. They would all squeeze into the rusting
blue van with her mother at the wheel, take the obligatory tour of
the former spa town with its neatly kept squares and side streets
lined with hotels now long past their Victorian prime, then happily
bump home together the ten miles or so to Dyffryn Farm.

It would have been unimaginable a week ago, waiting here on
a damp, chilly Saturday afternoon for the arrival from Oxford of
Professor Caradoc Bowen. The professor was unavailable when
she made the call the previous afternoon to Jesus College, but
his unsympathetic secretary, Mrs. Frayne, become suddenly more
accommodating when Julia boldly introduced herself as the wife of
one of his former students. She had heard about the professor's visit,
and would be glad to meet him at the station and drive him back to
Rhayader. It was Hugh's name that put the seal on the arrangement.
*Mr. Hugh Mortimer? Yes, of course I remember him—such a fine young man, and
a great favourite of Professor Bowen's. I'm sure he'll be glad to see Hugh again.* The
secretary proceeded to share a wealth of gratuitous detail concerning Bowen's itinerary, as well as her opinion as to his likely state of
mind upon arrival. *He hates to travel these days; he'll not be in the best of moods,
especially if he hasn't eaten; don't say anything to upset him, that's my best advice.* It
seems to Julia now, pacing nervously to and fro beneath the elegant
glass awning with its white-painted cast-iron columns and scroll-
work pediments, that to have come here today is pure recklessness.

The train arrives an excruciating ten minutes late, sliding into the station with a pungent smell of brakes. Julia stands off to one side, watches the passengers one by one as they step down on to the platform. Despite the fact that she has not seen Bowen for fourteen years, she is confident that he will be instantly recognisable. But she is caught off guard by a surprising rush of people, hulking teenage boys in muddied rugby kit, mothers with young children and shopping bags in hand, a few older people amongst the stragglers. She fixes on the most likely candidate, an elderly man with pure white hair and an air of erudition about him as he folds his newspaper and tucks it into his bag; then watches him settle a farmer's flat cap on his head and take a swig from a flask in his pocket as he makes his way to the exit. He smiles and winks at her as he hobbles past.

Some sixth sense makes her turn around, and she sees him then, standing by the door to the waiting room in a long black trench-coat and battered trilby with an old leather briefcase in his left hand and a long furled umbrella in his right. He looks oddly out of place, like a black-and-white actor in a colour film. *Don't say anything to upset him.* This phrase turns itself into a mantra, silently repeated over and over as Julia walks towards him.

'Professor Bowen? My name is Julia Llewellyn.'

He looks at her for a long moment. It is not so much the face that she remembers, with its aquiline features and gaunt, hollow cheeks, but the old-fashioned round glasses, the hawk-like gaze focused on its prey. He surprises her now by taking off his hat and offering a dry, firm handshake. 'Yes, of course,' he says. 'My secretary told me to expect you. I am glad to see you again after so many years.'

Julia hardly knows what to say next. She tries to remember the last time she set eyes on him, perhaps at some Jesus College event. It was before she and Hugh were married, certainly, because Bowen declined their invitation to come to the wedding, and things went wrong not long after that. She forces a smile. 'I wanted to speak to you, Professor. I hope you don't mind.'

He tilts his head to one side, a bristling white eyebrow arched almost imperceptibly. 'Well, as you can see, I am entirely at your disposal, if you would kindly lead the way.'

It is almost a surreal experience, reversing out of the parking space with Caradoc Bowen in the passenger seat. In spite of all that Julia knows about him—the long troubled history of his relationship with Hugh, his research on Owain Glyn Dŵr and Siôn Cent—he is almost a complete stranger to her. The image she has held in her mind, of the fiery Welsh nationalist, the eccentric scholar given to poetic and grandiloquent pronouncements, does not seem quite applicable to the elderly man who is now sitting next to her in the car, folding and refolding a large white handkerchief.

'As a native of this part of Wales, perhaps you are a student of its history?' Bowen's question seems friendly enough, but ambiguous, making Julia wonder if he means somehow to test her.

'Not so very much, I'm afraid.'

The professor now clears his throat, as if at the beginning of a lecture. 'The Romans were here very early on, of course. It was the Second Augustan Legion who built the fort at Castell Collen, just up there on the hill, in the difficult years after Caratacus's rising against Aulus Plautius and then the Boudiccan revolt. As you may recall, there were great fears that the Britons would rise again in the west after Suetonius Paulinus left his carnage unfinished at Ynys Môn. As Tacitus put it, *omne ignotum pro magnifico*, whatever is unknown is held to be magnificent. Unfortunately, with the possible exception of the bold Venutius, such magnificence as there was had to wait many centuries to be revealed.'

It occurs to Julia that Bowen is accustomed to a passive audience, that his purpose is less to inform than to impress with his depth of knowledge and rhetorical dexterity; especially so, in this case, because she is a woman. 'I'm curious about the name Caradoc,' she says. 'I believe it is derived from an original Brythonic form that would have been close to *Caratacos*, which would in turn have latinised to Caratacus. So you are perhaps named for a hero of the early British resistance?'

Slowly and deliberately, Bowen completes the polishing of his glasses. 'I'm afraid I had forgotten that you are a scholar of our ancient language,' he says. 'Your supposition is quite correct, and yet my given name has perhaps played even a larger role than this in Celtic history and mythology. Historians have recorded one Caradoc ap Ynyr, a sixth-century king of Gwent who was named in remembrance of the earlier hero, Caratacus. The same Welsh monarch also became the model for Caradoc Vreichvras, Caradoc Strong-Arm, who was stolen by the French romancers to become an Arthurian knight. To me, this suggests both an extraordinary degree of porosity between history and mythology, and a remarkable continuity of tradition between the pre- and post-Roman Brythonic cultures. Do you not agree?'

This last statement reminds Julia intensely of Donald; it is a line she might expect to read in his book. Her thoughts drift back to their last, inadequate conversation. She tries to imagine what he is thinking, how he will react when he sees her, how he will expect her to react. 'I think you met a friend of mine recently,' she says, 'Donald Gladstone.'

She senses Bowen looking at her with a renewed curiosity. 'Yes indeed, and I have found him to be a most thoughtful and determined scholar, though I cannot say whether he will be successful in disentangling the real Arthur—if there is such a creature—from the many threads that bind him. We are due to meet again tomorrow morning in Rhayader, as you are perhaps aware, to pursue a rather different project.'

Julia is tempted to ask the professor if she can join their expedition, but she stops herself short. What would she do, if he were to say no? By now, they are making their way out of the town, across the River Ithon and then west to intersect the Wye valley and the main road north to Rhayader. They drive on across a rolling upland terrain with lonely farmhouses glimpsed from time to time in the folds of the hills, Cerrigcroes, Gelligarn, Pistyll Gwyn. Caradoc Bowen holds his peace, breathing heavily and evenly as if he might have fallen asleep. When Julia glances across at him, she sees that he is staring intently out of the window at the passing landscape.

Soon enough, the looming bulk of Dôl-y-Fan above and to the right marks their approaching convergence with the Wye valley. Even allowing for the rain, they will be in Rhayader within twenty minutes, and she has not yet come close to what she really wants to say to him.

'I was hoping I could ask you something, Professor.'

'Yes, of course, if it is in my power to answer.' In her peripheral vision, Julia is aware of Bowen reaching into his pocket for his handkerchief, taking it out, putting it back again.

She speaks too fast, anxious to say everything before she loses her nerve. 'I have been trying to find out what really happened in Rhayader fourteen years ago, when there was an explosion at the Ellis engineering works. The official report said it was an accident, but the local rumour has always been that it was set off deliberately as part of the campaign against the Cwmhir dam. I believe you were in Rhayader around that time, and I'm wondering if you might know what really happened.'

She tightens her grip on the wheel, keeps her eyes fixed on the road ahead; but Caradoc Bowen is almost eerily calm in his response. 'May I ask, did you ever see the engineering plans for the dam?'

'No, of course not.'

'The blueprints and survey maps are still there in the British government archives, for anyone who is prepared to look hard enough. Were you to do so, you might notice that the flood waters would have extended farther than is commonly supposed, submerging not only the valley floor, Ty Faenor of course and the grave of Llywelyn the Great, but also, at the western end of the valley, the lower slopes of the hill called Moel Hywel.'

'Including Dyffryn Farm?' The words stick in Julia's throat.

'The Llewellyn family farm, amongst others, would have disappeared under the flood,' Bowen says, as if reciting some dry historical detail. 'The British planners were cautious at first in allowing the true scale of their plans to become known, having seen for themselves the damaging effects of the local resistance at Tryweryn. But there were some who were aware of it, including your father.'

Julia feels a creeping nausea now. 'Did you know him?'

'Yes, I first met Dai many years ago, and I was very sorry to hear the news of his untimely death. We had a good deal in common, your father and I, though it may surprise you to hear it. He was in his time a mentor to the young firebrands of Plaid Cymru, as was I to the members of Tân y Ddraig. Together, we meant to find a way to stop the construction of the dam.'

These words are left hanging in the air as Julia drives on past the entrance to Brynafon House and across the Tan House bridge to the southern edge of Rhayader, trying very hard to resist the logic of what Bowen has just told her. If his intention is to implicate her father as an accomplice in the crime that caused the death of Gwyn Edwards and the appalling injuries to Stephen Barnabas, it is more than can be believed. She speaks to him quietly now. 'You still haven't quite answered my question, Professor. I need to know what really happened at the engineering works, and whether my father was involved.'

Bowen takes his glasses off, recommences the polishing process. 'I will say only this. Dai Llewellyn was an honourable man and a true Welsh patriot, which of course you know better than any of us.'

Julia feels a kind of hatred now for Caradoc Bowen and his seemingly limitless powers of manipulation. If she could, she would stop the car and push him out into the rain. Hugh's role, at least, is now painfully clear to her. All along, he has told her as much of the truth as he could. He had no part in the violence, but he was forced to watch as Bowen conspired with her father. All his aloofness, his evasiveness on this question, this has been meant only to shield her from what he believed was the terrible secret of Dai's role in the bombing plot. Or to protect her father: this is the thought that comes to her now with the force of certainty. Hugh has acted not so much to spare her own feelings as from his sense of allegiance to Dai Llewellyn.

'Come and meet us tomorrow morning at nine o'clock, if you care to join our expedition,' the professor says, just as they are passing by the old grey clock tower in the centre of Rhayader. 'Perhaps in the end we may all find the answers we have been looking for.'

Someone has opened the front door of the Black Lion pub, sending a pool of welcoming light into the mid-afternoon gloom. Julia recognises the familiar figure of Gareth Williams, the long-standing proprietor and an old friend of her father's, who throws her a curious glance while he waits there respectfully for Caradoc Bowen to make his way inside through the pouring rain.

As she drives slowly away in the direction of Dyffryn Farm, her anger at Bowen is tempered by a sadness that winds itself quietly

around her like a shroud. It is a sadness for her father, whose memory she will treasure always, no matter what mistakes he may have
made in his past; a sadness for Hugh and all his misguided loyalty;
and a sadness for Donald Gladstone, for the chance not taken at
Trevethey Mill.

◈ ◈ ◈

WALKING INTO THE darkened, smoke-filled interior of the Black
Lion Inn after a long, solitary walk through the streets of Rhayader,
Donald cannot fail to notice a distinct lull in the conversation, an
indiscreet turning of heads, as his alien presence is registered by
the locals. It is a discomfort that is familiar enough from his days
at Bangor: he learned early on that there are places in Wales where
an Englishman feels his nationality clinging to him like some terrible affliction. As he approaches the bar, two of the older men,
pints in hand, show him the same baleful stare, then switch casually
into Welsh to continue their conversation. The dark-haired barmaid, grave and self-contained, glances coolly in his direction before
returning her attention to the row of unfilled glasses in front of her.

He takes in his surroundings at a glance, the plain wooden
benches and tables populated by a dozen or so Saturday evening
patrons, the smoke-yellowed walls, a neglected dart board, a cigarette machine and flashing jukebox in the far corner. There is a
narrow Victorian fireplace, unlit, with brass firedogs and cold ash in
the grate. On the wall above is the room's only unusual decoration,
a varnished wooden frame displaying a row of skulls arranged face
outwards in order of size: a shrew or mouse at the left-hand edge,
then emaciated visages of squirrel, cat, dog, goat, cow, and finally
the sweeping face-bones of a horse.

Approaching him now is a small man of about sixty with lively brown eyes in a round face, his nose reddened by drink. 'Dr. Gladstone, I presume? I am Gareth Williams, the owner of the Black Lion. It is my pleasure to welcome you to our modest establishment.' His rapid sing-song voice recalls the mining towns of South Wales, Gwilym Morgan in *How Green Was My Valley*. As he speaks, the left-hand side of his face is lifted up in a curious lopsided smile. 'I must say, you do look the part. A medical man, is it? I saw you examining my collection up there on the wall.'

'I'm an archaeologist,' Donald says. 'Human bones are more in my line, though I do come across the other kinds from time to time.'

'Ah yes, *homo sapiens*—that's where my collection has fallen sadly short.' Williams laughs, an infectious, high-pitched sound. 'Now then, will we pour you a drink, or just leave you standing here like a lonely English statue?'

'A pint of bitter, thank you. Has Professor Bowen arrived yet, by the way?' As Donald says this, he is aware of a new pair of eyes on him, a younger man at the far end of the bar.

'Yes indeed, he came in late this afternoon. He said he was feeling unwell, went straight upstairs. I thought to myself, there's a fine start to his visit.' Again the shrill, almost feverish laugh. 'Here's your room key now, number four, top of the stairs, then at the end on the left. Olwen, let's have a pint for Dr. Gladstone. On the house please, love.'

With this, Gareth Williams sidles away, leaving Donald to wait as the solemn barmaid, unmollified by her boss's familiarity, pulls him a pint of thin factory-brewed ale.

'Your first time in Rhayader, is it?' This comes from the man at the end of the bar. He is perhaps Donald's age, leanly built, with short dark hair flecked prematurely with grey, features firmly set into lines of worry or introspection. His dark-blue farmer's overalls are stained with mud.

'I've driven through a couple of times before,' Donald says, reluctant to commit himself to a conversation.

'And I've been here my whole life.' A handshake is offered, firm, measuring his grip in return. 'Ralph Barnabas. This Professor Bowen you mentioned, would he be a friend of yours?'

Donald can hardly deny the already admitted connection. 'Not exactly. We're working together on an archaeological project.'

Barnabas strikes a match, brings it up to the remnant of a hand-rolled cigarette, eyes narrowing as he inhales, then blows a stream of smoke out to one side. 'Here in Rhayader?' There is a note of disbelief in his voice.

'Up in the mountains. We're looking for a late medieval battle-site that has been lost to the historical record.' It is a calculated risk, a touch of condescension, not too much.

Another long pull on the cigarette, which is soon reduced to a small glowing nub. 'I'm wondering whether you might have been here with the professor when he last came to Rhayader?'

This feels like dangerous ground, but something in Ralph Barnabas's line of attack makes Donald want to see where the conversation might lead. He has not forgotten about the explosion at the engineer's office, the rumour that Bowen's militant students were behind it. 'I've only known Caradoc Bowen for a few weeks,' he says.

'But I assume you knew about him before that, what he did in the past?'

The chess game continues, thinking two moves ahead. 'I read a book of his a long time ago. I have a copy with me, if you'd like to see it.' Donald reaches into his bag, takes out the familiar slim blue volume: *Notes on the Welsh Rising* by C. H. R. Bowen. 'It's a history of the rebellion led by Owain Glyn Dŵr in the early fifteenth century. This has been Bowen's particular area of research.'

Gareth Williams comes up next to them, a greasy cloth in his hand. 'Not quite your cup of tea, is it, Ralph, all this rising up against the English?'

Barnabas drains the last of his beer, gives Williams a look that borders on disgust. 'Good luck to you,' he says, nodding in Donald's direction, then strides out of the pub without a backward glance.

After he has gone, Gareth Williams lays a familiar hand on Donald's arm. 'In case you hadn't noticed, Ralph doesn't like me very much. He wouldn't normally be seen dead drinking here, but he was hoping to catch sight of Caradoc Bowen.'

'Why should he care?'

'There's a long story.'

'I'd like to hear it.'

Williams gestures peremptorily at the barmaid. 'Olwen, a refill for our guest, please.' She draws another pint, pushes it back along the bar, and Williams leads the way to a table in the far corner, draws up a pair of straight-backed wooden chairs and gestures for Donald to sit. 'Now then, perhaps you knew they were once planning to put a dam across the Cwmhir valley, just out there to the north-east of town, to collect drinking water for the city of Birmingham. Some people thought it wasn't worth drowning a piece of Wales for that, so they decided to make a bit of noise to try and stop it.'

'I heard about that, the bombing at the engineering works. It all seems a long way in the past.'

'That's not what Ralph would say. It was his best friend who was killed, and his father, the vicar of St. Clement's, who had his legs blown off. Just after his mam died, too.' By now, Gareth Williams is leaning in close, speaking in a low conspiratorial voice. There is a stale smell on his breath. 'It was officially called an accident, the Reverend Barnabas made sure of that.'

'I'm not quite sure I follow you.'

'He saw who did it, you see. At least, that's what he said when he first woke up in hospital, though he wouldn't let on who it was. Ralph was standing there at his bedside when he said it. But Stephen Barnabas is a headstrong man. He told the inquiry something different, claimed he hadn't seen anyone after all, said it was down to his delirious state of mind after the accident. Now, if you're thinking that's maybe a little too convenient, you'd be quite right, but in the end they had to believe the sworn testimony of a man of the church.'

'He could have been telling the truth,' Donald says. 'I'm not sure why he would choose to lie about a thing like that.'

'Well, as to his reasons for it, you can decide for yourself, because he's never going to tell you in this life. There was nobody in the whole of Radnorshire who wanted the dam, except perhaps Dafydd Ellis who was going to get rich from it, but after that there wasn't much agreement on what to do about it. A great sharp wedge was being driven through the town, the militants against the pacifists, and Stephen Barnabas made it his duty to stop that if he could.'

Donald says nothing for a moment, picks up his beer glass and examines the contents. 'So where does Bowen come into the story?'

'He was here with us at the Black Lion. We've always had a great respect for Professor Caradoc Bowen in this establishment.'

'That doesn't quite answer the question, though.'

The familiar hand is back on Donald's forearm. 'Let me put it to you this way,' Williams says. 'I am sorry for what happened to Gwyn Edwards and Stephen Barnabas, and I'm not the one to say it was a sacrifice worth making, though some might be entitled to that opinion.'

Donald pulls his arm away, keeps a tight hold on his patience as he contemplates this strange and almost recklessly plain-speaking man. He is aware that he is being goaded, provoked into some statement he might regret. 'Why should you think it was the bombing that halted the building of the dam?' he says. 'It didn't stop them at Tryweryn.'

The half-sneering smile returns to Gareth Williams' face. 'You are quite correct, Dr. Gladstone,' he says, the melody gone from his voice. 'The bombing at Tryweryn did not stop them drowning the valley, and with it the ancient village of Capel Celyn. Perhaps that is why some bold Welshmen decided it must never happen again. Now, if you'll excuse me, I've some things I need to take care of.' With this he goes on his way, humming a sombre evening tune. He disappears through a door at the back, leaving Donald to hope fervently that he will not return.

By ten o'clock, the bar is almost empty, the regulars having mostly finished up and shambled off for home. With nobody left to serve, the barmaid is perfunctorily washing glasses and setting them out to dry. 'Were you expecting someone?' she says, with a knowing look and a surprising hint of sympathy in her voice.

'Yes, or at least I thought I was.' Donald pretends to shrug off his disappointment, picks up his bag and coat and heads for the back staircase. 'In case anyone happens to be looking for me before closing time, would you please come and find me? I'll be in my room, catching up on some reading.'

The floorboards squeak loudly underfoot as he turns the corner at the top of the stairs, treads along the corridor, opens his door and switches on the light. The unshaded bulb impinges harshly on a pale blue bedspread, pink floral wallpaper pasted around the difficult angles of the room. There is a strong smell of lilac and mildew. The curtains have been drawn as far as they will go across the small square window, the narrow gap between them admitting the twinkling illumination of a nearby street lamp. Donald lies down on the bed, staring up at the complex pattern of discoloured stains and cracks on the plaster ceiling, thinking about Julia and what happened at Tintagel. The stolen kiss on the bridge seems long faded into history, an event belonging to some other age of the world. He reaches for the yellow message slip in his coat pocket, sees Tim Watson's handwriting there and the number for Dyffryn Farm. He might ask to use the telephone downstairs; but it seems too late to call, and in the end he settles on the most straightforward explanation, that Julia has decided not to come.

For now, he diverts himself by unfolding his father's geological map. His eye is drawn straight away to a small area outlined in red at the left-hand edge of the map, and the Welsh placename, *Rhëydr y Tair Melltith*, Three Devil Falls. It is as remote a location as anyone could hope for, very hard to approach by road. He takes out his atlas, opens it to the pages showing central and southern Wales. With pencil in hand, he begins to trace out the most likely route.

By ten-thirty, he has lost all hope that Julia will come. Still not quite tired enough to sleep, he turns on the bedside lamp, pulls the cord above his head to switch off the main light, then props himself up on the bed with the two thin pillows behind him. Once settled in modest comfort, he reaches for the book he found at Hay-on-Wye, Giraldus Cambrensis and his irreverent account of his great Welsh journey with his fellow traveller, Archbishop Baldwin. Giraldus provides the good company he is hoping for, the pages turning surprisingly easily until he reaches a passage in which the author, while describing a reluctant crossing of a particular mountainous tract, makes a reference that chills him to the bone.

A grave-digger at Tregaron told us of a vale which is known to the locals as the thrice-accursed falls on account of the triple cascade that is to be found in its lower reaches. This man shared with us his grandmother's tale, that the valley is haunted by the magic of the ancient Britons, and that we should climb up there at our peril. We readily dismissed this superstition as a harmless blasphemy, making sure meanwhile to choose another route through the mountain passes.

Donald keeps on reading, trying not to think too hard about the timeless grievances of the old British gods, until the words finally begin to blur as alcohol and exhaustion do their work.

* * *

HUGH IS THERE in the kitchen at Dyffryn Farm when Julia gets back from Rhayader, sitting in the corner chair with the newspaper and a glass of sherry in his hand while her mother busies herself at the stove. She stops in the doorway, says hello to him as if it were an ordinary day at home, and it seems to her that this is a dream-like scene, twisting sharply away from reality.

'It's been a while since we had a proper dinner together,' Cath Llewellyn says with a spirited smile as they take their places at the long oak table. 'There's no need for us to stop eating, just because Dai's not with us.'

Julia does her best to play along with her mother's conceit. She can tell that Hugh is trying hard. He has brought a bottle of old claret rescued from the cellar at Ty Faenor after the recent flood, and now offers this as an accompaniment to her mother's improvised pot-roast. But she shakes her head when he offers to pour her a glass.

'I need to drive into town later on,' she says, trying not to look at the clock. Her mother notices the gesture, grimaces at her, a small emphatic warning.

'I could give you a lift, if you like?' Hugh says, innocently enough.

She does not repeat the thought that comes to her first, that he has already been drinking, that his father and mother were killed when they drove off the side of a road into a disused quarry in the Malvern hills. 'It's all right, there's no need.'

'Who are you going to see?'

Cath Llewellyn comes to her daughter's rescue. 'We're both going, actually. Olwen Williams has asked us down for a drink later on at the Black Lion. Perhaps you'd like to join us?'

It is a gamble, but a measured one. Hugh's antipathy to Gareth Williams' daughter goes back many years, to the time when he tried to kiss her behind the bar when she was fifteen, and she slapped him hard in the face. 'No, I don't think so,' he says, and to Julia he seems suddenly defeated, recognising the conspiracy that is at work against him.

Still he goes through the motions, and the dinner takes the time it takes, an hour and a half ticking by. Hugh drinks the wine on his own, telling them about his grand plans for Ty Faenor, how he needs to spend more time there to keep the place up. Julia sits mostly silent, thinking this is a strange state they have come to, pretending to have a conversation just because her mother is in the room.

When they have finished and he is getting ready to leave, she goes to the front door with him. 'There is one thing I wanted to ask you,' she says, her resentment edging towards bitterness. 'Why would you think it would be the right thing to do, to say nothing to me about my father's involvement in the Rhayader bombing?'

He looks at her in his cool, measured way. 'You've got it all wrong, Julia.' There is a kind of sincerity in his voice, a well-practised authenticity made more plausible by the wine he has drunk. But then something in his expression changes, the veneer of composure falls away. 'If you can't find a way to change the subject, perhaps you had better not speak to me at all.'

Julia can tell he regrets these words as soon as he has spoken them, but she cannot help thinking this is the only genuine thing she has heard from him all evening. 'Drive carefully,' she says. 'You've had far too much to drink.' She waits there on the doorstep as he walks back to the Land Rover, starts it up and drives slowly away down the hill.

Her mother is waiting for her in the front room. 'It seems to me he's doing his best, Julia.'

'You're not the one he's lying to, Mam.'

'In which case, we've all been guilty of the same crime this evening. Maybe you've already forgotten, I had to tell a lie on your behalf.'

Julia feels the full sharp sting of this rebuke. 'You're right, and I'm sorry. But I said I would be there, and I'm late, so I had better go.'

She drives too fast, fifteen minutes door to door in the pouring rain, pulls up at the side of the road a little way short of the Black Lion. There is a dim light on in the back room, where Gareth Williams, long separated from his wife, will hopefully by now have curled himself up on the sofa with his bottle of brandy and the Saturday-night film. Despite Gareth's long and loyal friendship with her father, Julia has never quite been able to bring herself to like him. From the earliest days, when she first went to the Black Lion as a teenager and he knowingly introduced her to the young Hugh Mortimer, she has felt him looking over her shoulder, watchful and proprietorial, passing judgment on her every move. He is the very last person she wants to see when she walks through the door of the pub. She leaves the wipers running for a few seconds, watching as they continue to sweep away at the glinting watery scene, then turns off the engine, gets out and runs to the door of the pub.

Olwen Williams is on her own behind the bar. She is an old friend, someone Julia has known her whole life. A few months earlier, she moved back here with her young family, and has now taken over the daily running of the place. 'Well now, here's a pretty thing the cat's dragged in.' She is diffident as always, but on the edge of a smile. 'How are you and your mam getting along at the farm?'

'Well enough, I suppose. Olwen, did you happen to see—'

'Did I happen to see an attractive man sitting here waiting for you for two hours? And being driven to distraction by my dear father, who grabbed on to him like a leech? Yes, I did. He's given up and gone to his room, half an hour ago now. He said to go and fetch him, though, if you got here before closing time.'

❖ ❖ ❖

IN DONALD'S DREAM, someone keeps knocking on the outside of his head. It is Mrs. Carwyn, at Trevethey Mill, telling him he has a visitor downstairs. He hears the knocking again, and now he is wide awake and on his feet and Julia is there at the door of his room. She looks a little breathless and quite lovely, it seems to him, with the colour in her cheeks and her hair damp from the rain.

'Can I come in?'

'Yes, of course.' He ushers her inside, closes the door behind her.

'I'm very late, I'm sorry. Were you asleep?'

'No—well, yes. I couldn't stay awake. I was trying to read my book.' He stoops to pick up Giraldus, fallen to the floor in a mess of open pages, sets the book down on the bedside table.

Julia smiles at him in her half-satirical way, but she seems tentative, unsure of herself. 'Do you mind if I stay and talk for a while?'

'You can have the chair, if you like.'

She takes off her coat, hangs it on the hook on the door, then sits down in the small wooden chair in the corner of the room. She runs her hands through her hair, pushes it back from her face. 'You must think me very selfish.'

'Why should I?'

'Because I ran away from you at Tintagel. Because I didn't call to tell you what had happened.'

'It's in the past now. I don't think you had much choice.'

'No, but it isn't your fault that my father died, and my husband came looking for me.'

The statement falls awkwardly, though Donald knows what she means to say. He smiles, tries to make light of it. 'I knew you were married. Why should I have been surprised?'

They fall into silence, Julia staring down at her fingernails. When she looks up at him again, she seems very close to tears. 'It has all been very unfair to you. That's what I wanted to tell you.'

It crosses Donald's mind that she need not have come quite so far, just to say this. In any case, there is nothing to be gained from continuing the conversation. He reaches for a change of subject. 'Your mother said you were going to get in touch with Caradoc Bowen.'

'I picked him up at the station this afternoon,' she says, shrugging in a faintly apologetic way. 'He invited me to come with you tomorrow.'

It is hard to understand why she would have gone to meet Bowen, but Donald decides to let it pass. He picks up the geological map from the floor and spreads it out on the bed. 'I can show you where we're going, if you like.' She comes over to sit next to him as he traces out the route. 'I'm guessing it's about two hours' drive, if we're lucky, although the last part looks a bit difficult.' He runs his finger along the line of an unmade track next to a small river that comes down from the mountains. 'It's probably one of the old drovers' roads, which were once used to drive livestock down from the hills and on to the lowland markets. They often followed the course of much older paths, ancient greenways that have been travelled since prehistoric times. My father and I once—'

It is the faintest of touches on Donald's arm that stops him in mid-sentence. 'There's something I want you to know,' Julia says.

'What is it?' he says, confused by her sudden intensity.

'I think my marriage is over.'

He cannot think of the right thing to say. 'Why are you telling me this?'

She lays her hand on top of his. 'So we don't keep misunderstanding each other.'

Donald turns to face her now, runs his fingers down her cheek. He pulls her towards him, holds her tightly in his arms, the dark green of her eyes, the softness of her skin, her faint perfume setting free the long-confined emotion. Their kiss is hesitant at first, provisional, as if they were sixteen years old, and yet there is a barely controlled tension between them. Julia pulls away from him, unbuttons her top and lifts it over her head. She leans over and slips the straps of her camisole away from her shoulders. He pulls off his shirt and jeans, then takes off her remaining clothes, doing it slowly, deliberately, his hands slipping down at last over the soft curves of her body. She turns her head to one side, closes her eyes. He hesitates now, but she whispers to him, tells him it's OK, she doesn't want him to stop.

▨ ▨ ▨

DONALD IS AWAKE in the darkness before dawn, his hearing sharply attuned to the noises of the night. The rain is still coming down hard, strong gusts of wind rattling the window. The other side of the bed is empty and cold. It takes him a second or two to remember precisely where he is, and what has happened, and to feel the full weight of his disappointment that she has gone. Making love to Julia, he felt the rightness of it, no sense of guilt or exploitation; and then, in the depth of the night, the indescribable feeling of her naked skin against his own. But now he can see that the constraint was all on her side, her eyes half-averted from his face even as her body responded to his, the shame of it barely suppressed even as her hands clung so fiercely to him. He switches on the light, finds the note she has left for him, its terse, pragmatic message only adding to his confusion. *It's late and I don't want to wake you. I'll see you in the morning, OK?*

Now he hears someone come out of the room opposite, walk slowly down the stairs and out of the back door of the pub. Something in the sound of the footfalls, a muffled clearing of the throat, convinces him that it is Caradoc Bowen who has been out on some mysterious errand in the midst of the storm.

▩ ▩ ▩

AT FIRST THERE is poetry in his dream, beautiful and stirring lines that paint a picture from the distant past. He sees a tall man standing alone, staring up a long sharp slope where a swift-flowing river cuts and weaves its way past smooth-faced rocks the colour of blood. His companions have gathered a stone's throw behind him, hardened warriors now anxiously regarding the familiar bear-like silhouette of their leader, conscious of the change that has come upon him, the feyness that is in his eye. The cool air is full of the soothing, treacherous rushing of the mountain stream.

The sun's edge breaks free of cloud: the world is breathless, flushed with light. There is movement now at the crest of the ridge, a shape is stirring there, a monster formed of upraised spear-tips dazzling white. They watch in silence as this beast unfolds its wings, turns its baleful eyes upon them; then, with a great screeching cry, takes flight down the slope towards them. It is their leader who gathers their courage, rallies them to a steep track that cuts high across the valley wall. Faster they climb, pain and fear clutching at their chests, until at last they come to a place where the path broadens out in a shape like an axe's head beneath the cliff, then falls away almost to nothing. Grimly they gather there, caught in a trap of their own making, as the sun begins its long slow decline. In the sky above, the carrion-birds circle knowingly for the coming feast.

The scene begins to fade, slipping from our dreamer's memory, leaving only this: a sound like a distant waterfall, sighing, whispering to him across the void.

Do you not know me, crab with broken shell?
Black raven I am called, the voice undying
My body turns to dust but my curse lives on
In rock and branch and mountain stream.

He is awake now in a darkened room, his pulse racing with a cold and familiar dread. Outside in the night, the rain is coming down harder than before.

Three Devil Falls

I T IS A pristine blue-sky morning, the clouds all swept away, the hills and fields scrubbed fresh and new with the rainwater pooled ankle-deep in every dip and hollow. Julia's mood swings from nervous excitement to trepidation as she drives down from Dyffryn Farm to the lower slopes of Moel Hywel and the lane that runs south and west along the valley to Rhayader. She finds that the only way for her to calm herself, to quell the anxious speculations and dissonant voices, is not to think at all, to count the sheep fleeing from the verges, the bends in the road, the crows on the fence-posts watching her as she goes by.

On East Street near the market cross, she runs into Owen the greengrocer for flowers, then cuts back through the side streets to St. Clement's church, parks against the wrought-iron gates and walks over to the newest graves clustered in the corner of the churchyard. She stands there for a while looking down on her father's plain-spoken epitaph, *Dai Llewellyn, devoted father, husband, artist, farmer, Welshman.* These are the words he chose for himself years ago, during some mild winter illness, to represent his soul to posterity. She cannot help smiling at the thought of it, Dai there in bed with a bad cold or the flu, pondering long and hard on the proper ordering of his vocations, worrying over the precise effect he would make on casual passers-by in decades and centuries to come. Now she feels only forgiveness for the mistakes he may have made in his life. She steps forward, lays down her flowers one by one, lilies and poppies, bright white and vivid red, then hurries away just as the tears start to blur in her eyes.

The Black Lion is no more than a short walk along narrow streets of whitewashed stone cottages with brightly painted front doors, well-trimmed patchwork gardens now long past their spring and summer best. Julia bows her head as she passes by, striving for anonymity, though some of the people who live here have known her all her life. Donald is waiting for her outside the pub, leaning against the wall next to the front door. He looks tired, his hair in disarray, his face unshaven.

'I'm glad you're here,' he says. There is something hopeful and uncertain in his smile.

'Did you think I was going to abandon you?' She wants to reach out her hand to him, but she is aware of the darkened windows of the pub, Gareth Williams surely there watching them from inside.

'I couldn't be sure.' Donald shrugs, an almost casual gesture, and it occurs to Julia that he, too, has rehearsed this rendezvous, coached himself on how he should act.

'Well, here I am. Are we ready to go?'

'Yes, and I'm afraid our distinguished professor is not in the best of moods this morning. We shouldn't keep him waiting.'

There is a deliberate, decisive quality in the way Donald ushers her towards the narrow passage that leads along the side of the pub to where his car is parked out at the back. Caradoc Bowen is sitting in the cramped rear seat of the Morris with the window wound down. His eyes are closed, his head slumped awkwardly on his chest. Julia feels a stab of irrational fear.

The professor opens his eyes with a start, gathers himself, then fixes her with his impatient stare. 'You may be assured that I am neither asleep nor yet quite dead, but merely resting after a poor night's sleep. Now, if you are both finally ready, I should like to propose that we leave without further delay.'

Bowen remains quiet as they set off through the Sunday-morning streets of Rhayader. His reticence imposes a similar state on Donald and Julia, who are forced to restrict their conversation to the essential details of navigation. The road atlas in Julia's lap is open to a page showing the whole great sweep of the Cambrian mountains through central and southern Wales. Tracing her finger along the route Donald has marked, she is reminded of their journey together to Solsbury Hill, of how the world has changed since then.

Soon they are heading out of the town towards smooth green hills rising gradually to a high dark hinterland. It is a view Julia's father would have chosen to sketch, the nearer slopes etched sharp and clear with a telling detail or two—a broken-down wall, a hovering bird of prey—merging into a fainter, shadowed, elusive suggestion of the distant uplands. He always said it was not a great art that he strove for in his landscapes, but a pure quality of Welshness, if such a thing could be achieved by the exercise of pencil-strokes alone.

Caradoc Bowen now speaks abruptly into the gathering silence. 'We are presently travelling along the western edge of the old Welsh *cantref* of Maelienydd,' he says. 'If I may be forgiven for borrowing a description from a long-dead poet, this was once a storied realm made mighty by great wars and fruitful land.'

The line is from Virgil's *Aeneid*, drummed into Julia by a fervent classicist in her first year at Wadham. Donald glances across at her, grimaces faintly. 'Perhaps you are somewhat exaggerating its claims, Professor Bowen?' he says.

She holds her breath for the inevitable reaction, but the professor's response seems only weary, or perhaps disappointed. 'You may have forgotten that Thomas Malory laid claim to Maelienydd as the kingdom belonging to Leodegrance, father of Guinevere, whose descendants strove here for many centuries against the oppression of the Mortimer earls. There was almost a happy union of the two, white dragon and red, when Edmund Mortimer married Catrin, the eldest daughter of Glyn Dŵr, but that dream was lost when Edmund perished at Harlech Castle and Catrin was taken to the Tower.'

Julia knows all the bitter history of it, as Caradoc Bowen must be aware. It is from Edmund and Catrin that Hugh claims his Anglo-Welsh descent. Bowen pauses for a moment, and she wonders if he means to coax her into joining the conversation; but soon enough he resumes his solemn narrative.

'It was into these mountains that Glyn Dŵr disappeared after the tragedy at Harlech. He was almost a broken man by then, broken by Gilbert Talbot who prosecuted the siege, who took away the wives and daughters of Owain and his followers and starved his many comrades to death. His only sustenance in those last days was the powerful mythology that his bards and his seers—Siôn Cent the most prominent amongst them—had woven about him during the years of his ascendancy. There was a purpose in his life that was not yet fulfilled. It was his strongest belief that the red dragon's song could still be heard echoing faintly in the valleys, if one only knew where to listen.'

'But do you think there's a danger in knowing too much about him?' Donald says. 'If we were to find his grave, look upon his mortal remains, some of that mythical aura would be destroyed. Perhaps we're not supposed to know what happened to him at the end.'

Caradoc Bowen's response is scarcely above a murmur. 'Owain Glyn Dŵr is a far deeper mystery than you suppose, if you imagine his life and death may be so readily encompassed. It has been my own great work, my *lapis philosophorum*, to recover even the barest essentials of what he once was. Are you proposing that I simply abandon the attempt?'

Julia is glad that Donald does not try to prolong the discussion. Instead he keeps his own counsel, a small frown of concentration creasing his brow as he forces the Morris along a series of narrow roads that twist their way up from the valley floor. When at last she steals a backward glance, she sees that Bowen has closed his eyes again, his hands to the sides of his head as if in some great effort of recollection. Donald catches her eye, and his smile is reassuring to her.

They are approaching a part of Wales that Julia has never visited before, beyond the last of the upland farms and on into the harsher terrain that runs for many miles to the south and east. The landscape is familiar to her in its rugged lines and craggy hollows, its hues of dun and green, but there is also a certain unsettling wildness that comes from a sharpness in the contours, a depth of blackness in the shadowed slopes, a sense of chilly isolation in the barren summit ridges stretching up to the glassy blue sky. As the miles pass by with no sign of human habitation, the loneliness of it begins to prey upon her peace of mind.

At length they come to a dramatic traverse along a little-used road that carries them high above the wall of a long, glacially sculpted *cwm*, then a final steep descent into the lower reaches of a deep riverine cleft carved into the mountainside. They make a turn on to an unmade track that follows the valley upstream. The car lurches uncomfortably along the muddy, rutted surface, bringing them perilously close to the river running in full spate just a few feet to their left. After two or three difficult miles, the track comes to an abrupt end at a place where the remnants of an old stone bridge make a fragmentary span across the river. On either side are steep slopes covered with deep thickets of stunted ash and birch. An old wooden sign, badly weathered, tells them they have reached their destination, *Rhëydr y Tair Melltith*, Three Devil Falls.

Donald stops the car in the shelter of the wooded hillside. 'This is as close as we can get,' he says, as he shuts off the engine and opens the driver's door.

They walk together to the riverbank, pause there to watch the tumultuous rush of brown-tinted water foaming white over the stones, dazzling with glints of sunlight thrown from the chaotic surface. Not far upstream is a place where the river surges out from a broad rounded space, a natural amphitheatre hollowed from the rock. There is a cliff perhaps a hundred feet high; and then, both beautiful and intimidating, a great flood-charged cascade thundering over the edge and into the pool beneath. It seems impossible that there could be enough water gathered in the upper reaches of the valley to sustain such an astonishing flow.

The professor stands quite still for a moment, staring back along the track, the way they have just come. Then without a word he sets off upstream, leaning heavily on his walking stick as he moves deliberately through the tumbled rocks. 'I hope he doesn't think he can climb up there,' Julia says, seeing the determination in his step.

'I expect that's exactly what he's planning to do. We'd better not let him get too far ahead.' There is something in the way Donald sets off in pursuit, a boldness and strength of purpose, that reminds her of the way Hugh used to be in their early days together. She follows along more slowly, shocked by the sudden intensity of the guilt that comes rushing in on her.

Fifty yards short of the falls, the professor stops to rest. To Julia he looks deeply unwell, ashen-faced as he gazes up at the wall of cascading water. The roar has become almost overwhelming, resolving itself into a many-layered sound with a dangerous rumbling like thunder at its core. The cool fine mist that has been drifting over them has intensified to a soaking spray that forces them close in to the lee of the cliff.

'As we have already seen from the map,' Bowen says, straining to raise his voice above the noise of the flood, 'what we seek is much higher up, where the stream first cuts its way down from the mountain heights. That place is quite inaccessible, now as in Glyn Dŵr's day, except for one very difficult route that requires an ascent above the three waterfalls for which this place is named, the lowest of which we see here before us.'

From where Julia is standing, the cliff-face makes an impenetrable barrier all the way around, its sheer surface for the most part obscured by a thick growth of scrubby trees and bushes that have somehow gained a purchase in the rock. The obvious conclusion has remained unspoken, that there is no possibility of making such a climb as Bowen suggests. 'There's no way up, Professor Bowen,' she says. 'It's too dangerous even to think of trying it.'

'There is a path,' Donald says. 'We just need to find where it starts.' Sheltering close in against the cliff, he takes out a map and traces the route they have followed so far: from the road to the unmade track to the place where they are now standing ensnared in a dense web of contour lines. 'Here,' he says, pointing to a thin dotted line that starts on their side of the lower waterfall and runs up in zig-zag fashion to the top of the second cascade.

Within a few minutes, they have found what they are looking for. Behind a thick screen of overhanging branches, they uncover the lower reaches of a rough staircase hewn into the rock. Bowen sets his walking stick decisively on the first step. 'I do not ask that you accompany me,' he says.

'We're hardly likely to turn back now, Professor,' Donald says.

The climb is made by numerous long traverses across the face of the cliff. Julia drops a little way back, settles into a rhythm of slow, measured strides, content to move along in her own space. She finds her senses sharply attuned to her surroundings, feels the wisps of cool mountain air against her skin, rocks and leaves and branches trodden underfoot; the rushing of the waterfall layered behind other more immediate sounds, a skittering of stones dislodged from the path far below, the harsh rasping cry of a raven disturbed from its roost, taking wing across the valley. Ahead of her, Donald is solid, familiar, reliably himself. He looks back from time to time to check that she is keeping up, and she takes comfort from it.

▨ ▨ ▨

DONALD FOLLOWS CLOSE behind as Caradoc Bowen makes a fretful, laboured ascent with many feverish glances over his shoulder. Perhaps his anxiety is not to be wondered at; they are, after all, on a journey that may in a sense complete his life's work. Bowen may truly believe that the academic world is watching, that others are hot on the same trail, that his peers have not, after all, entirely dismissed or forgotten his work. Is it Cambridge he fears, or the Welsh universities? This all seems a harmless enough conceit.

For now, Donald has other, more immediate preoccupations. Thirty yards below him on the path, Julia could as well be a thousand miles away. It seems a self-imposed exile on her part, a deliberate closing-off of communication, as if she means to pretend they are complete strangers: as if she is already regretting their ephemeral romance, and would undo it if she could. The uncertainty he senses in her is an injustice he finds very hard to take.

A final turn, and Bowen is waiting for him at the point where the path comes out of the trees. He is breathing heavily, leaning on a smooth-sided rock for support as he looks out on one of the wildest and most starkly beautiful settings that Donald has ever seen. The second of the three waterfalls is now some way below them, lesser in height than the first, but equally powerful in the force of the water flowing over the top. A long and treacherous slope of tumbled boulders leads down to a narrow rocky channel through which the river continues its rush to the brink of the fall, where for an instant it seems to pause, its turbulence gathered into a smooth edge like molten glass, before slipping over for its plunge to the pool below.

All around them now, the mountain slopes come sweeping down in complex, overlapping folds that keep the higher reaches of the valley hidden from view. Donald's eye is drawn inexorably to the sunlit upper slopes with their many shades and hues of grey and green and (this he sees with a sudden rush of recognition) a dark reddish-brown exposed in the upper strata. Without a doubt, they have found his father's promised St. Maughans formation, the famous Welsh red sandstone.

'You will note something of particular interest up on the heights,' Caradoc Bowen says, his hand shaking a little as he points with his walking stick. Donald sees it straight away, three huge interlocking stones in silhouette at the top of the ridge. 'It is known to us in Wales as a *cromlech*, the entrance to a neolithic portal-tomb.'

Donald has come across many such structures along the Celtic fringe of Europe, though he has never seen one in quite so majestic a location. He is reminded of Giraldus Cambrensis and his account of the grave-digger of Tregaron. *This man shared with us his grandmother's tale, that the valley is haunted by the magic of the ancient Britons, and that we should climb up there at our peril.* Lucy would say that this is a sacred valley, a place where the aura of the old gods is at its strongest.

Now he sees something he did not notice at first, a thin grey line running across the steep slope beneath the clifftop tomb. It may be no more than a quirk of the rock strata, but it looks more purposeful than that, perhaps a track made by mountain goats in ages past. Looking more closely, he can make out a second path separating from the first and climbing up to the top of the cliff.

'Such locations play a particularly important role in Welsh mythology,' Bowen is saying. 'They reputedly make a gateway between the world of mortal men and the otherworld, where the heroes of the past live on.'

Donald recognises the professor's oblique reference to the Song of Lailoken, to the poet's description of the death of his 'Arthur', Owain Glyn Dŵr, at the hands of the giant Madarakt, and the events that follow:

> We bore him up to the highest clifftop, gate of the otherworld
> Laid him beneath a linden tree, the shield-wood powerless now
> The words unspoken on his lips, the life we saw still behind his eyes
> No more than the trick of light and shadow on the rock.

Bowen's evident excitement is sharply contained. 'We must find a way to climb higher, if we are to prove our case.'

His meaning is clear enough. The scene does not yet fit the description in the Song of Lailoken, the last desperate refuge below cliffs raised like bloodied fists high above. That place must lie in the upper section of the valley, somewhere beyond the last waterfall. But now they have reached the end of the path, whose makers intended it only to bring sightseers safely to the top of the second cascade for a chance to see the stunning view that now confronts them. Somewhere up ahead, the third waterfall can be heard but not seen, hidden from view by a turn in the valley. If they are to continue, they must improvise a route down the steep, boulder-strewn slope to the river's edge.

Donald is glad to feel Julia's hand on his arm as she comes up behind him. 'I'm sorry to be so slow,' she says to him, quietly. 'I'll try to keep up.'

After a tense few minutes of scrambling, they find their way safely back down to the river. They follow its twisting course for another half-mile until at last the uppermost of the three waterfalls comes into view, a pure white cataract dropping to a tumultuous landing in a pool ringed with sharp-edged rocks. It is a daunting sight at first, a steep cliff-face whose top section is partly obscured by an overhanging ledge of rock. Looking more carefully, Donald can see many natural steps and handholds that should make it possible even for Caradoc Bowen to find a way up.

Julia comes to stand next to him, close enough that they are almost touching. It cannot be entirely in his imagination, the confusion he senses in her, the wish to make things right. His pretended indifference flies away to thin air; he wants nothing more than to take her by the hand. Instead they stand there in silent communion no more than a finger's breadth apart as the waterfall surrounds them with its chaotic, elemental sound.

'Are you ready to carry on, Professor?' Donald says, when he can bear it no longer. 'I think we're almost there.'

He is on the verge of leading them forward when he is stopped in his tracks by a new intensity in Bowen's expression, a series of murmured imprecations that he cannot quite catch. There is a noise from behind, boots scuffing on rock.

※ ※ ※

JULIA'S FIRST THOUGHT is that Hugh knows everything, that he has followed her here, hunted her down like an errant lamb escaped from a field. She stares mutely at him, wondering how she should feel, glad that Donald is standing guardedly, resolutely next to her.

But Hugh seems genuinely shocked to see her. She can sense the effort it costs him to keep his voice under control. 'I didn't know this was going to be quite such a party.'

It is Bowen who responds to this. 'You are very bold, Hugh, to come here speaking such mockery.'

'I am hardly mocking you, Professor Bowen. As I recall, you were the one who invited me to join you today. I didn't expect we would have so much company, that's all.' Hugh's gaze flickers to Donald, then back to his wife. 'Why didn't you say something to me, Julia?'

She remembers now, Bowen's phone call to Hugh at Ty Faenor. Seeing him standing there gazing coolly at her, she feels a twist of guilt and shame. 'I'm sorry, I had no idea he had asked you to come.'

'Why should you be surprised? I have stood with Professor Bowen in a dozen valleys just like this.' Hugh's restless glance falls back on Donald. Abruptly, he offers his hand. 'My name is Hugh Mortimer.'

'Donald Gladstone.' They shake hands in a brief, perfunctory way.

'Dr. Gladstone is an archaeological colleague of mine, from Oxford,' Bowen says.

'A new recruit for the search party, Professor? Does this mean it's the real thing this time?'

Caradoc Bowen raises his rasping voice above the sound of the falls. 'It seems to me, Hugh Mortimer, that you are a man without true convictions. Or perhaps it is merely the courage that is lacking. Once I thought we might have changed the world together, but I have badly misjudged you. For that I shall forever be sorry.'

'Changed the world?' Hugh's words seem to summon half a lifetime of contempt. 'We were just boys playing games, and you did everything you could to exploit us.'

'For some of us, it was never a game,' Bowen says. 'It was the fate of Wales that was at stake, the survival of our ancient homeland. But it is clear to me that I have been wrong to put my faith in the Mortimer family. Over the centuries, there has been a great deal of Welsh blood on their hands.' The professor turns away from them now, takes his walking stick in hand and begins to pick his way through the tumbled boulders in the direction of the waterfall.

▨ ▨ ▨

HUGH MORTIMER TAKES a step towards Bowen, but Donald moves to block his path. They are both tall, Donald an inch taller. 'I think you had better stay where you are,' he says.

His adversary stops three feet in front of him, holds his ground. 'Those are brave words,' he says.

'Please just let him go, Donald,' Julia says. 'They need to work it out for themselves.'

Hearing the urgency in her voice, he steps reluctantly to one side, allows Hugh to brush past him with a cursory glance and follow Bowen to the base of the waterfall. There is a brief, animated conversation between them; then Hugh approaches the cliff-face and begins to climb. He makes swift and easy progress until his upward path is blocked by the overhanging ledge. By this time the professor, following more slowly in his wake, has reached a long, smooth section of rock. Hugh is shouting something, gesturing with his hands, his voice lost in the rushing of the water. Finally he seems to turn away from Bowen in disgust. He resumes his climb, works his way around the overhang and on up to the hidden section above.

Looking back later on this moment, Donald will find it impossible to say precisely what happened, whether a foothold gave way beneath Hugh Mortimer as he tried to find his next step, or whether something else caused the cascade of loose stones that fell towards the professor from above. What he sees is the sickening sight of Caradoc Bowen sliding off the cliff-face, clutching at a last desperate handhold, losing his grip and slipping almost gracefully into the violent downward rush of the waterfall. It is only a matter of seconds before Donald is there waist-deep at the edge of the pool, clinging with one hand to a sharp-edged rock, desperately lunging, missing, lunging again, unable to reach the professor in time. In the end he can only watch helplessly as Bowen's lifeless body is swept away downstream.

Ty Faenor

JULIA IS AWAKE late into the night, her chance of peaceful sleep destroyed by images of a drowning man. Less than half a day has passed since she drove away with Hugh from Three Devil Falls with Caradoc Bowen's body laid out in the back of the car, leaving Donald alone in the wilderness. The events at the waterfall are imprinted vividly in her mind, Donald's desperate efforts to reach Bowen, Hugh joining him at the riverbank, helping to pull the lifeless body out of the water, Julia somehow calmly directing their futile attempts at resuscitation. In the end, there was nothing they could do but carry him back down the valley, the famous professor reduced to a slight bundle of cold, damp, empty skin and bone, his eyes unseeing, all his knowledge vanished from the world.

Hugh is the one who has borne the brunt of what happened, taking charge of Caradoc Bowen, all the gruesome banality of it. He dropped Julia at Dyffryn, then drove away in the Land Rover with the professor's body wrapped up in an old oil-stained blanket.

There was a phone call from him later, telling her he had taken care of everything, there would be no need for her to speak to the police. A cousin of Bowen's in his home town of Dolgellau would handle the funeral arrangements. Hugh had spoken to the chaplain at Jesus College, and a small service would be held in the college chapel as soon as it could be arranged, though Hugh made it clear he would not go to it. He has done more than anyone could have asked, and Julia is grateful for that. She tells herself she will drive over to Ty Faenor, try to find a way to talk to him properly, though she hardly knows what she will say to him.

As she creeps to the top of the stairs, she hears her mother stirring in the room next door, on the verge of waking from some troubled dream. 'Is that you, Dai? Where have you been?'

'It's only me, Mam. Go back to sleep.'

Julia sits down in the kitchen with pen and paper, begins writing a note to Donald, explaining everything to him. She has promised to stay with her mother for another couple of days before heading back to Oxford on Tuesday night. She will call him as soon as she gets home. It seems a thin and inadequate means of communication, but she will not try to see him again in Rhayader, where she feels beset on all sides by people who know too much about her, who are watching her every move.

Now she can hear the creaking of her mother's footsteps on the floorboards above. She finishes more hurriedly than she intended, seals the envelope, writes Donald's name on the front. First thing in the morning, she will drive down to the Black Lion and leave the note with Olwen, who can be relied upon to make sure he gets it before he leaves.

DRIVING ACROSS THE wooded lower slopes of the Cwmhir valley, Donald winds down the windows, lets the cool air flow over him as he tries to make some sense of where he stands with Julia Llewellyn. What should have been the best thing to happen in his life has been followed only by death and destruction. The note she left for him, with all its uncertainties, the things she did not say, offers no useful evidence as to her true state of mind. There is the promised phone call, and whatever the future may bring. For now, it is best to remove himself from the confusion, to find some wide-open space where he can clear his head and be on his own.

An interminable hill brings him down at last into the hamlet of Abbeycwmhir with its small and diverse collection of buildings, a pub, a parish church, a Victorian gothic mansion. He leaves the car at the side of the road near the river, then walks out across an expanse of muddy green fields strewn with the broken remnants of Cwmhir Abbey. A smooth marble slab marks the traditional burial place of Llywelyn ap Gruffydd, Prince of Wales, who died by the treachery of the Mortimers in December 1282. His body was laid to rest here in holy ground as the White Monks sang a mass for his soul.

More than a century later, the poet Siôn Cent came down from the hills with an English price on his head as the spiritual architect of Glyn Dŵr's rebellion, finding refuge in the simpler guise of a Cistercian monk, Brother Siôn of Cwmhir. According to Caradoc Bowen, it was here at the abbey that Siôn composed the Song of Lailoken, the poem that became the professor's greatest obsession. In his mind's eye, Donald tries to raise up the shattered walls, join up the massive bays of the once-imposing nave, but his imagination fails at the task. This seems a lonely place, oppressed by its sense of lost history, the weight of the silence in the depths of the valley.

A small plaque tells something of the history of the abbey. Donald's mild interest soon turns to an intense curiosity.

THE BUILDING WHOSE RUINS ARE SEEN HERE WAS ESTAB-
LISHED IN 1176 TO HOUSE A MONASTIC COMMUNITY THAT
WAS DRIVEN OUT OF THE CWMHIR VALLEY A DECADE EAR-
LIER BY HUGH DE MORTIMER, EARL OF HEREFORD. THE
SITE OF THE ORIGINAL MONASTERY, FOUNDED IN 1143 AT
THE EASTERN END OF THE VALLEY, IS NOW OCCUPIED BY
THE MANOR HOUSE OF TY FAENOR.

He does not allow himself to stop and think, in case he should
change his mind. From where he has left the car, it is a walk of perhaps a mile along the course of the river with rough pastures rising
to tree-lined escarpments on the right and left. There is a north-
ward turn on to a narrow lane, not much more than a track heading through a tunnel of foliage, then over the river and on between
thick hedgerows opening out to gently sloping water-meadows on
the farther side. A sharp left-hand turn brings him face to face with
the seventeenth-century manor house of Ty Faenor, a substantial
three-storey structure: the Welsh seat of the Mortimer family.

Having ticked away a slow minute waiting for a response at the
front door, Donald walks around to the back, where he finds Hugh
Mortimer leaning against a wooden fence in torn blue overalls
stained with mud and engine oil, drawing deeply on a cigarette.

'It's the archaeologist,' he says, betraying no surprise, and Donald can tell from something in his voice that he has been drinking.
'What can I do for you?'

'I've come to ask if I can have a look around your house.'

Hugh's smile has a faintly acerbic edge. 'Are you thinking of
buying the old place?'

'No, it's not quite my style. I'm more interested in what's underneath it.'

'So you would be. And there was I thinking you might at least name a good price.' Hugh stubs out his cigarette, pushes himself away from the fence and heads in the direction of the back door. 'You'd better come in.'

They walk up a short flight of steps into a crooked entrance hall, then through to a spacious drawing room with a frayed old French sofa and armchairs arrayed in front of a wide brick fireplace filled with congealed grey ash. Hugh takes a whisky bottle and two heavy crystal glasses from a shelf.

'Drink?' Donald nods his assent, watches as his host adds a generous measure to each, hands him a glass and points him towards an armchair. 'I'm curious, how long have you known Julia?'

Conscious of Mortimer's eyes on him, Donald settles himself carefully into what must once have been a lavish woven upholstery. 'We met at Oxford. I was a student at St. John's.'

'An old flame?'

'No, that's not it at all. We hardly knew each other back then.'

'But you know her now?' Hugh drinks half of his whisky, stares down into the glass. 'Are you having an affair with my wife?'

Donald's reply will fall well short of answering the question, but he holds his nerve. 'Do you think I would have come here, if I was?'

'That would be a bold move, certainly.' Hugh smiles grimly at this, and it seems to Donald that he makes an abject figure, standing there radiating an aura of tobacco and alcohol and some less tangible thing, broken dreams or frustrated ambition. 'So, perhaps you would like to tell me why you're suddenly so interested in my property?'

Donald takes a sip from his glass, sets it down on the wooden floorboards. However poor the remaining card in his hand, this is the moment to play it. 'I think something important was once buried here.'

'What kind of thing?'

It is pure instinct that has brought Donald to Ty Faenor; he has no idea at all of what he might expect to find. 'I can't say for sure, but it's related to the Cistercian monastery that once occupied this site. I've read that it was one of the Mortimers who forced the monks to abandon it.'

Hugh sits down on the armrest of the sofa. 'Ah yes, the unfortunate Cistercians. I'm afraid my family did them no favours at all. Are you familiar with the noble history of the Mortimers, Lords of the Welsh March?' His irony is reinforced by a faint expression of disdain. 'It was my own ancestor, Hugh de Mortimer, who drove the monks out. They returned a few years later to build a new abbey on a site a mile to the west. When that building was destroyed in turn, bits of it were used in the walls of this house, which always struck me as a double injustice.'

'Have any traces of the monastery been preserved here at Ty Faenor?'

Hugh gives him a long, searching look, then empties his glass, gets abruptly to his feet. 'There is something I can show you. I suggest you drink up—you might need it.'

Back in the entrance hall, a heavy batten door with ornate black ironwork is opened to reveal a set of brick steps falling away into the darkness. 'The house was completed in the 1650s,' Hugh says, 'with three upper storeys and a basement floor for the servants and the kitchen, which we are about to see. Another forebear of mine, Sir John Mortimer, drew up the plans and was the first to live here.'

Donald remembers the name from Caradoc Bowen's journal article. 'The book collector?'

'That's far too simplistic a label,' Hugh says. There is a hint of impatience now in his voice. 'John Mortimer was a devout Catholic who took his inspiration from his faith. He made it his mission to find and preserve what had been lost in the dissolution of the monasteries in the sixteenth century. There were manuscripts, certainly, but also many religious artefacts that he had collected on his travels.' Hugh does not expand on this comment, instead picks up a large electric torch that has been left just inside the door. 'I'm afraid we'll have to make do with this,' he says. 'We were flooded down here recently, and we haven't been able to get the power back up.'

By the time they step down on to the brick floor of the cellar, they have reached a surprising depth below ground. There is a powerful smell of damp, a waft of chilly humid air. Hugh scans the torch beam back and forth, revealing heavy stone walls and a high ceiling festooned with wires and pipes. The space around them is reverberant with the sound of dripping water, the creaking of timbers above their heads, a strange metallic clicking and scratching from some distant recess.

They walk on into the shadows, Hugh lighting the path ahead as best he can, revealing a profusion of antique domestic debris: wooden boxes full of mildewed papers, brown bottles still half-full of dark liquids, a rusted mechanical device with springs and levers that looks like an old animal trap. Donald counts ten paces to the farther wall, where they stop in front of a broad, deep recess in the crumbling brick.

'This is the original kitchen fireplace,' Hugh says. 'When my grandfather first came here sixty years ago, he installed a modern kitchen on the ground floor, and moved everything upstairs with the intention of having this chimney blocked up. One of the workmen was laying a row of new bricks when he accidentally put his hammer through the back wall, uncovering a disused passage running down behind the chimney.' Hugh plays the torch beam over a small square door set into the back of the fireplace. 'As far as we can tell, the passage was sealed up during the original construction of the house. This door was added in my grandfather's time.'

'I assume you know what's on the other side?'

'Yes, only too well. When I was eight years old, I got myself shut in there overnight.' Hugh speaks as if this might have been a deliberate accomplishment, an obscure rite of passage for younger members of the Mortimer family. 'I had only the rats for company, and then the pitch darkness, after my batteries ran out. But I take it you're not scared of the dark?'

Far from being afraid, Donald is busy finding his archaeological bearings, computing the probable ground level in the seventeenth century versus the twelfth. There is a heavy bolt, rusted but easy enough to slide, and the door yields to a few sharp tugs. 'I'll need to borrow the torch,' he says.

Rather than the expected muddy tunnel, the beam illuminates a set of stone steps leading down into the darkness. Donald notes the quality of the dressing, the squareness of the edges and the snugness of the joins: the hallmarks of a master mason. He is forced to crouch low through the door, then descends a dozen steps to a flagstone floor submerged in several inches of water. Ahead of him is a long narrow chamber supported by a series of perfectly executed Romanesque arches. Matching them instinctively to the familiar architectural sequence, he decides that they must predate the early English gothic with its pointed lancet style: this stonework is at least as old as the mid-twelfth century. At the far end of the chamber, a series of long stone receptacles have been pushed up against the walls on either side.

Donald feels the water seeping into his boots, but also a quickening of his heartbeat as he steps through the first of the arches into what can only be the crypt of the old Cistercian monastery. According to the story told by Giraldus Cambrensis, Geoffrey's attempt to reach his new bishopric at St. Asaph ended prematurely in or around 1154, the generally accepted date of his death, at 'a small monastery then recently established at a place called in Welsh *Cumhyr*'. If Giraldus's tale is to be believed, Donald has found the burial place of Geoffrey of Monmouth.

For now, he holds his excitement firmly in check. Crouching down next to one of the stone vessels in the confined space at the far end of the crypt, he lifts off the heavy rectangular lid and brings the torchlight to bear on the contents. The beam illuminates a tangled collection of bones in varying shades of darkened ivory. He notes the narrow and graceful radii and ulnae, the more substantial femurs and humeri, a quantity of dislocated metacarpals and metatarsals. There is a skull there, too, perfectly intact. The other coffins yield similar results.

Donald stands up and takes a step back, troubled by an unsettling awareness that all is not right. His former mentor John Evans, describing a similar discovery made long ago, had an apt phrase that comes back to him now. *The smaller bones from the hands and feet were sprinkled throughout, like the seasoning in a stew.* The fact that the remains are in such disarray is a sure sign that they have previously been turned out and carelessly put back. Most tellingly of all, there are no grave goods of any kind, none of the religious artefacts that would be expected in monastic burials of the medieval period, when monks were typically sent on to the afterlife with the emblems of their religious status. There is no question at all in his mind: some time in the past eight hundred years, these coffins have been plundered by thieves.

Hugh is waiting for him at the top of the steps leading down to the crypt, his expression impossible to read in the dim reflected light. 'Did you find what you were looking for?'

'No, unfortunately not.' It seems audacious, to say the least, to suggest that one of the sets of human remains lying below may belong to Geoffrey of Monmouth, and to prove it will be impossible. In any case, there is no question of sharing his theory with Hugh Mortimer. 'But the crypt is a remarkable thing. Why has it been kept so quiet?'

'My grandfather always said whoever was buried in there should be left in peace, and I suppose I agree with that.' There is a surprising earnestness now in Hugh's voice. 'It was presumably what our ancestor intended when he built the house.'

Donald's mind is racing now. 'Do you know if he ever removed anything from the crypt?'

Hugh gives a strange, bitter laugh. 'Sir John was a passionate collector, certainly, but I haven't heard that he was a grave-robber.'

By the time they emerge into daylight in the main hallway of the house, Hugh Mortimer seems entirely sober, his cool reserve fully restored. 'Please give my regards to Julia,' he says, as he ushers Donald in the direction of the front door. 'Just in case you happen to see her before I do.'

Divitiae Grandes Homini

RRIVING LATER THAN usual at the riverside offices of the Oxfordshire County Archaeology Service, Donald finds a surprising tumult for a Tuesday morning, with a team just heading off to a dig on the site of a new housing estate at Didcot. Officially, he should be going with them. He tries to slip through to his desk unnoticed, but Tim Watson is waiting there to ambush him.

'Sorry to disturb your peace and quiet,' Tim says, 'but there are two things you might want to know about. First, the revised bone-dating results have come in from King's. They sampled skeletons at the top and the bottom of the pile, and got the same date, plus or minus. Late second to early first millennium BC, that's what I'm hearing. Paul Healey won't be best pleased. Secondly, there was a call from one Dr. Rackham at the Bodleian Library. It sounds as if she would very much like to speak to you.'

Donald takes a moment to absorb these presumably unrelated messages. 'Thanks, Tim. Why don't you head down to the site with the others? I'll try to join you later on.'

Margaret Rackham is waiting as promised in front of the Old Bodleian, next to the bronze statue of the Earl of Pembroke. Despite her claims to the contrary, she is hardly inconspicuous, wrapped up in a bright red overcoat, her thick grey hair disarrayed by the wind gusting relentlessly around the courtyard.

'I'm very pleased to meet you, Donald,' she says. 'I dare say you have far better things to do than slog all the way across Oxford in a howling gale, just to see me.'

'The pleasure is mine.' Donald finds himself warming straight away to the unsuspected irreverence of the distinguished Bodley's Librarian. 'I was supposed to go to a building site near Didcot power station today. This is better.'

'Well, I am glad to hear it. And I am so very sorry about what happened in Wales. It must be very hard to take.' What might have been a mere platitude is given greater eloquence by a quality of directness in Margaret Rackham's speech, a deep intelligence and sincerity in her surprisingly bright blue eyes.

'It has been a very strange few days,' Donald says.

'Yes, for all of us,' the librarian says, 'but for you more than most, I imagine. May I suggest we walk somewhere, rather than go back indoors to the Stygian gloom? And then perhaps you would tell me what happened at the waterfall. I have had only a brief sketch of it from the chaplain at Jesus College, who spoke to Hugh Mortimer after the accident.'

They strike off down Catte Street towards Radcliffe Square, heads bowed down into the wind as Donald recounts the bare facts of the accident. Dry leaves are swirling in the gutters, greyish clouds scudding overhead.

'It's a pity you had to witness it,' Margaret Rackham says. 'But if he had to go, I am glad he went out in such style, like a character in a poem. He would have wanted that.' She glances curiously at Donald. 'How did you come to know Julia, by the way?'

For a strange, disorientating moment, Donald is not quite sure how to answer the question. What comes first to his mind is the room at the Black Lion, the feeling of Julia's body against his. 'She once helped me out in a game of Scrabble,' he says.

'I imagine she would be a powerful ally in that game,' the librarian says, smiling. 'When she came to see me about the Siôn Cent manuscript, I did try to warn her there would be trouble, and now I cannot help feeling responsible for what has happened.'

They walk in a slow loop around the Radcliffe Camera, then find a table in a café housed in what was once part of the church of St. Mary the Virgin. Here they find the familiar Oxford incongruities, gothic windows and medieval rib vaults overhead, the hissing of steam and the smell of coffee, the murmuring of erudite conversation, a random tinkling of teaspoons and chinking of cups. The librarian raises an imperious hand to a brooding waitress who seems to recognise her, breaks from her reverie and bustles over to take their order.

'Well now,' Margaret Rackham says, when the waitress has gone, 'I expect you're curious about the letter I mentioned on the telephone.' She hands him a small white envelope addressed to her at the Bodleian Library. It is imprinted on the back with the return address of the Black Lion Inn. The badly smudged postmark shows that the letter was processed the day before at Rhayader post office. 'When it arrived this morning, I had not yet heard the news, so as you may imagine it struck me a little strangely at first.'

Donald opens the envelope to find a single folded sheet of writing paper covered with a small and ornate script.

My dear Margaret,

Though many years have passed since we last found common cause, it is without hesitation that I turn to you now for assistance. This will doubtless strike you as a moderately premature and perhaps indeed a shocking thing to speak of, but I have reached an age at which such precautions become necessary.

I write to request that, in case of my untimely death, you will look to the proper disposition of my books held at Jesus College and especially to the preservation of a certain manuscript that is already in your care, namely, the poetry book of Siôn Cent containing a series of bardic verses collectively entitled the Song of Lailoken. I trust you will remember it well, for we have spoken of it many times in the past. Without question, it is one of the most important Welsh manuscripts ever to have crossed the threshold of the Bodleian Library. Should you wish to find someone to advise you on the interpretation of this remarkable work, there is one young scholar, the Oxfordshire county archaeologist Donald Gladstone, who has come to understand its true significance.

In closing, may I also urge you to remember the wisdom of Lucretius in matters of life and love and death, *divitiae grandes homini sunt vivere parvo aequo animo*.

Yours in friendship,
CARADOC BOWEN

Donald finds the librarian looking at him with an intense but kindly scrutiny. 'He had very few friends later in his life,' she says. 'It seems that you became one of them.'

'I'm not sure I could make such a claim. I had only met him a couple of times.'

'First impressions were always important to Cranc Bowen.' Margaret Rackham smiles sadly, sending deep wrinkles radiating across her cheeks.

'Do you know how old he was?' Donald says.

'I don't think anyone can answer that question. Cranc's indeterminate age was part of the aura he liked to wrap around himself. I can, however, confirm that he was young once.'

The coffee arrives, delivered by the same intense-looking waitress. Margaret Rackham takes a sip, grimaces into the cup. 'Since you haven't asked, I should tell you, in the interests of full disclosure, that Caradoc Bowen at one time confided in me as a close friend, almost more than that. It seems an odd thing to say now, but Lucretius was the subject of a long-running debate between us. I am a classicist by training, you see, and Cranc knew his Latin poets well enough. I was never very fond of the philosophy of Titus Lucretius Carus, being perhaps of a more stoic than an epicurean disposition, and so he would always make a point of quoting him to me, looking for something we could both agree on. One day he came up with a promising line, *Quod siquis vera vitam ratione gubernet, divitiae grandes homini sunt vivere parvo aequo animo,* "But if one should guide his life by true principles, man's greatest wealth is to live frugally with a contented mind." You might say it started out as a sort of private motto between us, but in the end we adopted it almost as a creed, as a way of saying we would never be together, romantically speaking, that instead we would each try to live a joyful life of the mind. Does it surprise you to hear all of this?'

'A little, yes.'

'Of course that was all very many years ago, before his obsessions got the better of him. Speaking of which, I've been meaning to ask you, Donald, whether Bowen ever told you about his dreams?'

'I hardly knew him well enough for that.'

'I'm afraid none of us knew him well in recent years. I had forgotten about the dreams until fairly recently—until Julia came to

see me, in fact. Cranc once described to me how a voice would sometimes speak to him in his sleep, telling him of a violent death that
was to come to him. He said there were vivid images as well, almost
too life-like for an ordinary dream.' Margaret Rackham pours milk
into her coffee and stirs it with a teaspoon, stares distractedly at the
tiny whorls and eddies on the surface. 'In the old days, it seemed to
be of no real consequence. There was even a time when he used to
joke about it to me. He would say he had the advantage over most
people, because he knew precisely how he was going to die. But later
on I think it became quite distressing to him. He stopped talking
about the dreams, though I don't think they ever went away.'

'Did he tell you any of the details?'

'Yes, as a matter of fact he did. He said there was a particular
kind of death in his dreams—he called it the threefold death. It
was always one part of this triple death that happened to him. He
saw himself living wild in the forest, crushed by falling rock. Or
attacked with sharpened sticks as he tried to cross a bridge. Does
this mean something to you?'

Donald feels a small icy finger creeping up his spine. 'The threefold death is a common motif in Celtic mythology. The prophet
Lailoken is said to have predicted his own death by stone, stake, and
water, and the same theme was captured in the Song of Lailoken.'

'Yes, I remember those lines very well. *Belak-neskato she was named,
the death-wielder . . . Threefold life she promised me, and threefold death.* It always
seemed to me that there was something strange and fascinating in
the way Siôn Cent introduced this terrifying murderous woman, as
if she had crawled out of some gruesome underworld. It seems odd
to say it, but that's who Cranc thought was speaking to him in his
dreams. It was the death-wielder who told him how he was going
to die.'

'I had no idea it had affected him quite so deeply,' Donald says. He feels deeply saddened by the thought of what Caradoc Bowen was forced to endure, the bitter loneliness of his obsession.

Margaret Rackham leans back in her chair, looks him steadily in the eye. 'There's another aspect of this that you might find interesting. Cranc told me he often heard the sound of water in the dreams, a rushing, raging torrent. He said it was water that would kill him in the end. Does that strike you as a little strange?'

'I'm not quite sure what you're suggesting,' Donald says, though her insinuation is clear enough. He remembers something now, Bowen at the Black Lion, leaving his room in the small hours. Did he experience a dream of dying that night, then go out into the storm to post a letter he had written to Margaret Rackham?

'The self-fulfilling prophecy is a well-documented phenomenon in psychology. It is a prediction that causes itself to become true by means of a positive feedback between belief and behaviour. I do have to wonder, Donald, if he killed himself. In a court of law, one might be forced to introduce his letter as *prima facie* evidence.'

All Donald's instincts rebel against this idea; of all the explanations for Caradoc Bowen's death, it is the one he least wants to believe. He can still picture it in the sharpest detail, the moment when the professor slipped from the rock. There was a cascade of stones from above, enough to cause him to lose his footing. If he had wanted to jump, he would simply have jumped. 'No, I don't think that can be true,' he says. 'It would make no sense at all. He was only thirty feet from the top of the waterfall. It was everything he wanted, his ambition of almost half a century, to climb up there and see Glyn Dŵr's lost valley for himself.'

It was a simple, tragic accident, this is what Donald tells himself, though another unsettling thought comes to him now. From where he was standing on the cliff-face, Bowen might have been able to see that the way up was too steep, that it would be impossible for him to get to the top, to reach the highest part of the valley where he hoped to find the place where Glyn Dŵr fought his last battle.

The librarian holds him for a moment in her shrewd gaze. 'Well, perhaps he was still haunted by the ghost of Belak-neskato, who-ever she was. Meanwhile, we must honour Cranc's wishes, and do what we can to take care of his books. I shall first need to make some arrangements by telephone. Would you kindly meet me in his rooms at Jesus College in, say, an hour's time?'

    ▨   ▨   ▨

JULIA HAS SPENT the morning cleaning the upstairs rooms, con-centrating on the details, leaving everything spotless and shining. When she was younger, growing up alone with her parents, she used to think of the farmhouse as a member of the family, a watchful elderly uncle with its own bluff, reliable personality, always to be treated with respect. Something of this feeling returns as she goes about her work; there is some comfort in the thought that she is helping to ease the old house into this quieter new phase of its long and arduous life.

When she comes back down to the kitchen, she finds her mother briskly sorting and organising, working with a fierce determina-tion to take control of her domestic world. Every pot and pan has found its appropriate shelf, every ladle and spoon its proper hook. Dai's favourite corner has been tidied up, his drawing things put away, his fleece-lined slippers no longer there on the floor next to the chair.

Cath Llewellyn takes off her apron, comes over to the kitchen table. 'Sit down and talk to me for a moment, before you rush off.'

'You're not making it any easier,' Julia says, pulling up a chair.

'Don't be thinking I'm going to fall apart without you, my love.' There is a combative note in her mother's voice. 'I always used to tell your father when he wouldn't stop talking, I'd give anything for a bit of peace and quiet. I suppose it would have been simpler just to send him out to the shed.' They share a knowing glance, then burst into laughter at this perfectly drawn image. If Dai were here with them, he would be laughing the hardest of all.

'I've been meaning to tell you,' Julia says, when they have fallen silent again, 'Ralph Barnabas offered to help out on the farm, if you need it.'

'That's thoughtful of him, but I don't want to hear any more fussing about how I'm going to manage. My life is going to be simple enough from now on. It's you I'm more worried about.'

'I'll be fine.'

'Of course you will, my dear, and I'm the Queen of Sheba. Have you thought about what might happen next?'

Now they have reached the crux of it, but Julia has no good answer. 'I just need to get back to my ordinary life,' she says.

Her mother looks at her dubiously. 'I'm not sure what's going to be ordinary about it. Will Hugh go back to Oxford as well?'

'I have no idea. We haven't discussed it.'

Cath Llewellyn smiles wearily, reaches for Julia's hand. 'I'm guessing it might all depend on your archaeologist friend. Well, you'll do what you must do, my love.'

※　※　※

WALKING INTO THE study that Caradoc Bowen made his own for half a century or more, Donald is shocked by the quality of blankness and absence in the cold, musty air. Bowen's secretary, who has unlocked the door for him, seems uncomfortable being in the room at all.

'I worked with him for nearly forty years,' she says. Her formidable presence is much reduced, her face drawn in severe lines that speak of a staunch refusal to betray her true feelings. 'It's hard to believe what's happened.'

'I am sorry, Mrs. Frayne.' There is nothing else to be said.

'Well, I'd best leave you to it. Dr. Rackham should be up soon.'

Left on his own, Donald paces over to the other side of the room, where Bowen's map of the old *cantref* of Maelienydd is hanging on the wall next to the fireplace. As he runs his eye along the dark contours of the valleys, he is filled with grim thoughts of cliffs and waterfalls, the professor's dreams of his own death.

Now there are footsteps outside the room, a murmur of conversation. Margaret Rackham comes bursting in, her bold presence dispelling all lingering ghosts. 'I hope I haven't kept you waiting? One doesn't like to spend too much time alone in the mausoleum.' She takes a thick envelope out of her bag and hands it to him. 'I think you might find this of some interest. It was waiting for me in my office, hot off the press, so I haven't had a chance to read it properly myself. I've sent a copy to Julia as well. Anyway, first things first. Help me with these, would you?'

Following the librarian's precisely delivered directions, Donald drags a stack of large plastic crates into the room, then separates them into three groups. 'It's a straightforward system,' she says, 'tried and tested on more than a few Oxford dons who are sadly no longer with us. Over here, books that should go to the Jesus College library or the Bodleian for proper cataloguing. Here, other items that may have a residual value to the university. And here, things to get rid of or donate to some worthy cause.'

Violet Frayne now reappears at the door. 'Do you have everything you need, Dr. Rackham?' she says.

'Yes, thank you, Mrs. Frayne. Perhaps you would like to stay here and keep an eye on us?'

'I'm afraid I don't think I could bear it, if it's all the same to you.' With this, the secretary turns her back on them and hurries out of the room.

'In which case,' Margaret Rackham says, 'I'm going to start with these awful old tea things, which have been in constant use for fifty years, if I had to guess.' A teapot and several heavily chipped mugs depicting Welsh churches and cathedrals are tossed unceremoniously into a crate in the third group. 'If you would start on the book-shelves, I'll see what I can do with all this paperwork on the desk.'

A fierce quietness falls on the room as Donald begins work on an impressive collection of history books, early editions of works by famous deceased authors, Myres, Stenton, Collingwood, Gibbon, Tacitus, Herodotus. After a while, he begins to see that the whole collection is arranged in a reverse chronological order based on subject matter rather than authorship, with occasional volumes shelved incorrectly as if to entrap the unwary reader, A. J. P. Taylor's *Bismarck* set alongside the *History of the Peloponnesian War*, Salway's *Roman Britain* next to Jacob's *The Fifteenth Century*. Donald's efforts to discern a pattern or code in these misplaced titles prove fruitless, however. In the end, everything goes to the Bodleian crates.

He has reached the end of the last shelf when his hand falls on a book that had been pushed back behind the others. The title is embossed in gold on a faded blue cloth cover: *Three Lives of the Poet*, edited by C. H. R. Bowen. He sits down on the corner of the desk and begins to read, finds a surprising dark poetry of war and death and futility, raw bardic verses that were made to be spoken from a hilltop in the wrenching aftermath of battle.

To red-sky hill we flew like arrows in the night
Through the lands of our kinsmen blighted by strife
The dark host behind us, blooded, blades eager in hand
Death's herald beckoning us with black-glinting eye.

To red-sky hill we came, it was where our world ended
They could not know how hard we would fight
A hundred spears in hand, hale and strong we held them
Death's herald beckoning us with black-glinting eye.

'Some of those poems are quite striking,' Margaret Rackham says, breaking a long silence. 'I persuaded him to publish them, though I rather think he would have preferred not to.'

'Is this his own work?'

'Cranc was always a bit mysterious about that. He claimed these were bits of old verse that just happened to be in his head, as if they were nursery rhymes he had learned as a child, even though he could not remember having done so. I'd like to take that book with me, if you don't mind. He never did give me a copy.'

Donald hands the slim volume to her. 'That's the bookshelves finished, anyway.'

'Which just leaves us with the store cupboard. Violet tells me it hasn't been much used in recent years, but I suppose we should have a look. You never know what skeletons we might find.'

Donald forces open the cupboard door, causing flakes of white paint to drift to the floor. Inside is a cramped, musty space fitted on three sides with heavy wooden shelving, leaving just enough room to walk inside. The shelves are filled with ageing stationery supplies, boxes of pencils, bottles of ink and other writing paraphernalia, stacks of yellowed, curling paper, an old manual typewriter.

'I should think we can just throw all this stuff out,' Margaret Rackham says.

'Just a moment.' Something pushed against the back wall catches Donald's eye, a large wooden chest with heavy iron bands and an elaborate lock. He crouches down to examine it more closely. The method of construction and the quality of the patina suggest that this object is at least a few hundred years old. Gently, he manoeuvres it out into the room.

'I think I know where this came from,' the librarian says. 'Cranc brought it back from Ty Faenor with the book collection. He promised me he would send it over to the Ashmolean.'

The chest opens easily enough, revealing several compartments containing a collection of religious objects, cups and chalices and chains, most of them so heavily rusted as to be almost crumbling to dust. There is a separate drawer in the bottom with a jumble of smaller artefacts, simple metallic crucifixes, some decaying fragments of cloth, several brooches and clasps of the type that might be used to secure a monastic robe.

'It's a sacristy chest,' Donald says, 'a place where vestments and religious vessels would be kept in a church or a monastery.' He has not forgotten what Hugh Mortimer told him about his antiquarian forebear and his collection of religious artefacts. 'If I had to guess, I would say it once belonged to Sir John Mortimer, the original owner of Ty Faenor house.'

Margaret Rackham breathes out slowly. 'And Cranc just stuck it in the cupboard and forgot about it? I must say, I'm not very surprised. If he didn't consider it interesting, he would have assumed that no one else would, either.'

'He was probably right to doubt its significance. These items are too far decayed to be of much archaeological value.'

'That's a pity. Shall we get it moved out?'

'I just want to check one thing.' Looking at the design of the chest more closely, Donald can see that there is something not quite right about the carpentry, the proportions of the top rail. 'We may yet be in luck,' he says. 'Chests of this kind often included secret compartments where valuable documents or other items could safely be stowed. Let's see what we can find.'

Running his hand around the inside of the rail, he is not surprised to find a small wooden key which, when depressed, allows him to open a small compartment built into the rim. Inside, there are several objects made of gold: a cross and bracelet, a jeweled chain, a ring formed of two delicate rosettes joined by diamond-shaped connectors. Donald cautiously picks up the ring and lays it in the palm of his hand.

The librarian takes out a beautiful antique silver magnifying glass, just as an ordinary person might pull out a handkerchief or a set of keys. 'Here, try this.'

Donald trains the glass on the larger of the two rosettes, which was presumably intended to face upwards when the ring was on the wearer's finger. There is a classic floriated border, then what seems to be a single stylised letter in the centre, though it is crusted with dirt and difficult to make out. He turns the ring over to examine the second rosette. There is a similar floral design around the edge and another single letter in the middle, which at first glance looks like a capital *N*.

'I have an idea of what this might be,' Donald says, 'but I'll need a second opinion.'

'We'll ask Violet to find a box for it,' Margaret Rackham says, 'and then you can run it over to the museum. I shan't come with you, though. I'll only slow you down.'

Twenty minutes later, Donald is sitting in the office of Dr. Elaine Standish, assistant keeper of the Anglo-Saxon and medieval collections at the Ashmolean. She is young, in her early thirties, with the wiry build of a distance runner and a faintly superior air of well-informed scepticism. Donald knows her only slightly, from a chance meeting at a symposium where she spoke with impressive authority on the archaeology of parish church graveyards in the English midlands.

'I wouldn't get your hopes up, if I were you,' she says. 'Ecclesiastical jewellery often turns up in medieval church burials, but bishop's rings are not the usual thing one stumbles across. What exactly is its origin, do you know?'

'Yes, I believe I do. It was removed from a Welsh monastic crypt in the seventeenth century by an overly zealous antiquarian collector.'

She raises an incredulous eyebrow. 'That's an impressively detailed provenance. Let's have a look, shall we?'

Donald opens up the small padded box and hands her the ring. 'It's not my area of expertise,' he says, 'but I've seen a similar design somewhere before.'

Elaine Standish turns it over to look at the underside, whistles faintly. 'Yes, I see what you mean,' she says. 'It is similar in some details to the ring of Ahlstan, ninth-century Bishop of Sherborne, which is now in the V&A. Ahlstan's ring seems to have been the archetype for a style that became very popular in the later medieval period. This looks like the real thing—it's one of the finest examples I have ever seen.'

'Can you make out the letters?'

'It needs some cleaning up, but I'm seeing a *G* and an *N*. No, perhaps an *M*. *GM*—does that mean something to you?'

'Yes, I think so,' Donald says. 'May I?' He cradles the ring delicately in his palm. 'I think what we have here is the episcopal ring of Galfridus Monemutensis—Geoffrey of Monmouth, Bishop of St. Asaph.'

THE SOUND OF a car pulling up in front of Dyffryn Farm fills Julia with a sudden foreboding. Opening the front door, she is relieved to see that it is not Hugh, but Ralph Barnabas climbing out of his rusty white Ford van. His pickaxe comes out with him, swinging at his side as he walks towards the farmhouse.

'I'll be starting work on the walls up in the top fields,' he says.

She feels a small surge of relief and gratitude. The news of Bowen's accident will be common currency by now in Rhayader, but it seems that Ralph has not come here to talk about it. 'It's good of you to help my mother out,' she says.

'No, I don't mind. I think it was hard for Dai to keep up, towards the end.' It is a familiar puzzled expression he has, squinting against the brightness of the afternoon sun. 'You'll be off soon, then?'

'They're expecting me back at work tomorrow.'

'I'm sure we'll be seeing you again before long.'

There is something too possessive in the way he says this, but she dismisses the thought. Casual conversation was never Ralph's greatest strength. 'Yes, I'll be back up in a couple of weeks.'

His gaze shifts awkwardly away from her. 'There's something I wanted to say to you now, before you go.'

Please don't say anything to me at all, this is what she wants to tell him; but then again, there is no reason for her to show him such disdain. He is not to blame for anything, apart from still having feelings for her. 'What is it, Ralph?'

'It got me thinking, that's all, what happened at the waterfall. There are some things you don't know about Hugh Mortimer.'

Julia would ask him to stop, to go away and leave her in peace, if she could bring herself to do it. 'Please just say what you have to say.'

Ralph stands there working the sharp end of his axe into the gravel. 'I know you went to speak to my dad about the accident, but he won't have told you the truth about it.'

'Why should he lie to me?'

'Because there are things you're not supposed to know.' It seems a prepared speech he gives her now, lines he has been rehearsing for fourteen years. 'I was the only one who was with him, you see, when he woke up in hospital, and that's the only time he ever said what really happened. He saw who it was, running away right there in front of him just as the explosion went off. There was no mistaking it, he said, Hugh Mortimer was the one he saw. I thought you should know, they could have your husband for murder if they could prove he was the one who set the fuse.'

Julia's first reaction is simple disbelief. 'You wouldn't have said something before, if you've known about it for so long?'

'That's because of a promise I made to my dad. He said it was just a mistake, he couldn't send a man to prison for it.' There is something cold and calculating in Ralph, the way he looks at her now. 'I want you to know what your man is capable of, that's all.'

Now she turns away from him and walks back into the house, slams the door shut behind her. Her mother meets her at the foot of the stairs. 'What did he say to you, love?'

Julia feels so utterly defeated, she hardly knows how to respond. 'Nothing you want to hear.'

Cath Llewellyn lays a hand on her daughter's arm. 'Don't forget, Ralph has loved you since you were seven years old. It's like your father used to say, you were always the one to bring them hovering around you, the brightest flame they ever saw. I don't think you ever really understood that.'

It is true, Julia has never viewed her life in quite this way before. She imagines shrieking black creatures in the air around her, the burned-out shells of those who have come too close.

In the end, she makes a more hurried goodbye than she intended, winds down her window and waves to her mother with a cheerfulness she does not feel as she drives off towards Cyncoed Lane. At the bottom of the hill, a left turn will take her towards Abbeycwmhir and the Ty Faenor estate. She turns to the right, in the direction of Rhayader and the main road to the south.

＊＊＊

SETTLED LENGTHWISE ON his sofa in the cottage at Iffley with the television on, Donald finds himself glancing frequently at the telephone, willing it to ring. It is rare for him these days to hear his mother's voice, but she comes back to him now with one of her gentle, proverbial admonitions: *A watched pot never boils, Donald, go and do something useful while you wait.* Margaret Rackham's envelope is there unopened on the table next to him, but he has no appetite for whatever glories of the Bodleian Library it might contain. For now, he is glad of the BBC and a rerun of a classic comedy, a pet rat on the loose in a seaside hotel.

It is close to midnight, and he is in the kitchen cracking eggs for an omelette, when the call finally comes. The third egg is a disaster. He abandons it at the side of the bowl, runs to his desk in the front room and picks up the phone.

'Julia? I'm glad you called.'

'I'm so sorry. It took me a long time to get home.'

Are you there on your own? Can I come and see you? This is what he wants to ask her, but does not. On the desk in front of him is a formal notice from the University of Oxford.

A Memorial Service will be held in Jesus Chapel for Caradoc Hywel Rhys Bowen, B.Phil. M.A. Oxf., Emeritus Fellow and

Tutor in Welsh History, Politics, and Literature, from 11:00 am
to 12:00 noon on Wednesday, 26th November.

'Will you go to the memorial service tomorrow?' he says.

She hesitates, and he curses himself silently for asking the wrong
question. 'Honestly, I don't think I can face it. I've seen a little too
much of that kind of thing recently. I could meet you afterwards, if
you like?'

Hearing the suppressed hope and expectation in her voice, he
feels a small surge of elation. 'I'll wait for you at noon at the college
gate,' he says.

'I'll be there,' she says. 'I promise.'

An hour later, Donald is still wide awake, turning through the
pages of Margaret Rackham's document with a growing sense of
excitement. It is a detailed description of manuscript TF 97B, the
poetry book of Siôn Cent, which has been stabilised by a team of
conservators at the Bodleian and then analysed in painstaking detail.
The authors begin by describing what has been revealed about the
provenance of the manuscript. Carbon dating carried out on the
first section, the parchment folios that have been badly affected by a
mould infestation, shows a surprisingly early date, within fifty years
of the end of the sixth century AD. Detailed analysis of these folios
has allowed some parts of the text that was originally inscribed
there to be deciphered. The fragments that have been recovered were
all written down by the same scribe, who freely announces his name
in a colophon on the very first page via a simple Latin formulation,
Cantigernus me fecit. At this point, the report makes a small digression
into the hagiographical literature.

According to Jocelyn of Furness, in his life of Kentigern (in
Latin, *Cantigernus*; in Welsh, *Cyndeyrn*) written in the late twelfth

century, this saint during his exile from the Brythonic kingdom of Strathclyde (circa 570 AD) travelled to Wales, where he
founded the Celtic monastery of Llanelwy—the church on the
River Elwy—as the Welsh still call the town of St. Asaph. Several converging lines of evidence lead us to the conjecture that the
earliest parchment section of the present manuscript is one and
the same as the 'book of Cyndeyrn' cited by the poet Siôn Cent
as a source, and that its author is none other than St. Cyndeyrn
himself. When appending his own bardic poems to the manuscript, Siôn bound them in as a separate section comprising the
higher-quality vellum sheets found in the latter part of the book.
His 'lost' ancient source was, as it were, hiding in plain sight in
the same set of covers, camouflaged by the devastating effects of
the penicillium mould.

Further analysis of the early pages has uncovered traces of
numerous texts written in Cyndeyrn's hand, together making a
rudimentary history of the early British kings. These materials
may be of some interest in their own right, although the extent
of the mould damage has unfortunately limited what we have
been able to recover. Transcripts and rough translations of what
remains are presented in an appendix to this report.

Prefacing these historical texts, and also written in St. Cyndeyrn's hand, is an unusual series of verses composed in an early
form of Welsh. The extensive fragments of this poem that we
have been able to read, together with its title in Welsh, *Cân Lailoken* (Song of Lailoken), indicate that this work is substantially
the same as the similarly titled poem written down in the later
(vellum) section of the same manuscript by Siôn Cent. Hence
it is apparent that the Song of Lailoken was first written down
not in the fifteenth century, as Professor Bowen supposed, but
somewhere near the end of the sixth century. Siôn Cent was not

its author, and the battles it describes predate the campaigns of Owain Glyn Dŵr by eight hundred years at least, prompting the intriguing suggestion that the poem offers a glimpse into a far older bardic tradition.

There are, however, some important differences between the two redactions of the poem, Siôn Cent's and the earlier version written down by St. Cyndeyrn. First, Siôn has cleverly rendered his text from the sixth-century Brythonic or primitive Welsh into a form of Middle Welsh that would have been comprehensible to people of his own time, while retaining many of the archaisms of the original. Of particular note in this regard is his choice to translate the name of one of the characters in the poem, rendered by the original scribe as *Arto-uiros* ('bear-man', suggesting a totem or epithet applied to one deemed to have unusual strength or power), as the more recognisable Welsh *Arthur*.

Secondly, the rousing final stanzas of the poem, beginning with the line (from Professor Bowen's translation) *Thus our champion fell to earth, not dead but deeply sleeping*, do not appear at all in the original version. This section of the text, we may suppose, is entirely Siôn Cent's own work, thereby lending support to Caradoc Bowen's assertion (which our analysis in no way contradicts) that Siôn intended to use his version of the poem as a call to arms to the men of Wales, urging them to rise up in support of Glyn Dŵr's rebellion.

It is almost too much to absorb at once. For now, Donald focuses his attention on the authors' comment that certain texts found in the manuscript form a 'rudimentary history of the early British kings' and 'may be of some interest in their own right'. He can only smile at the degree of their understatement. A glance at the translations in the report's appendix shows him that Cyndeyrn compiled a chronology of real and mythical kings, from Aeneas to Brutus to Androgeus and Tenvantius to Ambrosius Aurelianus and his brother Uther Pendragon. The obvious convergence with the early chapters of Geoffrey's *Historia Regum Britanniae* seems evidence enough to support Donald's idea that Geoffrey's ancient book (the work he claimed as his source for the *Historia*) and the book of Cyndeyrn both drew from some earlier common source that has since been lost. And yet there is another, more dramatic interpretation of the evidence, one that he is at first hesitant to accept, lest some flaw in his logic should bring the tower of speculation crashing down.

A noise from outside, the wind catching at the branches of the old yew tree in St. Mary's churchyard, brings Donald sharply back to the present. He closes the report, switches off the bedside lamp: not because there is any chance of sleep, but to make a quiet calm space for himself to think. As he lies there in the darkness in a state of intense awareness, he forces his thoughts back into their proper analytical track, examines his reasoning in almost painful detail. It is the episcopal ring of Geoffrey of Monmouth that finally seals the argument. This is the tangible proof he has hoped for, a physical object that connects Geoffrey to the original Cistercian monastery at Cwmhir. When the discovery of the ring is joined up with the findings in the Bodleian report and the story told by Giraldus Cambrensis, a plausible chain of events begins to emerge.

Geoffrey's ill-fated journey to his new diocese of St. Asaph ended prematurely at the Cwmhir monastery, where he died and was laid to rest along with his ring and his other tokens of office, as was the medieval custom. According to Giraldus, Geoffrey brought his precious ancient book with him on this final journey. It remained at the

monastery after his death, and was later taken for safe-keeping by
the monks when they were driven from that site by Hugh de Mortimer. The book remained in their possession, and eventually found
its way to the new abbey when it was built on a site farther west
along the valley. This is where Siôn Cent came upon it, this manuscript 'which fate has brought to my hand', when he went into hiding at the abbey more than two centuries later. He felt so intensely
possessive of it that he bound a collection of his own bardic poetry,
including his own version of the Song of Lailoken, into the back of
the same book.

The thought that stays with Donald as tiredness finally overtakes him is this. Far more than simply drawing on a similar tradition or a common source, the book of Cyndeyrn, the damaged
parchment section of manuscript TF 97B now held safely in the
Bodleian library, is one and the same as Geoffrey's ancient book in
the British language. It is the archaeological discovery of a lifetime.

'Be Thine Despair . . .'

OMING DOWNSTAIRS EARLY on this foggy Wednesday morning, Julia feels a true lightness of spirit, a sense of opportunity in the new day. She throws the kitchen windows wide open to let in the cool autumnal air, then picks up the phone and dials the number for Dyffryn Farm. It is still not quite dawn, but she can be sure that her mother will be up and about.

'Are you all right, my love? I was worried about you, driving all that way alone.'

'I've driven a car on my own before,' Julia says, smiling. Her mother's proprietorial tone is as comforting to her now as it would have been irksome when she was seventeen.

'Well, I'm glad you called. I wanted to let you know, Hugh came over here yesterday evening.'

Julia's equanimity is dashed away to nothing. 'What did he have to say?'

'Not very much, honestly. I think he just wanted to check in on

me, make sure everything was all right. He told me he was planning
to drive back to Oxford first thing this morning. You haven't seen
him, I suppose?'

The question leaves a sharp splinter of anxiety. Julia glances
reflexively out of the window to the front of the house. 'No, I haven't
seen him.'

'I don't know everything that's happened between you, my dear,
but you do need to speak to him.'

'He knows where to find me, if he wants to talk.'

There is a real exasperation now in Cath Llewellyn's voice. 'Call
me back, would you, when you've had a chance to think about it
properly?'

After she hangs up, Julia can only think of getting out of the
house. She grabs her coat from the hook by the door, picks up her
coat and gloves, runs out of the back door and down through the
cool misty garden to the shed, wheels her bicycle out through the
garden gate and rides off towards the Woodstock Road and onwards
to the offices of Oxford University Press.

It is comforting to see the familiar face of Colin, the security
guard, eyeing her with a curious, kindly smile as she walks through
the door. 'Up with the larks today, Miss Llewellyn? It's good to have
you back.'

It is not yet eight o'clock, and the office is almost empty. As
Julia's colleagues begin to drift in, she finds herself quietly fending
off the sympathy of those who feel obliged to come and talk to her,
to find the right words to express their regret at her father's death.
Perhaps they also know about Bowen's accident, though she has no
idea how far that news has travelled; certainly no one mentions it
to her. She feels a vague sense of dishonesty as she gives simplified,
inadequate answers to their well-intentioned enquiries.

Going through her backlog of post, she finds a thick envelope from the Bodleian, photocopies or other materials she has requested from the library. She sets it to one side, unopened. There is a large stack of word-slips that have come in while she has been away. To distract herself, she begins browsing desultorily through them, but the earnestness of the OED's readers, usually a source of amusement and appreciation, is jarring to her today. She cannot find the proper degree of enthusiasm for the challenges of etymology and form, the nuances of definition and derivation; the meaning of *oppugn* versus that of *depreve*, the variant legal and grammatical usages of *elide*.

Just as her attention begins to wander, her eye falls on a copy she has made of the Song of Lailoken, marked up with her detailed linguistic annotations. The poem brings back unwanted images from Three Devil Falls, the sound of Bowen's voice shouting above the noise of the cascade, but still she feels drawn to pick it up. Speaking some of the verses back to herself in the original Welsh, she finds that they flow along with a pleasing kind of mellifluous intensity.

> Cyntaf yn nheml y ffurfafen, cylch cywrain cewri
> Safai ein gelyn yn syberw ar ei charreg echryslon
> Belak-neskato ei henw, triniwr angau
> Yn tywallt gwaed gwŷr a laddwyd deirgwaith
> I dorri syched y sarff wen, deirgwaith sychedig
> Nen-ddiafol a ddug gylch y cewri o'r gorllewin pell
> I wneuthur yma'r lladdfan gysegredig.
>
> Arthur a roes fywyd i'n gwroldeb
> Ymladdodd â'i dau amddiffynnwr, Araket a Madarakt
> Mân-dduwiau paentiedig ar y ddaear, ni thyciodd eu nerth ddim
> Y cyntaf a deimlodd lafn Arthur, dihangodd yr ail o'r maes

Yna ein ceimiad a lamodd yn uchel a bwrw'r hudoles ddu i lawr

A'i rhwygo o'i heisteddfan erch.

Sylw ni roddais i sgrechfeydd ei holaf anadl

Einioes driphlyg a addawodd im, ac angau triphlyg

Fy nhranc y gwenwyn ar ei thafod.

It is only the outlandish names in the poem, *Belak-neskato* and *Araket* and *Madarakt*, that stick harshly in her throat, as if they belong to some distant, alien tongue. She underlines them boldly in red pencil.

There is a quiet tapping, and she looks up to see her friend Otto Zeiss standing next to her desk. 'Good day, Julia,' he says, in his precise, Viennese way. 'I am glad to see you back, but now it seems you are already very deeply embedded into some problem or other.'

'Your timing is uncanny as always, Otto,' she says, smiling, as she hands the poem to him. 'I can't think of a better person to help me. I would like you to tell me, if you can, what kind of words these are, and in what kind of a language.'

Otto sits on the edge of her desk while he skims the text. 'This is very interesting indeed,' he says, smoothing a hand over his bald scalp. 'So far, I have no idea about it at all, but I will see what I can find out.'

An hour later, Julia is staring out of the window at a one-legged robin hunting for worms on the rain-dampened paving slabs. She tries to put herself inside its tiny head, to imagine its sharply delimited view of the world, the process of avian cognition that sends the signals to make it hop, peck, flutter, hop. She wills it to take to its wings and fly, but to no avail. The unsheltered sky holds no attractions to rival this glistening concrete expanse populated by defenceless, wriggling invertebrates there for the taking.

'You are finding something remarkable to look at outside?' Otto is back there at her desk. 'Well, my brain has only room for one remarkable thing at once, and so you must tell me about it later. For now, I have been thinking about your interesting poem, and perhaps I have found a kind of answer to your question. If you would like to hear it, I will try to explain.'

Julia pulls up a second chair, ushers him into it. 'Tell me,' she says.

'So, we start with the strange name *Belak-neskato*. Evidently its origins are not to be found in Welsh, nor in any language that is familiar to me. Something in its construction made me think first of those languages that are not of Indo-European origin, as is well known in the case of Basque and certain relatives and precursors. Most paleolinguists would agree that the Basque tongue, which is still widely spoken in the border regions of Spain and France, is the only surviving language of western Europe that is derived from the original languages of the Paleolithic. You are familiar with that story, of course.

'Unfortunately, this took me straight away beyond my area of expertise, but a check against the standard Basque dictionaries offered some interesting clues, and so I went to my bookshelves and dug a little deeper, to an extinct language called Aquitanian which is a precursor to Basque. A number of inscriptions in Aquitanian dating from classical times have been translated by reference to their Basque equivalents. From this limited lexicon, two particular correspondences seem to have some possible relevance. I have written them down for you here.'

With evident relish, Otto unfolds a sheet of paper from his pocket and lays it down on the desk.

Aquitanian *belex*, *-belex*, *-bel(e)s* = Basque *beltz*, *bele* = black, crow, raven

Aquitanian *nescato* = Basque *neska* = girl, young woman

'From this, we are perhaps permitted to conjecture that the construction *Belak-neskato* is an ancestral form of the Aquitanian *Belex-nescato*, which could be translated as "black-woman" or perhaps rather the more symbolic "raven-woman". As to this lady's protectors, *Araket* and *Madarakt*, I have so far found no linguistic clues at all, beyond the plausible assumption that they are rendered in the same ancient language.'

'What if I asked you to make an educated guess, Otto?'

He smiles at her now. 'Yes, I was hoping you would ask. If I were to make a hypothesis based on the context in which the words are used, I should say that they refer also to totemic creatures, companions to our raven-woman. Perhaps these are the names of other totems that we find commonly in the Basque mythologies, symbols of strength and courage such as the boar and the stag. As to how these errant words ended up in the middle of a medieval Welsh text, I could not possibly say.'

Julia waits until Otto has wandered dreamily back to his desk on the other side of the office before dialling Donald's number. He picks up the phone straight away. 'Julia, I'm glad you called—'

'Listen, there's something I wanted to ask you, about the poem.' Suddenly she is talking to him in an excited rush, about Otto Zeiss and Basque and Aquitanian, animal totems from the distant past. 'How can it be, Donald? How could such a language ever have been spoken in Britain?'

He is calmer, more measured. 'It's perhaps not as unlikely as it sounds,' he says. 'Most archaeologists agree that the island of Britain was repopulated after the last ice age, perhaps ten thousand years ago, by peoples who travelled up the western coasts of Europe from the glacial refuge of north-eastern Iberia. They would have spoken a language that was an ancestor to modern Basque. It was possibly the

main language spoken in Britain before the arrival of Celtic speakers
in the early centuries of the first millennium BC.'

'Can you make some sense of it, though? How these words got
into the poem?'

There is a silence now on the line. 'Not quite,' Donald says at
last, 'though I do perhaps have an idea. I'll see you later on, OK? We
have a lot to talk about.'

THE CHAPEL OF Jesus College is a narrow, chilly space that seems
to sap away what little warmth there is in the late autumn air. Its
bold Victorian pavement of marble, alabaster, and glazed encaus-
tic tiles sweeps through a broad gothic arch to the chancel and
the vivid stained glass of the east window. Next to the altar, the
young college chaplain, earnest and clean-cut, waits patiently as
the late arrivals find their seats. Donald sits there quietly surveying
the congregation, trying hard not to shiver in the sepulchral cold.
He exchanges a glance with Margaret Rackham, who has a bench
to herself at the front beneath the chancel arch, then casts his eye
along the triple ranks of upright wooden pews on either side. Along
with a few people of Caradoc Bowen's own generation, frail and
inscrutable old men who have the look of former spies and civil
servants, there are many familiar faces from the current Oxbridge
establishment, incumbent professors of poetry and history side by
side with younger aspiring dons for whom Bowen was of interest
mostly as an immovable object blocking their upward path through
the scholarly hierarchy.

There is a touch on Donald's shoulder from behind, a whisper
in his ear. 'I was hoping I might find you here.' It is an unmistakable

American voice. He turns his head, catches Lucy's knowing smile. 'I have something to show you,' she says. 'I'll see you outside afterwards, OK?'

The chaplain clears his throat, looks meaningfully from left to right, gathering their attention, waits for the hush to fall; then launches into a short, surprising oration, his delivery slowed and softened by the expanded syllables of the south Welsh coast. 'Caradoc Bowen was not a religious man. Not, at least, in the sense that one typically uses the term in my profession. Those of you who knew him will no doubt believe as I do that he would not thank me for sharing with you the traditional pieties of occasions such as this.' There is a faint murmuring now from the pews: of agreement, or perhaps of modest indignation. 'Professor Bowen was above all a remarkable scholar, an unparalleled authority on the bardic traditions of the Celtic peoples and their influence on wider British and European history, prehistory, and culture. He wrote widely on the medieval poetry of Wales and the role of mythology in shaping the national character and political fate of that country. In his younger days, he was a noted oratorical poet, and indeed I trust I do not overstep the mark in suggesting that, had he been born into another age, we might have seen Caradoc Bowen in the company of the greatest Welsh bards, Aneirin and Taliesin, Iolo Goch and Siôn Cent, whose work he so much admired. And so, with the late professor's bold poetic spirit very much in mind, I am honoured to introduce to you the distinguished Bodley's Librarian, who will give a brief eulogy on behalf of the university.'

Margaret Rackham stands up without ceremony, walks up to the pulpit and pauses for a moment, gathers her thoughts, then looks her audience unflinchingly in the eye. 'Today I would like to share with you one aspect of Caradoc Bowen's life that has almost been

forgotten,' she says. 'When he was a young man, he first made his
name with a dramatic performance at the national Eisteddfod, the
Welsh literary and cultural festival, which in that year was held
in his home town of Dolgellau in the shadow of the sacred peak
of Cadair Idris. In that famous recital, he rejected utterly the neo-
Druidic pomp and ceremony introduced by Iolo Morganwg in the
eighteenth century in favour of a quiet, captivating, song-like delivery of his own poetry as well as certain verses that he said were of
more ancient origin than his listeners could begin to comprehend.'

She pauses now, smiling faintly at the restive congregation.
'Cranc Bowen lamented the irremediable decay and ultimate loss of
the Welsh bardic tradition, a process whose beginnings he dated to
the century following the failure of Owain Glyn Dŵr's revolt. Along
with this tradition went a great body of Celtic verse reaching back
at least to the time of Aneirin in the fifth and sixth centuries, and
possibly a thousand or more years before that. Only a few poor fragments were captured in medieval times in the Great Books of Wales.
As far as Cranc was concerned, this was the precious lifeblood of
the Welsh nation. He saw it as his role to preserve what was left of
it in any way he could.

'Bardic poetry was Caradoc Bowen's heart and soul, and so it
might seem curious to memorialise him through the work of an
Englishman, and a Cambridge scholar to boot.' Now there is an
unmistakable nervous shuffling in the audience, but Margaret Rackham continues undaunted. 'Thomas Gray was nevertheless a poet
he greatly admired, and I can think of no more fitting memorial
than the extract I shall read to you from one of Gray's own favourite
works, the final lament of a Welsh bard pursued by the soldiers of
Edward the First as they crushed the life from a nation whose resistance had fallen with its hero, Llywelyn ap Gruffydd, now laid to rest

beneath a marble slab in the solitude of Cwmhir. Though close to his own end, Gray's forsaken prophet foretold a time of reckoning for the English crown, a new dawn and a brighter day for his own people.

> 'Fond impious man, think'st thou yon sanguine cloud
> Raised by thy breath, has quench'd the orb of day?
> To-morrow he repairs the golden flood,
> And warms the nations with redoubled ray.
> Enough for me: With joy I see
> The different Doom our fates assign.
> Be thine Despair, and sceptred Care;
> To triumph, and to die, are mine.'

> He spoke, and headlong from the mountain's height
> Deep in the roaring tide he plunged to endless night.

※ ※ ※

LUCY IS THERE at Donald's side as they file out of the chapel into pale crepuscular sunshine filtering through persistent layers of morning fog. She is over-dressed and theatrical in a flowing blue floral dress and elaborate matching shawl, drawing curious stares and admiring glances from the younger dons who are milling around in the quad.

'That was a strange choice of reading, don't you think?' she says. 'Almost as if our distinguished professor had intended to kill himself. You don't suppose that's what happened, do you? I heard you were there to see it.'

'I really don't want to talk about it, Lucy.' Beyond his ordinary irritation at her, Donald is still thinking about Margaret Rackham's eulogy. 'Why are you here, anyway? You didn't even know him.'

'Paul Healey told me about it.' She gives him her best sardonic smile. 'He said I'd probably find you here.'

Donald takes a moment to interpret what she has just said to him. 'I didn't know you were on speaking terms. It's only a few weeks since you humiliated him on national television.'

'Actually I had dinner with him in Cambridge last night. Paul has asked for my advice on Devil's Barrow, now it's come out that his bone dates are all wrong. You'd be surprised, we have become quite good friends.'

Seeing the mordant look on her face, Donald decides to leave this cryptic statement alone. It is not the first time he has thought her capable of getting her way by sleeping with Paul Healey. 'Let me ask you something, Lucy. Imagine that your magical chalice-woman lived at the beginning of the first millennium BC, as the dating now suggests. What sort of a culture do you think she inhabited?'

He is gratified to see a look of surprise flicker across her face. 'I didn't know you cared. But since you ask, I think she lived in the final days of the matrilineal society that once held sway throughout Old Europe. Each tribe had its powerful female shaman, the triune mother goddess made manifest on earth, venerating the cup and the cauldron as symbols of the magical power of the earth to bring forth life and sustenance. She was, in my humble opinion, one of the last great shamans of a vanishing culture.'

'But don't you think it's possible the culture had somehow become debased by that time—the triple goddess as a three-headed white serpent, to be propitiated by human male sacrifice in the form of a gruesome threefold death?'

'Which was the hallmark of the incoming Celts, not of the indigenous Britons. Clearly she was the victim, and not the aggressor.'

Lucy's complacency is infuriating, goading Donald to challenge her; but he refuses to give her the satisfaction. Instead he leads the way to a quieter corner of the quad. 'I need to ask your advice about something else.'

She lays the back of her hand against his forehead. 'Are you feeling quite well today, my love?'

'You know it's a last resort for me.' He smiles at her, despite himself. It is a very long time since he last had a normal conversation with Lucy, least of all on a topic of mutual intellectual interest. In the past, they would always end up arguing, passionately in the early years, acrimoniously later on, as they came to despise one another's point of view. Now he is badly in need of her professional advice. 'I've been thinking about the work you did in the Balkans.'

Her laugh is entirely disarming. 'That's not quite what I expected you to say. What is it you want to know?'

In their early years together, Lucy began an ambitious study of the deep-rooted folkloric traditions of eastern Europe, desperately (in Donald's view) trying to glean some support for her matriarchal vision of Old Europe. What he remembers most, apart from her constant over-interpretation of the evidence, is the surprising robustness of the traditional tales that were handed down by local storytellers, the themes that were preserved with remarkable consistency over time and space.

'Something Margaret Rackham said about Bowen and his ancient verses at the Eisteddfod got me thinking about the bardic system, and how well it could work over a long period of time. If a poem was passed on orally from bard to bard for many centuries before it was first written down, would you expect the original text to be faithfully preserved, or would it diverge into something quite different?'

Lucy looks at him now with a shrewd little twist of the mouth.

'Well, as any good public schoolboy could tell you, one example of what you've just described is the poetry of Homer, the *Iliad* with its story set in the Trojan War. There's an entire body of theory that explains how phrases such as *eos rhododaktylos*, for rosy-fingered dawn, or *oinops pontos*, for wine-dark sea, hew to a certain metrical pattern that makes them easier for the poet to compose and for others to remember. So the answer is yes, it is possible for specific lines of text to survive over many generations. Is that what you were hoping I would say?'

'I was curious, that's all.'

She grabs dramatically at his sleeve. 'I do hope you'll tell me if you're on to something big, Donald? Give me proper credit in your book?'

'I'll be sure to send you a signed copy.'

Lucy seems cheerful now, almost radiant. 'Talking of which, I'd like you to tell me what you think of this.' She hands him a thin brown envelope. 'Whenever you have a chance.'

'I'll have a look later on, I promise.' Donald puts it in his jacket pocket. He glances at his watch; only a few minutes to his rendez-vous with Julia.

Lucy seems momentarily distracted by something behind him. 'And now all of a sudden you seem to be in a hurry. I was hoping you might buy me a drink.'

'I'm supposed to be meeting someone.'

'Well, some other time, dearest. And by the way, how is your friend Julia? I thought she might be here.' Lucy does not wait for an answer, takes him by the arm as they walk, leans in close. 'I've been thinking, Donald, you're far too caught up in your Arthurian world. Julia is like Guinevere to your Lancelot, and we all know what happened to her in the end.'

▨ ▨ ▨

FROM FORCE OF habit, Julia follows the route she would usually take to the Bodleian, the cut-through from the Lamb and Flag pub to Parks Road, then down past the library to the Radcliffe Camera, finally looping back along Brasenose Lane to Turl Street and the entrance to Jesus College. Just as she arrives, there is a steady stream of people filing out of the college grounds. Leaving her bicycle propped up against the outside wall, she runs a hand through her hair, walks up to the gate.

She catches a glimpse of Donald in the corner of the quad, facing away from her, deep in conversation with a woman who looks immediately familiar. It takes her only a second: this is Lucy Trevelyan, whom she saw on the BBC talking about Devil's Barrow and the magical chalice. She can see straight away that there is an intensity and an intimacy in the way Donald is speaking to his ex-wife. Lucy hands something to him, smiling, and he puts it in his pocket. Now she catches sight of Julia, holds her gaze for a long moment. There is a look in her eye that speaks unmistakably of ownership, of forbidden territory. And why should Donald not fall back into Lucy's embrace? She is an attractive, intelligent, imposing woman who knows everything there is to know about him; whereas Julia, by comparison, hardly knows him at all. Her claim on him is one night of love in a seedy bedroom at the Black Lion Inn. Lucy takes Donald by the arm, smiling, whispers something to him as they walk.

Julia ducks around the corner out of sight, gets back on her bicycle and pedals away through the familiar streets, keeps going until she finds her way to Christ Church and the path that leads across the meadow to the river. She sits there for a long time on a bench by the water, watching the mallards gliding in perfect arcs, wondering how it would feel to go through life like that, contentedly circling.

⊞ ⊞ ⊞

DONALD WAITS AT the gate for half an hour before knocking on the door of the porter's lodge.

'Can I help you, sir?' The hoarse voice carries with it an aura of mild irritation and stale pipe tobacco.

'Do you have a phone book, by any chance?'

'Ah yes, I see,' the porter says, emerging partially into the daylight. He is wearing a faded blue jacket and matching tie emblazoned with the Jesus College crest, silver stags on green. 'You're not the first person to be properly stood up at the college gate.' He gives a low chuckle as he turns back into the dim interior of the lodge. 'Be with you in just a second.'

Donald finds the phone number under Mortimer, makes a note of the address and the house name: *Cair Paravel*, one of the self-important donnish residences of north Oxford.

'I don't suppose I could use the phone?' he says. 'It's a bit of an emergency.'

The porter taps the side of his nose. 'I shan't tell,' he says. 'Be my guest.'

There is no answer at the Mortimer house. Donald walks back up to Broad Street, finds a wooden bench near the entrance to Trinity College and sits there watching the passing cyclists. After a while, he takes Lucy's envelope out of his pocket, fumbles it open with chilly fingers. There are two folded pages inside, the introduction to a book: *The Last Prophetess*, by Lucinda Macaulay Trevelyan. She begins in her trademark hyperbolic, provocative style.

The British soil is finally giving up her deepest secrets. The recent unburyings at Devil's Barrow have bequeathed to us a magical chalice whose like has never before been seen, the arms of its protector still wrapped about it, the wracked remains of her guardsmen piled beneath her in the burial mound. We picture this woman as the earthly interlocutor of the mother goddess, perhaps the last of the great prophetesses of Old Europe. Are we not entitled to ask whether her magic is still alive in the landscape of Britain?

He screws the sheets of paper into a ball. A little while later, with a small twinge of guilt, he smooths them out as best he can, tucks them into the back of his notebook. As he does so, something falls out from between the pages, a drawing done in pencil, the one Julia gave him at Trevethey Mill. The picture shows an imposing cliff-face in a landscape of desolate Welsh hills. This is Craig-y-Ddinas, where Arthur and his knights have been sleeping for centuries in a cave deep within.

There was something Donald's father said to him when they were talking about his book. *If only we could get back to the original names of things, names that are settled deep into the bones of the landscape, we would learn a great deal about our distant ancestors.* He digs in his bag for the geological map, traces his finger from the lower part of the valley to the top of the third cascade. Two inches to the right, just beyond the densely massed contours that indicate the face of the eastern cliff, is something he did not pay much attention to when he first looked at the map. It is the symbol for an ancient long barrow or burial chamber, and written next to it in a small antique script is its traditional local name: a name that is unremarkable in its way, but now fills him with a sudden exhilaration.

He tears out a blank sheet from his notebook, pauses to gather his thoughts, pencil in hand, then sets down the most careful letter he has ever written in his life. At the end, he adds detailed directions and a small hand-drawn map. He tucks the sheet inside Lucy's empty envelope, reseals it and writes Julia's name on the front, then runs back to his car parked at Gloucester Green, drives up to St. Giles and on in the direction of north Oxford.

The Old Way Down
from the Mountain

IT IS A comfort to Julia, seeing Emma Speedwell pulling her battered blue Volvo into the gravel drive shared by the two neighbouring houses. Emma, always in a hurry, shouts a cheerful hello as she runs inside. Turning the key in the front door, Julia sees a letter there, a brown envelope pushed half-way through. She opens it, takes out a single sheet of paper filled with Donald's precise, angular handwriting. The first line hits her like a blow to the stomach. *I looked for you at the college gate, but perhaps you changed your mind.* What follows is a beautifully crafted letter telling her of Geoffrey of Monmouth and his bishop's ring, his desperate final journey and the fate of his ancient book, the true meaning of the verses that are written there. The letter closes with a vision that first came to Donald at Trevethey Mill, when Julia was drawing a map of the Welsh mountains on a paper napkin. In his mind's eye, they are walking hand in hand as they climb up to a high valley and look out together on a view described in an old poem they both know by heart.

Within minutes she is in the car, reversing out of the drive. As she pulls away, she glimpses something in the rear-view mirror that stops her short, freezes all logical thought. Hugh's Land Rover is coming along the street from the other end. The traffic light is amber changing to red at the Woodstock Road as she makes the turn too quickly, heart pounding, then drives away as fast as she dares, cutting through the back streets, heading out of Oxford to the north and west.

By the time she reaches the Cheltenham road, making slow but steady progress through the banks of fog still lying heavily across the Thames valley, the crisis is over. In time the traffic thins out, the fog lifting as the land rises gradually to the west. The Oxfordshire farmland slips easily by, the faint green haze of the winter wheat now making its mark on the November fields.

She turns on the radio, tunes to the BBC playing music that is twenty years old, a nostalgic soundtrack of her youth. There are sharp memories of her final summer living at Dyffryn; then a song that transports her to the springtime of her first year at Wadham College, not long after she and Hugh first met. They are walking hand in hand along a narrow, penumbral space between high college walls. Somebody familiar is coming towards them from Radcliffe Square, a tall boy with reddish-brown hair, good-looking in an awkward, gangly way. She feels the colour coming to her cheeks, thinks to disengage her hand from Hugh's, but it is too late, the gauntlet must be run. It is only a couple of weeks since she was with Donald at the Ashmolean Museum, listening to his earnest explanations of cartouches and scarabs and hieroglyphs, then to the Randolph for tea, all the while sensing him falling for her, basking in the glow of his evident admiration. She cannot recall precisely what was said as they passed each other on Brasenose

Lane, perhaps just an uncomfortable greeting tersely returned, then
on with their lives.

⬚ ⬚ ⬚

DEEP INTO THE lower reaches of the Wye valley beyond the Welsh
border, Donald finds himself in the state of heightened awareness
that sometimes comes upon him when he is alone on a country road.
This sensation grows to a spine-tingling intensity, as if some old
British magic is speaking to him along the quiet, meandering lanes
and the hills and dells where the morning mist is still gathered. He
looks out on the passing landscape with a rare depth of understanding, sees banks and ditches and sunken lanes with their own stories to tell, hedgerows anchored by ancient pedunculate oaks with
twisted arms outstretched towards the sky. Fragments of poetry are
in his head, *On a green hilltop we made our stand, spear-tips trapping gold of
sunset . . . At nightfall we fell like thunder down the slope . . . think'st thou yon
sanguine cloud has quench'd the orb of day? . . . To-morrow he repairs the golden
flood, and warms the nations with redoubled ray.* Then the outskirts of a
small town, drab grey cottages, a petrol station and a pub, enough
to banish this temporary enchantment. His thoughts return to the
present world, and to Julia Llewellyn, and to his hopes for what the
day might bring.

It is early afternoon by the time he reaches the old drovers' track
that leads alongside the river to the base of the falls. It seems a
far different place, the river much diminished, flowing smooth and
tranquil over the rocks, a fine mist veiling the upper slopes. He gets
out of the car, takes out the map to orientate himself, then looks in
vain for a path that might lead up to the higher ground on the eastern side of the valley. The slopes on either side are steep and topped

by treacherous crags. As far as he can see, the only way forward is along the river to the lower waterfall, where he climbed up with Julia and Caradoc Bowen.

He walks a little way back along the track, follows it around a few bends of the river. Finally, as he is retracing his steps to the car, he sees what he is looking for. Ahead of him, the track seems to come to an abrupt end as the valley narrows towards the waterfall. Now he can see that it would at one time have turned sharply to the left and crossed over the bridge that once spanned the river at this point. The original path can still be traced on the far side, running up a hillside now thickly clad with bushes and small trees. This is the old way down from the mountain. He walks over to the riverbank and sits down with his back against one of the ruined stone footings of the bridge. For now, there is nothing for him to do but wait.

JULIA CAN SEE the Land Rover five cars behind her. The first rush of panic soon subsides to a quieter, more rational anxiety. She might have expected it: seeing her drive away from the house at speed, Hugh has followed her all the way from Oxford. In any case, there is no way to avoid this confrontation. Ahead of her now are long, straight stretches with nowhere to stop, then a series of sharp bends as the road climbs up to the higher ground of the Forest of Dean. He is gaining steadily on her, and making no attempt to keep out of sight. She puts on her indicator, dives off to a steep, narrow lane on the right. It is signposted to a village they once visited on a long-ago happy weekend spent exploring this landscape of secret woods and hills. They always meant to come back.

She drives no more than two hundred yards, pulls over in a narrow passing-place and waits there with the engine running. She can see him in her wing mirror as he makes the turn and accelerates down the hill. He pulls in close behind her with a sharp squeal of brakes, squeezes the Land Rover on to the grassy verge and opens the driver's door. Instead of coming to her car, he crosses the road to a place where a gate leads to a farmer's field. For an anxious few seconds, she stays where she is, wondering if she should simply drive away from him, try to lose him in the country lanes. Instead she turns off the engine, gets out and walks over to join him.

'Ralph Barnabas told me he was going to speak to you,' he says, almost casual, not looking at her. 'Is that why you're running away from me?'

She feels wrong-footed by this statement, thrown off balance. 'I can hardly believe it's true, what he said to me.'

'Why is that? Because you don't think I'm capable of such a thing?'

Looking at her husband leaning against the gate, the grim set of his face as he stares out across long sloping fields left fallow for the rough winter grazing, Julia sees someone who has become a stranger to her, who has nothing to do with the Hugh Mortimer she used to know, so bold and strong and inspired with the noble possibilities of the world. She opens her mouth to speak, but he holds up his hand.

'No, don't say anything, please just hear me out.' He turns away from her, the words coming now with a quiet intensity. 'I don't think you ever quite understood about Caradoc Bowen. He was such an extraordinary figure in the early days, not like anyone else we had ever seen. We were young and idealistic and determined to change the world, and he spoke to us as if we had some grand purpose in life. He filled us with the romance of the Welsh rebellion, told us Owain Glyn Dŵr was Arthur returned to the aid of his people, and he alone knew how to find the place where Glyn Dŵr fell in battle and crossed over to the otherworld. If Bowen chose to cast himself as a modern-day Merlin, who were we to say he was not?'

Hugh looks sharply at Julia, as if to see if his words have meant something to her. His face is pale, his eyes rimmed with red. 'Then he offered us his greatest challenge. Where, he said, was the next Arthur, the next true champion of Wales? He was looking at me when he asked that question. He was looking straight at me, with my anger and my self-confidence and my pedigree coming all the way from Glyn Dŵr. He saw something in me, and I responded to it. If he was prepared to put his faith in me, how could I not believe myself to have all the makings of a Celtic hero from the past?'

'It was what you wanted for yourself,' Julia says. 'Bowen didn't force you—'

'No, he didn't force me into anything,' Hugh says, 'but he had a real power over me, and he knew how to use it. The plan to dam the Cwmhir valley was the catalyst he had been waiting for, the perfect opportunity to exploit my anger. He told me about the deal my father had made years before with the British government, trading away the future of the Ty Faenor estate in return for some tawdry aristocratic favour. Then he said it wasn't just Ty Faenor, that Dyffryn Farm would also go under the flood.'

Julia knows this story from Caradoc Bowen, but the thought of it still has the power to shock her. 'So the two of you told my father about it, but said nothing to me.'

'Should we not have spoken to him?' In the look Hugh gives her now, so full of unconscious condescension, she reads the whole story of their marriage. 'Dai met us at the Black Lion with Gareth Williams and some of the local Plaid Cymru men, all of them fired up to do whatever was necessary to stop the construction of the dam.

Some people thought your father was the ring-leader, but it wasn't that way at all. He was the voice of reason, telling us we should steer clear of violence. We should remember what happened at Cwm Tryweryn, how the bombing there hadn't done any good in the end, Capel Celyn still went under the flood. But Bowen was a captivating speaker, and Dai stood no chance against him. I remember your father took me to one side just before he left, tried his best to calm me down. He said he had been like me in some ways, in his youth, and he knew what was burning inside me. But I was not strong enough to walk away from Caradoc Bowen.'

Hugh falls silent for a moment, concentrates on flexing the toe of his boot against the metal gatepost. 'In the autumn, we met up in secret at Ty Faenor with Gwyn Edwards, one of the Plaid Cymru men who had been at the Black Lion. It was agreed that Gwyn would work from the inside. He was used to handling explosives from the time he spent with his father in the slate quarries, and he was already working for Dafydd Ellis as a junior engineer. It would be a simple matter for him to stay late one evening and set the whole thing up. All I had to do was stand outside and keep watch. But something went wrong, he was standing over the dynamite when it went off.'

It is a cruel trick of Julia's imagination, the colourful picture that paints itself: the destructive effect of explosives on the human anatomy, a wave of blood and body parts. She finds herself clinging to the only redemptive thought she can find, that her father was not responsible for what happened. He tried to prevent it, and he would be bitterly dismayed if he knew she had ever thought otherwise.

Now she would like Hugh to stop, but there is a relentless quality to his catharsis. 'Just as Gwyn Edwards was being blown to pieces, and just as Stephen Barnabas was having his legs ripped from his body, I was running away like a helpless coward. The explosion knocked me off my feet, and I picked myself up, and I ran off along the railway tracks without so much as a glance over my shoulder.'

The way he is looking at her now, it seems he is waiting for some reaction. What is there to say? She has been trying to get to the truth of what happened, and now she knows, and does not want to know. For a bewildering moment, she wonders what crime her husband has just confessed to. Accomplice to something: murder, attempted murder, manslaughter? She speaks quietly to him now. 'I'm not sure what you expect from me.'

'I expect nothing at all,' Hugh says. 'Perhaps you'll want to go to the police. I've never had the courage to do it myself.' He pushes himself away from the gate, turns to face her. 'But I hope you will find a way to forgive me.'

Julia has an image in her mind now, the young Hugh waiting there in the darkness by the railway tracks, so arrogant and self-assured and entirely in thrall to the messianic visions of Caradoc Bowen. In the end, the logic of it twisted cruelly back on him. He was torn down by failure, by the insupportable weight of Bowen's expectations. What Julia feels mostly is a sadness that comes from knowing what he might have achieved, but did not; what their marriage might have been, but was not.

And there is another picture that she will not easily forget, a rushing waterfall, rocks sent tumbling down from above, Bowen grasping desperately at a last handhold before falling to his death: Caradoc Bowen, who was the only person alive who knew for sure what Hugh's role had been. She cannot say precisely what he is guilty of, but at this moment, more than anything else, she wants to be far away from Hugh Mortimer. As calmly as she can, she walks back across the road to her car.

'Please, Julia,' Hugh says. 'Stay and talk to me.'

'I'm glad you told me the truth,' she says, 'but I need to be on my own.' She closes the door and starts the engine. As she drives away from him, around a bend in the lane and out of sight, she has a final glimpse of him in her mirror, standing there transfixed as if she has just sent him into oblivion.

⬚ ⬚ ⬚

SITTING ALONE AT the riverbank, Donald turns his thoughts back to Caradoc Bowen, to this brilliant and troubled man who in some respects got things so right, yet also came to get them so terribly wrong. He pictures Bowen as an intense young scholar in the depths of his research on Siôn Cent, immersing himself in the treasure trove of previously unstudied manuscripts that he found at Ty Faenor. It is not hard to imagine his excitement at coming across Siôn's poetry book full of his unknown early work: and its crowning jewel, a poem written in a strange, archaic form of Middle Welsh, the Song of Lailoken. Perhaps he felt some magical connection to Siôn Cent, a sense that it was his fate alone to discover these verses and make them known to the world.

Bowen wrote swiftly to Margaret Rackham with his first translation of the poem, not yet sure what it might all mean, but certain that he had found something of deep significance. His first mistake came early on. He took at face value the evidence of the manuscript, which seemed to tell him without a doubt that Siôn Cent was the author of the Song of Lailoken. Why should he not believe this, seeing the poem written out there in Siôn's own hand, with its heroic message that seemed so perfectly to match his own conception of this great Welsh bard? According to Bowen's interpretation, Siôn Cent was a prophet in the Merlinic tradition, seer of Glyn Dŵr's rebellion and a central figure in its early success. He created the Song of Lailoken as a means of burnishing his leader's

mythical aura: it was a poem to be read or sung aloud, to inspire
a renewed fervour in Welshmen's hearts. His verses were carefully
crafted to reinforce the popular mythology of the Celtic hero
cast in the mould of Arthur, the one who does not truly die, who
remains at the fringes of the mortal realm, waiting to return in his
people's time of trouble. To his impressionable Welsh audience,
Glyn Dŵr *was* Arthur returned as champion of the red dragon in
the hour of need.

In some essential aspects of his analysis, the professor was
entirely correct. According to the sober assessment of the Bodleian
Library report, Siôn Cent was indeed responsible for the final two
stanzas of the poem, the lines that Bowen declaimed so memorably
to Donald in his rooms at Jesus College. But Siôn did not write the
earlier verses of the poem, which were made at least eight hundred
years before his time. Far from being a Merlinic concoction on the
part of Siôn Cent to commemorate the battles of Glyn Dŵr, the
Song of Lailoken speaks of much older, deeper secrets than Caradoc
Bowen can possibly have imagined.

To come to a proper understanding of the poem, Donald must
reach all the way back to the latter years of the sixth century AD,
when St. Cyndeyrn established his monastery on the banks of the
Elwy river. At Donald's first meeting with Bowen, the professor
spoke of an old Welsh tale describing Cyndeyrn's encounter in the
forest with the poet Lailoken, who was once a bard in the court of
a British monarch of the Old North. Driven to the edge of madness
by terrible visions of a battle he had witnessed, Lailoken predicted
his own threefold death by stone, stake, and water. It is almost irresistible now for Donald to conclude that the Lailoken story is more
than a mere folktale, that it preserves an echo of real events: that
Cyndeyrn did indeed meet Lailoken on his travels, and committed
to writing a poem he heard the old man recite.

❖ ❖ ❖

WITH THE AFTERNOON drawing on, Julia finds herself trapped in a thick fog on the main road from Monmouth and the Welsh borders across the Vale of Usk. What little traffic there is has bunched up into a small convoy strung together by the sharp glow of red taillights. From time to time, the car ahead disappears entirely, forcing her to drive on alone inside a silent white shroud, doubting the reality of her surroundings. Every time she tries to speed up, the fog seems to gather itself anew, curling and eddying against the glass, filling the car with a cold pale light.

There is a prickling of anxiety now, a sense of natural forces arrayed against her. She counts the hours since she left Oxford, imagines Donald still waiting for her, hopes fading, as twilight falls across the valley. The sun breaks through at last, still well up above the horizon as she drives on past Abergavenny into the eastern fringe of the Black Mountains. She pushes up to seventy on the empty road that leads to Crickhowell and Brecon and finally to the narrower lanes that will take her up into the wilderness.

❖ ❖ ❖

DONALD FINDS HIMSELF pacing upstream towards the lower waterfall, back downstream to the ruins of the old bridge, ideas crowding in on him from the empty sky. The Song of Lailoken describes how the one called Belak-neskato in her death-throes laid a bitter curse on her adversary, the poet who calls himself the crab.

I did not heed her last-breath's screeching
Threefold life she promised me, and threefold death
My doom the venom on her tongue.

Margaret Rackham hinted at a connection to these lines in the poem when she spoke of Bowen's intense dreams of a kind of threefold death, his visions of being crushed by falling stones in the forest, assaulted on a bridge by an enemy wielding sharpened sticks, drowned in a raging flood. Thus Bowen's own death was also in a sense foretold: with his strange premonitory note sent to the Bodleian on the eve of the accident, he seems to have guessed that his time was near. Perhaps there is, after all, a thread that connects these three elusive characters, Lailoken and Siôn Cent and Caradoc Bowen. They were the successive inheritors of an ancient poem, and each in his own time became obsessed with these strange and troubling verses. Did each of them in the end also come to suffer his apportioned part of the threefold death? The prophecy of Belakneskato was fulfilled at last when Caradoc Bowen, the final victim of her curse, fell into the torrent at Three Devil Falls.

Donald sits down once more at the river's edge, tries to halt the irrational galloping of his thoughts. There is no place in his scientific world-view for avatars of an earlier age. Margaret Rackham described Bowen as suffering from a kind of psychosis: she thought his death was self-inflicted, an act of prophetic self-fulfilment. If he suffered from dark dreams of his own death, this was the unhappy result of his fixation on a poem that he came to believe had a personal, oracular meaning for him. If he lost his footing as he made a dangerous climb up the waterfall, this happened only because, in some final act of acceptance or resignation, he placed himself deliberately in harm's way.

❖ ❖ ❖

THERE ARE LONG shadows now from the line of hills to the west, making a strange light that begins to play tricks on Julia's senses.

Turning a sharp bend, she brakes suddenly at a fork in the road, certain that she saw the silhouette of a woman in a dark cloak standing there, a hand outstretched; but it is only the blackened fragment of a dead tree leaning across the verge. She stops the car, takes out Donald's map, tries to find her bearings. It is clear enough: a turn to the right will bring her on to the track that leads alongside the river to Three Devil Falls.

Now she is so close, something makes her hesitate. She gets out of the car and walks over to the tree. There is a strange sound in the air, something whispering from the rim of the valley, glancing off the folds and ridges, mingling with the wind and the rushing stream. It is a woman's voice, a simple phrase endlessly repeated, Julia's mother speaking to her along some magical southerly path through the Welsh bedrock from Dyffryn Farm. *Do what you must do, my love, do what you must do.* But now the words are changing, losing their benign intentions, and she is not so sure.

Leaning back against the trunk of the tree, she sinks her head in her hands, tries to shut out the insidious whispering, this malicious trick her mind has chosen to play on her. When all is quiet once more, what comes to her first is a memory of her father cursing at the kitchen stove, trying to light it with damp wood on a cold April morning: angry at her for the news he has heard from the treacherous Gareth Williams, that she has been seen in the company of Robert Mortimer's son. She remembers the look on his face, half-joking and half-serious in the intense way he had sometimes. He told her she should always try to take the right path, even if another way seems easier. Her mother was there in the room, turning her back on him. You were never quite so wise yourself, Dai Llewellyn, she said.

She plays through scenes from her past, imagines going the other way at every turn, where that would have left her now. Instead of leaving Donald standing outside the Randolph Hotel after he kissed her clumsily on the cheek, she takes him by the hand, walks on with him down Broad Street to a future without Hugh Mortimer. Instead of leaving him alone with Lucy Trevelyan at Jesus College, she walks boldly in through the gate. Instead of abandoning Hugh at the side of the road, she finds a way to go back to him, to repair the shattered fragments of their married life. Instead of getting back in her car and taking the right-hand turn, she goes to the left, keeps on driving until she comes to some new crossroads where she might hope to choose a path that leads to a simpler life.

❖   ❖   ❖

DONALD CAN HEAR a noise in the far distance, the humming of an engine. The more closely he listens, the more it seems to fade away. By now, he is almost sure that Julia will not come. He imagines her still at home in Oxford, ashamed, confused, remorseful perhaps, his letter disregarded: Hugh Mortimer there at her side, coolly avowing his undying love for his wife. Still, he will wait for her until the last moment, just in case.

It is Julia, in the end, who had the right instincts about the Song of Lailoken. When they met at the Randolph Hotel, she suggested to him that there might be some connection between the poem and Paul Healey's archaeological finds. At the time it seemed an impossible leap, to imagine that the remains unearthed at Devil's Barrow, the woman with her arms wrapped around a ritual chalice decorated with the symbols of stag, boar, and raven, the three-headed serpent, were somehow what the Song of Lailoken was *about*.

And yet there is now some real evidence that can be brought to bear. The dating analysis from King's College suggests the late second or early first millennium BC for the human remains in the barrow, and Margaret Rackham's team at the Bodleian has shown

that the Song of Lailoken is at least as old as the sixth century AD. If
the poem recited to St. Cyndeyrn was derived from a long-standing
Celtic oral tradition, it could be far older than this, as Lucy with
her Homeric insights has shown him. Is it possible that the poem
was learned by the bard Lailoken as a young apprentice, that it was a
story passed on to him from some earlier generation: then captured
for the first time in writing by St. Cyndeyrn, who heard it from
Lailoken in the forest?

Once the new linguistic evidence is added to the mix, the convergence that Julia originally proposed becomes harder to resist. Otto
Zeiss's plausible theory suggests that the alien words in the poem,
Belak-neskato and *Araket* and *Madarakt*, are the names of animal totems
taken from a language that was spoken in Britain when the first Celtic
peoples, contemporaries of the heroes of the *Iliad*, were exploring the
coastal Atlantic routes to the north. The Song of Lailoken carries
an echo of the forgotten time when they came into contact with the
descendants of the original post-glacial settlers, the indigenous Britons whose ancestors were the builders of Stonehenge.

There is a story here that badly wants to be told, a tale of the
terrifying raven-priestess dispensing death to her own people, thirteen male warriors chosen with special care to satisfy the gruesome
demands of the white-winged, three-headed sky god:

> Belak-neskato she was named, the death-wielder
> Draining blood of men three-times slain
> To slake the white serpent, three-times thirsting
> Sky-devil who bore the giants' ring from farthest west
> To make this hallowed killing-place.

The remains of Belak-neskato were discovered at Devil's Barrow,
still clutching the magical chalice on which her raven totem was

depicted with those of her twin protectors, the stag and the boar,
Araket and Madarakt.

> Painted petty-gods on earth, their strength availed them nothing
> The first meeting Arthur's blade, the second flew the field
> Then our champion leaping high struck down the black enchantress
> Tore her from her gruesome perch.

The warrior Araket fell at the sky-temple to the sword of the hero
Arthur, and was laid to rest alongside Belak-neskato whom he had
tried to save. Buried with him were the antlers of the great Irish elk,
which he had worn as a symbol of his unearthly power. Beneath
them in this mass grave were the bodies of the thirteen victims of
the threefold death. Madarakt escaped that day, but would return to
challenge Arthur in a final battle at the crooked vale.

▨ ▨ ▨

DONALD OPENS HIS eyes, sees Julia standing there looking down
at him with her beautiful, ironical smile. 'I hope I'm not too late,'
she says.

He climbs to his feet, disorientated, takes half a step towards
her. 'No, I'm glad you're here,' he says, reaching to take her hand.
'There's something I need to show you.'

The crossing is challenging but not perilous, a series of jumps
between the broken-down footings of the bridge. The path on the
other side is steep and tumbled with boulders, but they are able
to find a way up, scrambling through thickets of stunted ash and
birch. Soon they break out of the trees to a narrow ridge that climbs
steadily up the eastern side of the valley. The slope becomes gradually more sheer, but there is a firm footing underneath and a narrow

but well-defined path carved through heather now shading towards the dark brown of winter. This track can be seen curving up far ahead of them, summoning them to the higher ground.

By now they are walking in single file, distracted by the difficulty of the final pitch across the top of the valley wall. They come around a broad shoulder of the hillside to a place where the track splits in two. Above and to their left, a short, steep climb will take them to the very top of the cliff. Ahead of them, the full sweep of the valley at last comes into view, the river cutting and weaving its way past smooth-faced rocks the colour of blood, its jagged course making the shape of a wolf's-head smile as it finds its way down from the rim of the valley to the top of the uppermost waterfall, where Caradoc Bowen fell. The path in front of them opens up to a rocky ledge, a broad, tapering space shaped like an axe's blade beneath tall cliffs rising to great rounded sandstone crags glowing bright red in the light of the setting sun.

'Does it look familiar to you?' Donald says.

Julia comes to stand next to him, takes hold of his arm. 'It's like a scene from a fairy tale.'

He would not have thought to say it this way, but she has captured it perfectly. This is a view that has remained unchanged across the centuries, the same rugged landscape that was once described in a heroic tale of the red dragon pitted against the white, crossing stone circles and rivers and mountainsides to a last battle beneath the blood-tinged cliff where Arthur felled the giant Madarakt even as he was himself struck down.

'I think that's exactly what it is,' Donald says. 'But there's something missing from the story.' He points to the narrow path that branches away from the main track, leading sharply up the hillside. 'We need to climb up to the top.'

▨ ▨ ▨

DONALD STEPS UP at last to a broad slab laid by human hand at the edge of the cliff. In front of him now are the three great stones, a tall upright on either side with a huge curved capstone raised on top. Together they form the entrance to a grass-covered burial mound, a doorway to a dimly lit tunnel disappearing into blackness. On another day, in another place, he would be studying this tomb as a scientific archaeologist, examining the details of its construction, wondering at the possibilities of excavation. But he finds himself in a far different frame of mind as he stands there staring into the portal, shivering with a chill that has nothing to do with the coolness of the mountain air, the fast-approaching sunset. It is not a sense of fear, but a disorientating awareness of the scale of human time, the centuries that have gone by since anyone passed this way, into the darkness.

He takes out his father's map, to settle himself, to be sure he is not mistaken. The name of this place is clearly written there, *Drws-Arthur*, Arthur's Door, a throwback to a far-distant event described in the closing lines of the Song of Lailoken.

> We bore him up to the highest cliff-top, gate of the otherworld
> Laid him beneath a linden tree, the shield-wood powerless now
> The words unspoken on his lips, the life we saw still behind his eyes
> No more than the trick of light and shadow on the rock.

Donald conjures up the scene, allows himself to believe that it might be true: that this remote and rugged place, unchanged across the centuries, is where the warrior *Arto-uiros*, the bear-man, fought his last fight and was carried off to the otherworld where his wounds might be healed. There is an entry in the *Annales Cambriae*, the fragmentary tale of Arthur's final battle written there by Welsh monks whose grandparents' grandparents had heard the story whispered to them as children.

Gueith Camlann, in qua Arthur et Medraut corruere.
The strife of Camlann, in which Arthur and Medraut fell.

As he stands at the windswept edge, looking along the valley to the tall sandstone crags raised like bloodied fists in the declining sun, the real Arthur feels almost within reach.

Julia comes up beside him now, stands there quietly with a charming curious expression on her face. He takes her by the hand, and together they walk past the staring entrance to the tomb, then on around the burial mound. On the northern side, a small grove of trees has somehow found enough shelter to survive on the exposed cliff-top. The trunks are stunted and twisted, scarred with deep entwining furrows, and amongst them stand the hollowed remains of some earlier generation. Donald pulls Julia close to him, feels the physical presence of her, the warmth of her body against his, the rightness of being here with her. He looks up at the knotted black branches against the orange sky with the buds of next year's leaves almost ready for life. Though he cannot quite be sure, he thinks they might be linden trees.

Chronology

2400 BC	Completion of main stone circle at Stonehenge
1000*	First contacts between Celtic-speaking peoples and indigenous Britons
750*	Homer: the *Iliad*
43 AD	Claudius begins Roman conquest of Britain
407	Withdrawal of Roman legions from Britain
500*	Siege of Mount Badon
540*	Gildas, *De Excidio et Conquestu Britanniae* (*On the Ruin and Conquest of Britain*): earliest reference to Mount Badon
555*	St. Cyndeyrn (Kentigern) establishes a monastery at Llanelwy
573*	According to Welsh mythology, the prophet Lailoken flees to the forest
600*	Aneirin, *Y Gododdin*: earliest poetic reference to Arthur
731	The Venerable Bede of Jarrow, *Historia Ecclesiastica Gentis Anglorum*: widely regarded as the first true work of English historical scholarship

828*   Nennius, *Historia Brittonum*: lists twelve Arthurian battles, including Badon but not Camlann

970*   *Annales Cambriae* (*Annals of Wales*): lists two Arthurian battles, Badon and Camlann

1138   Geoffrey of Monmouth, *Historia Regum Britanniae* (*History of the Kings of Britain*) including the *Prophetiae Merlini* (*Prophecies of Merlin*): introduces Arthur, King of the Britons, and the prophet Merlin to a wide audience

1152   Geoffrey of Monmouth consecrated Bishop of St. Asaph

1154*   Death of Geoffrey of Monmouth

1190*   Chrétien de Troyes, *Perceval, le Conte du Graal*: progenitor of the medieval 'romance' tradition of Arthurian literature

1400–1415   The Welsh rebellion of Owain Glyn Dŵr

1416*   Death of Owain Glyn Dŵr

*approximate or tentative date

Guide to Welsh Pronunciation

Despite its formidable appearance, the Welsh language follows generally simple rules of spelling and pronunciation. The principal Welsh names and placenames in the novel are pronounced roughly as follows.

Camlann = *kam*-lan (with two short vowels)
Cwmhir = koom-heere
Cyndeyrn = *kin*-dayrn
Dyffryn = *duh*-frin
Owain Glyn Dŵr = *Oh*wain glin doowr
Plaid Cymru = plide kumree
Rhayader = ray-uh-der (with the 'uh' barely sounded)
Siôn Cent = shon kent
Tân y Ddraig = tahn uh thraig ('th' as in 'the', 'ai' as in 'eye')
Ty Faenor = tee vynor